FLYING TO PIECES

ALSO BY DEAN ING

The Big Lifters

Blood of Eagles

Butcher Bird

The Nemesis Mission

The Ransom of Black Stealth One

Silent Thunder

Single Combat

Spooker

Systemic Shock

Wild Country

DEAN ING

FLYING TO PIECES

A TOM DOHERTY ASSOCIATES BOOK NEW YORK

This is a work of fiction. All of the characters and events portrayed in this novel are either fictitious or are used fictitiously.

FLYING TO PIECES

This book is printed on acid-free paper.

A Forge Book
Published by Tom Doherty Associates, Inc.
175 Fifth Avenue
New York, NY 10010

Forge® is a registered trademark of Tom Doherty Associates, Inc.

Map by Mark Stein Studios

Design by Sara Stemen

Library of Congress Cataloging-in-Publication Data

Ing, Dean.
Flying to pieces / Dean Ing. — 1st ed.
p. cm.
"A Tom Doherty Associates book."
ISBN 0-312-85741-1 (acid-free paper)
I. Title.
PS3559.N37F59 1997
813'.54—dc21 97-6275
CIP

First Edition: August 1997

Printed in the United States of America

0 9 8 7 6 5 4 3 2 1

For Rob and David,

who helped wrangle the little winged beast.

ACKNOWLEDGMENTS

My brain trust of vintage throttle jockeys, especially Ted Voulgaris, contributed much with hair-raising accounts of the propeller era. This time, they were aided in some areas by airmen Bill Knowles, Dan Denney, David Guerriero, Wayne Reavis, Smithsonian aircraft wizards Tom Alison and Rich Horigan, music maven Karen Kammerer, the lovely and radiant Peter Sage, marine engineer Mark McAdams, and our family Alaskans, Glenn and Valerie Ing-Miller. Though the following tale is—like Fundabora—chiefly fictional, I learned that its central wild-hare idea is rooted in fact; more than one stash of "pickled" Japanese treasures have actually been found hidden in the manner, and for the purpose, described here.

For background lore on the Nippon of the 1930s I am indebted to author John Patric, whose wanderings through Japan yielded, in 1943, the wonderfully readable *Why Japan Was Strong*. Scholars of that period, and of strategic warfare, will find this book brimful of astonishing insight.

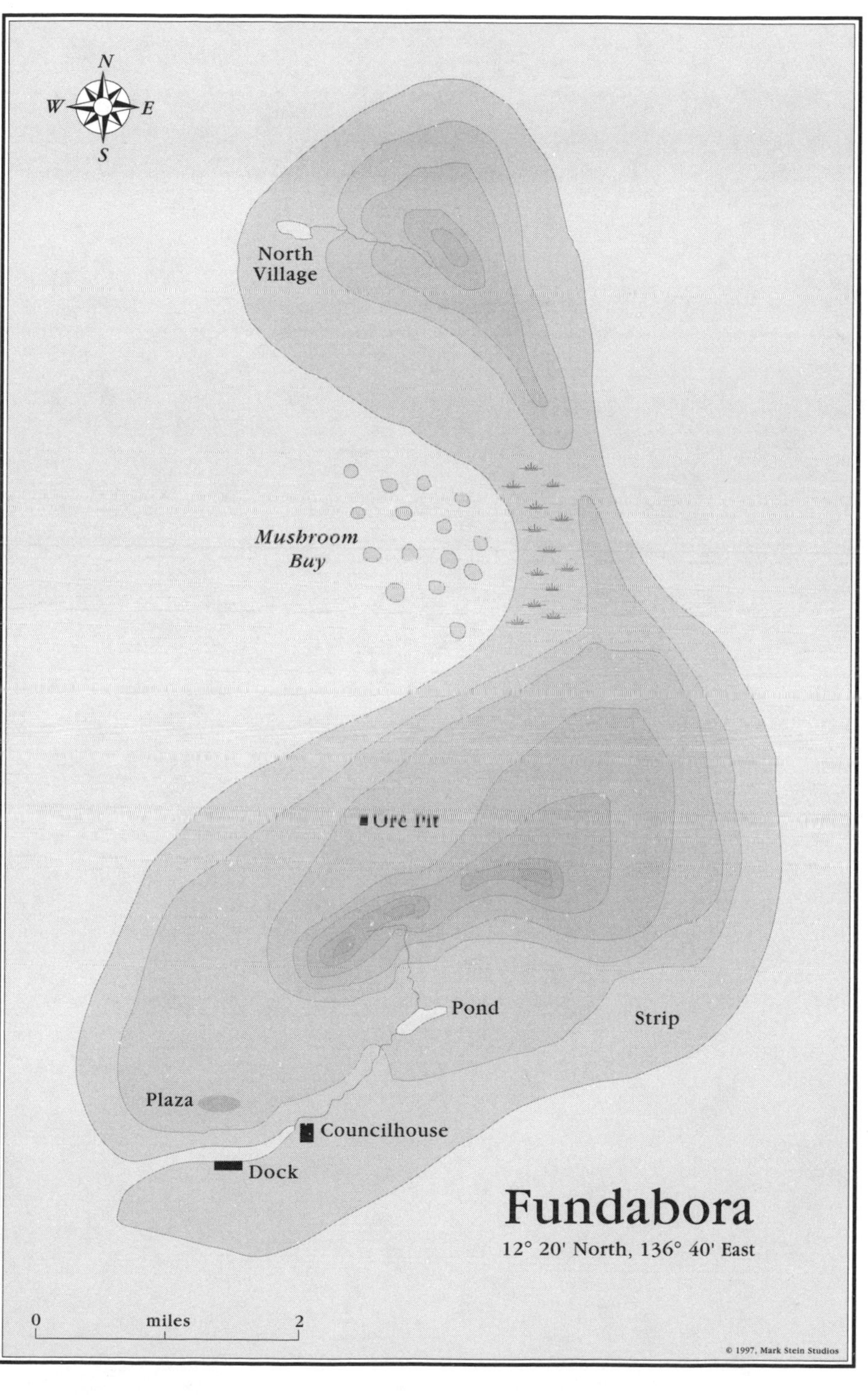
N
W
E
S
North Village
Mushroom Bay
Ore Pit
Pond
Strip
Plaza
Councilhouse
Dock
Fundabora
12° 20' North, 136° 40' East
0
miles
2
© 1997, Mark Stein Studios

FLYING TO PIECES

PROLOGUE

If Elmo Benteen hadn't raised so much hell at his last B.O.F. party, he might have lived to throw another one. Or maybe not; Elmo was loopy as a bedspring, having fought off half the tropical diseases known to medical science and too much of the VD. By now, Elmo's organs had become stony where they should be soft and, he admitted on his deathbed, soft when they ought to be hard. Every surviving member of the Boring Old Farts agreed he was past due; Elmo was a legend, but it had taken him more than eighty years and damned near that many airplane crashes. The only surprise was, it was finally his innards that crashed.

That's not strictly true. Elmo had a second surprise for his B.O.F. buddies, and at first they thought it was just the stuff running through tubes into his arms that was doing the talking. Some of them figured he hadn't converted all those smuggled Cambodian rubies to money, and maybe that was what he meant by a huge stash. But after a little judicious illegal entry, when the last words of the late Elmo Benteen finally became clear, most of the B.O.F.s emitted variations of, "I don't believe a word of it," or, "This gives a whole new meaning to 'risk capital,' " or, more succinctly, "At my age? No dice."

But there are a few old pilots like Wade Lovett who, smart enough to survive to retirement age, are still dumb enough to sucker themselves into a box canyon, or beneath an anvil cloud, if the reason seems good enough to risk flying to pieces. When the reasons include several millions in cash and a paragraph in aviation history, these few will step forward, betting that experience will bring them through. Amelia Earhart had lost that bet and Fred Noonan with her, two generations before in the same corner of the world where Elmo Benteen later recorded his great stash. But most of the B.O.F.s remembered Earhart as a pilot of great courage and indifferent skills, and themselves as "good sticks"—superior pilots. They also figured that, if ol' Elmo had got in and out again with a whole skin, the risks would be chiefly financial. So much for the wisdom of Boring Old Farts.

Actually, the trouble didn't start at Elmo's deathbed; it all began when he declared a National Emergency . . .

1

Even though the city reached out westward toward Rolling Hills, Kansas, the air traffic from Wichita's Mid-Continent Airport kept Wade Lovett's condo affordable because some folks don't like to live under an aerial on-ramp. Still, for each housewife who wakes up fearful whenever a Boeing's low pass shakes dust motes into her moonlit bedroom, some solitary wing nut like Lovett smiles without waking.

No mystery about that. For many years Wichita has been home to half the aircraft constructors in the country, and the area boasts more aircraft freaks than farmers. When a bug decorates his windshield like a Jackson Pollock, the driver twangs, "Wow, must've been a twin Piper." That's how many airplanes infest Wichita, and their thunder roars a duet of future money and past adventures to old guys like Lovett. No wonder they smile in their sleep.

But Lovett hadn't done much smiling when awake lately, though the business of trading used aircraft was going well at his hangar. When he padlocked the big multifold hangar doors that cloudy afternoon in late April and climbed into his sporty silver Mazda coupe, Lovett tried to avoid replaying the litany of downers that, he felt, would've had the prophet Job dancing with fury.

He *knew* he should've kept his Ford pickup with the winch and liftgate, because you can't shoehorn a goddamn crate full of Lycoming engine into the trunk of a goddamn racy foreign coupe. But he'd traded up to surprise his seventeen-year-old grandson, give the beloved elitist twirp more reason to enjoy his summer visit, and three days ago Chip had provided his own surprise, writing to say he wouldn't be coming after all. Downers Number One and Two.

Number Three was the defection of Mayday, who had checked out, "gone west" in pilot's parlance, augured in, all right then goddamn it, *died*, with what the vet said was a full cargo of kidney stones. He had raised that fool from a kitten the size of a flea's hood ornament, a fiftieth birthday present from a woman whose name he'd now forgotten. That made Mayday, what was it, nearly thirteen when he bought the farm. It had taken Wade Lovett longer to get over Mayday, his only housemate, than seemed possible. *You wouldn't think a satisfied loner in his sixties would go all misty-eyed over something with a brain the general size and usefulness of a mildewed walnut*, Lovett told himself, squirting the Mazda north on Tyler Road, ignoring the towers of cloud to his left that were backlit by God's own rosy runway light. And suddenly he felt guilty.

It was one thing to verbally abuse the talkative black tom to his whiskers, so to speak; tell him that any cat who would stand meowing before a closed door for an hour when an open one was in plain sight ten feet away, well, such a cat was dumb as a radish and deserved his imprisonment. Mayday's gaze had always said he understood those jibes were just male-bonding bullshit by a man who had nobody else—barring visits by Chip and an occasional pretty lady, *needed* no one else—to talk to, evenings in the condo.

It was something else, though, to debase Mayday's currency when he was no longer current. It wasn't fair, it was mean-spirited.

"I'm sorry, Mayday," Lovett said aloud, easing from the flow of traffic, then toward parking slot #16.

What was worse, Wade Lovett was chiefly sorry for himself, and knew it. He turned off the ignition and sat blinking at his windshield for a long moment and someone pulled into slot #15, doubtless the new neighbor he hadn't met. He didn't care to meet him now, either. Was this how you felt when old age crept up on you? Maybe he should get another kitten, and as soon as possible.

He got out of the car, shaking his head, and muttered, "One Mayday was enough."

"Isn't that a cry for help?"

Lovett turned and saw, over the top of the adjacent classic porthole Thunderbird, big brown eyes regarding him with honest interest. They belonged to a woman who could hardly see over her little T-Bird, perky side of fifty, and he realized he had spoken aloud. "Sometimes it is." He smiled by reflex. "Looks like you could use some help yourself."

She let him take one of her bulging grocery sacks and, sure

enough, she was the new tenant next door, and by the time Lovett sat alone in his kitchen to sort his mail he had agreed to a martini later in the evening. He still got invitations like that because his thick graying hair was still unruly and his dimpled killer smile apparently ageless. He still accepted the invitations if the lady seemed mature enough to take little disappointments in stride. All his life, one way or another, Wade Lovett had eventually disappointed women.

He tossed the junk mail to one side and used the blade of his Swiss Army knife, the one that would fillet a bass, to slit the single personal letter. The return address was Irvine, California, so he figured in advance it would be from old Elmo Benteen.

It was a single xeroxed page declaring a National Emergency at the offices of Bentwing Associates—Elmo went through associates like a dose of salts through a fasting guru—on a Friday evening two weeks hence. Lovett knew there would be maybe forty copies of the B.O.F. letter, because more than half of the hundred-odd Boring Old Farts had already cashed in their short snorters; and of that forty perhaps half of them would be able to make it to the boozy reunion known to them all as a National Emergency.

The B.O.F.s had no officials and only two requirements: you had flown military missions around the Pacific or China-Burma-India—Korea and Southeast Asia counted, too—and in the process you'd got your tailfeathers caught in a crack by some desk dildo, maybe a general. A court-martial helped you in, but one "no" vote by any member kept you out, so the really bad bastards never qualified. Garden-variety bastards were common, though; and if you didn't consume alcohol, why the hell would you attend a National Emergency anyhow?

The B.O.F. title had emerged from a Carews Booze-scented blowout in Darwin, Australia, back in '42 when the Japanese Navy was practically in the harbor. Some transport pilot, scheduled for the duration to fly many tons of explosive cargo very slowly and unarmed through a sky full of Mitsubishi Zeroes, said his only remaining ambition was to live long enough that his war stories would qualify him as a boring old fart. That became a toast, and the toast became a rallying cry, and when some smartass dreamed up an unofficial patch the Boring Old Farts got a slogan, too; stolen, naturally, from the First Troop Carrier Command. The patch showed two winged purple shafts crossed over a pipe and slippers, with a legend beneath: VINCIT QUI PRIMUM GERIT; He Conquers Who First Grows Old, or, The Old Fart Wins.

It was understood that the member who called an emergency footed its bills except for breakage and, now and then, bail; those blowouts were not exactly formal affairs and you didn't bring your wife because she might get into a dustup with one of the strippers. It had been nearly a year since the last bash and Lovett smiled to reflect that old Elmo, now in his eighties, was still kicking. Lovett was pleased to see that the emergency was to be held in the Bentwing offices, which meant Elmo's hangar at John Wayne Airport in Orange County, with the planes booted outside and a bunch of tables for the girls to strut on. He'd done that once before.

"Wise move, Elmo," Lovett muttered. When the bottles started flying in formation, they wouldn't hit anything beyond the hangar. The B.O.F.s had tried hiring American Legion halls, private clubs, and in one case, a country club. The tabs for wear and tear had proven greater than those for food, booze, and entertainment combined. Actually, they had it down to a science by now. You put your keys, along with everybody else's, in the same box with a combination lock when you came in. If you couldn't work the combination a few hours later and then find your way out of a hangar, you had no business operating a vehicle. Some people said those weren't just awfully exacting standards. The hell with them.

Lovett toyed with the idea of passing on this one. It would be a long cross-country alone to Southern California in his VariEze, a swept-wing little two-holer he had built from Rutan plans when plastic airplanes were still exotic. He would hear the same stories again, tell some of them himself, like the time over Korea when one of the Mighty Mouse rockets fired from his own F-84 started doing slow rolls until he passed it, and his slipstream sucked it toward him like a big explosive bullet with his name on it. The Mighty Mouse wasn't a smart munition, but neither were you if you trusted it. This one was so dumb it sideswiped his wing without taking half of it off.

Yeah, stories like that, some of them embellished with each retelling. The problem, he realized, was that the B.O.F.s really *were* boring old farts now to most outsiders. And it would be a long flight back, nursing a hangover. On the other hand, he could spend a night or two with his daughter, Roxanne, and more to the point, Chip would be there. Lovett's hesitation was more bullshit, and it didn't take him in. He scrawled, "Hold a tiedown space for my VariEze" on the xerox and sought an envelope for it. With all the oddball aircraft Elmo rented out to the more adventurous of the Hollywood crowd, surely there would be room.

And this time, with most of his fellow Farts pushing seventy or more, maybe it would end without major trouble for somebody.

Yeah; riiight.

2

Lovett inverted his schedule at the last minute after calling Roxanne, and flew first to Santa Cruz. It seemed that Chip had a piano recital on Wednesday night and Roxy hinted that, first, the kid would appreciate his granddad's putting in an appearance, and second, a little culture wouldn't hurt her father any. Lovett sighed and complied. Sure, it might cost him a sale in Wichita, but you couldn't expect Roxy to think along those lines. Unlike her father, Roxanne needed more money like Manuel Noriega needed more zits.

Moving to Santa Cruz with Tess after the divorce, Roxanne Lovett had grown tall and comely like her mother. Right on Tess's schedule Roxy had married Tom Mason, a regular guy, the only son in a "good," meaning flush with real estate, Santa Cruz family. Tom had lived long enough to influence his son Childress—Chip—and, thank God, Tom had hit it off right away with Wade Lovett in spite of Mason family reservations about a clapped-out old test pilot who traded noisy little airplanes for a living.

Tom Mason had reared Chip to the age of ten, cheered him at Little League and steered him toward respect for Lovett, before a zonked trucker bunted Tom off the Coast Highway one night. Along that cliffside stretch, a man who leaves the macadam doesn't need an airbag; he needs an ejection seat with chute attached.

After that, Roxanne Lovett-Mason raised Chip. With Mason money and a full-time maid in her yuppie Santa Cruz chalet, Roxy had plenty of time to redirect her son in genteel ways. She remained her mother's kid but she still loved Wade, wrote him faithfully three times a year, and had no objection to letting Chip spend a few weeks in Wichita every summer as a birthday present.

"He thinks you're from the Planet Gosh," she once told Lovett, then gave her other reason with an ominous murmur; "and there is very little surfing in Kansas." The surfing off Santa Cruz was, she felt, an altogether too-seductive competitor to Chip's piano lessons.

So when Wade Lovett greased his VariEze onto the runway at Watsonville Municipal, ten miles from Roxy's Santa Cruz place, Chip was waiting with his mom's mud-brown Mercedes.

Chip offered a hand as Lovett clambered down, and they traded boisterous hugs. "Jeez, when are you gonna quit growing," Lovett grinned up at his grandson who now towered several inches over Lovett's five-eight.

"Don't blame me for my genes, Pop. Sure you haven't shrunk in the rain? Here, let me roust your duds," Chip said, scrambling up to retrieve Lovett's soft luggage. The two had agreed, back when the boy had begun his summer visits and Lovett was still shaving ten years off his age to women who asked, that Chip would call him "Pop." Now the kid was man-sized, and if the term no longer fitted as well it was still an agreement. In the Mason family, agreements could be hard-won.

Lovett watched the youth's lithe motions with critical approval; surfing kept his slender body fit. Chip's hands and feet remained smallish, too small for a pianist really, his blond hair long and straight, his eyes the deep turquoise of Tess above a straight patrician nose. Though his voice had changed, it kept a light timbre, equally adept at quick-paced surfer patter and foreign music terms. Lovett hoped Roxy still bought the boy's clothes because they were elitist as hell. The shoes were Air Jordans, his black jeans had a designer label, and his blue silk shirt said the rest.

When they had the VariEze properly kneeling on its nosewheel and secured, Chip helped with the postflight inspection. Lots of guys didn't bother but, as Lovett had told him years ago, lots of guys found loose fittings or surface cracks later during preflights just when they were anxious to launch on time. Or they didn't find them, and paid the price in midair. A good habit, Lovett said, was easy to break. And so was your neck.

"You test any experimentals lately," Chip asked as they finished the job.

"Not for a while now," Lovett said, a vast understatement. It was Chip's proudest boast that his granddad had been a test pilot, though he hadn't done it for many years. It suited Lovett just fine that Chip knew so little about his time as Cessna's man in Southeast Asia back in the sixties. He'd been a civilian then, illegally flying ground support missions in an O-2A, a very special type of twin-engined Cessna. The O-2A was the Rambo of light aircraft, and it wouldn't get arrested for loitering with its retractable gear and rocket rails. If Chip ever met any of the other B.O.F.s and heard some of those stories about him, the kid wouldn't trust him on a tandem bicycle.

During the drive into Santa Cruz when Chip asked what else his pop was up to on the Coast, Lovett confessed. The kid knew better than to tell his mom too much about Lovett's present life. He hadn't told her when they spent a week in Wisconsin at the Oshkosh Fly-in, or about his discovery that two Heinekens had been one too many for a fifteen-year-old. "Some kind of fly-in this weekend," Chip guessed.

"Just a geezer patrol reunion at John Wayne Airport on Saturday," Lovett said. "Bunch of old farts telling lies, mostly."

Chip's grin and quick glance were too knowing. "The B.O.F.s, right?"

"Who's the satchel mouth told you about that?"

"You are. Bad company, you said, but some of their names? Bitchin', Pop. Who'll be there?"

Shrug. "At the rate they're corking off, maybe nobody but me and Benteen. It's his bash."

"*Elmo* Benteen? Jesus Christ and Rachmaninoff! Or did he have a son?" Chip's enthusiasm waned as fast as it had peaked.

"I believe he does—Del, or Mel, something like that. Elmo probably has fifty sons schlumping around the South Pacific. They aren't his primary topics."

Chip: "What is?"

Lovett: "He is. Elmo's your basic autistic adult."

"So he's still alive. Jeez, that's rad. You really know him?"

Lovett chuckled at this. "Maybe I should ask what you know about him."

"More than you think, Pop. I had this teacher that kept on about how spies changed history, so I started a term paper to get him cranked and ran across this unbelievable dude around World War Two who flew his black Catalina flying boat for Naval Intelligence."

"Elmo and his Black Cat. You did your homework, kid."

"Hey, I was stoked. And over twenty years later, Benteen disappeared in the Pacific, and turned up alive in, I think it was 'sixty-nine. The headlines called him, um, I forget," Chip said, and laughed. "Something gnarly."

"The Phantom of Shangri-La," Lovett supplied. "And don't think he'll ever let us forget it, either."

"Did you know he sold his story to the tabloids?"

"Never read 'em. But I know he'd sell his eyes if he got the right price," Lovett said.

Chip tooled the Mercedes down Capitola Road, shaking his head and uttering little bursts of merriment. "Oh, man. There's this book with a whole chapter on Benteen. Really neat shit. According to him, he'd been working undercover for the British for years, keeping tabs on French interests in the Pacific; and when he got famous again, they dropped him. Too much exposure. So he really gave them exposure. Bitchin'," he said again, and laughed. "Only 'A' I ever got on a history paper. And Elmo Benteen is a friend of yours," he marveled. "That is *so* cool."

"Elmo's like the Brits," Lovett said. "He doesn't have friends exactly, he has associates. Big sign on his hangar: BENTWING ASSOCIATES. Believe it."

Chip turned up the long, curving drive past Monterey cypress and flowering ground cover that, Lovett thought, must require a lot of upkeep. "Huh." Chip shook his head. "If he doesn't have friends, why is he throwing a party?"

And there, at the back of the house, was Roxy waiting with pruning shears in one hand and an armload of flowers, and in medium heels she was as tall as her father and as splendid as Tess had ever been, kissing Lovett with genuine warmth. "Let's get you out of this breeze," she said, taking his arm protectively. "That must be quite a trip alone for a man your age. How are you feeling?"

Abruptly, Lovett realized that she was equating his physical condition with that of his ex-wife Tess who, he'd been told, hadn't aged well. By now Tess was in stationary orbit around Jupiter in a region called Alzheimer Land.

He realized suddenly that Roxy had asked him how he felt for the second time. "Never ask an old guy how he feels, honey. Because he might tell you. He will give you details until you wish he were dead and in hell. Thank your lucky stars I'm not quite an old guy just yet. Tomorrow for sure, but not quite yet."

He was happy to have his daughter on his arm on any pretext, though, and they strolled into the solarium while Chip toted his luggage.

". . . so even if Chip won't visit this summer, I knew he'd enjoy nothing more than showing you off here. You're," she paused to find a metaphor her son would like, but it crashed and burned: "the Mark Foo of the air."

"Bummer," Chip said, aghast. "Mom, Mark got the liquid hammer a while back. Must'a tried to ride a real whale-choker. Augered," he added with an eyebrow lift toward Lovett.

"I can never keep it all straight," Roxy said with a helpless smile. "My son lives a double life—triple, if you count those little airplanes. Domenica?" She hardly raised her voice at all. "We'll have tea out here."

Lovett's glance swept past Roxy to Chip and he saw the youth's quick gesture, forefinger aimed into his mouth in a comic display of distaste. Chip might sip Herbal Heaven for his mom but he shared Lovett's preference for beer.

Their long-time maid, Domenica Sotomayor, sailed into the fern-hung solarium with the tea tray moments later and beamed at Lovett, who gave her a hug. "Guapa as ever," Lovett winked, and Domenica flushed with pleasure. She could never fit her rump into a washtub but she might fit nicely into a registry of great chefs.

Roxy poured, making a ceremony of it, and made polite enquiry about business in Kansas. "Okay, I suppose," Lovett replied, hoping to avoid shop talk. "I don't worry about it much so long as I can pay the bills."

Her glance sharpened. "Is it, um, becoming much of a bother, Dad?" Unspoken but hanging there: *at your advancing age.*

Some imp of perversity made Lovett lie: "The arithmetic's getting tougher. Maybe I should hire Chip to do it."

Her dropped gaze and nod said she had taken him seriously. "Not much of a career for a concert pianist, Dad," she murmured with a sad little smile.

They both glanced at Chip who, understanding Lovett's jape perfectly, was now trying to sip tea without laughing. "Hey, I've gotta push," he said, glancing at his watch. "Nap time. Honest."

"We just got here," Lovett protested.

"Yeah, but I'm gonna sweat buckets tonight," Chip said, and moments later he had disappeared into the bowels of the house.

To Lovett's puzzled look, Roxy said, "Pianists have to train, Dad.

He spent this morning with his Czerny exercises and he's winding up the program tonight with excerpts from Mussorgsky. After his nap he'll study the score."

"You mean he doesn't have to practice?"

"No, just read the score. His teacher, Karen Kincade, always says if it's in his head, it will be in his fingers. After he studies we'll dress and then drive to the auditorium."

"I brought a black turtleneck and sport coat. That okay?"

"I suppose it'll have to be," she said, and then her eyes grew round. "Oh my God," she said, and put down her cup as she rose. "His dinner jacket's still at the cleaners, and they don't deliver. Just enjoy yourself, I'll be back in a jif." And with that, she hurried out to the Mercedes.

Lovett sat quietly, watching windswept trees flex in a late summer sun, but looked up when Domenica padded into the solarium again. She had watched Chip grow from a stripling, from a "grom" in the boy's parlance, and evidently something of Tom Mason's regard for Lovett had rubbed off on Domenica during his earlier visits. "That kid has outgrown us all," Lovett remarked with a smile, referring to Chip's height.

"Childress outgrows many things. Not you," she smiled back, meaning something else entirely. "And not the ocean, as we had hoped."

"Give him time. He got a girl?"

Domenica made a *pfuh* noise, hands on hips. "Those girls who risk their necks on surfboards," she admitted. "Surfettes, he calls them. At least he is not named in any paternity suits. But that might be less cruel than the ocean," she said.

"C'mon, Domenica; if it were that dangerous Roxy wouldn't let him do it."

"Oho," she crooned, rolling her eyes. "She has tried. I will tell you this, because you are the *abuelo*, even if your daughter or your grandson would never tell you. Two years ago she put her foot down; no more surfing. And he put his own down; no more piano. Then she forbade him this and that and the other thing."

"Turning up the heat, upping the ante. You women know how to do that," Lovett conceded.

But Domenica went on in stealthy tones, almost a whisper: "And one evening they were arguing in the kitchen while I had *antojitos* on a hot griddle, and she told him again how painful it would be for him to continue his . . . ah, the word, defiance, yes; and he reached out in front of me and made a spider of his right hand, and put all five fingers down on the blistering steel of that griddle, as if playing a chord to deafen the devil, and kept them there until we could both pull him away."

"God a'mighty," Lovett said, and swallowed hard. "Maybe Roxy doesn't understand pain as well as she thinks."

"Childress told her much the same," said the old domestic softly, "while she was being sick on my clean floor and I was wrapping the boy's hand in ice. He wore a bandage on it for weeks."

"Don't tell me: when it came off, he went surfing again."

"Yes, but also practicing again. He is gentle, almost girlish in some ways, but if a thing is important enough to him," she said, and paused. Then she ended with a hands-out gesture and nod, an "as you see" clearer than words.

Lovett let his shudder pass, then began to chuckle almost soundlessly as he looked at the old woman. "Well, Domenica," he said through his tiny snorts, "he didn't get it out of the ground. I'm surprised it took her fifteen years to learn that."

"He laughs about it, too, when we are alone," said Domenica. Then, "*Bastardos machos*," she muttered.

Lovett did not know if he was included in the imprecation and he didn't intend to ask. "So Chip still surfs, and he still puts on a monkey suit to play the piano," Lovett said. "Something for everybody. I think we've all gotten off pretty lightly, considering."

"He is a good boy," Domenica agreed, and took Lovett's empty cup. "But his mother wishes he would grow up. So does her suitor, for what I suspect are his own reasons, but I should not be mentioning him. It is enough that she feels that way."

"And so do you."

"And so do I," she echoed, moving toward the kitchen.

Later, Lovett couldn't recall the early part of the evening's program because he kept drowsing off, prodded now and then by Roxy's elbow when he snored accompaniment to a young girl's Pachelbel or another youth's Chopin. He had no problem staying awake for Chip, though; the best and last on the program, young Childress Mason swept through his *Pictures at an Exhibition* with the Promenade and Limoges, then ripped and pounded through *The Great*

Gate at Kiev with such fervor that Lovett felt gooseflesh down his arms.

At the reception afterward, Chip stood a head above his surrounding throng and swilled pink lemonade, accepting his due, smiling mute apologies to Lovett who stood well out of the way with a plate of hors d'oeuvres. It occurred to Wade Lovett then that his grandson, erect in that spiffy dinner jacket, seemed to fit into the culture vulture crowd like patent leather. He could not say why that depressed him so.

Roxy introduced her father to a few of the adults, among them a smallish fellow with a pencil mustache, a faint accent and matching handshake, carefully slicked-down hair and a title of sorts: one Alexis von Wurttemburg. Perhaps it was the excess of jewelry on von W. that set Lovett's personal radar to jittering, or maybe it was the deep-set eyes or the fact that the little man seemed to be studying Lovett while wolfing thumbnail-sized sandwiches. He was among the first to leave the reception.

Lovett perked up when Chip introduced him to special friends as *the* Wade Lovett, test pilot. Chip seemed surprised to find his surfing buddy David Guerra, a sturdy compact model-builder, at a recital of classical music. "No choice, man, if I was gonna slap palms with your gramp," David admitted. "Hadda meet this dude."

Lovett found himself describing his swept-wing VariEze to David, as Chip went for a refill of lemonade. "They're pretty common now but when I built mine, people thought it was a secret weapon," Lovett concluded.

"On the phone this afternoon Chip's like, dropping a lot of hints about secret stuff," David mused, rubbing a chin that needed a shave. "He's like, 'My pop's on some mysterious mission to meet a retired spy,' and I'm all, 'You been warping on the wrong comix again,' and he's like, 'Naw, my pop's the real deal.' " David may have sensed their language gap when he noticed Lovett's eyes glazing over, and fell silent at this point.

Don't call your grandson a liar, Lovett told himself. "Well, that's a bit strong," he said. "But you never know what'll happen at a reunion." *Beyond a bunch of drunks doddering around a stripper*, he added silently.

"I don't suppose you could take me and Chip," said David wistfully. "It's a weekend."

"Afraid not, David. Anyway, why would you want to?"

David's gaze glistened with intent. "Oh, it'd be neat shit," he grinned.

"Sorry. The only outsiders will be waiters of voting age," Lovett said, "and uh, catering ladies."

"Catering to what," said David with a sly glance.

Lovett stared at the youth, dismayed at his adult grasp of things. "What hath TV wrought," he murmured.

Chip returned with a cup in each hand. David reached for one but Chip shook his head. "Hey, I'm parched, Dave, gopher your own. You don't drink liquids before a recital so I'm tanking now." To Lovett's quizzical look he added, "It's hard to keep your mind on Moussorgsky when you need to drain your lizard." Then, as an inside joke for his grandfather: "They don't put relief tubes on Steinways, Pop."

And of course Roxanne happened along with Chip's teacher, Karen Kincade, in time to hear Lovett explaining to David how you relieved yourself in an airplane. Lovett would have gladly spent the next few weeks getting to know the striking Kincade, even if she did tower above him, on the theory that the taller they are, the nicer they fall. But while Kincade seemed to enjoy the moment, Roxy's jaw-muscle twitch said, *'I might have known,'* and soon afterward she was driving her little group home before Lovett could embarrass her further.

"Interesting guy, this von Whoozis," Lovett said at one point, just to cut the silence. "I was hoping we could talk awhile."

"Alex isn't much for small talk," she said. "He's very charming but quite focused."

"On what?"

"Oh—finance," she said.

Lovett merely nodded. He didn't bother to point out that there's another word that defines finance: money.

By the time they'd shared two cups of decaffeinated coffee at home, Lovett sensed he'd been forgiven. Then Roxanne went off to bed and Lovett communed with his grandson for another hour.

Apparently his social radar had lit up a bogey in von Wurttemburg who, according to Chip, was an occasional fixture at the house. The youth was quick to dismiss von W., happy to talk about other things: his decision to study at the U.S.C. School of Music, for example, since surfing was nil near Juilliard and, around Eastman-Rochester, the only action was Niagara Falls. Lovett found himself impressed with Chip's progress, yet somehow uneasy at the boy's willing immersion into his mother's lifestyle. *I wish his father were still around*, he thought after a final midnight hug from Chip, and, *I wish I lived nearer.*

But before sleep overtook him, Lovett's thoughts took another turn. Old Elmo Benteen hadn't called a National Emergency in years. It justified Chip's question. If Elmo Benteen didn't have any real friends, why was he throwing a party?

3

Lovett launched southward early on Thursday, to avoid making Chip late for his first class. To make the trip deductible he intended to use part of the day to check on aircraft advertised in the trade papers. The moment he found something interesting, of course, his schedule went into an inverted spin and crashed. He might as well have tried to cruise the Smithsonian in five minutes.

There were bargains out there but, having written a few ads himself, Lovett's eye had developed a case of jaundice. RESTORATION 90% COMPLETE might mean that the owner had made 90 percent of the mistakes possible and hoped to dump this abortion on a complete idiot. LOW TIME could mean the engine had been overhauled by a cross-eyed maladroit who worried over those funny new noises coming through his firewall and was hoping to sell this deathtrap before the pistons started swapping holes. ALWAYS HANGARED could suggest the aircraft hadn't been flown since 1947—for good reason.

And the guy who said, "History is bunk" may have just bought a secondhand airplane. NO DAMAGE HISTORY sometimes meant the owner had a convenient memory for little things like scraped wingtips and propellers with an acquired taste for seagulls. When a prop went south while you were going north, you instantly had a glider, or pieces of one.

He landed at Taft to check on an aerobatic Acro Sport—held together by its paint, if Lovett was any judge, and not worth the money—then stopping again at Corona between mountain ranges that bounced the VariEze around. The tiny Wittman single-seater at Corona was worth a second look, a checkout ride and, on Saturday after a more thorough inspection, his personal check for the down payment. Once he got the little plane ferried home, he could renovate it himself; the little screamer might even entice Chip back to Wichita.

He flew to Santa Ana just in time for Benteen's National Emergency, an entire day behind schedule, only a short hop but in skies so crowded with air traffic that he felt like a gnat in a roomful of flyswatters. What do you call fifty Southern California lawyers flying joyrides? Air pollution, he reminded himself, taxiing to refuel before seeking a tiedown space. Some of his old colleagues would be tanked up on Benteen's booze already, though the real festivities wouldn't begin 'til dark.

It was sundown when Lovett strolled toward the hangar of Bentwing Associates, flight bag in hand. The assortment of aircraft towed outside, safely out of the reach of partygoers, looked as though someone had evicted a museum of flight. Elmo's Monocoupe, a long-distance racer of 1935 vintage, needed work. The Tiger Moth was older still but looked flyable. The Sikorsky flying boat, a genuine 1920s antique, was small by modern standards, lovingly rebuilt. Created chiefly from wood and fabric, such flyable relics brought top dollar and Lovett doubted if Benteen owned them outright.

Lovett entered the hangar unnoticed, his heels echoing a ghostly tattoo on the concrete floor. Someone had unfurled the B.O.F. motto, in gleaming satin a yard wide, to hang from a shattered propeller high on one wall. Four long tables had been shoved together, doubtless for the bimbo runway, faced by three more tables surrounded by folding chairs. *God, that's depressing*, Lovett thought. *There probably won't be enough of us to fill those three tables.* Two young guys resplendent in black had their backs to him, setting up the bar in a far corner of the hangar, strategically placed far from the chairs. Elmo's theory was, if you couldn't make it to the bar, you didn't need a refill.

In years past, dozens of men would have made the place more festive than bunting by now, lounging at the tables, scarfing down cold cuts with imported beer while they waited for the real action to begin. Now, Lovett could hear faint echoes of it all, which he discovered wasn't just his imagination. The earlier arrivals had all convened with beer in the hangar office, away from those hollow echoes. *Pretty soon we'll be able to do this in a phone booth*, Lovett thought as he entered the main office.

Of the dozen B.O.F.s lounging in the scatter of office chairs, the first to spot him was bearded, overweight Victor Myles. *It would be*, Lovett thought: Mr. Survivalist, a self-promoting writer whose neck always seemed to be on gimbal mounts lest he miss something worth scribbling about in the men's magazines.

"Condition red," Myles boomed in a cowpoke drawl, waving his corncob pipe as he spotted Lovett. "Hide your booze and broads, boys, ol' Lovett's back in town."

Lovett gave them his best smile, shaking hands all around with men he'd known for decades. In Benteen's momentary absence, Vic Myles had seated himself behind the scarred old desk and now he finished the tale he'd been spinning. "So then he says, 'Get an eye test, Myles, your broad's ugly as a combat boot,' and I says, 'Maybe, but she can suck a football through a garden hose.' And would you believe, a week later they were going steady."

Lovett decided the little group was primed to laugh at anything, even Myles's raunchiest lines. And teenagers wanted to hear this kind of stuff? Christ, they probably invent it, Lovett mused.

And Myles was no worse than some of the others, and he knew better stories than most. Spotting targets for Army artillery in Korea, Vic Myles had earned every right to wear that grungy Stetson, to walk the walk, to talk the talk. He'd earned a nickname, 'Hemingway,' from messmates in those days for the eye-popping porn he'd pecked out in his spare time. A gun nut who hung out with Army demolition teams, he'd become familiar with explosives of all kinds—and the stories about them that would curl horsehair. When Myles returned stateside in the fifties with an endless fund of fine-ground baloney, adventure magazines began to take his stuff, and in time he had developed into a passable scribbler. Much later the survivalist movement had made his articles popular, more so after Myles contracted with a CIA offshoot to instruct foreign nationals in handling explosives.

But for Myles, fame had been brief. Needing glasses, his beard gray, the man exuded an air of forlorn hope, as though remaining the focus of attention was proof that he still had the right stuff. Half listening, Lovett reflected that maybe that term should be retired until somebody found a way to define exactly what stuff was right. Good sticks came in every conceivable and a few inconceivable packages; there was stuff, and there was other stuff; and some of it turned out right.

Myles's face betrayed a trace of dismay as an old fellow shuffled out of the men's room. On the best day he ever had, Myles couldn't compete with Elmo Benteen.

Lovett forced a grin for the old man and said the right things over their handshake. What he felt like saying was, "Damn, I'm sorry, Elmo." At a guess Benteen had lost thirty pounds, his gait uncertain, the flesh drawn tightly over his cheekbones, that go-to-hell square grin of his now reduced to a set of cheap false teeth in a skull. Only the eyes were the same, still clear and lively, as if they could look into you and evaluate the man within.

Evidently they could read minds, too: "I know, kid, I look like shit warmed over," Benteen said, and waved a hand toward the framed photos along the office wall. "Look at those instead if you druther. And grab a beer." Benteen himself was nursing a non-alcoholic Kaliber brew.

Not many people could properly call Lovett "kid," and somewhere among those wall photos was one of a younger Wade Lovett with his arm around the shoulder of a middle-aged Elmo. In the photo's background, stark against silhouetted palm trees, squatted a huge old Consolidated Catalina, looking like a goose on wheels—and a dead-black goose at that. Those had been Elmo's glory days, rare old times for a man who had never finished high school.

Other photos showed Elmo in more recent years, sharing the frame with politicians, CEOs, film actors, a starlet or two. *Oh, he's led a high life,* Lovett conceded. It had been the kind of life that blurred the distinction between fame and notoriety. In a way, it was too bad Chip couldn't meet this living legend in the flesh, while there was still a little of it left.

But Elmo was pulling up his shirttail while one of the guys began singing, "A pretty boyyyy, is like a melodyyyy . . ."

"Well, you wanted to know what took me so long in the dumper," Elmo said, either pissed off or pretending, tugging at something to the left of his navel. Lovett was sorry when he craned his neck for a better look; he hadn't known about Benteen's colostomy bag. The old fellow showed off his synthetic intestine's orifice now to Crispin Reventlo, the only Brit among them. Evidently Cris had provoked this little demonstration with a remark, and must now live with the result. "Some of my innards are now outtards," Benteen explained.

Because Benteen was standing and Reventlo sitting, the hapless Brit found himself at eye-level with Elmo's little surprise, a pink pucker visible through that flaccid plastic bag which seemed grafted to Elmo's side with tape. "We knew you had guts, Elmo, but what's that winking back at me," he demanded.

"My butthole," Benteen said. "I wear it pretty high these days."

"He always did," Reventlo said in an aside to the others as Benteen rearranged his shirt.

"What'd he say?" This from Coop Gunther, whose ability to lip-read usually masked the deafness he tried to hide.

"Hey, that's nothing. Wait'll you see my catheter." It was Curran Quinn, reaching down into the front of his trousers, then blinking in pretended confusion. "Gee, that's odd. I had it in here somewhere," and then the competition heated up, half of the group with some kind of age-related peculiarity, the other half trying to appear envious.

One spoke up with, "My stainless steel hip feels okay, but I swear to God it squeaks."

Another: "It's a cruel fate to get mice in your pants."

"Oh, I dunno," said a third; "I could use a few nibbles."

A fourth: "Ow, the very idea hurts. You shouldn't say that around a guy who's just been circumcised at sixty-nine."

Myles: "Lemme get this straight: you tried a sixty-nine and got circumcised?"

"Lissen, Myles, if I can't get it straight by myself, don't try and help me 'cause that *really* hurts. Sure, laugh," said the complainer to old comrades, "but after I got my trim in the Bay Area from the San Francisco Clipper, which is what they call my doc, I hadda learn to pee all over again."

Reventlo's manner was droll: "I gather 'all over' is the operative phrase," he said.

"That's operative. This?" Patting his fly tenderly: "This is still in intensive care. My wife won't even let me into the front bathroom anymore. I level off for a bombing run on the commode and ease off a stream, and my shoes and my tie and the towel rack are all targets of accidental opportunity."

"It's just getting back at you now for all those years you've abused it," Lovett said, straight-faced.

"Okay, have your fun, Wade, but mark my words: get a trim job at your age and Mr. Wiggly goes cross-eyed on you. It's like he's never been sighted in, I'm as apt to get two streams as one and like as not they both hit my galoshes."

Even Benteen found this bizarre. "You wear galoshes to the john?"

"I do until my aim improves. House rules," was the reply.

"If you have to go in here," Benteen told him, "don't go in here. Go outside. Hell, it'll be dark soon anyway."

Lovett had heard stories about midlife circumcisions before, but never anything quite this plaintive. It wasn't the last tragicomedy of aging he was to experience that night as he listened, sipped his beer, and tried to feel festive.

Several late arrivals strolled in until Benteen's office was standing room only, and it took the caterer several tries before he got Benteen's attention from the doorway. "The ladies," he said, "have arrived." Lovett thought it was remarkable how fast a score of old guys could dodder out of a narrow doorway.

Lovett saw no women, but he could hear someone trying to cue a music tape somewhere in a side office and Benteen reminded the throng that they'd need a drink of some sort for the opening toast—a pointless reminder since the bartenders were already hidden, besieged by revelers ordering doubles. Lovett still had half his beer and decided to take it slowly this time, choosing a chair at random.

In moments he found himself flanked by Quinn and Reventlo, both with hefty glasses of booze. "How's it hanging, Quinn," Lovett said.

"Don't ask. I wasn't kidding about the catheter. And business isn't what it should be," said the affable Quinn, as though it was of no importance.

"Still putting your kids through at Illinois?"

"Nope, wife and I moved to Florida. I run a little FBO; Doris is mostly bedridden and I have dialysis every three days but it's doable. Non illigitimus carborundum," he grinned. That was more of their bogus Latin: *Don't let the bastards grind you down.*

Lovett nodded. An ex-Raven with missions over Laos, Quinn would probably still have his old spook contacts. If he was a Fixed Base Operator in Florida now, those contacts could be important. Once a handsome six-footer with the curly dark hair of the black Irish, Quinn had picked up some exotic bug in Southeast Asia and would carry its effects to the grave. Now he seemed to have shrunk a bit with a permanent squint that might be his old laugh lines, or possibly just worry lines. With Curran Quinn it was hard to tell. "I'd think your end of the biz should be good in Florida," Lovett said with a wink.

"Place is crammed with blacks and spics," Quinn rejoined, "and they don't fly, they try to hire it done with no questions asked."

Lovett found momentary eye contact with Reventlo. Quinn had never made any secret of his bigotry, but at least he told you up front. And he wasn't dealing with drug runners. Lovett shrugged and said, "So you turn down a lot of business?"

"Yeah, and sometimes I see who doesn't, and I take a few license numbers. Now and then it helps pay the bills." Quinn said volumes in those few words. With business flagging and medical costs in the stratosphere, he had the balls to play an informant role to the authorities. It could pay the rent. It could also get you seriously killed.

"Just watch your back, old man," Reventlo murmured.

Then Elmo Benteen made his way to a chair and raised his beverage, having graduated to a hearty ale. "Vincit qui primum gerit," he called, husking it as loud as he could. A score of stronger throats responded with the same motto, "the old guy conquers," and its thunder brought dust sifting from the hangar rafters as they drank. Lovett felt gooseflesh on his arms. For the moment, it was 1965, or even 1945 for some, and they were all ageless, peerless, dauntless. The eyes of some of those men glistened, and Lovett realized that this moment was what most of them had really come for.

The second toast was more of the group's tradition, with a moment of silence for those B.O.F.s who had "gone west" before them. Then Elmo announced the evening's agenda. "I've had a pig barbecued for you, South Pacific-style, and you'll get served like civilized folks. Of course there'll be some after-dinner entertainment," he smirked, "and I advise you to remain conscious 'til it's over."

He waited for the cheering to subside, then went on: "Because I have a little business proposition for you later. I reckon you all know a little about that accidental vacation of mine back in '68 . . ."

"Let's hear it for the Phantom of Shangri-La," someone called, to good-natured jeering.

Elmo's grin was sly. "Oh, I ain't a phantom quite yet, but stay tuned. Anyhow, what you never heard was this: I had the best reason in the world for not telling where I fetched up in that forced landing. In a way, it sure 'nough was a Shangri-La." No longer smiling now: "It should be, still. Oh, it may not let you live forever—but it'll stuff the deepest pockets you've got. And you'll be remembered as long as airchines fly, gentlemen. That, I promise." The throng had fallen silent now; something in old Elmo's manner said this was more than a tall tale. Again, Lovett flashed on the question Chip had asked. *Why is he throwing a party?* It seemed the answer would not be long in coming.

"I'll whet your curiosity this much," Benteen went on. "I tried for years to get backers for a return trip. Looks like I tried all the wrong folks. Every mother's whelp of 'em wanted too big a share and too much proof before they wrote a check. Starting with map coordinates."

Quinn pierced the silence with, "How big a check, Elmo?"

"Last time I ran the figures out with my kid, a hundred thou. Might take twice that much now, or so Mel tells me."

Lovett could hear murmurs of, "I'm out," and other words to the same effect.

"Might not be that much, though, if you have the gumption to do it up close and personal. Most of you runway rats were too busy gettin' domesticated until now," Benteen went on, visibly tiring. "It needs diplomacy, which ain't my strong suit; it needs some cash; it may need some heavy equipment. Mel can run anything with treads, so you'd have an operator. I'll go along 'cause I wouldn't miss it, and if I'm gonna get it done it'd better be soon. The question is, do we have a few guys who could use, say, a mill apiece?"

Quinn again, now in disbelief: "As in, million? A one with six zeroes and no decimal points?"

"Dollars," Benteen nodded, managing his patented grin again. "And that's all I intend to say for now." He waved a hand expansively. "Eat, cheer the ladies, and think about it." Had he not sat down, Lovett thought, Benteen might have simply fallen down.

While waiters served paper plates of succulent pork and salad, Cris Reventlo murmured what Lovett was thinking. "Can't say I like Benteen's looks."

"We can't all be fashion plates," Quinn rejoined, taking in Reventlo's tailored shirt with epaulets, his ruddy tan topped by a thick shock of white hair. In his seventies, the Brit was still erect, his bearing vaguely military as befitted a man who had flown Qantas and Air Micronesia jets for years.

"You know what I mean," Reventlo insisted, as a paper plate slid in front of him. The waiter moved quickly behind Lovett, served him a plate, then plopped down a very large and suspiciously dark drink.

"Iced tea is more his style," Lovett said, nodding toward Reventlo.

"Scotch highball, triple," said a voice with a laugh in it, a familiar voice that shocked Lovett, literally, speechless. It was Lovett's favorite drink, all right; and as he jerked around to verify the impossible, he saw his only grandson give him a horsewink as he hurried away for more plates.

Chip, here? Sweet Jesus, the kid was underage, hundreds of miles from home, and wearing the same damned monkey suit he'd worn the night before. No, two nights; time enough to sneak down here and weasel his way in as hired help—not that he needed the money.

"If you must open your mouth that wide, Lovett, stuff some protein in it," said Reventlo with an amused glance.

Lovett snapped his jaw shut, blinking, thinking furiously, not wondering how Roxanne would react because he knew only too well. Then, because there was nothing he could do about it—perhaps nothing he *should* do to a youth who could pass as an adult—Wade Lovett began to chuckle, and addressed his plate. The next time Chip passed, Lovett raised his scotch highball in a silent toast to his grandson, who cackled aloud and kept serving.

During his second helping, Lovett discovered that Cris Reventlo's wife had recently left him in Darwin after he bought into an Australian charter flight outfit and lost a bundle. Making money and losing it did not seem to concern Reventlo, who had too many skills to starve. The son of an English plantation engineer, Cris had grown up in Burma and was flying unlicensed from grass fields at sixteen. Then, as a youthful prisoner of war near Rangoon, he had learned Japanese before the war's end. He had never returned to England, but still spoke at times like a man happily lost in a time warp. Somehow, from Reventlo, it did not sound like an affectation; and women of a certain age seemed mesmerized by it.

When Lovett had finished his triple highball, another magically appeared to replace it. "Don't give me away, Pop," said a voice in his ear, and he turned to see Chip at his shoulder.

"Give you away? Right now I'd pay somebody to take you," Lovett muttered, with a look that was half amusement, half dismay. "I suppose you came for the floorshow."

"Nah," said Chip. "I saw them getting ready. Makes me feel sad to see women whose idea of formal dress is two Dixie cups and a cork." With that, Chip whisked Lovett's plate away and was gone.

Neither Quinn nor Reventlo noticed this interchange, intent as they were on positioning themselves for a better view as the opening strains of "St. Louis Woman" flooded the hangar.

The two showgirls had more help than they needed as they mounted the runway, and except for the four-inch heels they were as different as gin and tequila. The tall blonde might have come straight from Vegas, long-haired, bedecked in fur and costume jewelry with a headdress that made her seem to soar. The latina was more voluptuous with short dark gypsy curls, tricked out in lacy stuff that artfully failed to hide a great pair of legs. They strutted in unison, wearing bright commercial smiles, and made a parody of shy surprise to the calls of, "Take it off!" It was obvious that they would; and just as obvious that they would take their sweet time about it.

Then the music tape segued to a whispery piece from "All That Jazz" and Blondie began a stately slink, while Shortie took a folding chair onto the runway and appeared willing to wait her turn. But Shortie could not seem to find a comfortable position in that infernal little chair. She crossed her legs demurely, and showed fresh charms to her gallant viewers, and could not let the situation stand. She rearranged herself, leaning one arm on the chairback and hooking an ankle behind a chair leg, and became more scenic still.

By the time she tried straddling that chair, whistles and hoots of laughter proved that Shortie, not Blondie, was the feature of this segment. Shortie, in her contortions, may not have been in love with that little chair, but she certainly developed a close relationship with it, Lovett decided. He cheered her acrobatic efforts along with the others and was not surprised when Blondie found it necessary to unwind her colleague from some of those yards of lace before Shortie could divorce the chair.

Naturally, the blonde found her headdress a hindrance. Shortie, still fetchingly pretzeled in that folding chair, helped her get it off—all in cadence with the music. By the time they took their bows and promised to return, both performers glistened with perspiration and their audience had developed into two roughly equal camps, one fancying the elegant Blondie, the other more in rut for the smoldering Shortie. It was during the costume change that Lovett sought one of those nonalcoholic brews, while a few argumentative revelers sprayed one another with beer.

When Lovett regained his seat: "Good idea," Reventlo said, eyeing Lovett's beverage. "And since poor Elmo didn't follow your example he'll be courting a gyppy tummy, if I'm any judge."

Sure enough, Benteen had switched to harder stuff but then, so had a dozen others. The old fellow did look more determined than happy but you didn't withhold a man's booze at his own party, and Lovett only replied, "The man said to stay conscious," and took a swig of his Kaliber.

Act Two began musically with the tawdry, brassy, "The Stripper." Blondie's fresh costume began to disintegrate on cue, helped by snaps and Velcro, and by a few urgent hands from below, while Shortie, in a long cloak, collected the debris. Before long, she was practically down to the Dixie cups and cork of Chip's description. And then Shortie threw off her cloak and issued forth in Flamenco dress, with music to match, and all those petticoats didn't hold up very well either, but the blonde's faction began to clap, chanting, "Blondie, Blondie," which didn't impede the Spanish dancer at all.

But the spray from shaken beer bottles did. Any sober idiot can tell when a professional entertainer is pretending to lose her patience and when she really parts from it, but some drunken idiots cannot. That is when some other drunken idiot will launch a wild swing at Idiot Number One, causing Idiot Three to grapple with Idiot Two, and so on. With her runway teetering, Blondie slid into the melee and Shortie went to her aid. Lovett began to back away, holding his chair in front of him to shield his retreat, and tripped over someone trying to crawl under a table.

Usually, an audiotape of "The Star-Spangled Banner" has a certain calming influence. This time it had little effect. What sent a dozen men lumbering for hangar doors was the series of piercing blasts from a police whistle. There were those who said a police whistle ought to be the B.O.F.'s national anthem.

By the time Lovett managed to disentangle himself from fallen chairs and stand erect, doors were slamming all over the place. No police showed. A sobbing Blondie hobbled on a broken heel to the dressing room, grasping what was left of snapped ostrich plumes, while Shortie fed a stream of barrio invective to the caterer. Of the original partygoers, only half a dozen remained.

"Mayday, mayday," Lovett heard, and saw Cris Reventlo bending over their host who was either *hors de combat* or asleep at his table. The Brit's glance was searching as if for fighter escort, and Lovett reached them a step ahead of young Chip, who seemed untouched by it all.

"Aw shit. Who hit him," Lovett said, because he could see Elmo Benteen shake, his breath chuffing.

"Jack Daniels," the Brit replied, checking for a pulse. "The self-indulgent, bloody old fool; diet be blowed, he will have his fun even if it kills him."

"That's Elmo, all right, as long as I've known him," Lovett agreed.

"Get a shoulder under him," said Reventlo. "Wade, can you get some car keys from the strongbox?"

"Plymouth wagon, parking lot," Chip said, wasting not a syllable as the two men lifted Benteen, who seemed to have no bones in him. Chip sprinted out ahead of them and, as they stumbled outside, the youth was already wheeling a huge old '57 station wagon toward them. A pair of whopping surfboards lay stowed on the roof rack and the men clambered in from the rear door, the hapless Benteen unable to help.

"But what's this all in aid of," Reventlo called toward Chip. "He needs an emergency room."

"I could use a navigator," Chip called back, steering with one hand, holding a cellular phone in the other.

Lovett crawled forward beside the driver, found himself sitting on a huge bag of Doritos, noted a road sign as he belted up. Chip, meanwhile, was murmuring into his phone with inhuman calm. "Macarthur to Bristol, north to Hemlock. Got it. Tell them to expect us," he said, and put the phone into its dashboard cradle. Then, perhaps for Reventlo, he called, "Communities Hospital, five minutes."

"We're on Macarthur," Lovett said, as a freeway crossed beneath them. Chip had the old Plymouth roaring along now, passing other cars. "Cellular phone, huh? Chalk up one for the yuppies."

"We could be losing him, lads," Reventlo called over the din.

They didn't lose him then. They got Elmo Benteen to the hospital in record time, and Reventlo saw to the admission rigamarole while Lovett stayed with the old man, so much bigger than life for so many years, now so tiny on that gurney.

Minutes later, Benteen was wheeled away as Chip entered, having parked the car. Reventlo strode up to hear Lovett say, "They're getting him stabilized, whatever that involves."

"Stable? That will be a lifetime first for Elmo," Reventlo said, and turned to Chip. "Don't know what we'd have done without you."

Chip, with a shy smile: "I thought maybe Pop here could use a designated driver."

Reventlo stared at Chip, then at Lovett. "This is your son?"

"Grandson," Lovett said. "It's a long story, and even I don't want to hear it. For that matter, I don't yet understand it. But Elmo Benteen owes you, Chip."

A shrug from the youth. "It was an honor."

Reventlo sighed and gazed down the hospital corridor. "I just hope," he said, "the honor won't be posthumous for Elmo."

4

The samaritans mooched around the waiting room long enough for two of them to sober up. When Lovett suggested that the caterer had blown that police whistle, Chip laughed and pulled the little gizmo from a chain around his neck. "Mom made me wear it," he said. "The only musical instrument that helps when you shred your stick in a killer barrel."

Reventlo looked up. "Can that possibly be the Queen's English?"

"Don't expect too much when it's past his bedtime," Lovett told his old friend.

"When your surfboard breaks up in a monster wave," Chip explained.

"Ah," said Reventlo, and was satisfied. "The whistle was a piece of quick thinking, lad." Lovett nodded agreement. After a moment Reventlo went on with the reticence of a bygone era, "Lovett, ah, about bringing your grandson to a Boff extravaganza: we don't, um, well, it isn't done, you know."

"I didn't bring him in, he snuck in; Christ knows how I'm gonna square this with his mother," said Lovett in a fast monotone.

"You won't have to. She thinks I went surfing, Pop," said Chip patiently, then glanced away as a nurse padded toward them, gum-rubber soles squeaking on polished linoleum.

"Wayne Lovett," she said. "Mr. Wayne Lovett?"

"Wade," he said, standing.

"Your uncle is asking for you," she said.

"You're the only family he has here, old man," Reventlo put in quickly. *Shut up and go*, his tone warned.

Two floors up, Lovett was ushered into a room where he found Elmo Benteen behind a curtain, with tubes in both arms and another taped below his nostrils. "Aw Jesus, Elmo," was all Lovett could say.

The parchment eyelids fluttered open. Turning his head seemed to require heroic effort from Benteen, whose lips formed the faintest of smiles. "Just cut it too close with that sour mash," he said, so low that Lovett moved nearer. "Well, they warned me. Call it pilot error."

"Any landing you can walk away from," Lovett said, implying that all would be well now.

"Ain't walkin' away this time, kid," Elmo said. "Just as well it's you here. Some of the boys I could name might not wanta—share what I have to say." He was having more trouble talking now.

"They'll have you up and around again, nice as you please, if you just behave."

"You don't get it, Wade. Listen up, 'cause this is what you call a death or death situation." A long breath, as if marshaling energy. Then: "Early in '45, back when your fist was still a virgin, the Japs hid away a fleet of planes for an all-out suicide war when we invaded Japan."

"Kamikazes. I remember," Lovett put in, but Benteen cut him off.

"Shut up, Wade." Another pause, as Benteen's eyes closed. "This was bigger. Hundreds of planes, maybe thousands, stashed everywhere. More than they had pilots to fly 'em. They were recruiting high school kids as cadet pilots near the end, and we were finding late-model airchines hid away for years afterward, regular aerial armada. But the A-bomb scrapped the invasion plans. Damn good thing for both sides."

He fell silent for a long moment, and Lovett touched the thin wrist nearest him. The eyes opened. "Wade?" The hand groped for Lovett's, gripped with surprising strength. "*But they didn't find 'em all.* I found a half-dozen, maybe the last on earth in mint condition, in a cave twenty years later, after my forced landing. I believe they're still waitin' for the day that didn't come. It's a fuckin' bonanza, kid."

"Maybe they've been found by now," Lovett guessed.

"Bullshit. I paid attention and I'd have heard. So would you."

Lovett swallowed hard, knowing it was true. A Mitsubishi "Zeke" in flyable condition brought up to a million dollars, now that so few remained. After fifty years gathering cobwebs, they'd need a lot of refurbishing—O-rings, corrosion, fabric. Most of the aircraft flown as Zeroes in films were American trainers reworked to look something like a Zero. The real thing was almost literally worth its weight in precious metal. Lovett felt gooseflesh rise on his arms. He said, "Who else knows?"

"What I've said? A few, most dead now. Served 'em right—tryin' to hog the deal." A brief silence. "They never got the details, and there's a hell of a lot of islands out there. Two months ago—when medics said I was ready for scrap—I said damn straight I was ready. Bad enough I can't cut the mustard; now I can't even lick the jar. But what a shame to leave all those ol' airchines to rot, huh?"

"Elmo, hang in there. We'll get specialists—"

"You been monitoring the wrong frequency? I've had specialists." Another silence, and a subtle change in Benteen's breathing rhythm. "That Nip squadron belongs to any Boffs who'll put their butts on the line for it, kid, and those only; but see that Mel gets a share."

"I'll try, Elmo." The old fellow gave no sign that he'd heard. "Want to tell me how to find this bonanza?"

"All on map—hangar," Benteen managed to say.

Now the old man was fighting for breath and, in response to some unseen monitor, a blue-clad nurse whisked in. "You'll have to go," she said to Lovett. "Now. Please."

Elmo's gaze held Lovett's as he tried to continue but in moments, more blue smocks bustled in. Lovett, hands in pockets, slouched in the hallway listening to the futile efforts of the hospital staff. He was not thinking about maps as he muttered, over and over, "Aw, Elmo; damn it, Elmo."

It took Elmo Benteen another fifteen minutes to "head west," but at last the staff began to file from the room, not hurrying. Lovett caught the eye of the nurse, motioned her to him with an expectant look.

"He just slipped away," she said. "I'm sorry. This can't have been a surprise," she added, "with multiple organ failures."

"Did he say anything?"

She paused, then shrugged. "Nothing that made sense. Usually they don't."

"Anything at all," Lovett persisted, shamed that he would be thinking again about a navigation chart.

"He said, 'Mean old Bub Merle.' I think he tried to say it again, but . . ." A larger shrug.

Lovett nodded and turned away, wondering if there was any point in pursuing this fantasy further. He had known Frank "Bub" Merrill, a famed barnstormer and test pilot of roughly Benteen's age. "Mean" was hardly an apt description for Frank Merrill; "deaf as a cast-iron hitching post" would be more like it, during the old fellow's later years. In any case there was no point in looking Merrill up. A respected member of the B.O.F.s, cheerful to the last with his familiar, "Well, how you doin', stud?" the old boy had died somewhere in south Texas a year or so previous.

Lovett had not kept track of the time. When he found Chip and Reventlo, the youth was dozing but snapped back to alertness. Their faces fell at Lovett's headshake. "He knew damn well he shouldn't be drinking," Lovett explained. "I think he never expected to live past the weekend. And he didn't much care."

"And those hints he dropped, broad as a barmaid's arse, will just become part of his legend," said the Brit.

"Maybe part of ours," Lovett said. "He made a, uh, call it half of a deathbed confession."

"And you believed him?"

"I believe it's worth checking out."

"So who's to pick up the pieces? You Yanks have such quaint legal constraints," Reventlo said.

"I don't know. His son Mel, I suppose." A sudden image flickered across Lovett's inner eye: an air nav chart folded into some attorney's briefcase, hidden away from the people Benteen meant to see it and meaningless to anyone else. He said, into Chip's yawn: "But before tomorrow we've got to find something in Elmo's hangar." Then, infected by Chip, he yawned, too.

"Let me point out," said Reventlo as they left the building, "that it's already tomorrow. Are you sure you're up to it?"

"I have a million reasons to," said Lovett.

Chip broke a thoughtful silence as they left the parking lot. "Pop, let's not get into breaking and entering, okay?"

"Not if we're lucky. Tell you what: you drop us off and go get more coffee."

"I can stop on the way," Chip pointed out.

"Drop us off, and go—get—more—coffee," Lovett repeated very slowly.

"Gotcha," Chip sighed. If there was to be any break-in, he wouldn't be present at the time.

"This had better be very, very important," Reventlo warned.

"You decide," Lovett replied. "Remember Benteen never told anyone where he was marooned, back in '68? Here's why . . ."

The outside doors to the hangar offices had been locked, presumably by the caterer, but no one had thought to check the hangar doors. The two men shoved one of the towering door panels aside enough to squeeze through, then closed it again. The huge cavity inside was still littered with overturned chairs and stank of stale beer, lit only by a few phosphorescent tubes against girders above. Reventlo, hands on hips, surveyed the mess. "In the hangar, not in one of his aircraft outside," he prompted.

"So the man said."

"We're looking for a nav chart. Philippines? Indonesia?" Benteen's famed disappearance had fueled speculation into both areas, once upon a time.

"They fold to the same size, Cris," said Lovett, with the patience he might display to an idiot.

"You're lecturing me on ONC charts?" Reventlo vented a snort of derision. Operational Navigation Charts, unlike the sectionals used by stateside pilots, folded down only to briefcase size and were identified, not by some city name, but by a letter and number. "Righteeoh, then. Something between F-10 and, say, K-13." This was a verbal elbow in Lovett's ribs to remind him that Cris Reventlo, having flown commercial jets in the South Pacific, knew those charts like he knew the wrinkles in his skivvies. "Or it could be one of the little Jeppesen charts," Reventlo mused.

"Oh hell, we round up the lot then." They began in Benteen's office, finding numerous charts but all North American Regionals folded pocket-sized, most of them outdated.

Benteen's desk was a hollow-core door slab screwed down to a pair of metal two-drawer file cabinets spaced well apart. Tugging on a drawer, Lovett found it locked. "Cris, find us a pry bar."

The Brit raised his brows, shrugged, and turned to comply when a knock echoed. "That'll be the lad," he said.

"Let's hope so. I'll go," Lovett said, and left Reventlo deep in thought. He let Chip in and left the door unlocked, took a cardboard tray full of lidded containers and doughnuts. "Relax. We didn't have to break in," he said.

Chip's face shone with zeal. "What'd you find?"

"Cuban cigars. A bottle of Wild Turkey behind some books. Nothing we were looking for," said Lovett. "We haven't jimmied Elmo's cabinets yet."

But when they entered the office, the file cabinets were open, Reventlo pawing through one. "I knew Benteen wouldn't keep his keys safe," said the Brit without glancing up. "Manila envelope taped here in the footwell. Keys to cabinets, aircraft, God knows what."

"Hot diggity," Lovett crowed.

"Waiter, bring this man a cool diggity," Reventlo murmured.

"We'll take the other cabinet," Lovett said. Chip simply pulled the top drawer out and placed it atop the desk for Lovett, then knelt at the lower one.

Reventlo stopped to open his coffee and glanced at the others. "The lad knows a nav chart on sight?"

"Gimme a break," Chip muttered.

"Thought I'd ask," said the Brit, sipping. "Some fold to a size larger than sectionals."

"He's been my nagivator often enough," Lovett said.

"Nagivator," said Reventlo. "Precisely the word for them. Where were you when I needed you, Lovett?"

"At Elmo's bedside, and that's exactly where you needed me," Lovett rejoined, bickering good-naturedly.

"Unless this was his last great practical joke," the Brit said, pausing in his search. Benteen's sense of the absurd was well known.

"There is that," Lovett admitted. "Nobody's twisting your arm here, Cris."

The Brit laughed and resumed searching. They enjoyed brief spurts of elation, always followed by dismay to find charts labeled, KETCHIKAN, BILLINGS, GREEN BAY. At length they finished, frustrated, replacing paper in the cabinets, then relocking them. Over coffee and doughnuts, they talked it over. Surely, Reventlo said, some of those keys would open lockers near the workbenches across the hangar.

Dawn showed through high windows before they finished rifling through those lockers. Because a refrigerator makes an excellent low-temperature locker for volatiles, Benteen had one with a hefty padlock and chain. "Let me take the fridge," Chip said. "They're my favorite stashes. And don't ask, Pop," he said as Lovett turned to respond.

Chip finally admitted defeat after emptying ice cubes from trays and prying into plastic fascia panels. "Rivets in the ice trays, epoxy in the crisper, solvents and stuff," he reported as the others refilled lockers. "Nothing like a map. You're sure he said a map," he urged for confirmation.

Lovett, squatting, dry-washed his face. "Yeah, that was the word, he just—"

"Why not 'chart,' " Reventlo asked abruptly. "He should've said 'chart.' Shouldn't he?"

"You'd think so," Lovett mused, and stifled a mighty yawn, standing erect, stretching. "Shit. When isn't a map a chart?"

"For one thing, when it isn't to scale," Reventlo said. "We're missing something, lads."

"Yeah, a map of umpteen million bucks," Chip said glumly.

They strolled back to Benteen's office now, scanning the distant corners, the girdered heights, the shadows beneath work-benches. "I'll check the w.c.," Reventlo said, and fanned through the pile of magazines in the bathroom. Chip wondered aloud if a map could be among those papers they'd flipped past in the file cabinets, and Lovett agreed that could be the case.

At last Reventlo emerged from the little room with a headshake. "The lad's probably right. I propose we remove the contents of those cabinets, get some sleep, and peruse it all when we're fresh."

"Which is theft, any way you look at it," Chip said.

"Not if we put it back before anyone notices," said Reventlo.

Lovett, grinning wanly: "If you're not caught, theft ain't theft?"

Reventlo, spreading his hands: "According to my solicitor."

"Pass," Lovett said. "So far we haven't done anything to put my grandson's tail in a crack—well, not too deep a crack. I won't risk a felony. Of course, what you do after we leave, . . ." He stopped as his gaze flicked across the walls with all those framed photos, some large, a few too small to inspect from any distance.

Then, without the slightest hesitation, Wade Lovett stood up and marched with jaunty step to the smallest framed picture in the lot. Smiling, he lifted it from the wall. It was a wallet-sized black-and-white shot of two men standing beside a menacing, twin-engined Martin bomber of World War Two vintage, the photo's creases showing through its protective glass.

"Elmo and Frank Merrill, back when Merrill was taming that killer B-26 Martin built during the war," Lovett said, caressing the frame, smiling. "He didn't say Bub Merrill was mean. He was saying, 'Me and old Bub Merrill.' "

His smile faded as he turned the picture over, finding blank cardboard.

"Merrill tested your B-26 early in the war. I think Elmo had some input," Reventlo offered.

"Something to be proud of," Chip said. "I bet Mr. Benteen carried it with him."

"Of course he did," Lovett mused, now prying at the cardboard backing, clumsy in his haste. And there on the back of that photo, scratched in pencil, was an outline like a misshapen sock, perhaps two inches in its largest dimension. A single word, "strip," slanted down the heel. Below it were more scratches, and Lovett read them aloud. "136 degrees, 40 minutes East; 12 degrees, 20 minutes North," he said softly. "And maybe an airstrip."

Reventlo let out a long breath, then shut his eyes. "Ah . . . Philippine Sea, somewhere north of the Carolines," he breathed, smiling to himself.

"A half dozen cherry antiques," added Chip, awed by the notion.

"One—million—a copy," said Lovett, "if it's true." He peered again at the back of that photo, then tucked it into his shirt pocket. "First we get some decent charts of the area, and then call another National Emergency."

"Charts of what area?" The stern contralto voice from the doorway made all three males whirl in unison.

Reventlo, brazening it out: "Who left that door unlocked? Private conversation, young lady. I'm awfully sorry, but Benteen Associates isn't open for—"

"Let me tell *you* what's open, buster." She was fortyish, medium height and on the sturdy side, with cropped straight ebony air and a twinpeaks bustline and the apricot-tinted complexion of a Balinese. Her nose was a trifle too broad for conventional beauty, but common among islanders. Her stride into the office was brisk, her dark eyes bright as they flickered around the place. She wore slacks and sandals, and the hand that rested on her shoulder bag was scarred and callused. "A lot of private files are open. This is my hangar, so you bozos are trespassing. At least," she added, the almond shape of her eyes closing to slits, with a glitter as hard as obsidian. "Unless you're the debris from that goddamn wingding my old man threw last night. And judging by the kid," she pointed toward Chip, "I don't think so." She let her left hand glide into her shoulder bag. "Names."

Now Lovett stood up. "Could you produce some ID, ma'am? We seem to be off on the wrong foot this morning."

"Didn't think I'd need it," she sighed, pulling a smallish automatic pistol from her bag, letting it sweep the office casually. "I want names, and your asses out of here, in that order."

"Chip Mason, Jesus, lady," the youth said quickly, putting his hands up.

"Chip Mason Jesus," she said. "Never heard of you. Catchy, though."

"He's Crispin Reventlo," said Lovett, pointing toward the Brit and easing sideways to place himself in front of Chip. "And I'm Wade Lovett. And would you mind not pointing that—"

But she was already replacing the sidearm, sighing, her gaze softening with the slump of her shoulders. "Oh shit," she said softly. "The limey accent fits. And you're Lovett, huh? I suppose you could be the bunch who saw my old man off, so to speak. But unless he's found the fountain of youth, this is the youngest Boring Old Fart I've run across," she went on, still suspicious of Chip.

"I've got to use the john," said Chip, sidling away.

"Why now, just when things get interesting," she asked.

"Why not? When you pulled that cannon on us," Lovett rejoined, "I had the urge myself. This is my grandson."

"Little old thirty-two caliber, a cannon? Relax. I didn't know who you were," she said. "I'm still upset over my dad."

Reventlo found his voice again: "And that would be?"

"Elmo Benteen," she said, her eyes starting to brim over. "I've just come from the hospital. I guess they found my number in his wallet."

Lovett's jaw dropped. "Your father? You're not Mel Benteen!"

"And all this time I thought I was. Melanie, if that'll help," she said, ignoring the single tear that traced a handsome cheek. Her gaze seemed fixed on some great distance, as though reliance on anger might keep her less vulnerable. "The old fool. I told him and told him—but that's my problem, guys. And I, ah, I do need some privacy here. Stuff I need to find," she added vaguely.

Reventlo spread his hands as if offering an invisible basket to Lovett. "A fiver says I know what she's after, Wade. And even if she isn't, she's entitled to it."

The woman: "Entitled to what?" Lovett fished the little photo from his pocket, handed it over without a word. She looked at both sides, and shut her eyes for a long moment, and then tried a smile. As if to herself, she murmured, "When it wasn't in his wallet, I damn near peed my knickers. He once told me to look there."

"It was here on the wall," Lovett supplied, pointing. "He staged his last blowout so he could turn it over to us."

A quick glance at each of them. "You know, then."

"The lost squadron? Elmo said if it panned out for the Boffs, a share should go to you," Lovett explained. "Of course, we'll honor it."

"You damn well bet you will," said Mel with asperity. "Goddamn him, if he had just told me where those hulks are, I'd have been there years ago. Probably rusted to junk by now."

Reventlo and Lovett shared a wary look. "You intend to take part in an island recovery operation?"

"Just try and stop me. I was born on Bora Bora, guys; don't you know an islander when you see one? After stateside boarding schools—several of 'em," she grinned, not needing to explain, "he taught me to run heavy equipment hauling phosphates on Palau," she said evenly. "If I thought I could go it alone . . . but Papa spilled the beans, didn't he?"

Reventlo: "It crossed our minds that Elmo could be having his fun with us all, Ms. Benteen."

"Mel. Yeah, he might have done that to you. Not to me. I still don't see why he would've told an over-the-hill gang."

"You said it yourself: you couldn't do it alone, and Elmo must've known that. And there was nobody else he could trust to see that you got a share," Lovett replied.

"Some of us are still kings of the hill," Reventlo put in, standing more erect, straightening his tie.

Mel flicked her glance to Chip as he exited the bathroom. "And at least one of you is still a little prince."

"He won't be part of the operation," Lovett said quickly. "Still, I'll vouch for him."

"You'd better. All we need is to show up there," she said, handing the photo back, "and find the Confederate Air Force hauling our goodies off. Hell, we don't even know the legalities of it!"

"She's right, you know," said Reventlo. "We have some scutwork to do."

Lovett kept his answer civil with an effort. "I know that, Cris. Good Christ, we don't even know what questions to ask yet. But we're going to," he said.

"Without arousing any suspicions," Mel chimed in.

"So we're really going to do this," said the Brit in wonderment.

"Now really, are we, old man? Let me stress those last two words. Men half our age would be challenged. I, for one, need to get in shape if we're to be Tarzanning about on jungle vines, ducking natives who want our heads on poles."

Mel Benteen's nostrils flared. "You sure somebody hasn't already shrunk yours? That's insulting, you elitist asshole."

"She's a saucy bird," Reventlo murmured, blinking.

"She's an islander, for God's sake," Lovett told him, "who evidently learned the language at Elmo's knee." When he needed to concentrate, Lovett tended to look like a man with a migraine, placing one or both hands over his forehead. He put them there now. "Hold on, folks. Okay. Okay. I know it's crazy to rush into this, so let's ease into it. We can cancel the operation later, if it seems undoable. Maybe we will. But think what a windfall it could be!" His hands came down now. "It may be the chance of a lifetime. Meanwhile, we need each other on friendly terms."

"Don't count on it, pal," Mel said. "Just think of me as an equal who will pop you in the snoot if you deserve it."

"Snoot," said the Brit to nobody in particular. "Dear Goddy, the woman is Elmo in the flesh."

"You better believe it," she rejoined. "My papa may have been ashamed of me, but he didn't raise me to take a lot of shit."

"Right," Lovett said, with a glance toward Chip who seemed to be enjoying the woman's truculence. "So we take this one step at a time, exchange phone and fax numbers, and recall the faithful when we have more essentials. Who wants to locate the charts, and who checks out the location, and Lord help us, who hosts the next National Emergency?"

5

After his return to Wichita, Lovett's fax machine stayed hot throughout the next week. Several of those messages were Chip's: lowest air fares to Guam and Manila, inoculations suggested by government honchos, prices of inflatable boats and outboard engines, shipping weights. It warmed Lovett to think how seriously Chip, sworn to secrecy, was taking on these responsibilities when he had no hope of tagging along.

After a dozen amendments, Lovett's B.O.F. announcement said the usual cornball stuff about a National Emergency, this time to be held in his own hangar. But in a rare nod toward sanity, it included a page that was both proposition and warning in what he hoped were roughly equal parts. It began with Elmo's obituary clipping, a good half-dozen column inches, enlarged so that the more elderly Boffs could read it. Below the clipping was Lovett's postscript.

> If you were there, you know Elmo intended to give us a chance at one hell of a stash in the vicinity of his '68 mishap. Think big. Maybe it's there; maybe not, and there is only one way to find out without it getting on CNN. Elmo debriefed me on his way West. Show up for this only if you can take part in recovery ops. If you talk the talk, you must walk the walk. Funding may be a problem and you may be a partial solution. Think of this one as a boozeless business meeting with pizza, iced tea and only one female but I guarantee her as a surprise. If she doesn't dance on your Stetsons the surprise will be mine.

Lovett tapped a pencil against his teeth, uncertain at what he'd written. They had agreed that no mention of the site would be made, even among themselves, until the Boffs convened.

He dropped the rough draft as his phone rang. "Yo, Chipper," he said, brightening, and waited while his grandson spoke. Then, "I've slated my emergency for weekend after next. Don't expect a big turnout.—Whoa. You know I'd love that, but not unless your mom concurs. And I don't . . ."

His brows shot up at Chip's reply. Evidently, Roxanne had loosened her leash on the boy. Grinning now: "Come as soon as you like and stay as long as you can. Just tell me which flight to meet. Uh, one thing, though. I can't fund you, I'm scraping the bottom of my financial barrel.—Yep, selling my stocks, aircraft, maybe the VariEze if I get a halfway decent offer."

Now he waited longer, a wry smile fading as he doodled some numbers. "You know, I'm having trouble figuring out who's the grandparent here," he interrupted finally. "Okay, so it's loony. I'm entitled. If there's one thing worse than an old whippersnapper, it's a young fogey.—It's my decision, Chip. If you and Roxy weren't well fixed, I wouldn't be highrolling like this; but you are, and if it pays off I can send care packages to Fort Knox.—Hey, it's not as if I couldn't earn more.—You sound like Roxy. If I hear you say 'at your age' one more time, I'm gonna cut off your Coors. Quit worrying. It's my money and my risk, and I'm gonna take 'em both. Jeez," he finished, exasperated.

Chip made amends and promised another fax before he arrived. Lovett replaced the phone, put both elbows on his desk, and buried his face in his hands. *Maybe the kid's right*, he thought. What had Reventlo said? Men half their ages would be challenged. Most people would conclude that anyone in his sixties, converting most of his assets to cash for a treasure hunt into the Pacific, was crazy as a druggie's lab rat. All undeniably true. And yet . . .

And yet it was all coming together; *seemed* to be coming together, anyhow. Reventlo's UPS parcel full of charts had filled in a few blanks, including a little squiggle representing dirt with a name and a location that almost exactly matched Elmo's coordinates.

Melanie Benteen hadn't been idle either. Her Laguna Niguel address was near Laguna Beach, not exactly a low-rent district, so if she managed to lease her place on good terms as she hoped, maybe she could help with expenses. Meanwhile Mel was faxing information on Location X as fast as she could scribble notes from transoceanic phone calls.

Lovett wondered if anyone could have guessed that location from her notes, now in his possession. The tropical or subtropical Pacific was easy to guess, which narrowed it down to only ten million square miles or so. Narrow it further to accommodate Mel's data on Japanese occupation during the '40s, and you still had a million square miles to scan. Those charts from Reventlo, plus faxes from Chip, would have given too much away, which is why Wade Lovett kept the whole sheaf in a battered attaché case, within sight at all times.

He sold his sporty car and two aircraft in the following days, renting a subcompact and making arrangements to convert as much of his stock portfolio as possible. The figure he arrived at was a shade over $180,000, but that could evaporate fast when he started shipping major items—a leased crane and maybe a barge came readily to mind—to Location X. God only knew all the equipment they'd need, but he was guessing his funds wouldn't cover it all. Crispin Reventlo's resources were still a total unknown.

Someone in the States, he realized, should have power of attorney to free his funds and wire money to him as he needed it. Chip? Too young to qualify. Roxy? God, no; she might try to argue instead of following orders. *Who, then?* He hated to spend money on a local attorney, but it might be necessary.

He spent fruitless days showing off his beloved VariEze to prospective buyers, but none of them wanted to buy an aircraft in a disassembled state. If it was flying now, they said, why not sell it in flyable condition?

Because, Lovett told them, selling a whole aircraft you'd built yourself was a time bomb under your mattress. You sold it to Buyer One, who then sold it to Buyer Two, and ten years later Buyer Five's drunken idiot cousin stole it for a joyride and deep-stalled it hard enough to marmalade him on impact. Guess who *must* be responsible: you, the builder, must pay damages, having built a deathtrap for the innocent. Or so the goddamned lawyers had claimed, time after time, virtually sending both Cessna and Piper into bankruptcy in the process. The trouble this caused to smaller commercial and private builders was beyond belief. No, thanks, Lovett said. He would sell a disassembled bird, and let the buyer rebuild it. You might not avoid torts and retorts entirely, but from Square One you sure packed a lot of crushed ice into the average shyster's jockstrap—always a good beginning in the Litigious States of America.

Or the buyers could find airplanes in Mexico, where people were responsible for their own purchases—and where some airplanes were put together with duct tape and silly putty. The choice was theirs.

So far, they had chosen to keep looking. Try as he might, Lovett couldn't manage to feel crestfallen. Win or lose in the Pacific, it would be nice to know his flashy little wings would be waiting when he returned.

If he returned. Lovett was no pessimist ordinarily, but you could hardly turn over a shovelful of dirt in that part of the world without finding some optimist's bones. There was no such thing as a minor disease or a slight accident in a place that harbored germs from Saturn and might lie five hundred air miles from the nearest medic.

Prompted by that thought, he checked the time and cursed, realizing he was late for his shots, taking the attaché case with him. The tetanus booster was the least of his concerns. No matter how well he prepared, he knew there'd be some damn thing to hurdle at the last minute.

His first inkling of a Matterhorn-sized hurdle came on a Monday afternoon, two days prior to Chip's arrival, with a Mr. Collins who was roughly Lovett's age and who reminded him of a frog in a three-piece suit. The guy looked about as threatening as a day in May, wore a rep tie and had little nose-clip glasses, with sparse mousy hair combed artfully across his scalp. His business card was from Lincoln Properties Management in Omaha. He was acting on a rumor, he said, that Mr. Lovett might consider selling his business. His client chose to remain anonymous for the present, but Lincoln Properties was prepared to vouch for his sincerity.

The idea had much appeal for Lovett after he found that Collins did not jump like a toad from a hot skillet at the mention of a quarter of a mil. He ticked off the equipment on hand, the VariEze to be sold in pieces, the goodwill he had built up, the hangar itself—and then realized just how far it all failed to tally up to $250,000.

Collins remained unperturbed. He seemed more interested in Lovett himself—whether this was a retirement move, how Lovett was feeling about it, what he might consider next.

Over a steak and Chianti, the portly Collins revealed a weakness for word games: riddles, tongue-twisters, exercises in logic. If there was anything that interested Wade Lovett less, it was trying to think of something less interesting. That is why he deliberately made such a bad showing, in hopes he could turn the discussion elsewhere. He botched an easy "Anna's banned bananas" by multiple repetitions of the last syllable—"I know how to say it but I don't know when to stop," he lied. He flunked a simple problem in solid geometry, insisting that a three-inch cube cut into one-inch cubes would yield three one-inch cubes, resisting the impulse to say it was thirteen because the government took the other fourteen for taxes.

Most men would have called the game on account of idiocy at that point but Collins was made of more curious stuff, claiming Lovett's efforts were "capital, truly capital." He asked what Lovett had eaten for breakfast, and choked on his cheesecake when Lovett smiled and said, "Pussy, as I recall." And then Lovett added that all this intellectual work was giving him a headache.

Collins relented then, paying with an Amex card, and Lovett made no obvious reaction when his gaze swept the receipt Collins signed, and even upside down he could tell with an instant's glance that the name on it was not Collins but Collingwood.

And when "Collins," driving him home, asked what could be in that attaché case that made him carry it to dinner, Lovett said, "I haven't the foggiest idea, forgot the combination months ago. It just makes me feel good." And the little man smiled and said he understood.

Perhaps he thought he did understand. In any case, he accepted the offer of a nightcap and made no remark at the disaster area of Lovett's apartment, with half-empty cartons of Chinese takeout from days ago and back issues of *Kitplanes* strewn about like autumn leaves. "Sample anything that looks good and isn't green," Lovett said as he headed for the kitchen. The little guy sat on the edge of a chair already full of periodicals, knees together, looking at those cartons of leftovers as if wondering how far they could strike from repose.

Lovett's guest took a few sips of his martini before claiming he was late with a long drive ahead of him. Lovett wondered if he was going to have to remind the guy that his Chevy rental was still at the hangar. But Collins/Collingwood did a fair imitation of suddenly remembering at the door, and drove a bemused Lovett to his hangar. There he promised a follow-up call, and Lovett watched with mixed emotions as the man drove off.

Lincoln Properties might vouch for the sincerity of anyone they liked. But who would vouch for Lincoln? Not the Omaha directory assistance, nor nearby Council Bluffs, nor the city of Lincoln, nor Grand Island, as Lovett discovered from his hangar office simply because he didn't want to spend the rest of that evening in an apartment made empty by Mayday's absence. Either these property management folks were very exclusive or they flew false colors, Lovett concluded. He had experienced both. He did not expect to get that follow-up call, and turned his attention to a fax that had come in from Crispin Reventlo during dinner.

"Man oh man," he muttered, scanning it a second time. Reventlo wasn't sure, but thought he might have a chance to ferry an old transport from Oregon to Alice Springs. The plane was an ancient C-47, the Model T of the air in its civilian DC-3 version, which Brits called a Dakota and Americans had once dubbed the Gooney Bird. The big old twin-engine workhorse had many names, and a surprising number of them could still be seen galumphing slowly across primitive regions sixty years after their introduction. Douglas C-47s had flown cargo over the Himalayan Hump, towed gliders into combat, dropped paratroopers, hauled kings and cabbages and cattle and salmon, and had served as a sturdy gun platform against ground troops.

Several companies had existed solely to rehabilitate worn-out DC-3s, of which more than ten thousand copies had been built. Some of the weary had been turned into diners, mobile homes, even warehouses. One had been found on a farm in Canada, in use as a chicken coop; a year later it was flying again in South America. They groaned and grunted, ran rough, bounced like golf balls, their wings flexed like a hummingbird's—and promised to keep on doing it forever.

This particular old classic was being fitted by Everkeen with long-range tanks because, even by island-hopping across the Pacific, you needed a three-thousand-mile range to make it with any kind of decent fuel margin. And the C-47 had whopping big tires that could land on sand, and take off the same way. It would fly, more or less, on one engine until hell exported glaciers and it could be repaired by anyone with an A and P—aircraft and power plant—ticket. No wonder some rancher smack in the middle of the Australian outback wanted this one. According to Reventlo, there was no official cargo to be flown, which meant there was room for the strictly *un*official kind. That was the really good news.

The bad news was that the Aussie rancher wanted this old war horse picked up as soon as the tanks and maintenance were finished. "Damn and blast," Lovett said aloud. According to the schedule forwarded by Reventlo, the C-47 would leave for Hawaii the day before Lovett's National Emergency. That meant the Brit would have to make a wide diversion merely to get a snapshot or so of the island—

and to justify it to a copilot and flight engineer without giving the game away. Perhaps, Reventlo had scrawled, he could develop an imaginary case of cylinder weevils and use the landing strip Elmo Benteen had indicated. Either way, Cris could hardly be in Wichita and halfway to Hawaii simultaneously. "Ta," he had written.

Lovett realized it was only 7 P.M. in Portland, Oregon, where Reventlo awaited his airplane from Everkeen. He did not call the Brit, but spun his Rolodex to locate an Everkeen test engineer who, though too young to be a B.O.F., had built a VariEze like Lovett's. Well, not *exactly* alike; Lovett's nose wheel retracted only when it was supposed to and this guy's winged tricycle had a mind of its own until Lovett exorcised the gremlin for him.

The connection was good in more ways than one. "Nah, I'm in Wichita," Lovett told him, and reminded him of the favor he'd promised. "I believe you're refitting a weary old C-Fort with long range tanks there. I need you to keep it there for an extra week or so." Whereupon, the voice from Portland became slightly wary.

Knowing the engineer was a Perot believer, Lovett began, "Okay, so here's the deal," and after that it was a lock-in.

Lovett rang off and called Reventlo, who would not believe the news at first. "No, I bloody well can't be there because I'll be on the bleeding airplane for about a thousand years going bugger-all from those damned droning engines," he said irritably.

"Not if there's a series of minor delays at Everkeen that you can't affect," Lovett said, "and I am reliably informed that there will be."

"How can you do that? Everkeen doesn't do that. What the bleeding hell have you duh-done?" Reventlo was stammering by now.

"Actually, I don't know, and you don't want to know," said Lovett. "Nothing to jeopardize the flight. But if your schedule just happened to slip, I wouldn't fall over in a dead faint. Possibly several slips. As many as it takes to set your departure back, oh, say, ten days."

A long silence from Oregon. Then as if talking to himself, "If that happened, and I signed on a copilot and mech I fancied, at very attractive rates to the client, it might solve a lot of problems. I don't suppose our tough little Benteen bird is rated for multi-engine."

"I can find out," Lovett said. "I'm type-rated for those old ashcans and I could sign on either as flight engineer or copilot."

"When it sounds this slick, someone has usually greased my skids on a long slide into Shit Lake," the Brit responded, "but I've been there before. Let me put it this way: I am going to forget this call unless and until a series of bizarre incidents puts me on the bloody beach when I am supposed to be filing a flight plan. For the record, who's your inside man here?"

"For the record, none of your goddamn business," Lovett chuckled. "I just wanted you to be ready for a hop to Wichita, if fate fucks up your original plan."

Reventlo's sigh breezed through the earpiece. "I've had the fickle finger of fate diddling up my arse so long I've grown accustomed to the blockage."

"Explains why you're so full of crap," Lovett replied. "Listen, Cris, if you really don't want to make the meeting, I can undiddle your schedule."

"No, no, I'm beginning to like the idea." A moment's pause. "I may haunt a surplus store or two around Portland tomorrow; locate some emergency rations, all that sort of thing."

Lovett endorsed the suggestion and hung up after promising a vacant couch for Reventlo. He filed the latest fax in his attaché case and took it all with him when he locked his office, facing a humid night breeze. The apartment was still a howling mess but he could spare a few hours of cleanup before bedtime. What he truly hated was his new regimen of a three-mile run every morning, though he had to admit he hadn't felt better in years. Maybe, he thought, it was just the prospect of having Chip visit. Or maybe it was having a goal again. There was nothing like a big, preposterous, risky project to motivate a man.

Or to kill him.

6

Chip came in by commercial air two days before the meeting and claimed the guest bedroom as usual. "Cool," he said, gazing around at the apartment's unexpected neatness. He gave it the new pronunciation, "coowul," a reminder to his grandfather that if Chip Mason was no longer a boy, he was not yet entirely a man.

Protected by his elders, Chip still kept a youthful naïveté, and liked to quote some unknown savant to the effect that life was like a box of chocolates. Lovett hoped it would not shatter too many illusions when Chip learned that the box held half chocolates, half horse muffins; and that whichever you got, you had to keep chewing.

At least the youth had grown adult enough to worry about his integrity. "Friend of mine has a problem, Pop," he mumbled through a mouthful of BLT with cheese at the next morning's breakfast, as Lovett attacked its twin across the table. He got only a nod, Lovett's mouth being full. Sandwiches for breakfast had been Chip's choice; it was their habit to alternate the meal decisions. "Call it a loyalty problem," Chip added. And he sipped at his nonalcoholic Kaliber, which Lovett usually stocked.

When he had swallowed, Lovett said, "You pick your friends for what they're selfish about, Chip. If narrow self-interest is his only priority, don't count on him for much."

"No, I mean, two loyalties. He's promised one person to keep an eye out for, uh, what another person's doing. He loves that person. Both persons," he corrected.

"Love," said his grandfather, with an eye roll.

"Not jump-your-bones love; best-friend love," Chip explained. "Actually, they all love each other."

Lovett replayed the first part of that conversation to himself, nodding, chewing. Then: "So what's the second person doing that merits your spying?"

Chip flinched at that word as if struck; seemed to wrestle with it a moment, then could not stop a blush. "Nothing that I, my friend, can tell. Spying. Yeah, I guess." He pounded a fist on the table. "Yeah, dammit, let's call it what it is! Why do people do bad crap for good reasons? It only confuses things."

"Sorry, kid, but that's our big bad world—and welcome to it." Lovett thought he knew the problem in essence. He could worry around this Gordian knot with Chip for hours, or he could cut it. He chose to slash very gently. "So what does Roxy think I'm gonna do? Corrupt you? If that's it, don't take another swig of that beer. It looks like it might have alcohol." His grin proved that he was joking.

Chip's frown mirrored vexation. "Ah, hell, Pop. Am I that transparent?"

"Pure quarter-inch Plexiglas," Lovett replied, still amused. "And I'm not surprised she's worried about you. Look, you're all she has, and she knows damn well I'm not a Bobbsey twin."

A blank stare. "What's a Bobbsey?"

"I was born sixty years too soon," Lovett muttered. "Never mind. It means I'm not your standard model gramps with his laprobe and faithful old Shep by his rocker. My daughter knows that, bless her heart. The fact that you're here means she knows she has to let go pretty soon. She—"

"No it *doesn't*," Chip fired back, more vexed than ever. "Spying. Well, I don't do that, Mom. I should've told her that. And if I had, I wouldn't be here now. Or maybe I would anyway," he said, his face alight with grim satisfaction. "Pop, she sent me here. I even pretended I didn't much want to," he admitted. "That sealed it; here I am."

"So you got here by promising to, umm, report on how it goes." Lovett got a nod and a decision to speak, instantly reconsidered. He went on, "Well, then make your reports. I'll try to see there's no drunken orgies or high-stakes poker or mud-wrestling bimbos in the living room. It'll be an effort, but I'll try to make like a role model. Okay?"

But Chip had worked himself up to anger now, and would not be put off by these attempts to gloss over the problem. "It's not okay." His smile was brief and lopsided but, "Old Shep by your rocker, huh? Pop, they think you're *off* your rocker. Mom tried to weaselword around that, and I know she wants what's best for you, but that's what it comes down to. I mean, she sees her own mom every week, and I'm here to tell you the old lady isn't all there."

" 'Course not. She married me, didn't she?" Despite his efforts to keep this business on a trivial basis, Lovett knew his daughter's concern was genuine. He did not doubt that his ex got the best care Roxy could find for early senility. He also had no doubt that Roxy was used to getting her own way. "So your mom thinks it's time she took me in hand, now that her *other* son is nearly grown," he said, to prime the pump.

"Yeah," the youth snickered through his irritation. "And you know how hardheaded she can be."

"Whim of steel," Lovett replied, his W. C. Fields imitation, flicking an imaginary cigar ash.

"You're not taking this seriously enough, Pop," Chip warned.

Lovett shrugged. "Why should I? You're almost ready to leave the nest with that magical eighteenth birthday coming up in June, and it's her problem. What could she do?"

Chip's brows shot up, and he began to tick off items on his fingers. "Consult that pusillanimous little pissant, Alex the Wart, von Wurttemburg, who doesn't even know you, and get bad advice because the Wart wants to take over as her financial adviser." One finger down. Another went down with, "Hire some investigator to get your mental marbles counted. She did that, Pop. She could put your plans on ice for a while, that's what she could do."

"Jesus H. Christ," Lovett breathed softly. "That explains the guy I deliberately acted the fool for," he said, and slapped his forehead. "I'd love to see his report."

"No you wouldn't. I, uh, activated Mom's speakerphone and listened while she and the Wart talked about it. Some guy named Collingwood will testify on it. Whatever a dim cap is, it doesn't sound good."

"Diminished capacity. It's a kind of legal judgment," Lovett furnished, his own anger finally smouldering—partly at himself. To ease Chip's worry, he reached across the table and laid a hand on the youth's wrist. "Well, of course they could try that. Their problem is me. The day I can't convince a judge I'm still functional is the day I deserve to learn how to cut out paper dolls, if I still can."

"Right. And it'll cost you, and meanwhile your assets will be chilled, uh, frozen, and if you go on any trips you'll have to thumb your ride, and it might be seen as, well, whatever the Wart called it. Some legal term. I'm telling you, Pop, when that little squid waves a tentacle in your face, the other one's probably in your pocket."

"So he's already in your mom's pocket. Right?"

A sad nod of his head. "Looks that way. He's sooo refined. How could anybody with such refinement be other than genuine?" *Snort.*

Lovett pointed a finger at Chip. "You've just set my priorities for the day." He finished his beer and then added, "If they haven't already moved on this today, Roxy can freeze only what amounts to a tray of ice cubes tomorrow. And if I'm not dumb enough to let myself be served with any papers, and if it seems like business as usual otherwise, I can be the hell and gone out of reach before Roxy and von Warpdrive get their act together. I said maybe. Oh shit, oh dear, this is all I needed."

He stood up, licking mayonnaise from his fingers, taking their plates to the kitchen, talking as he went. "I'm not mad at your mom, Chip. Pissed, yeah. All right, a little mad, but she thinks she's doing this for the best."

"I know it," from the dining alcove. "I just don't like the way she got wind of you converting your assets."

"And how was that?" Lovett kept talking as he went into his bedroom and began to dress—with a goddamned tie, no less—as Chip followed.

"She was the one who spied. Listened in on the phone. I wonder how long she's been doing that."

Pausing to cudgel his memory, Lovett said, "She knows I'm headed for the tropics?"

"No, just that you've suddenly decided to clean out your assets to risk everything you own on something goofy. I flat-ass lied, said I didn't know. But she's sure it must be nutty as Granola."

"She's got that right," Lovett smiled, making a lousy Windsor knot. "But I know it's nutty. And I'm going to have fun at it, kid. If I had any lingering doubts, this settled 'em." Grumbling: "Roxy needed to talk this over with me first."

"She needs to turn that turd, Wurttemburg, out," Chip said.

Rough talk from a kid. Worse still, it sounded exactly like Lovett himself. *Rule One: they copy your worst habits first,* he thought. Lovett *tch, tch*'ed as he zipped up and slid into his best polished loafers. "She needs," he said, pointing his finger again, "the spanking I never gave her."

Lovett filled his pockets with the right junk, rubbed his hands together. "Okay, you drive, I'll nagivate. Hell, I gotta remember not to screw with the language that way; sounds like ol' rockin' chair's got me. Anyway, this may be a bad day for you but it'll save me some time, and we don't know yet whether we're too late."

"You're not nuts, Pop, just hyperactive."

"From the mouths of babes," Lovett said, waving the youth to follow as he tossed keys to him. "We're off."

"You know," Chip mused behind him, "sometimes I think maybe we are."

"Like I told Domenica, you didn't get it out of the ground," Lovett said, and cackled.

Lovett's broker, a wisecracking yuppie hoodlum named Peter Tyme, tried for roughly three minutes to talk Lovett out of disemboweling his account. When in full chat, Tyme could talk two hundred and fifty words a minute with gusts up to three hundred. "So just sit down and wipe that look out of your eye, Wade," he was saying, "and fill me in on—"

"It is five after nine, Pete," Lovett interrupted, staring at the clock on the one wall that wasn't mostly solid glass. "If you ever want another outrageous commission from me, you'll give me what I want right now instead of telling me why I don't want it when I damned well do."

Tyme rubbed his chin in doubt, then made an internal decision. "You're acting like a manic-depressive caught on the upswing, but what else is new? I can't just cash you out completely on the spot, Wade." Turning to his keyboard and screen, Tyme punched up the Lovett account, muttering as he scanned. "Market's open in the Big Apple. None of your stuff's in joint name, so I could sell in cash trade and give you a check for—how much of it do you want?"

"How much is all?"

With another look at the screen, Tyme grimaced. "Say, a hundred and fifty thou at current prices. WhichIcan'tpayouttoday," he rushed on.

Lovett began to seethe. "How much today? Right fucking now."

"I'd have to hold back, oh, ten thousand for three days 'til the trades settle. That's just the way—"

"Do it," said Lovett, relaxing a bit.

"Not quite so fast. Auditors will want some reason on this form, or my name's Chazz Keating, alias mud."

Lovett chewed his lip a moment. "Call it a gamble, Pete. Good odds, but a gamble. If, ah, when I come back, it comes back in multiples."

"You didn't say that, and don't say it again," Tyme warned.

"Well, shit, it's—another investment. Real estate," said Lovett, brightening. "Sort of a mining venture," he added. It was on the tip of his tongue to say, "offshore," but he held back.

"Mining venture," Tyme repeated, squinting at his client, shaking his head. "If I were the suspicious type, I could guess you're digging a legal hole for me to jump into. But this whole thing is your idea, and I told you not to, and you told me to go to blazes. Okay, sane people have been known to do that. Not that you qualify by any stretch of the imagination. You're sure you don't want to do lunch on me, think this over, settle down?"

"Dead solid certain. Watching that minute hand crawl unsettles me, for reasons you may discover." From the way his broker leaned back, he knew he'd said too much. He leaned forward and stared hard into his broker's eyes. "Pete, I have broken no law, and I've made us both some money over the years. Give—me—my—cash."

Tyme sighed, nodded, and addressed his keyboard, with occasional utterances to report sale prices. From time to time he would pause to glance Lovett's way, and always as if expecting Wade Lovett to suddenly levitate from his chair and go zooming around the ceiling. "Can't hand over cash, you know," he said during a lull. "I can make out a check you'll present to a bank, for the benefit of one Wade 'wild-man' Lovett."

Lovett gave that some thought, watching the clock's hands creep, feeling as if they were ants on his spine. "How many banks do you have this kind of buddy-system with?"

"Nearly a dozen, in Wichita."

"I want seven checks on the nearest seven banks, for twenty thousand each. And a printout of the bank addresses. I intend to pay them calls on short notice. Can do?" A nod from Tyme. "How long in minutes?"

"Boy, you're a piece of work. Half an hour, with luck. Are your hands sweating?"

"No, why?"

"They should be. Mine are," Tyme said with a doleful glance. "Most of the lunatics I know don't manage to hide it as well as you do." At one point he took a piece of printout and handed it over. It listed the addresses of seven banks in greater Wichita. Presently he turned back to Lovett. "I haven't cleaned you out; you still have an account and that makes some things easier. You don't want to hear me say, 'regulations'? All right then, rules." He hopped up and disappeared into the hall with a printout, leaving Lovett to stew about the time. His stride on returning was not his usual jaunty affair. "They'll be ready in a few minutes. Anything else I can do? Novocaine? Psychiatric evaluation?"

"Don't say that," Lovett pleaded. "You can tell me whether someone could have frozen my investments against my will."

"Court order," Tyme shrugged. "A circuit court can do that to protect assets." His eyes gleamed with conjecture. "At banks, too. I'm guessing you had that in mind, not putting all your nest-eggs in one basket. Don'tconfirmit," he said in a microburst, waving his hands before him.

"Who would deliver papers like that to you?"

"It'd usually be an attorney. Like the guy I see hassling our receptionist out front," he added, nodding at the clear glass wall. "I know that one. Biggest firm in town, biggest prink in Kansas."

Lovett knew that Roxy would gravitate to a big firm. He stood up, took one look, and turned his back on the scene. Though he didn't recognize the man with the receptionist, Lovett himself might be recognized. "I pick up the checks from the receptionist?"

"If I tell her to," Tyme said.

"Use that phone and tell her to the instant that shylock turns away. This may be a false alarm but—just in case the guy mentions my name, Pete, stroke him around. Gimme time to cash some small checks."

"I can try," Tyme said, smiling. "I don't get this kind of thing often. 'Course, when I do, I'd be smart to call our in-house attorney, and then sit here while they impress each other, before we got down to cases."

"How long would *that* take?"

"About three weeks, if I know those two," Tyme said with a grin of pure impudence. "You can go around and come back in the front way, if that'll help."

Peter Tyme stood, hands on hips, and watched Lovett disappear through a side exit while, through two glass partitions, he saw the approach of a natty little man-of-war complete with briefcase and, unless Tyme's eyes were faulty, grasping what looked like a folded court order as though it were a flaming sword.

One of those seven banks held Lovett's checking and savings accounts, and he hit it first while Chip waited, engine running. He used up twenty minutes because it takes a lot of time to count out several hundred big bills while cashing out two accounts and a whopping check. They scooted through traffic to two more banks. By ten-thirty, the rear seat of Lovett's rental car was strewn with a jumble of fat manila envelopes carrying more green stuff than the average flowerbed.

His brush with spastic colon came from the biggest bank in town. "If you'll just wait a moment," said the teller after consulting her inevitable screen, and started to whirr away.

But Lovett had seen her eyes narrow before she glanced back to him, and, "Just leave my cashier's check with me, please," he said, and she did.

He held the check, beginning to sweat, until a rumpled gent in a suit arrived with his paw outthrust, all smiles and bullshit and bonhomie. He was acting manager, he said, and he wasn't sure the bank had that much disbursible cash on hand.

Lovett's return smile was guarded. "What's the matter, didn't you guys install a big enough mattress?"

Well, not exactly, said the man, as if no joke had been made, almost as if this were a time for smiling, but not for joking. But if Mr. Lovett didn't mind, they would need some time to clear that check.

"A cashier's check? That's what these things are for. It's precleared," Lovett protested.

"Well, in a manner of speaking, yes. But occasionally some irregularity crops up. You know how computers are," said the manager, smoothly, without a blink.

Too smoothly. He hadn't actually said it *was* a computer problem; it might be a call-the-men-with-butterfly-nets problem. When he asked Lovett to sit down with him behind the carven low barrier, perhaps to have a cappuccino, Lovett saw five big letters invisibly blazoned across his forehead: S T A L L.

In or out of an airplane, Wade Lovett had always been able to sense the first buffet of a stall. He put the check in his pocket, sat down in a leather chair as if prepared to camp there until doomsday, and let the manager bustle off for that cup of java. When the man returned, the leather chair was vacant and the front door was slowly hissing shut, and Lovett was headed for the final bank on his list.

In that last bank, the computers were down. Whether that had anything to do with the fact that his transaction was conducted quickly, Lovett never knew, but by noon he had some hundred and thirty-five thousand in cash, plus a useless cashier's check that he tucked away in his attaché case. Who could say: one day it might be worth something.

Lovett changed into an old surplus flight suit at the hangar, kept all doors locked, and did not answer knocks until he heard Chip's three and two and one, in late afternoon. The kid was loaded down with brown bags; bottled drinks, a good ten pounds of sausage and cheese, and fruit in one bag. The other had rye bread, boxes of snack crackers and nonfat cream cheese on top, and below lay toilet articles with a change of clothes "—For my paranoid Pop," as Chip put it. The youth seemed to think his grandfather had gone from too little concern to unnecessary extremes of caution, but he carried out his instructions to the letter.

Lovett cheerfully agreed that all these preparations might be pointless but, he pointed out, "Better to have it and not need it than the other way around. Besides, most of this stuff will come in handy as munchies during the meeting. What's left won't survive several days in a lumbering old C-17."

Lovett wondered aloud if anyone had come to the apartment while Chip was accumulating the listed stuff. No one, said Chip. "Meter reader," he added offhandedly, "but I told him to come back tomorrow."

"The meters in my apartment complex are all grouped together," Lovett said evenly. His smile was faint and wry.

Chip, startled: "Not in your apartment?"

Lovett eyed his grandson for one pregnant moment, then began with a comically mocking, "Duhhh. Think about it; you ever notice twenty-four electric meters ranked like trophies on my wall? Now tell me again about paranoia, professor."

Chip sat down heavily and stared at nothing. "Pop," he said at length, "it's as if you were a fugitive from justice. But, I mean—they wouldn't shoot you or anything, would they?"

"Nope. Just serve me with papers; one of those cute little rigamaroles with its own set of rules. If they can't face me, they can't serve me. But let's say they managed that. Then if I tried to leave or spend my own money before a hearing was held, I *would* be breaking the law. That's where cops and threats of force might come in. I just—don't—know. I'm not a professional fugitive, you know."

"But a real gifted amateur," Chip said brightly.

The sound of knuckles on metal echoed through the hangar, and Lovett placed a restraining hand on his grandson's shoulder. "Doesn't matter who it is," he said softly. The knock echoed again, and Lovett could feel a tremor in the shoulder beneath his hand. For a few seconds he mistook intent for fear, until Chip's gaze hardened. "Maybe you can't afford to roust him, but I could."

"Don't. He's an officer of the court, I think. And process servers are always ready for rough stuff," Lovett said gently. They could hear footsteps moving away outside.

As they stashed their food, Chip remained subdued until he finally burst out, "I should call Mom. Tell her how stupid this is, try talking sense to her. We should both do that. If we don't, there's nooo way you can host a B.O.F. meeting here tomorrow night."

"You're right, I can't. You will, Chip."

Panic-stricken, the youth shook his head. "But where are you going?"

"Here and there, and you can help. If you want to, that is. Frankly, I could do it without you and it might be better if you flew back home. Roxy's probably chewed her nails up to the elbows by now." At this point the phone alerted them to a fresh fax message.

"S'posed to call her anyway," Chip muttered.

"Then call her," Lovett said, waving toward the phone which was cradled in his fax machine. They watched silently as a sheet of paper began to extrude like a tongue.

Though he did not yet read the message, Lovett's expression shifted gradually from thoughtfulness to one of good cheer. "I don't want you to have to lie to your mom on my account. Now listen carefully. Having just received this fax, I am going to fly out of here immediately. I have, um, new business interests on the coast, you see. Anyone who wants to conclude that I can't be found here has my blessings."

"But the meeting, Pop!"

"Oh, yeah. I've previously given permission for some group to use my hangar for a meeting. Not one of those boozy Boff blowouts Roxy's heard about, but a respectable business meeting of some kind.

Right?" Chip nodded in a kind of circular motion with a grimace that implied, "yes, but you've lost me." Lovett grinned and went on: "Promise me you'll hang around for that." A frozen instant between them. "Go ahead; promise me."

"Well, sure," said Chip.

"Good enough. And I promise to be back before—oh, Tuesday or so. Now call your mom as soon as I leave. She'll appreciate that."

He began to read Reventlo's fax now as Chip displayed his hands helplessly. "Pop, I don't know about this. I mean, if you'll be gone—"

Lovett heaved a long sigh. "I said I'd be back before Tuesday. I didn't say *how much* before." And with that, he winked and pulled his scarred old military-style helmet from its shelf. A lot of pilots wore Western-style hats when flying; their wide brims gave extra protection at high altitude from the ultraviolet rays that made skin cancer a real risk. Wade Lovett had the same protection in that helmet—and in a mishap, a thin layer of felt is no help at all.

At this time of day, adjacent hangars were closed. Lovett finished his usual meticulous preflight check inside the hangar, made certain that no strangers were skulking near, and taxied his VariEze outside with a parting wave to his grandson.

7

When Lovett taxied back after his half-hour jaunt in the VariEze, he saw Chip waiting with wheel chocks and a grin that stretched as wide as the hangar doors. Normally it is deliberate foolishness, alias a "Mr. Fumducker," to taxi smartly all the way into a hangar; brake failures are not unknown. But under the circumstances, this pilot felt he had no better option. The youth was talking before Lovett's canopy had fully raised. "I didn't tumble to your little plot 'til Mom had hung up. You were right, Pop; I didn't have to tell any lies, I thought you'd really lit out for Oregon."

Together, they secured the big doors again. Feeling guilty for his little deception, Lovett said, "I suppose you're in thick yogurt with Roxy."

A shrug. "Aw—not exactly. Would you believe, she thought I should've gone with you? Said from now on I must stick close to you in, swear to God, I quote, 'your time of need.' " An earnest frown accompanied his, "She really is worried about you, Pop. She isn't after your money."

"It'd go to you anyhow," Lovett told him. "My will—being of sound mind, and all that, as if anybody believed it now—puts it in trust 'til you're older. You and only you. Roxy doesn't know that," he added.

"Then Alex the Wart doesn't know it, either," Chip pointed out. "If he did, all this might not be happening."

"Screw von Wart, and screw the cockroach he rode in on," said his grandfather. He threw an arm over the youth's shoulder as they returned to his office, now in evening gloom. "We've got some lists and motel reservations to make, hair to wash, maybe some faxes to send, before tomorrow. As I said before, you'll have to be my welcome wagon because one thing I don't need right now is a high profile."

The little gathering of B.O.F.s, fewer than a dozen, trickled together over a period of hours during the following afternoon, not overly charmed by the conspicuous absence of booze. Each member demanded proof of Chip's claim, a proof obtained by wandering over to the sturdy coveralled and grease-smeared mechanic with unruly blond hair who worked on the VariEze in one corner of the hangar near a handy exit. It was Wade Lovett, all right, pulling that oil change. And to all, Lovett warned that they should simply forget him until they locked the doors for their scheduled meeting. "This open-door policy should convince some people I'm not here, and to anybody trying to serve me papers, I'm not. I'm in Oregon. That's why the peroxide job. Go swap lies with somebody else and tell my grandson the instant you spot a stranger." Naturally, Lovett's high crimes and misdemeanors became the hottest batch of guesswork among them.

Of all the members who collected there, Coop Gunther, a windburnt, scar-faced senior citizen with the proportions of a fireplug, was the only one who offered to limp away for a set of coveralls to help with the maintenance. Lovett admired the old boy, who would tackle any task, as Coop would say, "irregardless." That's the sort of work ethic you expected from old-time Alaskans.

Back in 1924, Gunther's mother had gone into labor on Kupreanof Island off the Alaskan coast while with his father, hunting moose for the larder as most Alaskans did; as many still do. Mitkof Island and the fishing village of Petersburg lay only two miles distant, but even today, every twelve hours the tide-swamped creek on Kupreanof goes dry as a bedouin's bathtub. With no bridge, no plane, and no way to launch their boat, Coop's dad delivered the squalling mite and named him Kupreanof, which nobody outside Russia and Alaska could pronounce in fewer than fifty tries; hence "Coop."

Everyone in the B.O.F.s knew why Coop would no longer fly; to get from his little outboard-and-snowmobile shop on Petersburg, old Coop had reached Wichita by seagoing ferry to Bellingham, then via Greyhound bus. He limped for the same reason that he lacked the last joints of two fingers: Coop's usual one-word explanation was,

"Alaska." The longer explanation had taken him on a lecture tour, and it was a skin-crawler.

Already a bush pilot in '42, Coop had joined the service he knew best, the Coast Guard, a beardless youth flying Grummans and PBY "Catalinas" during the war. He dodged a lot of flak when the Japanese invaded our Aleutians. Lucky Coop Gunther suffered not so much as a hangnail and lasted the next twenty years flying in what he called the brown-water navy. Newly retired from the Coast Guard, he rebuilt a dead man's Noordyne Norseman, an enormous single-engined slab of an airplane that some still affectionately liken to Paul Bunyan's Piper Cub. Then he contracted to fly high-grade gold ore out of a mine in Alaska's vast interior. Superstitious miners preferred to fly with lucky Coop. They did, at least, for nearly ten years.

Then one April night in the early '70s, Coop's Norseman began to collect ice in flight the way a shoplifter collects coats, layer after layer. The only real estate void of huge trees within two hundred miles was a frozen river surface and the Norseman was on humongous big skis, but skis do not have brakes and Coop's perfect landing ended in a perfectly godawful pileup at the river's bend. It was like Coop to thank Providence that nobody else had been in the plane because it was trashed to hell. No repairing his old Viking this time.

Coop couldn't see too well with only his flashlight and the flap of forehead that was hanging over his eyes, and all the blood that went with it. But he knew his leg was broken and, while splinting the leg with loosened tiedowns and a broken piece of aircraft tubing, he figured some ribs were cracked, too. No point in moaning about it, nobody to hear him anyway if you discounted the occasional gigantic Brownie lurching out of hibernation early, lean and mean and hungry as—well, bears are *always* hungry, and Coop had blood all over him. Why make more noise than he absolutely had to?

Coop passed out a few times that night and stopped trying to get out of the cockpit, pulling a hand-me-down Alaskan Brownie pelt around him. If it had helped a thousand-pound bear survive Alaskan winters, maybe it would work for lucky Coop.

Whenever he waked during the night, he could hear the mutter and groan of ice moving beneath the Norseman, grinding it, eating it by inches. The region had been unseasonably warm in previous days; the traditional sweepstakes among Alaskans, betting on the spring breakup of river ice, had already begun. And every year since God made Alaska, on the hour that river ice begins to break up, *every*thing on the river and much that adjoins it becomes a churning, horrendous maelstrom of white and blue and green and gray, with a thunder that can be heard for miles and which annually delivers house-sized boulders and eight-foot-diameter trees hundreds of miles to the sea. First-time viewers, reflecting that the Lord God promised He would not create a second flood, often fear that He has reconsidered.

The next morning Coop saw that the shore was only yards away. He thought he was too stiff to move until the river convinced him it was straining at its leash. He roped together what items he could reach and heaved them onto the ice, crawled out, and slid his goods to the forest's edge, while all around him the ice popped and strained. He needed most of that day to crawl high enough to build a shelter and a signal fire, and tossed his rope over a fir limb to haul his edibles beyond the reach of bears while the river waited.

It waited through much of the next day but, when it let go, the ear-splitting, cataclysmic flow carved away the prominence where he tended his fire. It took the tree where his goods were cached while Coop Gunther scrabbled backward on his elbows, watching the edge crumble toward him. Coop was convinced the river, and all that bad luck he'd always avoided, were coming after him.

The Norseman had disappeared downriver like crumpled tissue. Coop was left with a tarp and blanket, the .44 caliber pistol in his belt which just might just possibly stop a small Brownie at point-blank range, and what remained in his pockets. The warming rain collected in his tarp, but it denied him dry tinder as well, and Coop existed on his own fat and fiddlehead ferns for a week. The air search had been called off before he got another fire started and, suffering more from exposure than hunger, turned his belt into sixteen yards of leather fishing line with a hook pounded from the tang on its buckle. For bait he used a few of the grubs he had dug to eat from rotted stumps and with that bum leg he nearly drowned landing the first fish he caught.

A month later, Kupreanof Gunther bobbed downriver on a raft made by lashing two tree trunks together, carrying a smoked elk haunch for vittles, and was pulled off unconscious by two Tlingit kids with an outboard. He lost his leg below the knee and attained a brief fame, swapping his hollow prosthesis for a handcarved peg leg during his lecture tour, and made enough money for a down payment on a smaller cargo plane. Coop didn't insure the plane for its full value and, when it burned after a botched landing, a couple of his fingertips became crispy critters. Some Alaskans agreed that Coop's luck had turned on him. Others weren't so sure; losing a leg could be chalked up to bad luck, but when he started missing fingers too, they thought it began to smack of plain damn carelessness.

Ever since then, Coop Gunther sold and repaired equipment in Petersburg for the owners of snowmobiles, boats, chainsaws, and a few weirdos with lawnmowers. He knew that his luck was out to get even, and would talk about it when he had soaked up enough alcohol to put two ordinary men into suspended animation. But Coop still enjoyed the company of other pilots, and for reasons of his own, seemed ready to listen to a business proposition that might take him to the South Pacific. He had to look as well as listen, for Coop heard as much by reading lips as he did with his ears.

"Ever been out there," Lovett asked him as Coop passed quarts of oil to him.

"Nope. But there's a first time for ever'thing," Coop replied. "Plenty of boats go there, I hear."

"Not where we're headed, if Mel Benteen is right. It'd cost a few thou if you could, and going by air is free the way we're going. Only way to get there, Coop," Lovett rejoined. He watched Gunther's face fall at the news, knowing the old fellow's superstitious dread.

Coop Gunther leaned on an exhaust stack and stared at nothing for a full minute, then pushed himself erect and squared his shoulders. "Well, hell, nobody lives forever. I don't wanta die as chickenshit as I've lived," he said at last. This was the only hint Coop was to offer for a motive and Lovett shook his head in wonder. Not one man in a thousand had displayed Coop's fortitude during the first fifty years of his life.

As advertised, Lovett ended his charade at 6 P.M., and Chip scurried about, locking up. By drawing a few benches to the drinks-and-munchies table they found enough seating room for everyone. Most of the men gave plenty of room to Melanie Benteen. They were plainly nonplussed to learn that this proud-bosomed late arrival wearing slacks and heels and, like a badge of authenticity, an old Breitling chronometer on her wrist, was Elmo's kid, Mel. She managed to ignore the murmurs, chiefly along the lines of, "A bit beamy in the fuselage," and, "Yeah, but get a load of those nacelles."

It was Crispin Reventlo who called them to order. "Since this isn't a plenary session, lads, and we have no time to waste, let's get about it. The steak and kidney pie, I am assured, is on the way. Very well then, you Philistines, he's laying on some pizza," he amended to those who were already gagging for effect.

Quinn had his doubts. "So who was the delivery boy you and the kid shooed off a few minutes ago?"

Reventlo: "Thirty-year-old delivery boys with five o'clock shadow don't belong here. That one intended his delivery for Wade Lovett. What he hoped to deliver, we think, was a legal summons."

"Class will tell," Quinn chuckled.

"All Wade did was turn most of his assets into cash for what we're proposing tonight," Reventlo cautioned. "That doesn't make him crazy."

"We give up, then," said Victor Myles. "What did?"

"Foolish questions," Reventlo replied.

One elderly churl piped up, "Bring on Lovett. I never heard a Brit who didn't need all night to say hello."

Reventlo gave a pained look to his accuser. "You might keep a civil tongue in your head to the man who's arranged free air travel for you."

This was more like it. "I might. Drone on," said the man; so Reventlo filled them in on the last hours of Elmo Benteen. This was the first time that these men realized exactly what Elmo's treasure consisted of, and the news was greeted with slack-jawed awe by most of them. He finished with, "You'll be glad Melanie Benteen is part of the operation; most of what we know about the island, she dug up."

By now, Lovett stood nearby, shucking his coverall to someone's quavery rendition of, "Take It Off." He raised a hand for silence and got it. "You may as well know from square one: I'm committed to this thing," he began, and explained how he, Reventlo, and Mel Benteen had pooled every cent they could. It probably wouldn't be enough, he said, to transport a half-dozen Japanese warplanes undamaged to some repair facility.

From exactly which island, someone asked; and here, Lovett shook his head. "We've agreed not to talk about that until we're en route," he said. To the spluttered responses he said, "Look, it's obvious this is the crucial item, and somebody had to make some command decisions about it."

"So it's Commander Lovett, huh?" Vic Myles had never been one to pull a verbal punch.

"We all agreed," Mel Benteen spoke up. "So far, we're the only ones who've pooled our resources, done the legwork, brought you in on it. If you can't go along or help foot the bills, this is the time to bow out."

Some of the men simply sat quietly, as if shell-shocked, and thought it over; but a few were suddenly full of questions. Which country owned the territory? It was autonomous, said Lovett. Had anyone contacted the place officially? To this, Mel shook her head. When and how would the free air travel happen? The following Friday, said Reventlo, from Portland in a reliable old C-47 he would ferry. "This doesn't give us bags of time but," Reventlo added, with a wry smile toward Lovett, "absent Wade Lovett's peculiar luck, I'd have needed to leave even sooner."

No one turned the offer down without reluctance, but most had some compelling reason for a turndown. Lovett wasn't surprised that the few who kept their seats were chiefly men without close family ties. Bert Campbell was different. A freckled, balding redhead who favored big cigars and solid investments, Campbell owned a chain of airport restaurants and spent more time bragging on his grandkids than on his Korean War exploits. Whoever put the most money into the kitty, Campbell said, he would match that amount. But only after Lovett's little nucleus group satisfied him on a few questions of a business nature.

"I hope it's enough for you to know that I've already zeroed out my savings and dumped a hundred and forty kay into this," Lovett told him.

"It's not," Campbell rapped, no longer the affable hell-raiser. "Are we just supposed to descend on some island like so many locusts and sneak off with a bunch of possibly mythical aircraft that haven't been flown in fifty years?"

Mel Benteen: "We hope to get a contract signed before we show our hand. There's an airstrip to land on—or was. I would expect we'd pay a modest fee."

A snort from Campbell. "And which bunch of headhunters is so goddamn stupid they'd sign such a contract, assuming they can make an *X*, without knowing what we're after?"

"It's done all the time," Lovett said calmly, "and Mel says some English is spoken there, though we're not counting on anything at this point. We're going to suggest a mining venture. We'd ask for rights to anything under the surface: ores, metals . . ." His smile grew, recalling his claim to his broker. "If it's in a cave, Bert, it's subsurface."

Though these two had yarned, laughed, and caroused through thirty years of reunions, Bert Campbell took a deep breath and eyed Lovett the way gunslingers did it in Westerns. "Islander views on mining?"

"To be determined," Lovett replied with a shrug.

Campbell fired again. "Condition of that airstrip?"

Lovett, choosing a different kind of shrug: "Hard to say."

Campbell loosed a volley now, his brow rumpled with concern. "Active loading dock? Fuel and electric power? Roads? Native labor? Local taboos?"

This time Lovett made his shrug so exaggerated his head nearly disappeared into his shoulders, and amusement in the group was audible. It was well known to most of them that Campbell's outlook on risk capital was purest Scot.

"I don't like all these loose ends worth a damn," Campbell snarled to no one in particular. "What kind of iffy business is this?"

"The loose-end business," Lovett said, "and we don't dare go public with it yet to get those answers."

Mel Benteen stood up to face the increasingly irate Campbell. Lovett, prepared to cringe at her broadside, found that she could be even-tempered on occasion. "These are all good questions, Mr. Campbell. Most of them can be answered when we arrive on the island, before we're too heavily committed. But asking questions like these to the people who know—and that means contacting the island's leaders somehow—are exactly the questions that would kite their price out of sight. Be reasonable."

"I am reasonable. I'm so reasonable I'm not going to throw money away on a bunch of junketeering gumshoes taking a vacation in a South Seas paradise at my expense," said Campbell, getting up to leave, striding near Mel Benteen. Too near, because he could not resist a parting shot, staring at Benteen's cleavage. "Most likely this was all Reventlo's idea after he thought of you, lady, stripped for the tropics."

Most women throw a punch like a baseball. Mel Benteen's came in straight and fast with her shoulder behind it, a short left that caught Campbell in the solar plexus, and she was poised to deliver more. He doubled over and sat down hard on a chair. It happened to be already occupied, and Vic Myles grinned as Campbell plopped onto his lap, gasping.

"Watch your mouth, Jasper," Mel said evenly, one hand out and patting the air to ward off help or interference. "And if you get up swinging, better park your dentures first." Still staring at Campbell, who was getting his breath back, she went on, "The same goes for anybody else that hassles me about my gender. Clear?"

No one broke the silence until Campbell, rocking on Myles's lap, managed to nod and wheeze, "I guess I was out of line."

"Getting guys back in line is something I had to learn early. It seemed like a point worth making. If you're satisfied, I am," she said, and thrust out a hand.

Campbell shook and released it, finally drawing deep breaths again, standing up with a sheepish look around. "She's got a good left, boys," he said. To Myles, he said, "Was that a roll of quarters I felt, or were you just glad to see me?"

"Enough of this love-in," Mel said. "I'll still be glad to see you on this operation, buddy. If we're going to be depending on one another, our disagreements ought to be short and sweet."

"Thanks, but I'm out," the chastened Campbell replied, rubbing his belly reflectively. "Appreciate the offer, and good luck to you. It's just not a risk I'm comfortable with." He walked to the door, then turned with his hand on the knob. "Maybe I shouldn't say this," he said slowly, "but I keep thinking about the Greenamyer expedition." Without another word, Bert Campbell squared his shoulders and walked out.

When the door closed, Coop Gunther was first to speak. "I heard that, and I'm thinking about it too. Greenamyer damn near made it, folks."

The Greenamyer expedition, to recover a huge B-29 many years after its forced landing in Greenland, had cost one man's life and half a million dollars before its end, the survivors dejected, the aircraft a burned hulk destined to remain in a frozen wasteland, a monument to failed dreams. But before their final disappointment, Darryl Greenamyer and his friends had actually got the big plane taxiing. Their valiant, doomed effort had its detractors, but it had come within moments of total success and might never be forgotten as long as airmen swap stories or write histories of the skilled and daring.

Wade Lovett looked into the eyes of the remaining Boffs and saw gleams of dedication. Win or lose, he realized, they hoped to be remembered in the same way.

8

Lovett finally gave in on one detail that evening after Coop Gunther shamed him into it, with, "So what is it with you? I'm in, Myles is in, so's Quinn, but you still won't say where the friggin' island is! I'm a great-grandfather, Wade; you think maybe I'm old enough to keep a goddamn secret?" Lovett agreed then that the island had to be identified without further delay, for serious planning. In themselves, old Elmo's map coordinates said a lot. That close to the equator, the climate would be fully tropical and they'd have to cross virtually the entire breadth of the Pacific to get there. The name, Fundabora, meant no more to Quinn or Gunther than it had to Lovett, so Mel Benteen filled them in quickly.

Before World War II, Fundabora had been one of numerous islands under Japanese mandate, a hundred square miles of sunny innocence roughly halfway between Guam and the Philippines. The natives, when they happened to feel like it, exported phosphates, copra, and a few pearls on a ho-hum basis. When the Japanese used whips in 1942 as a wakeup call to their new wartime needs, virtually all of those dusky citizens simply sailed the hell away in outrigger canoes one night to what they imagined would be safety in the Philippines. They never returned.

The Japanese promptly imported native labor from other islands and turned Fundabora into a hell of forced labor camps with armed sentries and shore patrols. A single airstrip was pounded by manual labor into the southern tip of the island, but Fundabora became one of those points of land bypassed by the Allies in 1944, not worth its cost in American lives.

It was a matter of record that, when the Japanese abruptly abandoned Fundabora in 1945, their empire was preparing for an all-out, genocidal defense of its home islands. Secret stores of munitions were cached; fuel dumps were hidden; and literally thousands of aircraft were put away, many of them on what we now call Taiwan, earmarked to be flown by teenaged, inexperienced Kamikaze pilots in their final apocalypse.

The Hiroshima and Nagasaki bombs had been the gigantic exclamation points that stopped these plans in midstride. Many Japanese and virtually all Americans remained blissfully ignorant of the mass civilian suicides and banzai charges that actually did take place on Guam, Tinian, and Saipan; the merest foretaste of the carnage that Imperial Japan intended to trigger on its own shores when the Americans invaded the home islands in 1945. To that end, it pulled its soldiers back, and planned a final surprise attack that was quashed only by the emperor's surrender speech—a speech that some Imperial officers proposed to ignore until peaceable factions won out.

When starving native laborers broke out of their camps on Fundabora in mid-1945 they took their first good look at the whole island. Ousting a few soldiers, they found modest stockpiles of food, no Japanese left to guard that airstrip, and no visible aircraft for anyone to guard. Most of those natives elected to stay on Fundabora. For one thing, they learned that most nearby islands had been converted to bomb craters while Fundabora remained serenely beautiful with beaches of white sand and creeks descending from old volcanic promontories. Visitors used to say the island made Tahiti look like the black hole of Calcutta.

After the war, when nearby island chains became UN trust territories, Fundaborans felt they'd had enough laws to last them an eternity. They followed the lead of Palau and declared themselves an island republic, not subject to Micronesia's constitution or anyone else's. No one warned them that a country catches laws the way a dog catches fleas, and that its citizens should be careful to pick the kind of itch they want to scratch. No one else cared much that the Republic of Fundabora, left to its own devices, soon had a President-for-life, one Matai Pelele, who believed that might made right because he and his friends had discovered the cache of small arms left by retreating Japanese.

Because the new Fundaborans had been forced immigrants from other islands, postwar Fundabora reflected a mixture of island cultures. Pelele, a three-hundred-pounder of prodigious appetites, kept several wives and imposed an annual ritual in which men literally wrestled for tribal leadership. To no one's surprise, Matai Pelele defeated all comers. According to rumors at the time, it helped that his wrestling opponents were first treated to a few days of orgies while Pelele sipped papaya nectar and dispensed booze with a free hand.

Some years later a consortium bribed Pelele, whose phosphate deposits had been largely worked out under Japanese rule, to let them build a vacation haven with quaint cabanas and a sprawling white monstrosity of a colonial palace complete with indoor toilets and a gasoline-driven generator. The dock was improved for paying guests, cruise ships visited for a generation, and Matai Pelele kept himself as happy as one of the local giant clams. Happy, at least, until his accidental death during the annual leadership games in 1978. That was when his son, Jean-Claude Pelele, filled the presidential throne.

Jean-Claude, it was said, looked like his father; that is, like a copper-sheathed NFL defensive tackle. He liked women—a lot. He liked them so much, he could not resist sampling the more fetching ladies who rented cabanas only to find themselves bundled off for a midnight tussle with King Kong. When the Dutch consortium manager raised enough hell over the antics of young Jean-Claude, he got the attention he asked for, but not the sort he wanted.

According to one rumor, he escaped with tribal outcasts. No one off the island could say, since he hadn't felt like dragging thirty pounds of radio transmitter along with him. Another rumor seemed more likely; some Fundaboran splinter groups had reintroduced ritual cannibalism, a return to an older tradition, and Jean-Claude liked to keep his people happy.

By the middle 1980s, cruise ships no longer visited Fundabora, which for all commercial purposes might as well have sunk into the Philippine Sea. Especially where tourism was concerned, the place was a non-place. Fundabora still had sporadic contact with Manila, Palau, and Guam whenever trading ships happened by. Fundabora's chief export was now a trickle of pearls. Presumably, said Mel, Fundabora still maintained dock facilities and electric power. She doubted aloud whether they had anything very modern in the way of medical facilities.

It was obvious that Quinn, who needed kidney dialysis twice a week, could not leave the States for Fundabora. Quinn's argument—that he could kick in fifty thousand bucks and they'd need someone stateside with good contacts and a head for business—sounded better as the evening wore on. "Or you could airlift all that cash and take your chances," Quinn shrugged. "And if you do, you're as loony-tunes as some people already think you are. Do yourselves a favor, and don't."

The total assets of Lovett, Reventlo, Mel Benteen, and Quinn himself came to a bit over three hundred thousand, disappointingly small for such an expedition. Gunther had never made any secret of his near-poverty but for Vic Myles, the admission was hard. "The survival magazine biz is just about extinct," he told them, "and royalties on my books could be better. Truth is, if I can't wheedle an advance from a publisher on an expedition I can't even tell 'em about, I'll be in the same bucket with Coop."

It was agreed that Myles and Gunther could borrow something for expenses, since the two could pass as copilot and flight engineer, though Lovett also had his ratings. Their major advantage was the old Douglas transport. "We'll be refueling on U.S. territory part of the way," Reventlo pointed out. "San Diego to Kauai, then Mejit in the Marshall chain, then Rota. After that it's only a few hundred miles to Fundabora. Fake a medical emergency or something of the sort. Or we may have to overfly it and find our way back by fishing boat."

"Why not Honolulu and Guam instead," Myles complained, studying the charts. "Some joints there I haven't hit in years."

"Because we don't want to be any more obvious than we must," Reventlo said. "I've already filed for my refueling clearances. Miz Benteen has a list of your booster shots, and I advise you to look to your mosquito netting."

"Not to mention passports," Lovett put in. "If we manage to land on Fundabora, we must look like people who were bound for Australia, putting down for an emergency."

"I wondered about that," said Chip, looking up from the palmtop computer he was using.

Myles jerked a thumb toward the youth. "And how about the kid here? We gonna have to worry about him?"

"He's flying home tomorrow," Lovett said quickly, and smiled in Chip's direction. "Sorry, Chip. That's just how it is."

"I know it. Don't have to like it," the boy replied.

Myles glanced over Chip's shoulder and shook his head. "Never use those things myself," he said in his first friendly words to Chip.

"You pick it up fast," Chip murmured, and kept at it. "I can type twice as fast as I did with Mom's old typewriter, and editing's a snap."

It was long after midnight when the meeting broke up, Lovett electing to sleep on a cot in the hangar. He welcomed an excuse to avoid his apartment because, while Chip and Reventlo had agreed to share the master bedroom, Myles and Gunther would take the spare bedroom. That left the living room couch for Mel Benteen, by her own choice; and Wade Lovett had enough troubles without that. The Benteen broad, he thought, had more touchy triggers than a flotilla of naval mines.

For Lovett, the next few days fled like felons. He called Roxy to make certain Chip had made it home without a hitch, and thought it best to ignore her entreaties. After admitting that Chip had arrived home with all his parts intact, she wondered aloud if Lovett himself felt well.

"Sure, if you discount a touch of senility," he said, trying to keep it light. "Goes with the territory."

Evidently she missed the sarcasm. "We need to talk, Dad. I'm worried about you."

"We *are* talking, Roxy. And one of us is talking nonsense. If I stop right there, we can claim total agreement, hm?"

"What are you going to do?"

"Oh—toss hundred-dollar bills from tall buildings; try a system to beat Vegas roulette wheels wearing a pyramid on my head. Maybe consult a gypsy before I plunge on the commodities market," he said, reaching beyond the absurd. Then, more calmly: "Or maybe something a good deal less inane. You'll find out sooner or later. Until then, you'll have to trust me."

"I just don't want you to make any mistakes you'll regret," she insisted, with a catch in her voice that bothered Lovett more than he would admit.

"A little late for that, honey; I started early. And after sixty-plus years of risk I'm still suckin' wind, so give me a little credit. I swear to you, my marbles are all still in the sack."

"I know you think so," she said, now tuning up to cry, "and you sound all right. So did Mother, at first, until she forgot how to use a stick shift and then started forgetting things like making her shoes match. I'd feel a lot better if you'd tell me where you are; let me come and talk with you about all these sudden changes."

Lovett took a deep breath, maintaining his calm with effort. "Roxy, there's an old Chinese curse that says, 'May you live in interesting times.' Who would consider that a curse? Fat-cat mandarins who love the status quo, that's who; they don't want interesting times, they want everything nice and dull. No changes. And that means no possible improvements that might upset their lives.

"My life has been a little too nice lately. Too dull. I concede that I'm taking some risks, but they're mine to take, Roxanne. I truly, truly appreciate your concern, honey, but if you don't get the hell out of my way, Papa is gonna whack your bottom. I love you, Roxy, and I've got to go now."

He had hung up while his daughter was talking. He had never done that in all his life, and it bothered him for a long time.

Mindful of Coop Gunther's lack of funds, Lovett first offered to fly the old fellow in the VariEze. But, "I'll take a bus. Bad enough I'll climb aboard a crate I know inside out, next week," Gunther said. "Ain't no way you'll get me shoehorned into a little bitty plastic dart that won't haul more'n two guys and looks like it's flyin' ass-end forward."

Vic Myles had an editor or two to bamboozle, promising to meet them in San Diego before the 2,500-mile first leg to Hawaii. So it was Mel Benteen who accompanied Lovett to Portland, after he saw Chip off on his flight home. At least she didn't try to tell him how to fly. On reflection, he realized why: she'd spent her youthful years flying with Elmo. When it came to taking criticism of his piloting prowess, Elmo Benteen had ranked right up there with Hermann Goering.

Portland had its share of surplus stores, as Reventlo had promised, and Lovett did not stint on his supplies. He said nothing about the rolls and cans of composite materials he added to the tool crates. Most of his B.O.F. fraternity might hoot at Kevlar and epoxy, but you could build an airplane with them using only hand tools and somehow, Lovett thought, he doubted they'd find any metalworking machine shops on Fundabora. For all they knew, any aircraft they found might need rework before you could even tow it.

And besides, Lovett just plain liked the sound of "advanced composites" better than "retarded aluminum."

As Reventlo signed forms on Friday, Mel helped Lovett stow their supplies aboard the transport while Gunther made their preflight inspection. With a few courtesy lights in that cargo section and a functioning toilet in the rear, the old plane seemed downright luxurious. They were in the air by noon, Gunther uneasy and up front with Reventlo because the dual controls, he claimed, at least gave him the illusion that he could wrestle with his luck. Lovett strapped himself near Mel Benteen in a sturdy old bucket seat next to the windows, and his pocketful of cheap foam earplugs found a willing taker.

"When those engines aren't quite synchronized they drive me nuts. Reminds me of Dad's Catalina," Mel said above the din of big radial engines.

"They should," Lovett replied. "This one was refitted with the same Pratt & Whitneys. We used to call 'em 'Briggs & Strattons' but they get you there."

If they got you there, they did it at a leisurely hundred and fifty miles an hour. As Reventlo and Gunther flew south past Oregon's Coos Bay, their two passengers were wandering up and down the plane's length, checking tiedowns, silencing the little buzzes and rattles of sympathetic vibration that made a C-47 sound like an airborne junkyard shaken in a sack.

Mel distributed fruit juice and chicken salad sandwiches as they droned down the San Joaquin Valley. "Think of this as *noblesse oblige*. First guy who treats me like a flight attendant scares up his own coffee," she told them, but no one was that foolhardy.

They landed in San Diego before sundown, where Victor Myles met them during refueling. As promised, he had picked up a few cartons of in-flight meal packs. "I brought a few other things," he said, nodding at a cart that was loaded to its capacity. Myles wore hiking boots and his shooting jacket had its pockets stuffed.

Lovett's stare at the heap of goods was disbelieving. "You forgot the pipe organ."

"Naw, it's in there someplace with the bull-fiddle," said Myles. "Hey, a survivalist goes prepared. Ah, some of my stuff is a little, uh, delicate, so let's treat it right."

Reventlo, after signing for the fuel, turned and regarded Myles with misgivings. "Define delicate."

Myles, boosting a huge duffel bag up with Gunther and Mel assisting, puffed, "You know—delicate, sensitive."

Reventlo waited until the fuel man had driven away, all too aware of Myles's work with explosives. "Sensitive as in breakable, or as in boom?"

"Yeah," said Myles, wrestling a heavy carton.

"All this stuff comes back off right now," Lovett said.

Myles faced him squarely. "Those planes we're after? According to you, Elmo said they're in a cave. We don't know how much dirt or how many trees we gotta remove to get 'em out. Who wants to take a year doing it all with picks and shovels? Come on, goddammit, let's have a show of hands!"

Reventlo blinked, looked at Lovett, and shrugged. "I hate to admit Myles is right, Wade," he said. "But if I'm unaware of what he's brought, I needn't declare it."

"I dunno," Lovett hedged.

Myles grabbed up a carton sealed by duct tape, deliberately dropped it at his feet. Lovett had time only to flinch before Myles picked it up again and said, "You think I nurse a death wish? Every detonator is packed so far away from the next one, it'd be no worse'n a firecracker."

Reventlo smirked. "Every *what*, Victor?"

"Desecrator," Myles said quickly. "Distillator, deprecator. I forget," he said, with a vague wave of a hand.

"We all will," the Brit promised, and helped load the rest of what they would come to call the Myles piles. It weighed over six hundred pounds including the parachute and inflatable life raft that Myles hauled from one of his duffel bags after they were once again in the air, flying toward the faint remnants of sunset.

That equipment marked Vic Myles in several ways. First, because no one else had brought such stuff as personal equipment. Second, because, while the plane's emergency equipment included a big inflatable raft, it contained no other chutes and Myles was not the man to trust anyone else's equipment. Third, neither was he the sort to offer his stuff to the only woman aboard. *Well, she wants to be one of the guys*, Lovett thought, and fluffed out his bedroll so that he could sleep on the metal floor, a tiedown across his torso. Summer or no summer, you could frost your buns off at ten thousand feet.

He awoke to the tang of coffee, and to a faint scent of orange blossoms. Because dawn had overtaken them he could see that Mel Benteen had copied him, snuggled on the floor plates in her mummy bag nearby. So near, in fact, he was inhaling the scent of her hair. He chalked up his budding erection to his need to urinate—or maybe it was just the coffee—and wriggled from his bag. He put on his Nikes and moved forward toward Reventlo who sat on one of the forward seats of the main cabin with a hamper at his feet, sipping from a mug and regarding him with amusement.

Lovett yawned and scratched himself, ready to be irritable on short notice. "What's so damn' funny? And who's watching the store up there?"

"To question one, no comment. As for question two, Gunther's checking Myles out on the instruments. Nothing like playing flight instructor to rebuild a man's confidence, eh?"

"You noticed, then."

Reventlo pulled a plastic mug from his hamper, filled it by pumping the top of a gallon-sized thermos, handed it over with a waggle of eyebrows. "You could say that. I do not believe that man breathed until we reached cruise altitude. I saw only the whites of his eyes for three hours. He was trembling like a hound passing peachpits, old man."

"You know how he feels about his luck," Lovett said, and grimaced at the hot stuff coursing down his throat.

"Stalwart lad, our Coop Gunther," said Reventlo, making a gesture with his mug as if making a toast. "If I were in that deep a funk, with ears that aren't that keen in detecting the odd noise, you could not pay me enough to climb aboard this thing. Incidentally, I found out that the control cables here," he tapped lightly on the floor plates covering cables that operated the tail surfaces, "were all retensioned. Again."

"Twice? What for?"

Reventlo smiled to himself and sipped. "Because, as if you didn't know, on its first checkout flight last week, every time this wallowing sow nosed up or down, something toured its underbelly rumbling like a bowling ball. No telling what it was, so they had to scope it out. You wouldn't know anything about that, I suppose."

"Nope." Lovett realized that, to find what was rolling loose in the plane's belly, they'd had to disconnect the maze of cables, find the problem by hauling the big plane's nose up and down with jacks, then carefully retension every blessed cable before the plane could be pronounced airworthy. "What was it?"

"A ball bearing. A one-ounce steel ball that any idiot could have inserted into one of the aluminum channels. Two days, Wade. I hope you're proud of yourself."

Lovett sipped and sighed, and tried not to look guilty. "We're here, aren't we?"

Now Reventlo chuckled broadly. "Oh yes, we are indeed. Every mother's son of us, thanks to you." He saw that his mug was empty, got up, and toed the hamper. "La Benteen will want some of this. I'll go and see if Coop's sweat has unfrozen from his forehead."

"He seems to be managing."

"A child could do it," Reventlo said, and disappeared forward through the bulkhead door into the forward cabin, known to air crews as the flight deck.

Lovett went aft, used the toilet, and found Mel Benteen waiting when he emerged. She brushed past without a word. *Bitchy before her coffee*, he decided, and took flight attendant duty, going forward with three of the meal cartons. The bulkhead door was locked.

It was Myles who opened it in good time, having left the controls to Gunther. Reventlo sat behind them, kibitzing from the radioman's seat, a Dick Francis paperback in his hands. The Brit saw Lovett's questioning glance around. It said, "Something wrong here?" Reventlo gave a faint headshake and wink, jerking his thumb toward the aft cabin. "Checkouts can be irksome; we've got enough strange egos up here as it is. But thanks for the rations, mate."

With a sigh, Lovett went aft, reflecting on Reventlo's weird speech patterns after a proper Brit childhood, his teens in a Japanese prison, and later years among Aussies. His "myte" for "mate" had sounded pure Strine.

Lovett immersed himself in a Micronesia guidebook until he fell asleep, which was very easy to do in the thin air. Mel Benteen shook him awake in time for him to see the big number *35* painted at the end of the runway at Lihue, Kauai. He set his watch back two hours and rubbed the stiffness from his neck, welcoming the dense warmer air.

Myles fairly bubbled with good cheer after landing the "C-Fort" with reasonable ease. In fact, everyone seemed in high spirits, laughing easily, elbows prodding ribs, and Lovett put it down to the excitement of this last, resounding geriatric hurrah by men who had thought they were past such things.

During their refueling only Reventlo left the plane, making a call to his Aussie client. With a combined total of over two hundred years' flying experience, the group simply knew too many people in the flying business and contrived to avoid chance meetings. It was agreed that Lovett would take copilot duties on the next leg to Mejit in the Marshall Islands, but they elected to wait and catnap until evening for their takeoff. That way, they would arrive at Mejit with the early light. At nightfall, the C-47 lumbered aloft under Reventlo's control for that 2,200-mile jaunt.

The third time Reventlo excused himself to leave the flight deck, turning the controls over to Lovett, the American eyed his friend closely. "What're you guys doing back there, smoking dope?"

Reventlo paused in the aisle. "Whatever can you mean?"

"I mean the way you're acting, and don't try to deny it. You're laughing at my feeblest jokes, which is not your style. You look out at two thousand miles of blackness ahead of us and you grin like a gremlin. And every half-hour, you jump up and leave me here."

"Just keeping abreast of the card game," said the Brit, and closed the door behind him. He returned in a half hour, and in the same mysterious high spirits.

Much later, Gunther came forward to sit behind them. Now and then he irritated Lovett with a chuckle that was practically a demand for attention. Presently he said, "Past the point of no return?"

"Well past," Reventlo said.

"Maybe I can take Wade's seat awhile. You play poker don't you, Wade?"

"Used to. Boring," Lovett said.

"I promise this won't bore you," said Reventlo. Gunther snickered like a truant.

Lovett discarded his instant vision of busty Melanie Benteen losing at strip poker, removed his headset, moved into the aisle. "Okay, but this had better be good," he warned.

"We think so," said the Brit. Lovett moved aft toward the dim cabin lights, closing the door, peering toward the group that sat draped in sleeping bags.

Gunther eased himself into the right-hand seat. "Think we'll need earplugs?"

"Absolutely. I'm not at all sure," the Brit replied, "that we won't need to lock that door against a mutiny."

Over the numbing drone of Pratt & Whitneys, they heard Lovett's despairing wail of, "*Jumping Jesus Christ on crutches,*" and then they both began to laugh.

9

As Lovett's cry resounded in the cargo cabin, a tall figure scrambled to its feet, passing a book-sized computer to Mel Benteen. Judging by the screen, they had been playing poker using a game program in the little gadget. "It's okay, Pop," said Chip, backing up against their cargo.

Lovett put hands to his temples, still aghast. "Okay that you're a stowaway? Okay that your mother will call for U.N. troops? Okay that you've popped up twice among my friends who wonder why the hell I let you do it, and never mind the fact that I didn't? Which okay is it that I've missed?"

"Relax," Vic Myles drawled. "The kid's okay. It's you that we should have doubts about."

Moving his hands down to his hips, Lovett stared at his old colleague. "And what's going through *your* mind, Vic, besides the usual jet stream?"

"He didn't exactly stow aboard, I kinda stowed him in a duffel bag; if he was any huskier or less flexible it wouldn't've worked. Everybody knew it but you. When we spent the night at your place, the kid blew us away with this little computer. He made a pitch I couldn't refuse that night. Hell, we need somebody who can do that stuff, Wade!"

"Plain old playing cards aren't good enough," Lovett marveled.

"Keeping track of expenses," Benteen said quietly. "Listing our needs. Making notes, dossiers on officials. Composing a few contracts. And Myles can't mark cards on a computer screen," she added slyly.

"Nothin' to do with cards," Myles burst out. "The kid promised to let me dictate my manuscript if I'd get him aboard."

Lovett trembled with quiet fury. "You were bribed by a seventeen-year-old. A new low. Congratulations."

Myles glanced at the other conspirators. "The kid is underage?"

"He said he was of age," Benteen accused, with a glance toward Chip.

"I didn't say *what* age," Chip replied, but had the decency to look sheepish. "I'll be eighteen in a couple of weeks."

"A technicality," Gunther shrugged. "He's acting more like an adult than some folks I could name. What were we s'posed to do? Card him?"

Lovett ignored that. "You're flying back from Mejit," he said to the youth. "I can't be responsible for you, Chip. For one thing, you're not eighteen yet. You don't have a passport."

"Yes I do. Just because you don't have to doesn't mean you can't, and Mom got me one when we went to Mexico last year," said Chip, producing the little blue booklet from his jacket. "I even got my shots. You don't have to be responsible for me. In fact," his smile was poised halfway between ingratiating and impudent, "Mom wants me to be responsible for *you*."

Lovett digested this in silence for a long moment. Then, "You're telling me she knows you're here?"

"Well . . . not here, as in *here*, exactly," Chip said, pointing at his feet. "She kept on at me to find out what you were up to, so I gave her the line that's worked so well for you."

Lovett: "Namely?"

"It's a mining venture."

"On bleeding Fundabora?"

"No way," the youth said hotly. "I did say we'd probably be camping out, uh, somewhere in the Southwest."

"You just didn't bother telling her it was *eight thousand miles* to the southwest," Lovett said, outraged.

Chip toed a nonexistent rock. "Well—she didn't exactly ask that exact question. Not exactly."

"I can't imagine why, exactly," Lovett said, with furious mimicry. He thought for a moment. "Benteen, Myles: you all knew about this but me. That explains why everybody's been snickering at me as if my fly was at half-mast. Thanks a load, Chip. But you're going to be the load, back from Mejit on the next commercial flight to the States."

Chip could not meet his grandfather's gaze but Mel Benteen had no such problem. "I doubt it. Chip, here, entertained us the other night with his account of your famous mental breakdown. All right then, your supposed breakdown," she amended to head off his objection. "Point is, I'm on the boy's side in this. You try shipping him back and I swear I'll tell the authorities on Mejit you're wanted back in the States as a man who's about three rowboats shy of a navy. A couple of calls to Wichita should verify that, I imagine."

"It occurs to me that 'fair young maid' is an oxymoron," Lovett told her.

"If you expect me to curtsy, dream on," she said. "Don't forget, this youngster got my dad to the hospital, trying to save his life; I owe him. And I know damned well Myles was tickled over the idea that he can double his writing output once he learns to use that computer."

"So that's your angle, Vic? You wanted a free secretary to take dictation and you elected Chip as a basket to hold your trash." Lovett did not seem to realize he was balling his fists.

Myles saw it, though. "I wouldn't, old son. I've got twenty pounds on you."

"More like fifty," Lovett snarled, "all of it suet. I won't hit a woman but I can kick a pig's butt."

"I don't have to take that," Myles growled slowly, with a great show of getting up the way John Wayne might have gotten up.

"Yes you do, you ponderous piece of shit," said Lovett, stepping forward.

Myles took a step back then, his bluff called, and looked past the others. "Cris, we have a problem here," he said.

"Told you so," said the Brit, who had left Gunther at the controls. "Wade, if you're going to set about punishing us, you really should begin with me. And then Coop, and so on. And after that, always assuming you manage it because I used to be a fair dinkum scuffler too, you can bring the plane into Mejit by yourself.

"Look here, the lad has earned his wings, wouldn't you say?" He waited for Lovett to answer and, without one, went on: "So say all of us, Wade. Every one. Young Chip damned near suffocated in that bloody sea bag, because his mother wanted him to take care of you and, for reasons that totally mystify me, he wants to stick by you. We had to smuggle him up to the flight deck while you slept. He hid in the flight engineer's cubicle when you came forward. We thought our little show was up the spout for a moment there."

Lovett stood indecisive, looking from one to another of them. Then he fixed his grandson with an angry gaze. "Chip, did you tell these—faithful houseguests of mine—that I was going loopy?"

Chip took a long dry swallow and a longer time before saying, "No sir. But I might have let them think so if they wanted to."

"You might have," Lovett prompted.

"Yes, sir, possibly I might have," in a voice so small it was nearly lost in the drone of engines. "Just possibly. If they really, really wanted to think so."

"And when we get to Mejit and I haul your gangly rump to Air Micronesia and aim you toward the States, and my great and good friends here all tell the authorities I'm a candidate for a very large canvas overcoat, what will you tell them?"

The last vestige of Chip's smile was gone now, but somehow he stood taller. "That they're all full of shit, Pop. You're sharp enough to slit a razor, edgewise. But I still think you're making a mistake."

"But you'll abide by it," Lovett persisted.

A three-beat pause. Then Chip dropped his eyes and said, "Yes, sir."

"Well, I'm almost sorry, because that's the right answer; and you're right, I *am* making a mistake, sure as hell. You remember that when you reach Fundabora."

It took Chip Mason a second or so for that to sink in, and as it did, he lifted both fists aloft with a "Yessss!" before stumbling forward to embrace his grandfather. Lovett could feel the youth's arms trembling with relief, and fought to keep moisture from his own eyes.

A hand clapped Lovett's shoulder as he heard Coop Gunther say, "Takes a good man to know when his kids are men, too."

"Well hello there, Coop," said Reventlo in mild surprise. "And who, may I ask, is flying this thing?"

"The autopilot," Gunther rumbled. "Won't hurt none, and I didn't wanta miss this."

"Interesting," the Brit said, still calm, "considering that the autopilot's been out of commission since San Diego."

Gunther said only, "Whoa," very quietly, then scuttled forward, limping as hard as he could go.

"That's not true and you know it," Lovett said softly.

"I lie occasionally," Reventlo agreed with perfect equanimity, "especially if it helps convince an old comrade that lady luck isn't a vengeful bitch. Even though any sensible man knows she is."

"I won't let you down, Pop," Chip said into Lovett's ear, moving away to recapture the sleeping bag that he had worn like a comforter.

"Yeah, right," Lovett answered, with a headshake toward the rest of the group. "I suppose it'll be useful, having somebody to record our last words."

"It's gonna be history, Wade," said Myles. "And I'm gonna write it from a whatchacallit."

"Data base," Chip supplied.

"Yeah. Strict accuracy," Myles boasted.

"That'll be a welcome change," Lovett rejoined, and followed Reventlo back to the flight deck. He said little to the men at the controls, musing on his decision as the C-47 made its stolid way toward the Marshall Islands through a limbo as dark as the inside of a boa constrictor.

The plain truth, he knew, was not so much that he feared Chip would let him down. What bothered him most was that, if Lovett himself should prove unequal to this mission in some way, his grandson would know it. It didn't improve his mood to know that histories are written by the winners, that Victor Myles had a contract to write this particular history, and that Myles needed a win of his own so much he would need to create a few losers as counterbalance. It wouldn't be the first time; Lovett had read some of Myles's stuff and thought of it as wannabe nonfiction. On paper at least, the hero with a Victor Myles byline was recognizably Victor Myles.

On one count, at any rate, he could rest easily for a while. Roxanne Mason was used to Chip's camping out and, by now, probably imagined her son settled in a tent somewhere in Arizona where roughing it meant his portable TV couldn't get the public access channel. The instant she suspected the truth, large satellites could ride Roxy into orbit. There had to be some way to forward little bogus "all's well" messages to her from stateside. *I guess that's one thing we can use Quinn for*, thought Lovett, drifting into a nap, hands under his armpits to avoid the chill.

He awoke in time to relieve Gunther, and banked the big plane around for a landing precisely on the 7 of Mejit's single three-thousand-foot runway in early morning. It had been a while since he greased such a big hunk of metal onto a strip this short, but Reventlo talked him through it with only a few choice phrases. Their old transport was just the kind of aircraft that runway had been built to accept, and Mejit still stocked the aviation gasoline needed by rehabs, old airplanes that plied Third World airways.

It would be nice, Lovett thought, if people could be refitted and renewed so well. But wasn't that exactly what this little cadre of B.O.F.s had determined to do? A renewal of sorts, yes; that might be possible. They'd staked their piddling fortunes on it, perhaps their lives as well. But for most of us, pushing seventy or thereabouts, our personal engines are pretty much worn out, our control cables frayed, can't always trust our instruments—and Lovett sighed to think that, if they were airplanes, the FAA would've grounded them on sight.

Lovett's subconscious longed to swoop and glide with gulls to better enjoy the tiny coral island, the airport terminal building its largest structure. Dugout canoes, dark splinters on the beaches, waited below for occupants; near a tiny lake, neatly kept gardens welcomed an early sun. *God, please keep Your Pacific pacified,* Lovett prayed silently. When your runway was short, cracked, and five feet above high tide, you didn't need a typhoon to keep life interesting.

10

Rota lies near Guam but without its crowding, especially with faces that might be familiar to Reventlo. Once a pilot for Air Micronesia, or Air Mike in local jargon, the Brit could easily have found overnight lodging for his passengers. Instead, he organized the refueling and postflight routines at a time when most of the island life was at ebb tide, and they all prepared to sleep on the plane.

The night air was warm and so humid that, Lovett said, Rota's mosquitoes would be doing the backstroke. "This may be a preview of coming unattractions on Fundabora," Reventlo grumped as he opened the forward and aft doors to promote some kind of ventilation down the plane's length. "Break out your mosquito nets and don't, whatever you do, leave anything dangling to the ground. And spare us the Texan ripostes if you please, Myles."

Chip saw the others nod and frowned his puzzlement. Mel Benteen noticed. "Rats," she shrugged, and went on fluffing out her pallet.

"Tell me you mean, pshaw, pshoot, pshucks," Chip said, with a shudder.

"I mean rats," she insisted. "Bigger than a breadbox, hungry as a bear."

"Don't forget the upside," Myles leered. "If one of 'em bites you, you can ride him to the hospital."

"You guys are putting me on," Chip complained.

Benteen smiled. "Only a little. As for their getting into everything, Prince Charming wasn't kidding, and we don't need rodents in here with us. Mosquitoes aren't quite that big but they'll off-load you, given half a chance."

"I brought mosquito netting," Chip said. He did not react to her deft characterization of Reventlo, but it was clear she was not one of the charmed.

Myles saw an opportunity to expound on survival lore. "You don't want thin netting," he said, " 'cause it won't stay fluffed out without some kinda support. You need the newest stuff, like mine. I call this my safety net," he said, unfolding a seven-foot sack sewn from nylon netting, stiff enough to be crinkly. He got inside it, forcing it to a tentlike shape. "If the net touches you, the little bastards can nail you through the holes. Gotta learn to sleep without moving around."

Lovett studied the gossamer stuff he had brought. "You wouldn't have an extra, I suppose."

"Several," Myles said, grinning from inside his nylon cocoon. "Hundred bucks apiece. Don't look at me like that, Wade, the price is the same for everybody. You folks are flush." He shucked his netting to stir around in his backpack.

"Several," Gunther repeated, looking at his own net, comparing it to that of Myles. "Let me guess. You brought exactly six."

"I believe I did," said Myles.

"But you want us to buy them," Gunther went on.

"Personal property. Had 'em made up special," Myles said. "Nobody's twisting your arm, Coop. With all your experience, seems like you people would've learned about high tech nets by . . ."

"Forget it, Coop," said Lovett, peeling off five big bills from his pocket roll, dropping them in Myles's lap. "You'll want to count it, Vic. You'll need all the fingers on one hand," he advised, plucking the big wad of nets from Myles.

"Count this," said Gunther, with a matching gesture. "I druther use my own net."

Lovett tossed a wad of the netting to each of them, Gunther included, and sat near Chip as the others found comfortable places to sleep, distancing themselves from Myles in unspoken rejection. A tiny convenience light threw hard shadows on the cabin walls as Chip consulted the glowing screen of his computer.

Lovett watched for a moment as Chip silently typed, I DO NOT BELIEVE WHAT JUST HAPPENED, POP.

Lovett took the machine and typed, EVERYONE TO HIS MINOR VICES. LEARN NOT TO SWEAT THE SMALL STUFF.

HE'S THE SMALL STUFF. MICROSCOPIC, Chip typed.

Lovett typed, HE KNOWS STUFF WE MAY NEED.

Chip typed, HE *SAYS* HE KNOWS STUFF WE MAY NEED.

Lovett's final entry was, YOU GET SMARTER EVERY DAY. IN SOME WAYS I'M GLAD YOU'RE ALONG, KID. Aloud he said, "I'm packing it in for the night, Chip. Either the mosquitoes have found their way in here, or we're being strafed by a squadron of Zeroes."

From nearby, a chuckle from Reventlo and, "Hold that thought, lads. We may find a squadron of our own."

But Lovett didn't think about Japanese aircraft. He fell asleep wondering how long Roxanne would assume her only son was somewhere in Arizona and imagining a headline, something along the lines of INSANE DOTARD KIDNAPS GRANDSON.

The last of the in-flight meals got their share of suspicious sniffing but everyone consumed parts of it while the group considered a landing on Fundabora. Because the plane was so lightly loaded, they followed Gunther's recommendation: let some of the air out of the tires if you expect to land on stones, brush, and on a long-disused strip, God alone knows what else. A good pilot could cope with gooshy shoes, he said, as long as he knew they were only half-inflated; and the Brit answered Coop's challenging glance with a wink. It was Coop himself who partially deflated the big balloon tires, having done it many times in Alaska.

Then Reventlo, with Gunther beside him, fired up the Pratt & Whitneys. Lovett saw that Chip removed their external control locks, waved him aboard, and stood near the engine nacelles with a big fire extinguisher for the warmups. Big radial engines tended to make hellacious threats on starting, with fuel-rich puffs of smoke and a Chitty Chitty Bang Bang imitation. Brief fires from overpriming these old brutes were not rare, as Lovett knew, so he took his job seriously. And if you got a fire, the best way to put it out was to blow it out using the propeller. The fire extinguisher was for those times when you needed a next-best way. Lovett had seen a P-47 Thunderbolt burn to ashes once, after a crew chief saw that his cowl was afire and simply throttled back in panic. Sometimes intuition told you what to do. But with aircraft, sometimes intuition lied like a congressman.

With the engines muttering smoothly and his extinguisher stowed, Lovett buckled himself in and looked forward to see Coop

Gunther peering back down the long tubular fuselage, then jerked his thumb upward. Moments later they swung onto Runway 9 and used only a third of the long asphalt strip before that familiar dump-your-innards sensation of takeoff.

Receding below in full daylight, Rota made Lovett wish he had stayed to enjoy it. Supple palms leaned like rows of beautiful women, fronds flexed in unison with a morning breeze. Lovett was willing to overlook the fact that these particular women had armies of rats in their hair. Ten miles long and three wide, the island had good beaches and some of its roads were flanked by flowering trees. He saw a golf course under development and spotted a sunken ship in the shallows of a bay. Reventlo had said Rota's wild deer were hunted in season, which meant that even a pinpoint of land this small could retain some primitive areas.

Bicyclists dwindled to antlike proportions as the transport gained altitude; it occurred to Lovett that Fundabora was more than twice the size of this island, and that bikes might be the best way to get around. Well, they hadn't thought to bring any bikes. No doubt Fundabora, like Rota, would look better from aloft than from some dusty hillside trail on its flanks. He knew from Benteen's research that Fundabora was no flat coral islet but, like Rota, had its own little highlands.

He watched Chip, in the seat beside him, gaze back toward the island. "Wish you'd stayed here?"

Chip flashed him a grin. "Bitchin' curl out past the shallows," he murmured. "Miz Benteen says it's just a short hop now. Too bad a guy can't surf from here to," and now his eyes danced as he rolled it off his tongue: "Funnndabora."

"Long and short are relative out here. It's over six hundred miles, four hours," Lovett said, and remembered that he needed to reset his watch again.

Presently Myles ambled back from his flight deck kibitzing. "Too bad about the weather," he said easily. "Reventlo's elected to go around it. Hell of a local front building to the southwest; happens sometimes," he shrugged.

Chip scanned the bright blue heavens and the steely ocean, crystalline in their clarity. "Shouldn't I be able to see it?"

"You could if it were real," Lovett told him.

"Then why are we—oh, it's not real," said the youth.

"For Reventlo's client, who's upwards of three thousand miles from here, it's real enough. It's forcing us almost due west. Wouldn't be a bit surprised if we developed engine trouble after a while," Myles said, and clucked his tongue in mock dismay.

"Somewhere around Fundabora, for example," Chip said.

"For example," Myles agreed sagely. "Reminds me, I gotta break out my scope. C'mon, kid," he said, and jerked his head toward their cargo.

Lovett saw indecision on the youth's face. "Why not? We'll need a monocular to check out the landing strip."

"It weighs fifty pounds, solid brass, that's why not," Chip said, unbuckling. "He showed it to me. Artillery spotting scope, he said." Putting some of the Myles gravel in his voice: "Back when they built things right, he said. Jeez Louise, I bet he expects me to lug it around for him."

"Probably." Lovett's gaze at his grandson was placid. If Chip expected special catering from his grandfather after sneaking aboard, it was time he learned to fend for himself.

Chip had not exaggerated, and Lovett wandered back to look over the instrument. Mounted on plywood but meant to stand on a hefty tripod, the spotting scope was machined from heavy bronze castings, not brass, with a hooded objective lens that must have spanned three inches. Its eyepiece was an inch across, and it had ten- and twenty-power settings. With all its hand cranks and adjustments, the thing was as dated as—as—as a C-47, Lovett concluded. And you could probably dunk it into the Pacific without doing it much damage. Again, like a C-47.

No sooner had Lovett grasped the thought when a sharp icicle of awareness plunged into his stomach. The engine note had changed suddenly, and they were still hours from Fundabora. His companions did not seem to notice. He fought a powerful temptation to go forward, but Reventlo knew his aircraft.

The portside engine surged, then relapsed; the port wing dipped, recovered as the starboard engine revved to maximum power. A moment later both engines returned to normal, but not for long, because moments later the starboard engine developed its own gremlin.

It had to be a fuel problem, Lovett hazarded. But no, it might be—and now he scuttled forward. "Uh," was all he could say, because the starboard engine was snapping like a bag of bad popcorn.

"Come in, Wade." Reventlo looked back and grinned. "Thought that'd bring you forward. Like to play with Number Two?"

"I just *did* number two," Lovett said. "I am not known for my long-distance swimming, Cris. Do we have a problem here, or what?"

Reventlo magicked his controls and, in seconds, all was serene again. "If it's got you convinced, it should play to the Fundaborans," he said. "Thought I should have a go at a dry run."

"It wasn't that dry a run for me," Lovett said wryly. "One more little surprise like that and you're looking at a major laundry bill." He glanced at Gunther, whose smile lacked conviction. *He knew this was bogus but it wasn't that much fun for him*, he thought. "Okay, you've had your fun, and fuck you very much. Satisfied now?"

"Quite," said the Brit, craning his neck back. "Our other passengers don't seem all that exercised."

"They wouldn't be," Lovett rejoined. "They don't know about the other minor sabotages I called for in Portland. Enjoy," he said, and saw a look of dark surmise drift across Reventlo's face before returning to his seat. He had, of course, called for nothing of the sort. Still, he felt a petty childish joy knowing that a cold pang of uncertainty about his aircraft had gone through Reventlo's guts, too, for just a moment. Crispin Reventlo was, above all, a career flight captain; and few sensations are less welcome to the breed.

Bored with the guidebook and half-convinced it had been a waste of time since it didn't so much as mention Fundabora, Lovett let the steady throb of engines lull him into napping. He popped into full alertness, however, the next time an engine faltered.

His watch said the nap had been longer than expected. Shadows defined by the windows suggested early afternoon, and he could see his companions peering hard through their windows as one engine snorted while the other snarled harder to compensate. A mile below and perhaps ten miles ahead, underlined by a scrawl of white surf, lay an uneven dark mass. As they drew nearer it separated into a rich green with brown protrusions poking skyward, one of them almost to their present altitude. Though Wade Lovett had spent years in the tropics, something in his breast tripped his heart.

Twice, Lovett had visited Tahiti; had seen nearby Bora Bora and Moorea. Fundabora—for it could be no other island—had the same sort of breathtakingly raw volcanic pinnacles thrusting up from a tumbled carpet of greenery, the southern tors spearing higher, another to the north longer and more sawtoothed, reminding him of a High Sierra feature that climbers called The Minarets. Lovett watched the spectacle develop finer details, stunned by its matchless loveliness, until he realized two things. One, he saw no sign of any landing strip, new or old.

And two, they were descending below the height of that southern claw of stone. "Ohhh, shiiiiit," he muttered, and was not surprised to see Victor Myles scramble to retrieve his chest-pack chute.

Because a lower spine of stone ran between pinnacles that were several miles apart, Crispin Reventlo would say later that he thought he "had it all well in hand." But a sudden buffet of bad air lurked in that saddleback ridge, and before the pilot could coax both engines back to full power, the plane had dropped within yards of lush tropical foliage, a thin skin that covered vertebrae of solid rock.

Palms roiled in their wake. The saddleback fell away again immediately to lowlands. Lovett had a brief impression of thatched roofs and, nearer, swampy mangroves beyond the spine, and then Reventlo had the C-47 banking to the left, now with a thousand feet of air below them, following a narrow swath of beach with more primitive dwellings and outrigger canoes. Slowly, he regained altitude in an arc around the island's southern curve, one engine harrumphing and spitting again. If that was all for show, Lovett decided, he should vote the Brit an Oscar.

Right after strangling him barehanded.

Reventlo maintained his arc until they were perhaps a mile off the southern shore, and Lovett had the presence of mind to move in a squat across the sloped floor panels, buckling up again as he scanned the island. Still no landing strip to be seen but they had already passed a finger of lagoon, too regular to be natural, inserting a tongue of the sea into Fundabora's southwest tip. Cupped around the end of the lagoon lay a long white building in colonial style with small thatched cabanas trailing away from it like tacky little goslings from a mother goose. He could see tiny figures near the building, hands semaphoring.

Myles stormed past him, scrambling on the tilted floor. "Which door you want me to go out," he screamed into the flight deck. Only then did Lovett see that the survivalist had fully strapped on his chute.

"Victor, Victor," the Brit chided with exaggerated calm, "you skydivers appall me. I could never see why anyone would want to jump out of a perfectly good airplane." *Pop, whuff, whappity bam*, said the port engine.

Myles wasn't all that reassured. "This isn't a perfectly good airplane, it's a big aluminum potholder flown into a mountain by a maniac, and it looks like you're gonna try it again. You're not gettin' another chance at Vic Myles, pal."

"Nobody on Fundabora answered our distress call," Gunther called back to the Texan. "We hadda get their attention, right?"

"Well, you got mine, goddammit," Myles fumed. "And I don't see any airstrip and I want outa here. Somebody oughta live to tell about it."

"Take the rear cargo door then," Reventlo called. "But remember: that chute won't have time to open if you're nearer ground level than this. And ground level's going up again. Work it out for yourself, Victor," he finished, his attention still focused ahead.

Myles scurried back and Lovett went forward. "He's not trying the door," he told the Brit.

"I knew he wouldn't." Now they were making a wider circuit around the island, staying below its pinnacles. At some points the beach disappeared so that cliffs tumbled vertically to the sea. "Frankly, lads, I don't think we have a usable strip to land on."

"Sure we do," Gunther put in manfully. "Beach is plenty wide near those buildings."

"And it slopes," said Reventlo. "Sand is shifty, Coop."

"Not when it's wet, which it is," said Gunther. "Perfect for a landing with soft squishy tires. Big footprint. We used to—"

Lovett broke in. "You think maybe we should get a committee decision on this before you do it?"

"Point taken," Reventlo called back, tickling his Pratt & Whitneys into still more hiccups. "We can fly on to Leyte and charter a boat, I suppose."

Meanwhile the plane described another arc, turning around the island's northern tip and following an inward curve of beach. "More roofs," Chip was exclaiming to Mel Benteen.

"Different tribal style; that's odd," she replied, then noticed Lovett. "I hope Master Reventlo's enjoying himself up there," she said.

Lovett sat down to buckle in. "Not a lot. But he's willing to put down on the beach if you'll chance it."

"I thought, the airstrip," Chip began.

"Sing out if you see one, guys. I'm afraid Elmo invented that part," Lovett said. They all, including Myles, stared at him silently. "Hey, it's decision time, everybody. The beach now, or a chartered boat from the Philippines in a week or so."

"Manila! Or Leyte. Just promise me Reventlo won't be our skipper," Myles said instantly.

Lovett looked at the woman. "Mel?"

She shut her eyes, licked her lips in a way that was strangely appealing, opened her eyes again after a long breath. "Abstain," she said. "I don't know enough to judge it."

"Chip?"

The youth looked at Lovett, then the woman, and swallowed hard. "You're not abstaining, are you, Pop?"

Lovett shook his head. "Even Coop thinks they can grease it in, and he's still not in love with his luck. I may be sorry, but this way we hit Fundabora today. Six beaches; no waiting."

Myles: "You hadda say 'hit Fundabora,' asshole?"

"No. That was just for you, Myles," Lovett smiled.

Chip, without further pause, but flicking his gaze toward Myles: "I say let's hit the sonofabitch now," Chip said, and managed something like a devil-may-care grin.

Lovett knew his young devil cared very much, grandstanding with the panache of youth, but only nodded before toiling forward again on floor plates that changed slope like a sloop's deck.

Reventlo was looking out his portside window as Lovett leaned in. "You haven't voted, Cris."

"As it happens, the best stretch of beach is fairly near their tawdry Taj Mahal. The man from Alaska has convinced me," said the Brit. Gunther seemed ready to make a reply, but kept silent.

"Then it's one for Manila, one abstention, and four to hit the beach while the surf's up," Lovett said, wondering how that would serve as last words.

Reventlo let his actions speak. As he banked so that the narrow lagoon was visible at Fundabora's southwest tip, the big plane began to make noises attendant to flaps lowering, big wheels dropping from nacelles, and engines smoothing out, Gunther called back: "One thing about a real survivalist, he won't take dumbshit chances. Ol' Vic is real as they get. And you better get ever'body strapped in good and tight, Wade; there won't be much landing roll with the gooshy shoes on this ol' Gooney Bird."

As Lovett hurried back, he called, "Buckle up aft of the cargo. Anything that jars loose might come forward!" As he took his own advice with Chip at his side, a tiny piece of his awareness nagged at him. It calculated the sudden movement of four people, say seven hundred pounds, twenty feet rearward as the plane flared out for its landing. Fourteen thousand foot-pounds of imbalance in an airplane that was lightly loaded, at the very moment its harried pilot was juggling more variables than a pro quarterback. It would be just dandy, his calculating cortex growled, if his advice caused poor Reventlo to stall his nice shiny C-47. The Aussie client would be short one airplane.

The expedition could be short six lives.

11

Reventlo did stall the big plane. He did it the way aviators were taught to do it for carrier landings in the old days, about one foot above that sloping deck of wet sand, timing it so perfectly that when its wings were abruptly robbed of lift, the big transport dropped like a stone for twelve paltry inches and never even bounced. On landing it rolled only a few hundred yards before Reventlo coaxed it up the sloping beach near the tree line, safely above debris marking the highest recent tides. Lovett added his whoop to the cheers and then, with fidgeting hands, loosened his seat belt. The whirl of propellers slowed, became individual blades, and stopped. The crew's collective sigh seemed to pressurize the cabin.

Myles was out of his chute almost as fast as he got into it, stroking his beard, swaggering to the aft cargo door. "No sweat," he proclaimed. Reassessment on short notice was a Myles virtue.

Reventlo came padding back ahead of Gunther, dry-washing his face. "I'd forgot I was a praying man," he confided, "but guess wot, mates, it still works."

Lovett gave the Brit a thumbs-up. "Maybe the Lord helps those who help themselves."

Gunther, with a shaky laugh: "He sure helps those who have ten thousand hours as flight captains," and to this Reventlo made a slight, mocking bow.

The aluminum steps were quickly secured and Vic Myles was first to step onto the sands of Fundabora—perhaps because it would look good on paper one day. He stared back along their tire tracks for a moment before making a fast retreat back up the steps, diving for his backpack. "Welcoming committee," he said tersely.

It was either that or an impromptu track meet, Lovett decided as he leaned outside to look. He could hear Myles entreating Reventlo to crank up the engines again, just in case, and Reventlo refusing on the grounds that the last thing they needed was to decapitate some curious native with a whirling metal prop he couldn't even see. Benteen and Chip withdrew the steps and stood by the cargo door, ready to swing it shut.

Lovett heard a distinctive sound and whirled to see that Myles had jacked a round into the bore of a .45 automatic. "For God's sake, Vic, don't wave that thing in their faces! They're not carrying spears; they seem to be happy."

" 'One may smile, and smile, *and* be a villain,' " Reventlo quoted, watching a score of natives run toward them. Myles lowered his sidearm from sight. They could hear cries like those of children, faintly at first, but from the throats of men. When they finally approached the plane they were plainly winded from running, the first to touch the plane capering in delight, teasing the laggards. They carried no weapons, bare chests heaving from the exercise, wearing only knee-length wraparound skirts or apronlike loincloths. Few wore footgear. Most of them were adults, and all were male. Some had frizzy hair and black skin, though most had skin of a coffee tint and the straight hair of Polynesians. Lovett began to smile back at these people, the very image of grown children in vibrant health. They did not stay winded for long.

Some of them were shouting gibberish that sounded like ricochets off familiar language because that's exactly what it proved to be. Mel Benteen, with her years on various islands, had warned early-on that this might be the case. She listened for a moment before she moved forward waving, then sat down cross-legged in the cargo opening. "Pidgin. Let's see if mine works," she said to the crew.

She called out something very much like an Aussie "Goodday," and got the same in return, with an "apinoon," from one. She pointed at him, a husky specimen with a prominent scar on his breast, who fairly glowed with good looks. "Yes, apinoon. Well, it *is* afternoon," she said in aside. Then, with a formal smile: "Youfela awrite?"

The replies included several "All awrite" as the men crowded near, but not too near, their voices pitched for good humor instead of machismo. They seemed much intrigued by this person who dressed like a man, had a commanding presence like a man, but filled a blouse like no man they had ever seen.

"Tell them not to muck about with the plane," Reventlo begged. He had seen several of the curious folk rapping knuckles on the tail, crawling beneath, one inventive goof already starting to play on the drum-tight tail fabric as if it were a set of bongos.

"Please, all you goodfela no brakem ship. Touchem ship maybe bun pinga, ship mashem pinga, nogood, you no pogip mefela."

"Jesus, I almost understand that," Chip said in awe as he squatted low beside her. "What's a pogip?"

"Forgive," Benteen muttered in explanation, then waved her hand at him in an obvious brushoff. She had a more important conversation going. To one sally by the big strapping specimen who by general consent became the spokesman with Benteen, she said, "Solly, all 'em fela belong me no tok pisin."

The fuselage echoed with Myles's stage-whispered, "What's that about pissin'?" Benteen gave him a wave-off too, but had to repeat her next phrases because she was trying too hard not to laugh. At her next pause, she did turn toward Myles. "I said I was sorry but none of my people here talk pidgin. You guys really must let me concentrate, okay?" Myles stroked his beard and sat back on a lump of cartons to listen. All the male crew members darted looks at one another. It had never occurred to them that if Melanie Benteen, by necessity, became their spokeswoman, she would begin as their leader.

Somewhere in the near distance, the emphysemic sputter of a small engine echoed among the trees. More natives began to arrive now, some because ten-year-old legs cover ground more slowly, and some who evidently filtered through from beyond the tree line. Lovett looked for women but saw none. Most of the younger children were obviously boys, lacking even a stitch of clothing. He noted that one of the adult late arrivals wore trousers and a shirt, a strikingly handsome youth in sandals with the eyes of a deer but vaguely Asiatic cheekbones. Unlike the others he squatted quietly near the trees on dry sand, slender arms folded across his knees, but smiling as if he knew a secret or two. Lovett got the distinct impression that the young man was smiling directly toward Chip.

And when he glanced to one side, he got a distincter impression that Chip was returning the smile. Benteen seemed to be doing "awrite" with her musical mefela, youfela pidgin, but, Lovett mused, it might have been better to start with kids. No words, just kids.

Presently Benteen placed a hand on Chip's shoulder. "Ee sonson disfela yellagrass belong head," she said, and pointed to Lovett whose hair was indeed yellow. By now the entire crew was grouped near the door. "Disfela he fightem machine," she said, indicating Reventlo. "Disfela he goodfela alltime docta machine," pointing to Gunther, and finally a thumb jerked toward Myles. "Fela kip grass belong face he sabby paypa tok, fight black stick," she said. To this, the Fundaborans reacted in some awe; even the smiling youth in sandals seemed to take note.

"That's a few too many for me," Chip murmured. "Fight black stick?"

"Works with a pencil; paper talk. He writes," she said quickly, eyes dancing. Lovett had not thought to wonder if Mel Benteen had kids of her own; certainly she showed less animosity to Chip than to the others in the crew.

Another few minutes and Benteen was blinking, touching fingertips to her forehead. She evidently called the dialog off with some discussion about "kaikai," standing up and waving, and the crowd began to disperse. Most of them simply moved up through the trees rather than trudge through sand again, and Benteen closed her eyes, grimacing. "God, it's been a long time. Translating something I only half-know gives me a ripper of a headache. Pidgins differ. I can make this one out, though. Do we have some aspirin? A jolt of Bushmill's would do."

Reventlo found a soda still cold from the flight, and passed three aspirins to her as the others sat near to hear her summary. "I think it went well. I've said the plane is tired, so we can't go zooming around until we've doctored it. They suggest we wait while they bring us some food; you can tell something about their culture from that."

Chip: "That's kaikai, right?"

"You're a quick study. Yeah, kaikai is eat, food. Their offering it is a very good sign, though they could be stalling for time to see how to treat us. One thing though: if they offer food, you've got to taste it."

Myles: "No problem. I could eat a horse and chase the driver."

"Uh-huh," Benteen said, unconvinced. "Remember that if the main course is raw grubs or fried grasshopper. Sometimes they make beer by having toothless old ladies gum the mash and spit it into a bucket," she added, relishing the dismayed *O* that appeared in the middle of Myles's beard.

Chip grinned at Reventlo. "I think she said you fight the airplane," he confided.

"By the Lord Harry, that's not far off," he said. "But I know you have to use some leeway with the Queen's English when you speak pidgin."

"No shit, Sherlock," Benteen sighed, pinching the bridge of her nose. "You know how to say, 'piano' in most pidgins? Big fella box, you fightem teeth, he cry."

"Coo-wull," Chip said, and laughed. "My piano teacher will bust a gut."

"Fundaborans keep a few words from Spanish, a little Chinese influence; nothing of Japanese, thank God. Pidgin Japanese is tough." Benteen gnawed her lip, frowning, thinking. "It's an old-style pidgin but they're fairly hip. The plane is an aerocanoe—and get this: up the beach a few miles is what they call an aerodrome! Might mean a hangar or a runway."

"I should very much like to know where the hell they hide it," said Reventlo with a touch of surliness.

A new voice, diffident and low-pitched—though even the largest of these islanders seemed to avoid deep tones in ordinary conversation—made six necks swivel as one. "The island hides it. The field was overgrown when I was small." The young fellow in trousers and sandals had walked silently through the sand and now stood near the plane, big-eyed and friendly and, despite the broad islander nose, handsome as carnal sin. He might have overheard everything Benteen said.

"You no tok pis—oh hell," Benteen chuckled.

"I do," said the youth, and extended a hand. "I must. I teach school here. I am Oht—Keikano," he corrected himself quickly. "First names are customary. I should not confuse you."

Benteen was first to shake that hand, naming herself as "Mel," followed by the others. "You could have saved me some trouble," Benteen said, her smile awry.

"First contacts can reveal much," said Keikano with a faint lowering of his head. "We must talk soon, you and I." Then, smiling at Chip: "If you have a piano teacher, maybeso, mm, perhaps you play."

"Some." Why boast that he was a budding concert pianist?

"President Jean-Claude has a," he paused and said the next phrase for Benteen, "*bebe* bik piano in the Councilhouse. No one can play it. You, perhaps?"

Benteen shrugged at Chip. "Large baby," she supplied.

Chip, surprised and pleased: "A baby grand piano? Sure, why not?"

This seemed to puzzle the youth as he repeated the question. "Why not? But I think it would please him. And it would please me very much."

Benteen quickly explained that the expression meant "yes." "You don't get many strangers here, do you, Keikano?"

"Only commercial traders. Chinese, Japanese, Filipino, Papuan. They take our pearls, some copra. No phosphates for long time now. They bring fuel, medicines, books, dirty movies. So," he went on with a change of pace that was bewilderingly abrupt, "the 'why not' is corroquial?"

"Colloquial," Benteen said, nodding.

"I can spell it. My mouth cannot," Keikano smiled. "Sometimes. You can help me. And I can help you," he said pointedly to Benteen. "Rongi and others will be back soon with a feast for you, and I am sure Minister Merizo will come too. We must talk now." And Keikano beckoned for Benteen to leave the plane.

Benteen did as she was asked, slinging her shoulder bag on, and the two trudged up into the tree line, the native taking her hand in comradely fashion. Their words faded quickly into the background of gentle surf noises, the whispering heartbeat of every Pacific island.

"I don't like them separating her from us like this without a handheld." Reventlo hopped down to the sand to begin his postflight inspection and added, over his shoulder, "We don't know a damned thing about them, really."

Their pricey little handheld two-way radio transceivers were state-of-the-art stuff with multiple frequencies, a far cry from the huge old walkie-talkies and scarcely larger than short-range modern toys. Better late than never, Lovett burrowed into their cargo and laid out their four handhelds, one of which Myles appropriated instantly. For a fleeting instant Lovett wished he had demanded that Myles buy the thing, but in a pettiness contest Vic Myles was a sure winner.

"We know Benteen packs a little persuader in her bag," Lovett said with a chuckle. "I sure haven't forgotten that. Time to worry when she pops off a few rounds. And I'd worry about the other guy."

"I'm keeping ol' Betsy right here," Myles said darkly, thrusting the heavy automatic under his bush jacket between belt and skin at the small of his back.

Gunther, climbing down stiffly with a handheld unit to follow the pilot: "You really call that fuckin' thing ol' Betsy? I'm glad you're along, Vic, you make me look real classy."

When he had gone: "Only class I worry about is the one I teach: survival," Myles muttered.

"Some of us think you charge too much tuition, but never mind," said Lovett. He continued to watch the tree line, rubbing the stubble on his chin. "Myles could be right, Chip. Ever since Captain Cook, whites have misjudged island cultures. In some places they're as open and friendly as a yard sale but they'll steal your skivvies while you're wearing them. In others, I'm told, letting them see the soles of your feet is like flipping 'em off, only worse. Just watch what people do and be careful, okay?"

"Okay, Pop. Believe it or not, I've been cramming on the Pacific. I even know this isn't really the South Pacific since we're north of the Equator."

Lovett nodded and continued to scan the foliage. He heard Benteen's contralto laugh once, his anxiety level dropping as the ambience of Fundabora seduced him. Its beach lay all around them, sparkling off-white, its surf lulling, and a flash of color in the trees proved that rats hadn't killed off its bird population. He began to trudge into dry sand, strangely encouraged by the Swiss army knife he felt in his pocket, a device as bulky as a hand grenade and a hell of a lot more useful. Somewhere in it, he suspected, lay a kitchen sink if only he knew how to tease it out.

Crispin Reventlo had already announced that he was satisfied with his walkaround inspection, and Lovett was feeling light-headed in the midday sun, before Benteen and the schoolteacher emerged onto the beach, still talking easily. Young Keikano took his leave there, waving as he disappeared in the riot of greenery, and moments later they heard the whirr and snivel of a small engine dopplering away.

"Fairly decent perimeter road in there a ways," Benteen told them. "The guy's got a scooter left over from Biblical times. Ever hear of a Cushman?"

Most of them had skinned elbows on those chugging little two-wheelers before Benteen was born, and Myles said so. "That means they have some technology we can use. That schoolteacher kid mentioned fuel and movies; like we figured, somebody's got electric power here."

Benteen found her half-consumed soda and chugalugged it like a man. "I think all the modern blessings must be concentrated around that Pelele goon; God's gift to women," she said finally.

"So the power is where the power is," said Lovett, and saw her head tilt. He went on quickly, "That's not the truism it seems; I mean, he'd keep things like electricity and fuel as symbols of clout. Pretty standard strongman tactic in lots of places. Lucky we have inverters and fuel of our own."

"Something worrisome about this setup," she said, studying her deck shoes as she swung her legs from the doorsill. "Can't place it yet. Maybe it's just because the elders of this entire population were shipped in here piecemeal during the war and kept behind barbed wire as forced labor. I can tell you this much: if young Mr. Keikano knows there are other aircraft on Fundabora, he's an accomplished liar."

Reventlo had found a soda for himself and, between sips, said, "Very well: you're our Maggie Thatcher. If it wasn't about aircraft, what state secrets did your young academic share?"

Benteen laughed aloud, which took ten years from her age. "You won't believe it. He told me I hadn't fooled Rongi—that's the big gorgeous hunk I was talking with earlier—and the others for a second. *They could plainly see I'm a woman*," she said, with a headshake of wonderment. Then, in mock despondency: "Woe is me."

"What's his problem," Chip asked.

"He said I should've, well—covered up. Worn something that doesn't give me away. Apparently it's too late now."

"Yeah, the boobs are outa the bag," Myles said.

"One of them certainly is," she replied, staring at Myles for a long instant. "The point is that Keikano was doing me a big favor, in his mind, because it's an important factor here. Their Mr. Rongi was humoring me but I mustn't try to be your leader when we meet Fundaboran high society. Women's lib hasn't washed ashore here." She looked around. "What, no rousing cheer?"

"Not with that pistol of yours so close at hand," the Brit assured her.

"Our small arms are something we should probably keep out of sight. I'm willing to continue to translate but even Keikano assumes we will have a single leader. I mean, Christ, they've never known anything else!"

"Well," Myles drawled, easing forward.

"Forget it," she and Lovett said together.

A two-beat tableau. "I nominate Cris," said Gunther. "He's used to command and he comes on like Winston friggin' Churchill."

"Oh give over, will you," Reventlo muttered, slightly aggrieved.

Lovett: "Second the motion. He looks the part. Well, shit, Cris, you do. Just don't forget to confer with your ministers before you go declaring war or anything. Mel?"

With a sigh that might be half genuine: "I suppose so. Eagle-eyed elder statesman type, and we could do worse. Chip?"

The youth looked up in surprise. "I get a vote on the geezer patrol?" He saw one shrug, a nod, and three smiles. He fell silent for a moment. Then: "I admit this is partly my bias, but I vote for my pop. I happen to know he's got more invested than anybody else. He's a businessman who makes deals. And I know he can command when he needs to." He was grinning as he added, "I never saw anybody make so many good snap decisions as when he was one jump ahead of those airheads in Wichita."

An uneasy silence fell over the crew. "Strong showing," murmured Reventlo.

Gunther said, "Myles, who do you like that won't make me laugh right out loud?"

"I'll put my money on the duke of earl," said the Texan, earning another pained look from the Brit. "Sorry, kid."

"It's okay," Chip said, "honest. Doesn't matter now how you vote, Mr. Reventlo, you're elected and no hard feelings. I'm just more used to Pop being a leader. And he has yet to fly me through a grove of palms," he finished, his grin askew.

"He just never had the chance," the Brit said, winking. "Very well, I'm the figurehead. And, ah—Benteen?" She gave him an expectant glance. "In future, Benteen, please do us all the favor of staying closer to the, ah, more or less legitimate males in our little party. That means you will kindly, kindly, not go perambulating alone with the locals."

"I love it when he talks dirty," she murmured. The sexuality was exaggerated and bogus, but Lovett felt it still worked, and faintly damned himself for the feeling.

"I mean it." Reventlo's complaint was earnest, and he pressed it well. "You tell us women are chattel here, more or less, and a well-meaning native has as much as warned you already. Now I admit I haven't your background with island cultures, but I've spent time in this part of the world. You may risk your honor as much as you like another time, but we came here for the profit motive. We did not come here to play Menelaus to your Helen of Troy."

Chip sat erect, recalling his classics. "You think she'd get kidnapped, like in *Seven Brides for Seven Brothers*?"

"Or perhaps as in the rape of Nanking," Reventlo said darkly.

"I think, if you must be chattel, you must be *our* chattel. Someone's, any one of us—purely a formality, you understand."

The look Melanie Benteen turned on their elected leader was a salad of dismay and amusement, with a sprinkle of resignation as seasoning. "Whose," she asked in the tone of one holding a horsewhip.

Three men said, "His," at once, Lovett and Gunther pointing at Reventlo, the Brit pointing at Lovett.

"I love it," Myles grunted.

"I can see I've swept you all off your feet," Benteen said. "But if I'm to have any status—and I'd better—it's best if I'm your little cuddle-bunny, Reventlo."

"Cuddle-bunny. The mind reels," said the Brit, closing his eyes briefly. "Though I can't fault your logic, my dear. Or your taste."

"Don't, for a millisecond, imagine," Benteen began.

"That I shall leap slavering onto your nubile bones at my first opportunity? When dingoes lay eggs and run for parliament, and not a moment sooner."

"I've spent time in Sydney. I'm told some of them already sit in parliament," she reminded him.

"I stand corrected. Not even then, madam," he said primly. Judging by the Brit's high color, Lovett concluded that Crispin Reventlo's dry sense of humor pretty much blew away with the dust when he felt truly slighted. Now Lovett felt even better about their choice of a leader; there actually was an indefinable something in Reventlo that commanded respect.

By now they could hear the clatter and whine of some large machine approaching, still invisible through the trees. It might almost have been a small military tank but, as it bulled its way through underbrush to the beach, Myles broke into a smile. "A dinosaur," he chortled, "a goddamn dinosaur!"

The half-track vehicle made almost as much noise as a T. rex, the size of a truck, smoking like a cigar salesman, with wheels up front for steering, treads and bogies like a tank in the rear for traction. Fifty years earlier these sturdy relics had slogged troops and cargo through many a shallow swamp but, with side panels that would turn a rifle bullet, it was not the kind of vehicle that floated.

The driver wore a baseball cap, a huge belt with leather pockets full of tools, and not much more. Beside him sat a skinny gent of middle age and vast dignity who carried a flywhisk of yellow feathers that looked as though it had seen many, many better days, some of them on a trash heap. His brown skin seemed pale next to the black he wore: black-striped pants, black waistcoat, black cummerbund, black tie. The effect was marred by his lack of a shirt but as he eased over the low door without opening it, they could see that he wore black shoes, with cutouts for his bunions and toes.

Reventlo murmured, "What, no praetorian guard?"

"No socks," Chip marveled. "This dude is up to date." Then he saw young Keikano rise up from the cargo compartment to brush himself off, and waved. Keikano was too busy scrambling to the side of His Nibs to return the wave. The driver stayed at his post, blipping a pedal to keep the engine from guttering out.

"Can't be Pelele," Benteen muttered as she moved forward at the side of Reventlo, whose, "mm-hm" was almost inaudible. The Brit waved the rest of the crew back as he advanced with Benteen.

The potentates gazed at each other for a moment before the islander raised his flywhisk and spoke. When he did, the effect was electric. A stream of some unfamiliar language erupted from him in the basso profundo of a bullhorn. To Lovett it seemed as if he was making up for the light tenor used by the other men on the island. To hear a voice like this from such a little fellow was astonishing enough to provoke a smile, but young Keikano, with a look that was slightly grim, seemed to be setting an example. Laughter, he was telling them, was definitely not the best medicine right now.

When the islander fell silent, Keikano spoke. "Merizo, First High Minister of the Fundaboran Republic, welcomes you on behalf of President Jean-Claude Pelele. He invites you to unroll your mats in the councilhouse."

Reventlo gave a sage nod, as if thinking it over. "We thank the minister on behalf of Her Majesty the Queen and the President of the United States and, um, all that," he said, "but some of us must stay with the, ah, aerocanoe. Doesn't he speak anything else?"

"Some, but this is formal talk. And he means it as an order," Keikano said. The little minister was already speaking to Keikano, however, and the youth's face darkened in embarrassment. Keikano tried again: "The low interpreter forgets himself. The low interpreter will not forget himself again." Then he launched into the island language, presumably repeating what Reventlo had said.

Merizo thought about it for a moment and seemed satisfied that the formalities had been observed, because he began to speak pidgin, using the flywhisk to help his gestures.

Benteen, speaking loudly enough for the crew to hear, said,

"Merizo will provide a guard for the plane. He urges us to accept Pelele's hospitality to avoid giving offense. We'll be treated like presidents, which I think means like God Almighty."

"Tell His Exquisiteness," said Reventlo, with a bow from another century, "we'll be glad to go, bringing gifts—except for one who must stay and monitor the radio at all times in case our prime minister across the sea grows concerned."

Benteen gave him a long searching glance, but then began her spiel; something about a littlefela box alltime tok for bikbik headman bilong whitefela, and so forth.

After a few more interchanges and some seriocomic pantomime on the part of Keikano who now stood a pace behind his minister, Crispin Reventlo thrust out his hand. It was taken, after the briefest of pauses, by Merizo, as Benteen spoke in an urgent undertone. Reventlo completed a formal handshake, took three backward steps, did a military about-face to shame a Coldstream Guard, and climbed aboard the aircraft with Benteen following.

"Whatthehell was all that about," Gunther complained, unable to hear much of it.

"I think Keikano was trying to tell him to kneel," Chip said.

"I'm bleeding certain of it," Reventlo said, turning to bestow a thousand-watt smile and wave from the plane to little Merizo. "And bending our knees is not the right message, if I'm any judge."

"No doubt; the little guy's game is status," Benteen said. "It used to be bad form to turn your back on a high muckymuck, and I think you hit the right note. We need to talk some more with this Keikano character."

"At the moment," Reventlo mused, gazing out at the waiting Fundaborans, "we need to choose our sentry."

"And gifts," Lovett reminded him. "I'll stay behind, but I'll want a sidearm."

"Let me," Gunther put in. "I got a bum leg anyway. But I could fire up the Briggs and Strattons if I had to. Don't forget to leave me a walkie-talkie and a pistol," he added.

Myles dug into his own cargo, brandishing a device that had a folding stock and a shortish barrel. "Ever see one of these," he asked as he handed it over. "Don't forget whose it is."

"Grease gun," Lovett nodded, remembering its nickname from two generations back. "Ugliest thing General Motors ever made."

" 'Cept maybe a fifty-one Buick," Gunther said.

"I've got a fifty-one," Myles protested.

Gunther, checking the magazine with its stubby forty-five caliber rounds: "I rest my case."

"Rest your case on this," said Myles, giving him a stinkfinger salute.

"For the love of God," Reventlo burst out, "will you stop bickering? Our carriage awaits."

With a limited choice of gifts that they could afford to offer, Lovett chose two bottles of scotch and tossed a pair of MREs, meals ready-to-eat, to Chip. The MRE, in its olive drab plastic pouch, might not be a gourmet's dream but it came as varied entrees, provided a day's calories, and unlike older rations it would float. It seemed appropriate as a gift to an islander. In moments they were ready, or thought they were, and streamed out to the burping old half-track with a final wave to Coop Gunther.

12

If that half-track still carried shock absorbers, they had long since lost their erections. Lovett estimated that the vehicle clunked and bounced for two miles along the perimenter road before emerging into a broad expanse that once might have been a golf course. The open vista revealed a white building that dominated the middle distance, a rambling two-story affair curved in a crescent. A low porch ran the full length of its frontal curve, and columns met in arches to support the overhang. Small cottages stretched away from it in a sinuous line, protected by distant palm groves with the beach far beyond.

Though he could not see it clearly from that angle, Lovett knew from their overflight that a fingerlike lagoon intruded near those cottages, terminating in a pool flanked by the arms of the the main structure. It had looked idyllic from the air, but a closer look proved that everything had become seedy with neglect.

Nearer, grass fought a losing battle against some knee-high, all-encroaching ground cover—ivy with an attitude. Lovett had seen similar stuff in Southeast Asia; it left the impression that if you spent ten minutes within its reach it would strangle you like a python. The road of crushed shell curved between outbuildings and fenced areas that had once been tennis courts. Two curved metal buildings like huge half-buried barrels, probably surplus Quonset huts, were flanked by rusting vehicles, suggesting abandoned efforts to maintain the island's equipment.

"These guys could use a mechanic or two," Myles noted.

Young Keikano, sitting near Benteen, replied only loud enough to be heard by her and Lovett. "President Jean-Claude agrees. But if the repairs fail, the workman finds life—very unpleasant. Do not say I told you."

As they drew nearer the big central building, they saw scores of natives running to gather down the length of its covered porch, their knee-length skirts a pulsating riot of color.

Benteen: "Different tribe?"

Keikano: "Same people. They have dressed for you."

Benteen nodded as she noticed the handsome oaf she had spoken with before. "What special advice can you give for this?"

"Our President speaks some English but he may not wish to. Let your leader talk and you translate. He should offer the gifts. Smile and stand tall, but never higher than the President," he said, with a darted glance toward the little minister who sat ahead, unable to hear over the squeals and grunts of his vehicle.

Benteen passed this on to Reventlo, who hurriedly filled his arms with scotch and MRE packets. Lovett saw to his astonishment that Myles was dictating to Chip, who had his little palmtop computer open on his knee.

As the half-track rumbled to the building's portico, Lovett thought he recognized a few more of the Fundaborans, all of them lining up along the porch to flank the central entrance, adopting solemn expressions. Before that entrance was a high bench with an outsized, high-backed rattan chair in its very center. Ranked behind it stood a half-dozen bruisers, stern-faced and much overfed, holding carved, clublike wooden staffs.

Occupying that huge chair, flanked by half a dozen bare-breasted beauties, sat a huge bronzed fellow in glorious Technicolor. He stood up as the vehicle stopped; made a gesture. The engine clattered and died as little Merizo scurried from the vehicle to his place at the right side of his leader. Keikano was almost as quick, hopping to the ground, moving to stand at the left.

"My God, the man's a giant," Reventlo muttered, easing himself down with the crew members.

"Fee, fie, foe, fum," Chip agreed, the computer under his arm now.

Giant he was, in a vest of some native material brilliant in red and yellow, his lava-lava skirt of heavier scarlet stuff with black decorations and a broad straw mat the color of dried blood around his waist, worn like a cummerbund. He wore sandals on his size umpteen feet, keg-legged, with huge calves and arms to match. His face was fleshy but unlined, with a prizefighter's nose, button eyes deeply set and lively, no discernible neck, the big head crowned by a headdress of sun-yellow feathers that added half a yard to his height. Unadorned, he might have stood an inch under seven feet, tipping the scales at three-fifty or more. Lovett found himself thanking God the man was smiling as he came up out of his rattan throne in a curiously graceful surge and stepped forward.

For one pregnant moment, giant Fundaboran and starchy Brit faced each other with formal smiles. Then something seemed to click into place behind the big man's eyes. He thrust out an enormous paw, each finger armored with rings, and Reventlo took it after shifting his loot to one arm.

Lovett heard the faint exhalation, half sigh, half grunt, from Reventlo as the handshake lingered. Then President Jean-Claude Pelele's smile broadened into something more genuine and he released his prey as he spoke.

Benteen's forehead creased with effort. The words were totally unfamiliar but the voice was light in tenor, almost breathy, yet resonant in a chest cavity that would suffice for two ordinary men.

Reventlo smiled harder. Young Keikano translated: "In the name of Fundabora, President Jean-Claude Pelele welcomes the shipwrecked. We will help you get passage on the next ship. You have nothing to fear from us."

But something in the way Keikano said *shipwrecked* and *fear* lent a special urgency to those words. Benteen spoke low into Reventlo's ear: "Sounds like a claim for salvage rights."

As if he had not heard her: "We thank you for your welcome, but we were not wrecked, sir. We want only to rest our ship. We bring gifts to show our thanks." And with that, he held out his offerings.

Pelele took them, with a perplexed glance at the MRE packs and a delighted grin at his scotch. He handed it all over to the hovering Merizo; seemed to reach some internal decision; said, "Pelele can tok English allsame youfela," and grasped Reventlo in a one-armed bearhug. The demonstration must have meant something special to Fundaborans, who began to whoop and cheer while surrounding the strangers and gabbling in what sounded like pig latin from hell.

Pelele liked to look at Benteen; and whatever he liked to do, he did. She found herself crowding close to Cris Reventlo, shielding herself from the big man's gaze. Pelele's English was laced with pidgin, most of it readily understood. He might ask, "Name belong you," while pointing at Benteen, but after getting the answer he could also confide like a sailor on shore leave to Reventlo, "Good knockers."

Low benches were dragged onto the porch for the crew, who soon began to relax their wary stances. With her smiles, Benteen showed her relief that Pelele had so quickly discarded the formalities she'd been led to expect. The only ritual that seemed formal was in the sharing of some opaque liquid in a bowl, served in a cup of coconut shell in a grave silence broken only by someone's low chant to the plaintive beat of a small wooden drum. After his first experimental sip, Myles claimed it tasted as though someone had lost some mild Mexican peppers in muddy water. After two cups, Lovett wondered aloud why his lips were numb. Benteen set their minds at ease by telling them it was the local version of *kava*, harmless and nonalcoholic. Once the bowl was empty, the last vestiges of ceremony disappeared and platters of unidentifiable foods were placed before them.

Lovett wasn't sure when the seals came off the scotch, intent as he was on staying near Chip amid the friendly jostle of a hundred mostly naked men who'd never heard of deodorant. He did take a taste when the scotch was passed to him for a swig, and saw Chip take more than a taste, and then got involved with a serious-faced man who wanted to swap a tiny misshapen pearl for "small rocks bilong docta, fix head bilong missy bilong me, head alltime nogood," perhaps aspirin for his wife's headaches. He did not show interest in cash. Lovett expressed enthusiasm but could only say things like, "later" and "another time," which eventually became "long time soon" with a wan smile from the pearl's owner.

The formidable Pelele appropriated one bottle for himself, repeatedly asking the crew's names between pulls at the scotch until he had everything memorized. Little Merizo never strayed far from the giant's elbow though the youthful schoolteacher, Keikano, must have received some signal that his services would no longer be needed. Keikano took Chip in tow, discussing tidbits of fish and fowl, and then someone brought in a crock of what proved to be home brew, and for Lovett, after that, the sequence of events got a little hazy.

Lovett's hangover was not hazy, it was solid as a concrete overcast. He awoke to the last rays of sun, a spear of molten gold through an open window that fried his retinas and made him flinch. He swung his legs to the floor, blinking, and found he'd been lying on a rattan couch. Myles sprawled nearby on a double bed, snoring, one arm caught in mosquito netting. There was no sign of Reventlo or Benteen but Chip was sitting in a woven chair, gazing out of their second-story window as he talked into one of their transceivers.

"The drink was probably spiked, Mr. Gunther," he was saying, between staccato bursts from the sleeping Texan across the room. The radio squawked softly, and then Chip spoke again: "That's just Mr. Myles, snoring the twenty-one gun salute from the 1812 Overture. He was slugging that awful crap down like he had a leak in his neck. Serves him right. My pop is," he paused, glanced toward Lovett, waved and smiled, "here with me, too. Mr. Reventlo and Miz Benteen went easy on the drinks. Last I saw, they were on a walking tour of the building with the President. Make that a staggering tour. They took it pretty easy on that home brew, though, like I did."

More squawks from the radio, as Lovett walked to the window, willing to let Chip save him the trouble of talking. Below them in the driveway of crushed shell, the half-track's driver was sitting literally on his vehicle's engine, bent over its carburetor with water pump pliers. Lovett winced, shook his head. Because they chewed up fittings so fast, water pump pliers were a good mechanic's choice only after the failure of wrenches, fingernails, and teeth. Aircraft mechanics called them Mexican speed wrenches and kept them with plumbing tools. Lacking professional mechanics on Fundabora, these people were lucky to maintain anything more complicated than a teeter-totter.

With the sun's escape below the horizon, dusk came hovering in like a heavy gauze curtain. Lovett had forgotten how fast daylight became night in the tropics but that poor bastard slaving over a cold carburetor now had a lit candle to help him, and to blow him clear off the island if serious gasoline fumes were present.

Fascinated, Lovett watched, and then remembered the powerful little Maglite in his pocket. He could either concentrate on his headache or do something to take his mind from it. "I'm going outside, Chip, but I'll stay within earshot. You do the same, okay?"

The youth nodded, obviously keeping company with the solitary Gunther in the only way he could, and Lovett's step became steadier as he found his way to a broad stairwell. The councilhouse, he had learned before conking out, had been a postwar hotel for a decade and now, with peeling paint and tatters of old carpet, it reminded him of cut-rate lodgings in some one-cop Mexican town. He descended into a deserted lobby whose windowpanes had been removed, welcoming the sea breeze, hurrying outside to the half-track and its hapless mahout.

The native, a wiry fellow in his forties, jerked nervously as Lovett's footstep crunched on the drive's shells, then seemed relieved to see that it was only one of the strangers. He bent to his task again. Lovett twisted the Maglite to a medium-focus beam, pinched the candle out. "We don't need an open flame," he said.

The driver-mechanic straightened, took the flashlight in one hand to inspect it, handed it back. Lovett realized that the fresh dark smear on the instrument was blood, and that the native's fingers were a gory mess. After a few moments he saw that the poor ignoramus was trying to force a length of tubing over a hose fitting—had been trying for some time—without loosening the hose clamp. It seemed likely that he did not realize you could loosen or tighten a hose clamp, and for good reason: the clamp's little fingerholds were rusted tight.

"Let me try," Lovett said. The man made no sign he had heard until Lovett patted his wrist and pantomimed helping.

"Pipe belong bun wata," said the native, indicating the fuel hose, and straightened the kinks from his back. He watched as Lovett, with one finger, transferred a smudge of oil from a puddle on the engine to the corroded hose clamp, then produced his Swiss knife and used its tough little pliers to loosen the clamp. The native *ahhh*ed in awe. Lovett trimmed the shredded end of the hose neatly with his knife blade, the native murmuring in pidgin as he studied the operation, then shoved the hose onto its fitting and repositioned the clamp before tightening it. The native showed a lively curiosity about the "knife pinga pinch iron," meaning the tiny pliers, and soon the two men were ranging over the antique engine as Lovett was shown all the things that didn't work, or worked poorly. Some of the newer fittings looked like good hardware, but not the "A N" fittings America had made standard across the globe. Lovett guessed they were Chinese.

After a half-hour, they had fixed a few more small glitches. Lovett knew the fellow's name, Pilau, and began to have a smattering of pidgin. *Bun wata*, water that burns, meant fuel; *Lubbet* was Lovett himself. And he knew that Pilau was almighty anxious to get that brute of a half-track the hell out of the drive before his President returned.

Pilau knew how to prime a carburetor with raw fuel, which smelled like any other gasoline, and soon had his vehicle lurching off toward the Quonsets. Lovett's ears welcomed the silence for a long while but presently he could hear an exchange of distant voices inside the councilhouse and hastily wiped his hands on ivy leaves before entering the building.

Though no electric lights were in evidence, kerosene torches held by Pelele's men lent a warm flickering glow to the lobby and explained some of the carbon smudges on nearby walls. Lovett gave them a silent wave as he approached the group. The huge headman had three of his burly retinue, still silent and impassive, with him. Lovett saw no sign of the schoolteacher or minister Merizo.

Reventlo, with Benteen's occasional help, was explaining to the huge Pelele that it didn't matter whether they had transportation or not; his crew would find the airplane. Thanks ever so much, perhaps tomorrow they would sleep in the guesthouses, but for now they had business with the airplane. As for rounding up their sleepers, not to worry; they would manage somehow.

"I slept it off pretty fast," Lovett announced. "A splash of water should do wonders for Myles—uh, fella grass belong face," he added, manfully trying out his pidgin.

"Awright, youfella go, Jean-Claude don't give a shit," the giant said in mild exasperation. With that, he turned and set off down the hall from the lobby, arms swinging with elbows held wide, his guards one step behind. Robbed of torchlight, the lobby became a pit of gloom.

"We pissed him off, didn't we," Lovett asked, producing his Maglite again.

"It's not a difficult chore," Reventlo muttered, still looking at the retreating backs. "He's not used to being denied. Wanted us to be his guests tonight whether we liked it or no."

Benteen: "Give the man some credit, Cris. He's dealing with it better than a lot of headmen do. Uh, how many of those flashlights do we have with us, Lovett?"

"Let's find out," said Lovett, and led the way upstairs.

They found Chip and Vic Myles together sharing the light of a candle stub, Chip tapping away on his computer while a bleary-eyed Myles enveloped himself in the smoke of a corncob pipe and dictated. "About time," Myles rumbled, getting up. "What's for supper?"

"Whatever Coop hasn't eaten," said Reventlo. "We were afraid we'd have to drag you back unconscious."

"Somebody slipped me a stone-age mickey. Sure didn't last long though—hold it. Drag me? We don't get a ride?"

The Brit shook his head. "Under the circumstances I thought we'd be wiser not to beg one; let the beggars know we can fend for ourselves. Let's have a show of pocket torches, shall we?"

Only Chip and Benteen lacked a flashlight. Myles pocketed his candle stub—with all its odds and ends, that hunting jacket must have weighed ten pounds—and soon they were trudging through the path of white shell toward the beach. Myles poked his sidearm into the front of his belt though Reventlo said they should be safe enough. "Our friend Jean-Claude seems to be a benevolent dictator, and dictators run a tight ship. I suspect muggers would have a rather short career on Fundabora."

They proceeded along the broad swath of sand in starlight, the black of the treeline to their left and pale shifting lines of surf to the right, using their flashlights now and then to identify the dark lump that would become seaweed or a palm stump rounded by surf and sand. Civilization had its points, Lovett decided, but they were not points of heavenly light; with no smog, no atmospheric glow from nearby cities, Fundabora's sky remained pristine, unsullied by modern barriers to the stargazer. The sea breeze cleared foggy heads nicely though the sand made their calves ache, and they saved their lungs for the walk, venting sighs of relief when they saw a row of dim glows far ahead near the treeline. Myles found his second wind and forged ahead a few paces to the plane, only to find the cargo door closed. He rapped on it.

From inside, Coop Gunther: "I told you to get away from here; go on, scat!"

"It's us, Coop," Reventlo called.

Heavy footfalls, and the door swung wide. "Whyn't you let me know," the old man grumped.

The Brit followed Myles in, rubbing his calves as he took one of the bucket seats. "I gather you've had unwanted company, Coop."

"That little half-pint in the Halloween tux? Him and some TV wrestlers showed up about sundown. Skulked around in the woods awhile before he came out with one of the biggies to have another look around the plane, trying to look innocent as Laurel and friggin' Hardy. I was watching from the cockpit, didn't say anything 'til the big guy gave a tap on the rudder. Then I raised hell."

Lovett eased his aching butt to a seat. "We need these people to stay friendly, Coop," he said.

"We need an airchine in one piece, too. He does his tapping

with a goddamn six-foot club, Wade. But he ain't Gene Krupa and that ain't a snare drum back there, okay?"

Chip: "Who's Gene Krupa?"

Myles: "I'm gonna kill this kid."

Benteen, worried: "You didn't shoot, Coop?"

"Naw. Opened the door and cycled the bolt, though. It's a noise that gets attention."

"They might not recognize it," said Myles.

Gunther, with a snort: "If they didn't, from the way they moved out they both made a damn good guess. They gotta have guns here."

"I think," Reventlo mused, "you walked a fine line, Coop. Good on you; proves we can be serious, but not too bloody-minded. They were probably just testing to see if anyone was home. Ah, have you tried the comm set to check the weather? I'd hate to see our nice C-Fort become a—"

"Sea fort," Chip put in, his pun earning a groan from the Brit.

"CAVU ahead," Gunther nodded, a shorthand phrase indicating Ceiling and Visibility Unlimited—clear weather. "Checked just before dinner."

That reminded Myles of his belly again, and presently they were sharing the mysteries of a few MRE packs. Though these modern analogs of C-rations still got their share of curses, they would last until the blast of Gabriel and provided well-rounded menus. Each olive-drab plastic pack carried one of a dozen labels: chicken with rice, spaghetti with meat sauce, beef or chicken stew, even pork chow mein; all precooked, each with separate packets for crackers, cookies, condiments with a plastic spoon, and a powdered drink mix. Chip was considering one labeled "Chili con carne with beans" until Reventlo plucked it from him with, "Not in my airplane. Does 'fart in a space-suit' have a familiar ring?"

"If he did, it would," Lovett said. "At least he has perfect pitch." Chip sighed and tried the "Escalloped potatoes with ham," instead.

During and after the meal they compared notes in the glow of a single cabin light. From Lovett they gained the impression that, while such simple remedies as aspirin were known on the island, the common folk had to barter for them.

Reventlo and Benteen had stayed closer than Siamese twins during their tour of the councilhouse. "Actually, it might be wise to accept Jean-Claude's offer," Benteen suggested. "If we stay in the councilhouse, it will make negotiations simpler."

"Not unless we taxi the plane up near the place with those palms as a windbreak," said the Brit.

"Yeah, and keep an eye on our transportation," Coop said. "You two learn anything about the stash?"

Reventlo shrugged. "Not a glimmer. I noticed there are lights in the presidential suite, though. That means a working generator."

"In the harem, too," said Benteen, which brought several heads up sharply. "Well, I don't know what else to call it. I think it began as a little convention hall but it's partitioned off for, oh, a half-dozen of the poor things. Did you see the bamboo bars over their windows? They didn't pay much attention to us. Must be a boring life."

"Interrupted by an occasional night of sheer terror, I should think," Reventlo said. "Do you suppose any of his wives would have influence? You'd be the one to look into it, Melanie."

"I could try," she said. "And the sooner we find the best way into Jean-Claude's heart, the better."

"All the better reason to taxi the plane back and bed down in the councilhouse. There are plenty of rooms for us," Lovett pointed out, "and it sure beats sleeping here."

No one argued against that. They began to arrange their sleeping bags as Chip described his discussion with the schoolteacher. Before Keikano left the party, he had asked a million questions of Chip: whether the youthful American knew of any hostilities between Pacific islands; whether the aircraft would return, assuming they left soon; whether any of the crew was a doctor or nurse; and whether he, Keikano, might purchase a ride to some city.

"Wants to see the bright lights, does he," Benteen smiled sadly. "Lots of young islanders make that mistake. Without money they wind up displaced, disillusioned, drunk, or all three."

"Like the Klinkit," Gunther nodded, "in Alaska."

"I don't think that's it, exactly. And if he can pay with pearls, he's far from broke," Chip said, producing a lovely orb the size of a small pea, with a soft nacreous pink luster as though lit from inside.

"Ohh, *ho*," said Reventlo, taking the object between thumb and forefinger. Now he murmured to the pearl: "Any more at home like you, my dear?" Chip merely nodded, but Lovett thought the youth's eyes shone almost too brightly. Reventlo spoke to Chip again: "He just gave this away?"

"Uh—swapped him my flashlight," Chip admitted.

Lovett, who knew his grandson had brought one: "So that's where it went."

"Not a good idea," Benteen said. "Look, I know it's tempting, but we can make trades when we're warming up the engines."

"Never know when you'll wish you could buy that hardware back, kid," Myles put in.

For once, Benteen seemed to value Myles's input. "Let's not show much interest in pearls; not if we want a good price later. So young Mr. Keikano hopes to buy his way aboard. If not to see the big city—Agana on Guam would qualify, I imagine—then why?"

"He didn't say." Chip cudgeled his memory as the pearl passed among the crew. "I know he figures on coming back, though. Maybe on some supply ship. He says there are many things his people need."

Lovett: "Textbooks?"

Reventlo: "A Walkman with a hundred spare batteries, more likely. He could probably receive Manila or Agana from here."

Mel Benteen's short hair swung with her headshake. "It wouldn't surprise me if you were right, Lovett. Our Mr. Keikano seems to see himself as the island's self-taught braintrust. Take a gentle young guy starved for intellectual give-and-take, introduce him to aliens from the sky with technology he's only heard about, and watch him bend over backward to make friends."

"Or bend over frontwards," Myles said, holding one hand up, wrist limp. "I'm not sure his sandals make prints."

In such dim light, the others may not have noticed what Lovett did: Chip's blush. Benteen said, "More islanders have homosexual relations than you'd think. Whatever he is, Keikano is also trying hard to be our friend. Let's not undervalue that."

"You can keep your homo friends," Myles rumbled, then belched.

"Not on Fundabora you can't," said Chip. When he had their full attention, he added, "Keikano was telling me about some of the local customs. President Jean-Claude doesn't like gays much either."

Myles smirked again. "What's the penalty, as if I didn't have a good guess?"

"Death," said Chip, and the look that crossed Myles's face said his guess hadn't even been close.

13

Jean-Claude Pelele sprawled back at ease in the presidential suite adjoining his harem, his bulk virtually hiding the imported, once elegant, gut-sprung loveseat that supported him. Behind him, the most pale of his young wives let her bare breasts sway as she kneaded the massive muscles of his shoulders and neck, and by Fundaboran standards she was a stunner. She gave no indication that anything other than that massage had the slightest significance for her, gazing now and then toward Keikano without a glimmer of interest. And judging from the schoolteacher's return glance, this flower of Fundaboran loveliness might as well have been a construction of rags and sand. The two young Fundaborans had known each other from childhood and each could have told much about the other; things better left unsaid. Each accepted the other's lifestyle without judging it.

The President had waited, and asked questions of the uneasy Keikano who sat alert and cross-legged near his feet, until Merizo returned from his mission two miles down the beach.

Being no fool, the little minister never failed to stress the fact that he wasn't much of a physical specimen; no more of a threat to Jean-Claude than the schoolteacher, neither in the harem nor the bruising leadership games. Whenever a noisy arrival was in order, Merizo took the half-track, his beefy honor guard jouncing in the cargo section. When some stealth was required, as it was for his second foray to the C-47, his guards bore him along the crushed shell road. They usually moved at a passable trot carrying him in a chair between poles so his arrival back at the councilhouse was that of a rhythmically grunting, ten-foot centipede.

The suite was lit by a varicolored string of Christmas tree lights, half of which had burnt out, and a careful listener might have heard the faint chug of the engine-driven generator from the hotel kitchen. Though he had been carried all the way Merizo was panting, as might be expected from a man who'd been shaken, not stirred, in a box for two miles. He made no ritual of his entrance but took his familiar place on the footstool, higher than Keikano but lower than his President.

Jean-Claude had not exceeded his capacity for the awful mixtures he had swilled down earlier and his little eyes, obsidian marbles, gleamed as he addressed his minister. "The leader of the whites claims his plane is huge, and not damaged. He tells me they could leave at any time. Did you see evidence to the contrary?"

Then again, that is not exactly how he said it. Because Merizo had spoken one islander language in his early years and Jean-Claude another, they commonly spoke a Fundaboran argot that was derived mostly from pidgin, partly from the English-speakers who had operated the vacation spa during the Truman and Eisenhower administrations. What the prez actually said was, "Witefella masta say aerocanoe bikbik, he no brokim, byanbye fly past salwatta what time he choose. You bin see othaway?"

"The plane is bigger than any of those old Japanese things of ours. They left a sentry," Merizo said, more or less. "He had a gun and warned us away, but the plane did not seem to be torn or bleeding. If it had been hurt, I think they would have left a work crew to fix it."

"Then why did they land here," Jean-Claude asked, and was met by silence. He glanced at Keikano. "What do you think, Prettyboy?"

It had been years since Keikano had felt any resentment at the nickname; for that matter, the President used the same term for several other Fundaboran youths whose bodies were gracile where his was sturdy, walked softly while he stomped, urinated in solitude as he playfully pissed on the nearest dog. The average Fundaboran pooch soon learned to be very wary of yellow rain.

Keikano knew the rules. Keikano was very, very careful. In the local argot he said, "Maybe the sentry was working on the plane inside. I could probably find out from the young one. They don't watch their tongues much around me."

"You do that," said the prez; a clear mandate.

"But that will take much of my time. What of my other duties? Minister Merizo?" With this, Keikano underlined his obedience through the chain of command. The little minister usually wanted his translator near when strangers came to the island. When Merizo needed him, school was out. Small wonder that Fundaboran kids capered so freely. For them, school was a sometime thing.

But what was Merizo to do: countermand the orders of a boss who made three of him? Could, if provoked enough, grab him by whatever part was handiest and literally *make* three of him? "Is something wrong with your ears, or is it just your brains? Befriend the boy and keep us informed." After this pro forma show of truculence the little fellow beamed at his leader, a model toadie at his best. "The one with yellow hair did not seem very interested in pearls. I had him tested."

The giant levered himself up as if exhaling stale booze into Merizo's face might change the bad news. "Not interested? Then what in the dark pit are we to trade with? You must test them all, one at a time. Do it yourself; you know how to sense these things."

Merizo did, for a fact. It was a simple trick known to sellers of desirable things: watch the eye pupils for a sudden dilation that betrays inner pleasure and arousal. It was one of the many simple tricks by which Merizo held his positions: consultant, soothsayer, pharmacist, mystic, judge. "I will, Jean-Claude."

"Tomorrow!"

"I will, Jean-Claude."

"And none of those lumpy pieces of shit the Chinese don't want!" The pidgin word he actually used for inferior pearls was *pekpek.*

"All right, Jean-Claude! Enough." The hard edge in the giant's voice had finally met tempered metal in Merizo's last reply. As Jean-Claude Pelele and Merizo stared each other down, young Keikano and the half-naked wife looked away. It was not good to be present at these contests of wills, since now and then a threat or a reminder was voiced by one of the two men. Generally, Jean-Claude Pelele got his way. But he needed Merizo and, what was more, he knew it, and the ridiculous-looking little man knew he knew it. Without Pelele, Merizo had no police power. Without Merizo, Pelele had no covert action group. Jean-Claude Pelele might be an oaf, but he was clever enough to know that every government needs its cadre of spies—even incompetent spies. As the world went, so went Fundabora.

Keikano had found the word for that relationship once, in his tattered dictionary. The word was *symbiosis.* These symbiotes would keep each other well painted for public view as long as intelligent self-interest required it. Common folk who got too near when the paint flaked off had been known to have accidents.

"If you cannot see inside the plane," Jean-Claude said, "Prettyboy here may be able to discover what cargo they carry. If it is some contraband the Republic of Fundabora must confiscate it."

Merizo replied carefully. "I have heard that governments of the English speakers sometimes ship contraband of their own. Do we really want an invasion that could make stories of the Japanese years seem like a festival?"

While his headman was thinking that over, Keikano coughed; his way of seeking permission to speak. Jean-Claude gave that permission with a flick of a sausagelike finger. "No matter what they carry, sirs, we might convince them to return with whatever you like. They may be better as trading partners than as enemies."

"We cannot trust men with radios and airplanes," Merizo countered.

Keikano's retort was gentle: "Do we trust the Chinese and Filipino ship captains? Besides, these people could bring new radios to us, medicine, entire crates of video films."

Merizo would not have said so, but he had no intention of reintroducing radios to Fundabora. The damned things had always started rumors of democratic processes on Guam and Palau. Medicine was another matter: as the island's only dispenser of modern medicines, Merizo could further cement his power with newer pills, better unguents.

But it was the mention of videos that rekindled the light in Jean-Claude's eyes. Some years previous, he had swapped a small fortune in pearls for a palletload of Chinese ripoffs of Japanese video players and TV sets. When one unit failed, he simply hurled it into the lagoon and had another installed. It was sad but true that, when a tape of "Lingapoo Fux Deluxe" had been played a hundred times by folk who do not know how to clean the machine, cunning little Lingapoo's sexual gymnastics had to be viewed through an electronic snowstorm.

More than medicines, Jean-Claude Pelele wanted a lifetime supply of porn tapes. Southeast Asia produced many of the most embarrassing, but somehow the traders seemed to know that, on Fundabora, a real raunch tape was worth its weight in pearls.

"Also whiskey. Don't forget whiskey," Jean-Claude urged.

"Of course," said Merizo, who knew very well that the leadership games would be held as the year's longest days approached. Much free booze was needed for those few days. "But in the meantime, we must keep them here long enough to arrange it. And if they do not have a weakness for the oyster's child as others do, we must find what they do crave."

"Money, no doubt." Jean-Claude kept a hidden strongbox of money, much of it worthless. He had given up trying to decipher the forces that made the stuff hard to come by on one season, and hard to get rid of on the next. Traders always showed initial interest which quickly paled. It seemed that Jean-Claude's strongbox never held much of what the traders wanted. Pearls were another matter.

Merizo bobbed his head. "Maybe. Until we know more, we must treat these people with every courtesy. It will be your task to learn their cravings, Keikano."

As Fundabora's leaders went on with their guesswork, the schoolteacher let slender shoulders droop dramatically under the heavy load of this mission. Keikano made no objection, though, in fear that the two might reconsider. Keikano had scarcely dared hope that this strategy meeting would turn out so well.

In midmorning, a strange and frightening drone could be heard from the beach, and it grew louder by the second. It sounded to Keikano like God's personal motor scooter but, through a break in the palms, it proved to be the big plane trundling along the sand at a pace no Fundaboran vehicle could match. It finally stopped, propellers ticking over, to disgorge the crew's British leader and the yellow-haired grandfather.

Before a welcoming committee could be formed, the two marched smartly to the councilhouse. Keikano had walked for miles along perilous footing to complete a hidden agenda on the previous night, and needed no more exercise. He stayed out of sight until called for, then hurried to the lobby where the two whites, with the help of a tongue-tied guard, were slowly building a semantic block of monolithic proportions. "Welcome! It is I, Keikano," he called, with a few words of caution to the guard. The welcoming smile was genuine. "What may I tell President Jean-Claude?"

The ritual of handshakes done with, the tall gray-hair said, "We have decided to accept his kind offer, Keikano; that is, we will be pleased to sleep in the councilhouse if we can leave our, ah, aerocanoe here safely clear of salt winds and high tides. In return for a promise that no nati—ah, citizen will touch the plane, we will try to repair some of your broken machines. This is our way of thanking President Jean-Claude for yesterday's—oh, bugger!—and so on, Keikano. You understand how to put it, I'm sure."

Keikano trotted down the hall to find that his President was still being dressed by his wives, a process that often as not became a dalliance occupying much of his morning. Merizo, however, was busily polishing off the debris of what had been Jean-Claude's breakfast: pork, boiled eggs, a starchy unleavened disc that passed for bread, juice, and peeled mangoes.

When Keikano had faithfully reported on the whites, Merizo made a snap decision while mango juice trickled from his chin. "I will give them an official invitation to do these things," he said, with a meaningful look. Keikano nodded, knowing what that meant: let Merizo take credit for things the whites want to do anyhow.

Merizo led the schoolteacher back to the lobby and, drying his hands by rubbing them through his hair, made a little speech. It was Keikano who explained that they could park the aircraft, choose upstairs rooms, and make free with the rusting gadgetry they wanted to repair. "I will be pleased to guide you. It is a tradition," he explained vaguely.

The whites tried not to show too much pleasure but their faces betrayed something like excitement; eyes roving here and there, their speech tempo quick, their step springy for men of their ages as they began to off-load some of their goods from the plane. Merizo gave orders to the guards and sent one of them away beyond the trees to the nearby village with The Word: touch the aerocanoe and furnish entertainment at the next leadership games. That was not quite "touch it and die," but close enough.

Keikano came aboard the plane only after an invitation from the tall, handsome youth called Chip, openly curious about everything, needing only to peer at something before Chip explained it. The cargo, which was chiefly left in its tiedown straps, Chip dismissed with, "Food, supplies, spare clothes, stuff like that." Not an overly helpful appraisal but several cardboard cases were labeled MRE, and Keikano already knew that Jean-Claude had found the powdery sweet stuff in his gift packets. Found them, and wolfed them down as candy.

In two trips, the crew finished off-loading what they needed and closed the door of the big plane. The leader and his woman, after a muttered exchange, took one room; the yellowhair and Chip took a room adjoining on the left; and both the bearded one and the limping one took the room adjoining on the right. They still spoke as if they had nothing to hide from Keikano.

"Coop and I will take a look at their maintenance sheds," said the yellowhair to their leader. "Maybe check out the water system and light plant later; God knows what's in the tap water. Keikano, it'd be nice if you came along."

"I would be honored. We may find Chip helpful, climbing here and there on large machines," said Keikano.

"Sure, glad to help," Chip replied.

Now the tall leader spoke. "I thought the rest of us might take a stroll around the island, unless you object. See how the other half lives, and all that."

Keikano made a judgment call. "You are honored guests. Please yourselves. But I ask you not to go far along the high trail. The footing is treacherous and I would be, um, discipled? Disciplined, if you came to harm. I will guide you there another time if you wish."

"Rightee-oh. Well, we'll nip off, then," said the Brit, taking the woman's arm firmly. Keikano thought the glance she gave him was peculiar, as though vexed and amused as well. She seemed to do that a lot, and still wore trousers like a man.

The two parties, at Keikano's urging, chose from a huge bowl of ripe fruit in the lobby before agreeing to return for lunch and going their separate ways. Keikano innocently tried to take the hand of young Chip in islander fashion—a habit shared by same-sex pairs in many third-world countries—but the youth blushed and, with a smile that asked forgiveness, disengaged his hand immediately. They walked through scented breeze, inundated by the sun, to the distant Quonset huts while munching fruit.

At the open door of the first shed, the yellow-haired elder simply stopped with hands on hips and vented a long, low whistle upon looking into the shadowed innards. The one who limped, Coop, began to laugh. "Regular effin' time machine," he said.

Keikano squinted. "Excuse me?"

Yellowhair: "He means we haven't seen equipment like this for a long time." Then, more softly: "For Christ's sake, Coop, try not to offend him."

"I am not offended, sirs. These machines need help."

"You can say that again. More than help, they need a decent burial. What the hell—um, what did you ever use that old LeTourneau rig for?" He pointed to a huge, work-scarred earthmover that towered on tires eight feet high above a gutted, forlorn Toyopet sedan. Flecks of yellow paint adhered to its welded steel frame amid a generation's pitted coat of rust. The older of the men approached the nearest rubber tire, long devoid of air, and squatted to peer beneath the chassis. "Yep, it's what we used to call a belly scraper. Saw some of these building roads in Alaska."

"In the time of Pelele the First, great flat ships took our dirt from these, I am told."

Chip looked blank. "They bought your dirt?"

Keikano used the shrug he had learned from strangers. "Special rocky dirt. All gone now, leaving a great hole, roads overgrown."

The yellowhair grunted to himself, then said, "Exactly what kind of dirt? You mean like guano, from a cave maybe?"

"No, a great shallow basin larger than all these buildings. I think it was called *hunger*, in English."

"Hunger," the elder repeated in bafflement.

Keikano nodded, then frowned. "Something like it. I found it in a dictionary but it was not the same." He beamed suddenly: "Appetite! I am certain the rocky earth was called *appetite*."

"Sure, no wonder you couldn't find it," said the grandfather, and spelled it for him. "Apatite; phosphate. Somebody surface-mined a deposit and left a LeTourneau here. Can't imagine why." His words echoed in the shed.

The old one beneath the vast machine lent his own echoes with, "You sure can when you see the chassis weldments here, Wade. Cracked, rewelded, prob'ly not heat-treated, cracked again. Never haul twenty tons of ore again, but—hmm. Lousy repair job but I think—mm. Well, we don't have a big welder's rig anyway."

Keikano was quick to argue the point. A Japanese trader's marine engineer had welded a broken cargo boom using equipment in the next shed, he said. The old one replied that the job would be too great. When he had limped back to them, the old fellows traded guarded looks but said nothing more.

Chip, meanwhile, had located a gaggle of old scooters, all with the Cushman logo, all stripped to varying degrees. "Too bad these are so far gone," he said gaily, sitting on one dusty relic, gripping its handlebars.

"Shit, I've seen worse than this in Petersburg, hauling drunks from the pier to AlasKafe," said the old man. The elders began to poke around, muttering about filing points and cleaning plugs, whatever that meant. Keikano wanted to know. He also wanted to avoid the appearance of knowing. The English terms were entirely new to him.

Soon, with Chip searching the area to round up tools left on the floor for years, they had further delved into the guts of one Cushman, hands grimy, doing their magics with the aid of a miraculous device from the pocket of the blond grandfather. Under their direction, Keikano and Chip used wire brushes to abrade the rust from the vehicle's shell and steering. "Please, sirs, do not say I helped with this work," Keikano pleaded. "It would become another duty for me after you leave." The yellowhair chuckled and said it would be their secret.

At length, the men stood back and nodded. "We need light oil and gas now," said the older of the two. After some explanation—Keikano thought they wanted to oil some lights and did not realize *gas* meant fuel—the islander led them to the next shed.

Now the Americans laughed and groaned some more. The lathe, drill press, and electric hand tools had rusted as well, they said, but one day they might function again if anyone knew how to use them. Oh yes, they knew these arcane skills. "The driver of the half-track," said yellowhair. "Now he's the guy who could use this stuff. Hey, he has gas! Where does he get it?"

Keikano remained silent for a long moment. But these men did not need to know where the fuel dump lay; they only needed a few liters. "I think he gets it from a barrel outside," he said, leading the way.

Chip, rummaging about inside, discovered a half-case of motor oil while the men found that the hand-cranked pump, screwed to a battered fuel drum outside, actually delivered a hefty stream of gasoline. A clean container proved to be the hardest thing to find. "A little grit in a Cushman's fuel line can shut you down," the old man said. Keikano knew that, too, but did not say so. Eventually they filled a bunch of discarded San Miguel beer bottles—there were plenty of those tokens of Manila culture around—and carried them back to the LeTourneau shed. Five minutes later, with anointments of oil in selected spots, they let Chip operate the kick starter. And again. And again, this time with a listless chug on its last revolution.

More adjustments; and now, for the first time since Keikano was a child, that old air-cooled engine began to cough and snort and chuff and clatter and make all sorts of threatening noises. And the Americans were slapping one another's raised hands in some strange ritual.

"Let's get the shell and seat on this thing," said yellowhair, "and you can ride it back to the councilhouse."

"Oh no," said Keikano, backing away. "I am allowed only when Merizo tells me to. But if Chip rides it, I could ride behind without offense. The minister will be most pleased."

"It's loud as hell," said the one called Coop, "but nothing I can do about it. That old muffler's useless as tits on a sea urchin."

"The louder, the better," Keikano smiled; his own private agenda. And anyway, it was true that Merizo liked machines noisy.

"Whyn't you say so," said the mechanic, and took up a screwdriver, punching viciously at a hollow canister on the machine. And that is how Keikano happened to return to the councilhouse an hour later, deliriously happy, arms clasped tightly around the waist of the manly and unprotesting Chip, on a motor scooter that bellowed like a machine gun on wheels.

14

"Lots of progress, all of it trivial," Lovett said, the moment the barefoot native woman backed out of Reventlo's room leaving a platter of oddments as lunch for the six crew members.

"That's more than I can say," said the Brit, unsmiling, selecting a piece of something broiled on a bamboo skewer. "Though it was a bloody great tramp for one morning."

Vic Myles, hiking boots shed, rubbed his feet and groaned. "All that to find a bunch of rotted hulks," he said. "Shit; I don't even see much of a story in this."

Gunther paused, his cheek full of something chewy. "Don't tell me you found the airchines already."

"Myles thinks so," said the Brit. "We found aircraft, right enough, or what used to be aircraft, most of it smothered in undergrowth. They were Nip, and they've been there forever. If the schoolteacher hadn't said there was an overgrown strip, we might have missed it."

Mel Benteen, noshing a hunk of fresh pineapple, made a derisive sound. "You might've."

"Give our devil her due," Reventlo murmured with a mocking obeisance. "I'd say the strip hasn't been used or kept up since this resort shut down; small trees growing on it. But Mel noticed the shell underfoot, tamped hard once upon a time, and it's decently flat for half a mile, from a sheer cliff all the way to the beach. Let me tell you, lads, it took large brass bollocks to take off and land on such an unforgiving strip as that. I doff my hat to the Nips of yore." This, from a man who had spent years of his youth as a Japanese prisoner, was rare applause.

"The planes," Lovett persisted. "They aren't protected?"

A sad headshake from Benteen. "Junk. They've been vandalized, too."

"One of 'em by a Browning fifty, judging from the holes," Myles added. "Maybe a strafing run, maybe in flight. They were sure 'nough Zeroes at one time, though. Honest to God Mitsubishi Zekes." A sigh. "I mean, there's no way any of 'em are gonna fly again, Wade. An engine here, a wing propped up against a tree there. Stuff like flex hoses had been cannibalized, or completely rotted away. We might sell some of it as curiosities."

Lovett said, "Bet I know where some of the stuff went. That old half-track has hoses that never came from the Western Hemisphere."

"How many planes were there?" Coop Gunther was no longer chewing.

"What does it matter," Myles asked, choosing a tidbit to eat.

"You saw a lot of subassemblies," said Lovett, realizing what Gunther was getting at. "How many aircraft would they make?"

"Two or three," said Myles.

"Possibly four," said Reventlo. "I admit we didn't tally it all up very carefully. We weren't exactly enthused tramping around in the bush, viewing all those pathetic remnants. But I see your drift, Wade. According to Elmo, he found more than we did."

"You know some Hong Kong trader got here first, you just fuckin' know it," Myles muttered.

"No we don't," Benteen insisted. "My dad wouldn't have held such hopes for a few boneyard wrecks. His were protected."

"Not anymore," from Myles.

"I think," said Reventlo, with great patience, "she's arguing that the ones we found weren't what we're after. We've not been at it long enough to draw conclusions. But what's your news, Wade? You've got the look of a cockeyed optimist."

Lovett described the Quonset huts and their contents, not missing the interest in Benteen's face when he mentioned the earthmover. He finished by saying they might get most of those motor scooters running, a process sure to please the islanders.

"The big rig was a vintage LeTourneau?" Benteen was already smiling. "I suppose no one noticed how many axles or engines it had."

"Suppose again," said Coop. "No duals, only two axles and one engine."

"Sounds like an old L Ten Belly Scraper. For LeTourneau, that was dinky. Vee-twelve Detroit diesel, electric motors on each wheel, ten-yard capacity. I can chauffeur that," she said.

Gunther: "Yeah? Can you patch a tire big as a wading pool?"

Benteen: "The question is, can *you*? I was a heavy equipment operator, not a grease monkey."

"Lots more wrong with it," Gunther said. "But what I didn't wanta say in front of the schoolteacher is, maybe it's salvageable."

"Whatever in God's name for," the Brit asked him.

"Beats me. It was just an idea."

"We need better ones than that, and soon," the Brit reminded them. "I can't putter about forever on this island with an aircraft that's already overdue in Alice Springs."

Tropical noontime, with a full belly, is not a situation that promotes heavy thought. When Myles announced that he needed a nap, Gunther seconded the notion, following the Texan to the next room. From aloft, they had all seen a village to the north and Benteen wondered aloud whether young Keikano might give a guided tour later that afternoon.

"I can ask him," said Chip, who yawned as he closed the cover of his computer. He ambled toward the doorway. "He'll be downstairs somewhere."

"Take a transceiver," Reventlo told him. "For now, when any of us is without the others it's just good practice, chaps." With that, he tossed his own unit to Chip, who pocketed it and strolled out. "Wipe that worry off your face, Wade," he said a moment later. "He'll be safe with Keikano."

"Uh, huh," Lovett replied glumly. "I'm just not so sure he'll be safe *from* Keikano."

Mel Benteen had already stretched out on the big bed. Now, without opening her eyes, she intoned, "Lovett, are you wondering about your own grandson?"

"My Chip?" Then, angrily: "Are you completely nuts?"

"Not so crazy I don't notice you didn't answer my question," she said sweetly.

"Hell, no, I'm not concerned. Not in the slightest. Never. Not in a thousand—"

"One answer is plenty," she said. "I understand 'no,' unlike some genders I could name. So what's to fear from a friendly little sprite like Keikano?"

Put that way, Lovett's worry seemed an extravagance. He shrugged and changed the subject. "Fresh-squeezed juice is great, but

I'd love a cold glass of water right now. If we're going to be here awhile, maybe I should hang around this afternoon and check the local utilities while you're doing the grand tour."

"The toilets work, that's a plus," said Reventlo.

"Yeah, and lacking a filter system, what comes into 'em may be full of more crap than what goes out," Lovett retorted. "I'll take a look before we drink the water, okay?"

So it was agreed. Lovett sought his room to wait for Chip and to see how the bed felt, and closed his eyes while waiting. From somewhere below the stairs, he could hear a piano rendition of "Clair de Lune."

"We should be damned ashamed of ourselves," Reventlo grumped, with a glance at his watch. "Half the ruddy afternoon is gone." Their little party stood in the lobby as Minister Merizo gave orders to the half-track driver, Keikano standing by.

"Bitch all you want to," Myles retorted, "I feel like a new man."

"Anyone want to use that straight line," Benteen asked.

"Too easy; I don't accept charity," Lovett replied, grinning. "Besides, a little siesta was just what I needed. Coop, are you up to a long walk?"

"Won't have to, Chip's driving me on the Cushman," said the old man. "You gonna teach that mechanic, what'shisname, how to use a wrench?"

"Pilau," Lovett supplied, and saw the wiry fellow's head jerk at the sound of his name, although he was getting orders from Merizo at the moment. "I'll try. Showing him how a hoseclamp works just about doubled his fund of knowledge."

Privately, Lovett thought Pilau might be smarter than that. As the rest of his party moved off, Coop Gunther riding with Chip on the scooter, Lovett began by visiting what had once been a modern, sprawling kitchen. The water taps worked and the outflow was clear. Lovett pantomimed drinking, then said, "Okay to drink?"

"Pilau no sabby, alltime use stream. Masta Merizo ee say watta good. Lubbet go topside lookoutim dirt belong sweet watta," Pilau said, pointing upward.

Lovett understood most of that and let the native lead to a ramp behind the building that led to its flat roof. He saw why the ramp was without steps: two wheelbarrows and a scatter of shovels lay atop the roof near big metal tanks. A brief inspection showed that water was pumped from some distant source to a flat covered tank filled with sand, no doubt Pilau's "dirt belonging to sweet water." What filtered through the sand was then pumped into a tall holding tank. The whole business looked like an afterthought, but sand made a passable filter—if replaced now and then.

Lovett made his next question clear only after pointing to the heaps of sand that had long ago been shoveled off the roof to mound in the ivy. Pilau said it had been "maybe this many" wet seasons, showing four fingers on each hand.

"Too damned long," Lovett said, adding a "longtime, nogood" for bad measure. The barrow wheels were simple spoked iron circles that squealed on their axles like tortured parrots when Lovett tried to spin them.

Pilau, with a bright grin, recalled his lesson atop the half-track. "Slickwatta ee fix machine, no cry allatime," he said brightly, and trotted off down the ramp.

Alone on that rooftop, Lovett let the ambience of the island flood into him. The C-47 was a welcome presence, sun glinting from its aluminum hide in the near distance. The breeze was warm, pleasant. Somewhere below, a man laughed. Faintly, from much farther away, the breeze brought what could have been the chatter of a small engine, now waxing, now waning; probably Chip on that ancient Cushman. The air was blossom-scented, incredibly clear but no longer CAVU, with great cloud masses of cumulus lurking blue-gray on the horizon, tops rounded, bases flat as garbage scows.

"Flat as my bank account, if this doesn't pan out," he mused aloud, and then turned to see Pilau trotting up the ramp, carrying a tin can full of some insipid-smelling stuff. According to Pilau it was burnwater, but also slickwater—some kind of cloudy oil that, Pilau explained, came from "pinch kaikai belong coconut." It had to be coconut oil squeezed from edible copra, and before they left that roof Pilau had oiled everything on it that spun, or slid, or twisted, or looked to him as though it might someday want to. Once you got an idea into Pilau's mind, thought Lovett, the thing grew roots like a weeping willow.

Evidently Pilau had asked for help while getting the coconut oil, since a half-dozen sturdy natives came trudging up the ramp, propelled by the bass rumblings of Merizo from below. The men had short pithy phrases for Pilau and glances that said they weren't voting him citizen of the year. They did, however, know what to do. Two of them trundled the wheelbarrows away for fresh sand while the others removed the cover to the sandbed filter, then set about shoveling wet sand into the ivy twenty feet below. Pilau smiled and said if Lubbet was awright with the job, the two of them could go down and looksee machines belong iron string bring lightning—the electrical gadgetry and wiring, no doubt. Lovett began to appreciate that you could indeed say just about anything with a few hundred words of pidgin, though your exact meaning might be known only to God and the speaker.

The power console was in the kitchen, a place that had seen its share of open fires. Judging from the smudges and debris, charcoal fires had been built directly atop a big griddle. A pair of toothless women who could not have been much over forty were engaged in preparing food and watched without comment as Lovett peered at the outdated fuses. Several fuses were obviously blown, though a carton of replacements sat in plain sight. Lovett showed Pilau how to recognize a no-good fuse, and how to change it, and as he screwed in the first one he was rewarded by a sizzle, a hum from over that griddle hood, and a shower of sparks that sent the cooks wailing from the room.

Pilau muttered something like *pekpek*, and strode fearlessly to the stove hood with its big inoperative exhaust fan. Ten minutes later Lovett found the bare wire that had shorted out after its insulation had burnt away in some forgotten culinary disaster. In a utility room off the kitchen, a sturdy old electrical plant shared floor space with deep-cycle batteries, and here at least Pilau seemed to know his way around. A man belonging to bigbig canoe, said Pilau, had fixed the thing two wet seasons back. He had been paid with a few rocks belong oyster for his trouble.

By the time he heard Chip's little scooter again, Lovett had repaired several circuits shorted out by sheer invincible ignorance. Then he traced an extension cord—which was plugged into another, and so on, all the way down the hall to the presidential suite. Jean-Claude Pelele met him with a bright bogus smile that looked more genuine after Pilau described the old whitefella's agenda, but the big man soon tired of watching and padded into his harem to a chorus of birdlike welcomes. Lovett sighed, glimpsing a presidential hoard of bare young tits, as the door closed. Then he continued tracing that circuit.

This single circuit, one of only two with good fuses, had powered Christmas tree lights strung along the wall near a uniquely weird four-poster bed big enough for a family of six, or for one vast President with a flock of underaged wives. The multiple outlet also powered a floor fan, a large-screen TV, and a VCR set against the wall facing the bed. Add one more lousy five-watt night-light, Lovett guessed, and the whole damned length of wiring—the iron string that brought lightning—would have gone up in smoke. With several live circuits now, he could spread the load; maybe check out the book-sized panel and speaker next to that four-poster bed. Good ol' Jean-Claude would love that, he thought, stepping near it, holding his Rexall reading glasses still as he read labels under the switches.

At his back, Pilau's breathing was as loud as the beating of his own heart. In the next room, a throaty presidential chuckle suggested too much; and in the distance, familiar voices echoed through the lobby as footsteps scuffed up the stairs. Lovett reached out one finger, toggled a switch.

And heard ". . . like an old movie set . . . ," unquestionably Chip's voice, from the little wall speaker before he toggled the switch off again.

A prickly heat sensation crawled up his limbs to burst into gooseflesh at the base of his skull. "Why, the dirty son of a bitch," he whispered, then made himself smile as he turned to Pilau. "All okay," he said. He had intended to check other circuits but now he was in no mood for that. He headed for the lobby where he dismissed Pilau with a handshake and took the stairs two at a time.

He found the crew lounging in Reventlo's room, gave them a smile and thumbs-up, and then sat beside Chip, who was already busy at his keyboard. He said, very softly, "Can I write a line or two?"

"Sure, just give me a sec—," Chip replied, then blinked as his grandfather whisked the little gadget onto his own knee with a muttered apology.

"Hey, take a look, team," Lovett called as he typed. "Ever see a view like this?" He broke off typing to put a forefinger to his lips, then resumed. One by one, the others crowded around.

In full caps, Lovett typed, PELELE HAS INTERCOM & CAN BUG OUR CONVERSATIONS. HAVE WE SAID TOO MUCH ALREADY?

"Well I'm a dirty bastard," Myles muttered.

"It's a wise man who knows his worth," Lovett replied, then typed again: KEEP TALKING. Instantly, five voices began to prattle about the weather, the view, and empty stomachs, and Lovett handed the machine back to Chip with a helpless chuckle. "Subtle as a lightning bolt," he said. "Speaking of which—"

He told them about his experiences in the kitchen and atop the building. They laughed over Pilau's discovering oil, or at least its magical uses. "I wondered who it was, tromping around up there," Gunther said, pointing toward the ceiling.

"They're doing it for us," Lovett reminded them. "One good turn deserves another, I guess."

Reventlo, louder than necessary: "Nice chaps. But you know, we really should contact the prime minister from the plane before we eat. And I mean, all of us." His gaze said more than his words.

"No time like the present, your excellency," Benteen intoned with a raised eyebrow, and soon they were all trooping out to the aircraft.

Keikano, biding his time in the lobby, showed every intention of going with them until Cris Reventlo stopped him at the outer steps with a gesture. "No need for you, Keikano, we're only going to the plane," he said decisively. The schoolteacher wheeled and walked back inside without another word.

Fifty yards farther along, Chip said, "Uh, Mr. Reventlo, could you be a little—well, nicer? Keikano's got feelings, too, and if we have a friend here, he's it."

"Yes? And has our friend told you our rooms are wired for sound?"

A grudging, "No-o," from the youth. "But he may not know it."

"In any case, someone has to show a firm hand. By acclamation it happens to be me, for all my sins. Look here, Chip. We don't know whether Keikano's chatting you up out of a good heart, or a presidential order. Our best tactic is to keep smiling and stop giving our game away."

Once inside the plane, they opened the little emergency door near the flight deck to lessen the ovenlike heat of an aircraft interior left baking all day in the sun, then took seats to confer. "So these innocents are a bit more high-tech than we thought," Reventlo said. "I can't recall what we may have given away. Anyone care to try?"

No one could be sure. Lovett thought they might have lucked out but Myles was not so optimistic. "We talked airplanes; no one listening could've missed that."

There was no denying this. They chewed it over among them until Lovett slapped his hands on his knees and said, "Okay, we know they can listen. We don't know if, or when, they do. I say let's openly talk about how disappointed we are that those Zeroes are trash, and say the same things when we're in our rooms. Use their audio pickups for our own purposes."

Coop Gunther asked, "What does that buy us?"

"An open-and-shut case. We just happened to land here, and hoped to make it pay, but tough tittie—wups, sorry, Benteen."

"You'll never know, Lovett," she said in a languid murmur.

He shrugged. "Anyway, I don't know what else it might buy us but whatever we want 'em to believe, we say in the rooms."

Reventlo liked that. What the Fundaborans had to believe, he said, was that the crew no longer hoped to find aircraft in repairable condition. "That leaves us needing a reason to keep pottering about on the island."

"Minerals," Benteen said. "We already know they sold phosphates for years, and they don't seem very prosperous now. They might jump at a chance to sell mineral rights."

"Gives us a perfect reason to comb the damn island, too. We haven't even seen the interior. Say we find some real mineral deposit that looks even halfway good; we could scrape a road in there while we survey the island. Show me a politician who doesn't want a few more roads in his district," said Myles, regaining a little optimism.

Evidently it was infectious. "And that means fix up that ol' earthmover. It'll be mighty handy in case we strike paydirt," Gunther added, " 'cause we'll need something that can tow an airchine better than that half-track gizmo."

"It's making sense," said the Brit. "We've found a natural separation for two teams. Benteen here has actually worked mineral deposits. Myles should be our best man for her in the bush, with all that survival lore of his. Lovett and Coop are our best mechanics, staying chiefly in the shops close by. Chip can split his time between teams. So could I, for a few days."

Myles: "Why only a few days?"

Reventlo: "It may have escaped your notice that I have an aircraft to deliver, or become a wanted man. I can probably scare up another aircraft around Darwin, for a decent price. Something that will seat six and the odd bits of cargo. Fact is, chaps, I'm certain I could turn up something we can use."

"Boy, it'd be a real shame if you couldn't," Coop muttered.

"Not to worry," the Brit said loftily. "In this part of the world there are lots of weary Willies to be had for a song, if you don't mind them looking a bit scruffy. Better yet, most of them are equipped for island-hopping."

But Chip's brow remained furrowed. "I can't believe they'd let us loose on Fundabora without a guide. They seem to have picked Keikano for that, and he's not stupid. If we find those planes we're after, what do we do then? Convince him they're phosphate deposits? Lotsa luck, dude," he said.

"Won't matter if we have that contract signed," said Reventlo. "We'll just have to word the agreement so that *any* valuable materials under the surface are ours."

Benteen: "And if they turn out to be in a hangar somewhere?"

"Then Elmo was wrong, mates, and we're screwed. But we might even make the agreement include surface minerals and define aluminum as a mineral."

Lovett put up a hand for attention. "Look, we can thrash the contract details out later, when we have more insights into what Big Boy Pelele wants for his little island empire."

"That's well and good," said Mel Benteen, "so long as you don't think of that guy as a big dumb Candide."

Lovett smiled. "If not Candide, then who?"

"Try Idi Amin," she replied.

Chip, stunned: "You mean a cannibal?"

Benteen mulled that over, then said, "Not exactly. Just make sure he stays happy. If a third-world leader doesn't like the deal he's made, he might chew you up in ways that make the difference academic."

15

When it became obvious that dinner would be another marathon affair on the verandah, Reventlo only said, "This time, remember: moderation." Then he took his indicated place on a low stool near the feet of President Jean-Claude, Benteen on his left, Keikano hovering near. The rest of the crew found mats awaiting them, each member separated from the others, each presented with a fragrant lei.

Wade Lovett kept his analytical reserve for a time, then began to think how fetching Melanie Benteen looked when she had rearranged a lei blossom in her hair, a pale starburst against her own rich coloration. She wore a skirt with a fruit-salad print, presented to her in the village earlier in the day, which showed off a set of fine strong legs. Lovett had not seen her without slacks until now. It made him think about things he very much needed *not* to think about, especially when their focus was a heavy equipment operator who could punch his lights out.

Then the dancers appeared, and presently he became caught up in the festivities. Drums set the pace for barefoot young men wearing skirts, intricately painted designs on their bodies, and little else. Smears of red and black made fearsome masks of their faces. As the tempo increased they whirled clubs about them in mock battle, seemingly unaware of their audience. One by one, the combatants fell from pretended blows until one superbly muscled fellow symbolically defeated his last opponent. Lovett recognized the man by an old scar on his left pectoral, though the mark was partly obscured by whorls of red paint: under all those cosmetics was Rongi, the gent who had first greeted Benteen on the beach. Then, the drumming silenced, Rongi knelt before Jean-Claude. The Fundaborans erupted in militant cheers as Jean-Claude pronounced some kind of benediction, though Lovett thought the President's gaze at Rongi held more calculation than good fellowship.

The following exhibition was by only one man, a specialist of sorts. Lovett had seen more showy versions of the torch dance, but this young guy took chances that seemed truly dangerous as he flung the flickering torches about him like a baton twirler with a death wish. When he snuffed the torches in his palm at the finale, Lovett felt the pang himself. The torch dancer's face, however, remained absolutely impassive. Lovett wondered how that trick was done.

Not for long, though. Face paint scrubbed away, Rongi's group of dancers returned, to be met by young women who arrayed themselves opposite the men. It was at this point that Lovett realized the native on his right was nudging him. While the dancers chanted and postured in an obvious mating ritual, Lovett found himself trying to carry on a pidgin conversation with a man who wanted to trade a "rock belong oyster," marble-smooth and of modest size, for his wristwatch. By the time Lovett made his refusal clear the dance tempo had increased to match the drums, male suitors stamping and twisting before their partners, women gyrating their midriffs with bumps and grinds so rapid it seemed they must have been impelled by vibrators. On one level, Lovett appreciated the demonstration as art, genuine as fine sculpture, an innocent celebration of the continuum of humankind. On another level, thanks to all those undulating hips and pulsating boobs, he had a nice erection going. Again. *What is it with you,* he asked himself, knowing all too well. After a dance like that, he decided, they should all do a pantomime of sharing cigarettes.

After the last of the seminude dancers had departed gleaming with sweat in the torchlight, Jean-Claude invited his guests to his suite for further entertainment. Low stools had been brought in, arranged for the primitive ritual of video watching. Jean-Claude himself chose a cassette and punched appropriate buttons with a finger like a brown banana, then eased back on that small acreage of bed. Four of his teenaged lovelies crawled onto the same arena, then began to groom their lord and master.

Lovett thought their actions had a certain air of resignation, and of familiar habit. He wondered how far that grooming would go, but was determined not to look. Pelele probably wanted him to look. *Most Western politicians are exhibitionists at heart*, he reminded himself. *Probably the same everywhere, and damned if I'll give him the pleasure.*

Young Keikano had stayed close to Reventlo all evening for translating duties and sat near him now, eyes averted from the screen. Judging from his expression, Lovett thought the schoolteacher might be deeply humiliated.

With good reason. The video featured a brace of Asian women, several men, four apparent sexes and no discernible plot. The distinguished President made frequent commentaries along the lines of, "Bigfella he nogood for longtime, not fuckem allsame Jean-Claude, eh?" and, "Goddamn picture worse every time. Ol' Cris tell Lubbet fix machine, okay?" The videotape, Lovett realized, was simply frazzled with repeated use.

Before long, an urgent whispering began between Benteen and Reventlo; then between the Brit and Keikano, who quickly moved near the bedside and whispered to Jean-Claude. The giant loosed a guttural chuckle and thrust his girls away, striding across the room to shut off the machine. Anyone who didn't see the huge rigid digit that protruded from his skirt simply wasn't looking. "Ol' Cris he get young ideas, eh? Okay, Jean-Claude sabby," he said, still laughing, waving them along. "Maybeso swap wife byandby, change his luck."

When Chip decided to make Reventlo's exit a threesome, Lovett hurried to make it four, glancing toward Gunther as he left.

"Naw, I'll stick with Myles. He needs a chaperone," said old Coop with a guilty grin. Victor Myles sat filling his corncob pipe with the air of a man who intended to live and die in that spot.

Lovett thought Keikano's reaction was interesting. The schoolteacher had risen to follow Chip but, on learning that two of the whites intended to stay, took a position between his leader and Coop Gunther, face averted. Whatever his orders might be, Standing Order #1 seemed to be as liaison for any conversation that Jean-Claude Pelele might want with his guests.

In the lobby, Reventlo paused at the stairs, wryly amused at their predicament. Very softly: "Do we really want to go to the room?"

Benteen muttered, "Somehow I don't think our host would understand 'not tonight, dear, I've got a headache.' And I'm in no mood for faking moans and bouncing on a bed for five minutes."

Reventlo drew himself up. "Five minutes? Well, thank you very much for that disparaging remark, I'm sure. There's one cheeky bird," he added to Lovett. "I could make a case for that 'rutting Reventlo' skit but a walk on the beach might be the better tactic for us all. Jean-Claude can imagine what he likes."

A late moon hung in the west, casting ghostly shadows from the treeline, lending the trail of crushed shell a faint luminosity. They moved past the dark mass of the aircraft and on to the beach before Chip asked, "Does anybody know what a pearl is worth? They're really trying to push those things on me."

Lovett said, "Me, too. Guy next to me at dinner? Tried to trade me one the diameter of a pencil. Worth a hundred bucks or so."

A delighted laugh from Benteen. "The blind leading the blind; wonderful! Lovett, a cultured pearl that size, good lustre, perfect shape, might retail for twice that. These can't be cultured. They're natural."

"They're trying the same bait on us all, according to Coop," said the Brit.

"Cheaper, huh," Chip guessed.

"Four to five times more expensive," Benteen corrected. "Cris, you recall when the village matrons had me try on those sarongs? One of the old girls showed me a pearl the size of a jawbreaker; maybe twenty millimeter. Said the President wanted me to have it, if," she said.

"So drop the other shoe," Lovett suggested.

"If I'd drop both shoes for him; what did you think? My God, don't be naive! The woman was pandering for Pelele."

Reventlo sighed. "How much was it worth?"

"Ten thousand or so," she said. "That's retail."

"May I at least glance at the thing," the Brit persisted.

"You could if I had it," she said with some heat. "If I could see whether you're smiling I'd know whether to deck you for that innuendo, mister."

"Serves you bloody right. Five minutes my arse," Reventlo chuckled, then grunted as her elbow landed lightly against his ribs. "All right, truce. The fact is, I had a similar offer, and for the same taste of sweets, from Merizo."

Their companions forgotten, Benteen gasped. "Pelele wants your bod?"

"Don't be an ass, he was dickering for yours."

"You might have told me."

"And the same, my crumbling crumpet, to you," said the Brit.

"I'd say you must keep one of our transceivers on your slightly shopworn person at all times. You might've simply disappeared while trying on those sarongs."

"Begins to look like that." Her face darkened as she said, as if to herself, "If he has me mugged I'll perforate the son of a bitch. I will." Then, "Guys, I never intended to be a problem," she said, morosely.

"You're not," Reventlo said sharply. "I'll just have to make your position clear to our kindly host. They're getting ready for some kind of annual bash, according to Pelele. That may occupy what passes for his mind. Anyway, it shouldn't be an issue once we're not underfoot so much."

"And when'll that be," Lovett asked.

"As soon as I can manage it. Tomorrow, perhaps. It's time we set out our bait; so let's make a show of enthusiasm among ourselves over the mineral wealth we expect to find, when we're all back in my suite."

"He's got to know there probably isn't any left," said Benteen.

Reventlo's low laugh was merry. "Exactly. He profits; we don't. Should appeal to him."

On their return to the upstairs suites, they found Coop waiting to the tune of Myles's snores. Asked how the entertainment had gone, Coop only said, "You wouldn't believe that big guy," with an air of disgust as he shook Vic Myles awake. A series of silent nods said that, whatever it was, they'd all believe it.

They made small talk for a few minutes, enlivened by news of the upcoming leadership games. Only Benteen and Reventlo had heard these bits from Jean-Claude during the dances. By tradition, the festival always began with food, some of it from Jean-Claude's hoard of goods imported for the purpose. The major delicacy for the locals, said Benteen, seemed to be cheap boiled ramen pasta without flavoring; platters of it, mounds of it, shoals of it. "But *poi* tastes like library paste, so we shouldn't be surprised," she added. And of course all that pasta would be washed down with liquids of every description.

Another phase of celebration would be dances and what Keikano had interpreted first as free association, then as family planning. "The way Mayday did his family planning," Lovett suggested to his grandson.

"I've just gotta get a look at Keikano's dictionary," Chip smiled.

But all this activity was preamble to the leadership games that would begin with contests among children, then adults. These games included individual feats of strength and more feasting after which, said Reventlo, the top contenders were eligible to wrestle for the ultimate Fundaboran prize: the Presidency.

Their research on Fundaboran customs had suggested as much but, "Good God," Lovett said; "I'm not sure I'd want to watch."

"Oh, it'll be fair and aboveboard. Jean-Claude assured me of that," Reventlo said, with an arch of the eyebrow that added, *in his fashion.*

Coop Gunther gave them a perfect segue to their false goal. "Hey, what if the big guy loses out? Maybe we should wait and see before we work out an agreement for mineral rights."

The Brit: "A good point. That big strapping fellow Rongi seems to have been chosen by the villagers as their prime candidate. Personally I believe our friend Jean-Claude is the better man," he added, "but anything's possible."

The others nudged the bait around. Lovett said they'd simply have to trust the Republic of Fundabora to honor its treaties. Reventlo cautioned the crew to avoid any show of interest in mineral deposits.

But it was Chip Mason who planted the best piece of disinformation. "I know you've said those old aircraft parts aren't worth much, but wouldn't they bring a few bucks to a museum or a junkyard or something?"

Into a chorus of doubters, Lovett said, "Hold on; it's possible. You know, that might be what we could tell them."

Myles, overdoing it: "What? Listen, all that stuff is crap! I've seen it, and even if the jungle is full of it nobody in his right mind would want it."

Reventlo seemed to enjoy himself immensely, arguing the point, making their real purpose seem a decoy for anyone listening. He sealed his position with, "It may be useless as antiques, but it should be worth something even as junk when I land in Alice Springs." His expression said that was about as likely as a Fundaboran snowstorm.

"Yeah," from Coop. "Say we don't find any deposits worth mining. If we could sell that old metal, we wouldn't stand to lose so much. It's no good to the islanders anyway."

Playing the perfect straight man, Reventlo said, "But Coop, how would we get a lot of junk metal to a pier or to the beach?"

"We'll just have to try and rebuild that old earthmover, I guess," Coop said in "why me, Lord" tones. "We'll have to do it anyway if we find phosphates. Either that or have one shipped in."

A stage groan from Lovett. "I hope you realize what you're asking, Coop. We'd be fixing up a lot of equipment we'd have to leave here for the Fundaborans."

"Damn right I realize it, and I hate it, but we'd have to do it." This was a palpable lie from a man who loved tinkering on machines of any size.

"Whose side are you on, Coop," Myles put in. "It's a better deal for them than for us."

"Tell me a better plan if you got one," Coop rumbled. "All I can say is, you guys better find us some phosphates worth exporting."

Myles and the others promised to do their best. Chip, plying the keys of his computer, silently showed its screen. It said, AND WHAT IF NOBODY'S LISTENING NOW?

"I think we'll have some answers very soon," Reventlo said, knowing that the crew would take the right meaning.

On the following morning, Chip treated the councilhouse to an impromptu recital on Fundabora's small grand piano. Though the instrument was pitifully out of tune, Chip ignored its shortcomings and pressed on as if he weren't playing one lost chord after another. From inside the piano bench, Keikano had unearthed a mildewed cache of sheet music, and stood by to turn pages at Chip's nod. Since the massive Jean-Claude appeared to enjoy it, Merizo and the stolid honor guard dutifully stamped for applause whenever their President did.

Afterward, Cris Reventlo presented Jean-Claude with another bottle of scotch whiskey as an open inducement to some serious haggling. "I believe," he said, "we can do business to our mutual benefit."

Little Merizo, clad in his everyday black lavalava skirt and flywhisk, called Keikano from Chip's side to help clarify these jawbreaking words. As Reventlo began to explain his wishes, something in Jean-Claude's manner suggested that he wasn't exactly astounded by these overtures. "Traders allatime like swap for dead machines," he explained, after Reventlo mentioned the moldering junk near the airstrip. Asked what he would like in return, the dusky hulk spoke rapidly with Merizo, then with Keikano.

The schoolteacher said, "Fundabora needs medicines. Salve for sores that do not heal, and for the pains of the elders."

"Screw belong arm, leg, pinga hurt," Merizo put in, following some of this.

"He means joints—elbows, knees, fingers," said Mel Benteen, smiling at Merizo. "Arthritis, I think."

Keikano asked her to spell it, nodded when she did, then went on: "And headache pills. Medicine to stop tooth pains. That is a common problem here."

But the crew had not brought these things in quantity, the Brit replied.

"Get plenty Alice Springs island," said Jean-Claude. Reventlo said that could be done. The amount of medicines was set, after some haggling, at the weight of Reventlo himself.

"Plenty fucktapes, too. This many," the giant insisted, hands spread apart as if holding a bushel basket. Reventlo made a show of doubt at this, saying videotapes of that sort were expensive and rare.

Pressed on the point—for it was obvious that Jean-Claude Pelele would sooner forgo medicines than pornography—Reventlo agreed. "While I travel, my crew must stay and work, search for more metal, repair your machines," he said; and this, Jean-Claude accepted easily. "Old machines and aerocanoe parts we find on Fundabora, become our property," Reventlo went on, his manner casual.

Again, no evident problem. "Then it's settled. We will draw up a contract between B.O.F. Unlimited—that's us, sire—and the Republic of Fundabora, for us to, uh, put our marks on," Reventlo said at length.

Which created an impasse that needed some time to unravel. Mel Benteen finally managed to explain that "draw up" had nothing to do with pretty pictures, but was a sworn promise by both sides, written and signed. Since there wasn't even a rusty portable typewriter on Fundabora that worked, the document would be printed by young Mister Mason and young Mister Keikano. Merizo and his boss evidently did business with traders on a pure barter basis. They became very thoughtful when Reventlo claimed that each side was bound by the might of their respective governments to see that the agreement was kept.

Reventlo gave the impression that their business was nearly concluded, and the Fundaborans were glancing uneasily at each other, when the Brit said, "Oh, one more thing, just a detail. If we should find some dirt we like, B.O.F. Unlimited wants the right to take it."

It was as though someone had released a valve to let all the wariness trickle out of Jean-Claude Pelele. Why, he wondered in ponderous caginess, would his guests care about such a detail?

Well, they didn't care much, Reventlo shrugged, a vast truth he was now sure the Fundaborans did not believe. But minerals had been found there before, he reminded them, and his crew proposed to look around the island, just on the off chance.

But how would they remove the stuff if they found it, Jean-Claude wanted to know. That, Reventlo replied, was a problem they would find a way to solve. Perhaps heavy equipment could be shipped in; but it was barely possible that his mechanics might repair the existing machines, which would naturally become the property of B.O.F. Unlimited.

Not so naturally, Pelele answered. Ol' Cris could use it if he could fix it, but all equipment in those sheds remained, positively and absolutely, Fundaboran property. The big fellow entered into this phase of the haggling with the total confidence of a man holding four aces and, step by step, Crispin Reventlo let himself be driven from his position. The only concession he managed was the promise of free meals daily. Since the real issue was already in the bag, Reventlo was not the toughest negotiator in town.

At length, the Brit sighed and shook his head, agreeing that though his crew could have free use of the fuel and equipment around the sheds, Fundabora would retain ownership. Of course, he went on, all of this depended on their right to study the island without interference.

When he understood this, little Merizo made it plain that a short recess was necessary and ordered Keikano to accompany the crew for a short stroll. Myles suggested a foray to the airplane for another bottle of scotch to seal the bargain, and all seven of them trooped outside, uneasily quiet in the schoolteacher's presence.

As they reached the plane Chip patted Keikano's shoulder lightly. "Why such a long face," he asked.

Keikano looked as if he might burst into tears. "You do not like my face?"

Laughing: "It's a nice face, Keikano," Chip said. "That was colloquial. It means, why are you sad?"

The islander brightened, but only a little. "I do not belong," he said simply. They turned their faces into the sea breeze and watched as Reventlo and Myles disappeared into the furnacelike heat of the aircraft.

"Don't worry about it," said Lovett, who hadn't missed a word. "They ordered you to come with us. We understand."

"You do not understand. I do not belong there, either. That is why I am here."

Benteen, who had heard this in silence: "Keikano, is it possible you aren't a Fundaboran?"

"I am." And with this statement, a tightening of the gentle features, the faintest of slitting around the eyes. "I am, but not like them," he said, clearly enmeshed in some inner conflict, nodding toward the councilhouse. Then he drew the narrow shoulders erect and swallowed hard. "I am from the North village. Many of the people there are—not friendly."

"My God," Benteen said, her eyes widening. "That explains, um, well, we had no idea."

"Jean-Claude wants you to have no ideas," was the bitter reply.

Benteen: "Are the two ends of the island at war?"

"Not war," the gentle schoolteacher said quickly. "But the ways of the North village are—different." It was obvious that Keikano was pausing to choose his words with great care, and saying those he chose with some reluctance. "If Jean-Claude Pelele or Merizo knew I spoke of these things, I would—" and now he paused, shook his head. "They would soon have another educated fool to teach the children," was the amended version.

"No wonder you want to leave Fundabora," Chip murmured.

"I do not want to stay away. I want to bring good things to Fundabora. My—the elders need medicines; the children need clean paper, books. They need a President who cares," he burst out, as if ridding himself of something that tasted of bile.

"Why can't your village," Benteen began.

"Not my village now," said Keikano. "A few of us are tolerated everywhere, especially those who are no threat to the Pelele—gang? Yes, my dictionary says 'gang.' But if I am tolerated, I am not entirely accepted anywhere."

"Poor little guy," Benteen said. "But why can't the North village do their own deals with the trading ships, Keikano?"

"No moorage. The beaches, the rocks, no good for ships. And it is a small village. The North shore is not worth their trouble. Please, do not let them know I have said any of this."

Lovett, squinting toward the councilhouse, said, "But we really need to look over the whole island, Keikano. If they insist that we don't leave the south part, it could stop this whole agreement."

At that moment, a voice with foghorn insistence floated from the councilhouse portico: little Merizo, calling them back in his own jargon. Keikano turned and waved, then said softly, "That little land-crab." It seemed to impel him to another decision. "If they deny you the right to study the north part of the island, I will find a way to show you myself. I swear it."

As Vic Myles carried a bottle of booze in each hand, Reventlo closed the cargo door and approached them smiling. "Somewhere a great bell is tolling," he said, pointing toward the little man with the big voice.

Keikano fell in beside him, speaking quickly. "This is worth my life: they can hear you talk in your rooms. Do not say what you do not want them to hear."

"Well, I'm damned," said Reventlo, his gaze toward Keikano full of new surmise. "Does this mean they don't intend to honor the agreement?"

"I believe they do. But they knew you expected to give back the great LeTourneau thing." A pause, as they walked on. "I knew it. They need me to translate some of what they hear in your rooms."

"Thanks for the warning. We'll be careful," Reventlo promised.

When the crew had seated themselves near him once more, Jean-Claude announced that he had made a decision. His guests could range freely on the island as far north as Fundabora's narrows, a salt swamp area flanked by rocky heights. That far and no farther, he said, because he could not protect them against a few "crazyheads, bad bastads belong north end."

Reventlo tried to get a dialogue going on that topic but Jean-Claude would not elaborate at any great length. There were only a few, he said; outcasts that he, in his loving kindness, allowed to live without trouble so long as they stayed on their miserable end of the island. "No jail belong Fundabora, nogoods run away northend," he said with a beatific smile.

The Brit made a show of agonizing over this but eventually agreed. "We will draw up the agreement tonight," he said, rising. "Keikano can help us now, or he can study it tomorrow and suggest changes."

Keikano, ordered to remain with his President, tried to avoid a show of disappointment and waved good-bye as the crew trooped upstairs. For the next hour, the entire crew gathered around Chip as he dutifully typed out the agreement, dictated chiefly by Lovett. Its wording was simple, but it was deceptive in one respect. It agreed that B.O.F. Unlimited had no rights to search or lay claim to anything north of the swampy isthmus. It did not promise that they wouldn't snoop there.

16

"Easy on the sauce, Coop. We're to be two-wheeler Boffins today," Reventlo said, as Gunther tilted the scotch bottle. By midmorning, after a few unimportant changes of phrasing, they had all signed the agreement which Lovett laboriously printed in neat draftsman's lettering, witnessing thumbprints by Jean-Claude and Merizo. It was a unique document, both copies done in ballpoint ink on water-stained stationery with a letterhead emblazoned "Funisle Resort." The schoolteacher evidently kept a hoard of the stuff, a relic of times past. Now everyone was beaming, shaking hands, and passing that bottle around to celebrate the event.

From some moldy archival drawer, Keikano also produced a map of the island, complete with elevations. Murmurs rose from the crew as they studied the map; Fundabora, on paper, was a sweatsock with a fat elliptical foot seven miles long, two old volcanic prominences rising nearly eighteen hundred feet above the beach. The ankle narrowed to perhaps a mile at the swamp. Flanking the swamp lay that thin ridge they had almost flown into, rising to another spire at the island's broader northern "shin" end some three miles wide. It was there that, presumably, the "crazyheads" eked out a primitive living. Creeks meandered down from each prominence. "The map's dated 1957," Lovett said, and laughed. "The airstrip's plain as day."

"We need a copy of that sucker," Myles muttered.

"In good time," Reventlo said softly, folding his copy of the agreement inside his nylon windbreaker. He turned to Lovett with, "Well, chaps, let's all see to the maintenance sheds."

Myles and Benteen made mutinous complaints on the way until

the Brit pointed out that, the sooner they got several Cushman scooters running, the less time they'd spend walking. Jean-Claude watched for a time, swigging the rest of the bottle, before padding away toward the councilhouse.

Keikano had lunch brought to them and enlisted the half-track driver, Pilau. When Pilau seemed reluctant to touch the scooters, Keikano explained why. "You have seen the scars on his back and legs," he said to the Brit. "He took these machines apart years ago but could not fix them. He worries that he will be punished again."

"I'd like to flog his butt myself if he's the guy who boogered up these bolts," Gunther said, laboring over a cylinder head. "Somebody try and scare us up a socket set, maybe in the other shed. Nobody touches our tools in the Gooney Bird unless we abso-effin'-lutely have to." Coop Gunther was a typical mechanic, and his horror of losing personal tools was downright pathological. As all good mechanics knew, he claimed, the damned things grew little bitty legs and scuttled off to hide like cockroaches the instant you took your eyes off them. Sometimes, they even hid in other people's pockets.

In midafternoon, sputtering and cheering accompanied the revival of another Cushman scooter. While in the other shed with Pilau, Lovett heard still another do its Lazarus imitation two hours later. He found the oxyacetylene welding rig on its wheeled cart as Keikano had promised, tanks still heavy with compressed gases after years of neglect. Pilau, to prove his newfound mastery of all things mechanical, proudly oiled its wheel hubs before they trundled the welding rig to the other shed.

For Coop Gunther, the LeTourneau was clearly Job One. He actually hugged the big green oxygen tank after coaxing a useable flame from the welding rig. "This'll weld half-inch plate, Wade," he said. "But we can't waste any gas on scooters and shit like that."

No one argued the point. Their best estimate was that four Cushmans would remain serviceable for them, with five "hangar queens" to furnish spare parts. Pilau, who had now lost his fear of the scooters, beamed as they prepared to ride back to the councilhouse. Four Cushmans, eight riders.

And no brakes. They learned this when Chip careened past the veranda. "It won't stop," he called, fishtailing, Keikano gripping his waist for dear life as they continued along the drive.

"Nothing wrong with—ahhHH, SHIiiiit," thundered Coop, who had seen to the brakes of each scooter but now peeled off from behind Lovett, who rode smartly into the ivy and fell, damning his demon velocipede and Coop Gunther with equal enthusiasm.

Reventlo and his passenger, Benteen, let the ivy stop them without falling, both cursing and laughing as they slowed. Last of all came Myles with Pilau as his passenger, dragging his boots heavily to stop fifty feet beyond the councilhouse. The pungent stink of hot oil wafted across the clearing as Coop began the briefest of inspections. It didn't take him long to find the problem.

Pilau, of course, had carefully oiled the brake drums of all the scooters. It took Lovett a while to explain to Pilau that sometimes, a little friction can be a very good thing. It would take several days, Coop snarled, before those brake drums would grip properly. Until then, he added, the gah-damn Cushmans wouldn't come to a quick stop without a boat anchor and a short chain.

The following morning, Lovett got his first look at the overgrown landing strip. "I see what you mean, Cris," he said, leaving his scooter to walk among the lush jungle growth, swinging one of the machetes they had taken from the C-47. With those knives in their belts, Benteen observed, they looked like old yuppie buccaneers. "Pilots took off in the shadow of this bluff, facing the water. Good thing it has a downslope."

"Bugger their takeoff, think of the landing," Reventlo replied. "Overshoot and you were marmalade against the cliff."

"Goddamn Japs were outa their gourds," said Gunther, hands on hips, shaking his head in wonderment.

"It took great courage, I think," said Keikano quietly.

Gunther looked up at the schoolteacher and grinned. "I'll give 'em that. You gotta remember, kid, I fought those guys when I was your age; and I ain't the kind that forgets quick."

Keikano's smile was tentative toward Lovett. "And you?"

"I was too young then. Hell, I've owned three Japanese cars."

"Traitor," Coop said, only half joking.

"Once he's been shot at, Coop's the sort to hold a grudge," Reventlo said, poking into the undergrowth. "I was a prisoner of the Nips for most of the war, but I've come to terms with all that, years ago. Actually, I have a few hours in confiscated Japanese aircraft; I'd hate to tell you how far back that goes."

From near the vertical bluff came a hail from Myles. "Another twin-row engine," he called. A single circular "row" of cylinders indicated modest power; a twin-row suggested the more powerful military craft.

"If you are searching for big pieces, try there," Keikano blurted suddenly, and pointed far to the right of Myles. "I think no one has moved them since I was young."

"Since he was young," said the Brit to Mel Benteen. "Oh, to be sixty again!"

"Speak for yourself," she said tartly as Keikano led them to a spot they had not visited earlier. The schoolteacher's memory was good; soon after Myles added his machete to the party they had hacked away enough vines to reveal the skeletal remains of what had once been a two-place, fabric-covered biplane, its single-row engine ripped half away from the frame.

"Jeez," said Coop, studying the torn stubs of upper and lower wings, then libeled a famous American trainer. "Japs had Stearmans?"

"No. It's a Tachikawa—or was," Reventlo said, slashing at vines, ducking low. "I've flown them. A trainer of prewar design, dead slow, fixed landing gear."

"Fixed, my ass," Coop retorted. "It's sure retracted now."

"That's why it's here," said the Brit. "Looks as if he shed his wheels on his way in and ended up in the jungle."

Lovett, fingering shreds of ancient fabric that still adhered to wooden strips along the fuselage, shook his head. "This is not," he began, then realized that Keikano stood near. "This could be middle five figures, if you spent six repairing it."

Coop Gunther tested a slender wooden longeron, which broke with a punky snap. "Rotted plumb away," he said gloomily. "I don't think you could cart this off and have anything left."

Reventlo had moved to the rounded mass of the radial engine now. "Shattered his prop," he mused, "when his gear failed. That means he probably bent the crankshaft. This old Hitachi radial engine might bring a nice piece of change—or not. It doesn't look a very promising prize, lads."

"And it isn't where it ought to be," Myles chimed in. "You know what I mean," he said to Reventlo, with a sidelong glance toward the schoolteacher. "Let's get on with it." And Vic Myles set off into the brush again, swinging his machete.

The day wore on with more small discoveries, none as promising as the tattered wood-and-fabric biplane. When Chip began to skirt the base of the forty-foot bluff, his young Fundaboran shadow entreating him to be careful, Reventlo drew Lovett and Gunther aside. "This won't do, lads. At this rate, our young friend won't be long in figuring that we aren't all that anxious to find a mining claim. We've got to make copies of that map, and record what we find so we go about this more efficiently. And we do it in context of digging a hole here, a hole there—that sort of thing."

"Good ol' Jean-Claude could have his goons out watching, too," Coop said. "They're a whole lot more used to these creeper vines than we are."

"Shovels on top of the councilhouse," Lovett put in. "We should carry 'em, and use 'em now and then. But you're right about making charts. That's assuming Keikano will let us borrow his."

Coop snorted. "You kiddin'? One word from Chip and that little cutiepie would chew us a map outa his skivvies." Then, seeing the look in Lovett's eye: "Uh, sorry, Wade. You know what I mean. It's a lock, if Chip asks."

"I know exactly what you meant. Let's give him the benefit of the doubt, huh?"

Coop: "Which him?"

Lovett leveled a forefinger at his old friend. "He's my grandson, Coop. Shut—the—fuck—up."

When Coop Gunther saw that the finger was trembling with intent, he made a wry face and turned away.

"We can't have this, Wade," Reventlo said softly. "You'll have to ignore twaddle of that kind."

"Maybe you can pass the word then: stuff that crap when I'm within earshot, 'cause I don't want to hear it," Lovett growled, and resumed his inspection of the area.

He knew the chief reason he didn't want to hear those innuendoes: they supported his own suspicions. Wade Lovett knew several friends who had chosen the gay life, a few of them among the Boring Old Farts; courageous, hard-living, frankly homosexual guys. He'd heard all about the genetic bias theories, too. But deeply buried in Lovett's mind lay the conviction that environment shaped those biases just as profoundly. Chip's role models were chiefly female. *Okay, so he's a surfer, which is a macho sport. But Domenica says he's interested in girls only as surfing pals. And I didn't see any ripe little tomato hanging on his arm after the recital.* And there were those damned silk shirts, and Chip's lack of interest in the strippers, and, and—and it probably took more guts to admit you were gay than it did to ride a booming surf, Lovett admitted silently.

Very well, so why should Chip's choice of lifestyle bother him so much? The answer did not lie very deep. Lovett felt that the gay life was, for the most part, anything but gay in a hundred socially stigmatized ways. That social stigma might disappear in a hundred years but Chip wasn't going to live that long. The AIDS thing was another worry, even if it was an avoidable statistic to those who practiced safe sex. Lovett's suspicion was that Chip might be one of those talented youths on the cusp of sexual orientation; an experience here, a gentle shove there, could channel him.

And Wade Lovett hadn't the faintest idea how to provide the right shove; in fact, wasn't entirely sure what would be right for the only grandson he was ever going to have. *Too bad if you don't get any great-grandkids*, whispered some brazen imp from his subconscious. Maybe that was the real worry, he decided; *maybe I just want a little piece of immortality by proxy.*

Crispin Reventlo obtained the map of Fundabora later through Chip, and the youngster's eyes were bleary before he had finished his copywork that night. Only Benteen retained enough youthful vision for closeup work to help him draw six copies. Lovett and Reventlo managed to rule the gridlines that separated Fundabora into one-mile squares.

They had located the two-way wired room speakers easily, behind dusty wall hangings. Someone, probably a visiting engineer, had long ago removed the toggles that had allowed paying guests of FunIsle Resort to order breakfast. It was Reventlo's idea to leave them unsabotaged; let Jean-Claude think he was privy to their private conversations, he said archly.

Always mindful of being overheard, the Brit gazed at his copy of the map. "This is depressing," he said.

"It's a start," Benteen countered.

"Oh yes, like that first step of a thousand-mile march," he said. "Take a square inch at random—a square mile of Fundabora. Now let's say our 'mineral deposit' is fully five hundred feet wide. More likely smaller, but humor me."

"I get it," said Myles, from over his shoulder. "Christ, what a blanket of English overcast you are."

Benteen waved at the bearded Myles for silence. "You mean like, needle in a haystack?"

"Think of every bloody square mile gridded into five-hundred-foot squares. Roughly a hundred little squares per mile. How long will it take us to search the lot? Never mind," he went on, "Chip would have a long beard before we finished."

Benteen said it for them all: "Are you suggesting we give it up so soon?"

"I'm suggesting," said the Brit, "that we take a more logical approach. Concentrate on areas where," and now he made silent quotation marks by wiggling his forefingers, "our 'mineral deposits' seem most promising."

"I've thought that all along," Benteen said.

Lovett traced a finger along the beach line. "To begin with, searching these elevations doesn't make sense. Nor along here," he circled the regions around the old resort and the village a mile from it. "You wouldn't expect it at these elevations either," he said, indicating the rocky heights.

Myles: "Why not? Isn't that where you find most, uh, mineral depressions?"

"Use your noodle," Coop grunted. "Anything up there would be impossible to get down."

"Then how did it get up," Myles asked.

"A very good question, Vic. You tell *me*," Lovett replied.

"Oh. Yeah. I'm too tired to think straight," the Texan admitted.

"But that's a fair dinkum point of departure," Reventlo murmured, scanning his map. "We've seen some roads that weren't kept open. We need to chart them, see where they went. There had to be some ready access to this," he finished, pointing at the airstrip. "Actually it seems pretty simple when you bother to think about it."

Coop Gunther had been rubbing his leg where the prosthesis fitted. "I can't do any more hiking for a while; this thing swells up something fierce," he said. It shouldn't prevent him from working in the maintenance sheds, he added, limping off to his room.

Before they turned in, Reventlo and Lovett visited the aircraft where the Brit managed to contact Alice Springs terminal. Not to worry, he reported; they'd had trouble with dirt in the fuel, made a safe landing, and were flushing the lines. It might take a few more days. "I can't keep this up forever," he said as he flicked off the last toggle. "My bonus is already up the spout."

"If you gotta go, you gotta go," said Lovett. "Just make sure you come fluttering back with something that'll fly us all out."

"Even if I have to charter it," the Brit promised.

They walked back slowly, palm fronds hissing in the night wind above them. "What do you think of our chances now, Cris?"

"Impossible to say. We could strap those old engines into the C-47 and off-load them to storage at Darwin."

"For cash?" Lovett's tone said he doubted that.

"For proof," Reventlo corrected. "We might pick up more investors if we need them, given some hardware to show."

"Even if they don't know the site," Lovett persisted.

"*Especially* then. I'm not keen on letting our aces show."

They could hear that tone-deaf piano before they reached the councilhouse, and found Keikano sitting beside Chip, a coconut-oil lamp nearby smoking like a Cushman. "Hey," said the pianist softly, and got up to meet them. "I've got a favor to ask. For Keikano, really." The two men waited. "It's a biggie," he added. The schoolteacher remained on the piano bench.

"Can you say it here," Lovett asked.

"Keikano swears there's no bugs down here. If he's lying, it's his little butt. You'll understand when you hear the favor."

"If we hear it," Reventlo prodded.

Chip took a deep breath. "When you ferry the plane, he wants to go with you. He'll come back, really he will. But he feels like he has to go soon. No telling how long before another trading ship stops here."

Reventlo thought for a long moment before walking to the piano. "Keikano," he said gently, "I'd like to take you with me. And I would, even though you could have passport trouble. But how d'you think your President would react?"

Silence, and a lowering of the head. "I'll tell you how," Reventlo went on. "He wants you here. If you disappeared when I did, any imbecile could draw the right conclusion. Jean-Claude could make my crew very, very sorry, and I don't doubt he would."

The gentle mouth was trembling. "Then the rest of you must remain here?"

"We have to," Lovett said. "We signed a contract and we intend to honor it." Put that way, not quite a lie; yet it left a dirty taste in his mouth.

"The medicines you promised; the books, the supplies. Could you bring more, and sell it to me? I can pay with pearls, but Jean-Claude must not know of this."

Reventlo said that he might if he had a good reason. Then he cocked his head and viewed Keikano shrewdly. "You're a conduit, um, a contact to those people in the north, aren't you?"

Keikano swallowed hard and said nothing.

Reventlo smiled gently. "I withdraw the question. But if you were helping those people, would you tell me?"

More silence. Then, "No."

"Do those pearls belong to Jean-Claude?"

He might as well have slapped the schoolteacher. "They are entrusted to me. He would take them," spoken in disgust.

"Forgive me. I had to ask. Very well, Keikano, I'll bring extra medicines for you alone. Any special kind?"

"For elders with pains in the head, bleeding from the nose."

"Damn me, that's what I had," Reventlo chuckled. "High blood pressure. There's medicine for that, God knows I take enough of it."

"Could I buy some of yours?"

"I'd rather not. I can bring more, but it might not help. What you need, Keikano, is to get your old far—uhm, your elders, to a doctor; Guam, even Leyte. The trouble with these particular medicines is in getting the right ones and, once you start taking them, it's not healthy to stop. You can see my problem," he said, smiling sadly.

"And you can see mine," Keikano said, not smiling.

"I think so. I'm truly sorry I can't afford to fly you out of here. Perhaps when we all leave—but before that time, surely you could buy passage on a ship."

"I have tried. I was punished. Now, Jean-Claude has me watched when a trader is in the lagoon."

"Well, by God, when we leave, we'll get you out somehow."

A hopeful light flickered in the dark eyes. "Soon?"

"As soon as we find what we're after," Reventlo said, and offered his hand.

Keikano shook the hand with a tremulous smile and turned to Chip, who flung his arm around the slumping shoulders. "When I leave, you leave," he said, and this endorsement seemed to cheer the little Fundaboran. "Right now, I could sleep for a week," he added. The three crew members shuffled up the stairs, waving to the schoolteacher whose oil lamp made a moving pool of light on its way out to the verandah.

"I really feel for the guy," Chip said as he and Lovett arranged the mosquito netting on their bed. "For sure, he's got problems he doesn't wanta share."

"For sure," his grandfather echoed softly. At least his grandson knew that little Keikano kept a part of his agenda hidden. When it emerged, there could be umpteen kinds of hell to pay. "Chip?"

Just as softly: "Yeah, Pop?"

A dozen warnings, a hundred fears, all clamored to be spoken. Wade Lovett spent the moment sifting them all; found none he knew to be dependable. "I'm proud of you, kid." There was no answer. Chip Mason was already enjoying the sleep of the innocent.

17

During the next few days, Reventlo's crew split as they had agreed, Lovett spending much of his time with Coop Gunther and other ancient artifacts, Reventlo leading the reconnaissance team with shovels and machetes. Some of Coop's problems with the earthmover, and the solutions they found, bordered on the ridiculous. The LeTourneau's batteries were a hopeless case; as Coop put it, "Not just dead, Wade, they're friggin' petrified." And a diesel of eight hundred and fifty cubic inch displacement, he swore, couldn't have been hand-cranked by Arnold Schwarzenegger.

Here, at least, Lovett could offer hope; a quarter-mile away in the councilhouse was the light plant with its deep-cycle batteries. The exact opposite of lightweight aircraft units, those massive things may last over a decade; and many are equipped with built-in handles because, filled with stacks of thick lead plates, at first grunt they seem bolted to the floor. Lovett told Merizo they'd have to borrow parts for an hour or so if Jean-Claude was ever to get his "bigbig machine" running.

It was Pilau who took the hefty batteries from the councilhouse kitchen, trundling them back and forth one at a time in a wheelbarrow for each test. The native mechanic linked his units together under the watchful eye of Coop, who promised to educate him with a wrench over his noggin the next time he picked up an oil can. It was a hell of a way to do business but, on the fourth day, Coop nursed the huge V-12 engine into a thunderous mutter, mixing kerosene with engine oil as a passable fuel. After that, Coop's repairs went more swiftly.

Reventlo's progress was slower. They located two roads, neither passable by now, one track leading to a shallow pit where many tons of apatite had been removed. The other road seemed more promising, from the airstrip to the island's narrow ankle. Myles sweated off ten pounds flailing in jungle growths before he concluded that, if any caves lay near that swampy isthmus, they were too small to hold an airplane.

And each day Crispin Reventlo grew more restive. In late afternoon after their fifth fruitless day of searching, he proposed a hike along the base of those rocky heights above the abandoned open-pit mine. "We'll tell Keikano it's to look over the land, but the team knows what we're checking on," he told Lovett.

"You might tell me. Coop's pretty gimpy but I'd like to go," Lovett said.

"Bats. You see them now and then, at dusk. Not the big fruit bats; those little nippers that like to roost in caves. When they come out at dusk, they might give us a bearing."

"What does Keikano think about coming back in the dark?"

"He thinks we're mad as March hares; probably isn't thinking about pocket torches. But if we're going, he'll guide us. And we're going," he said firmly.

"Mad dogs and Englishmen hike on moonlit nights," Lovett misquoted, grinning. "We'll need every flashlight we can find."

They left Coop in his room with a transceiver and, with Keikano in the lead, took a footpath that skirted the steep rocky heights. Chip pointed out the mining pit below in the distance, a broad ugly scar the jungle was slowly reclaiming. A mile beyond lay a shallow bay, freckled with tiny islands, their bases worn narrower than their tops by wave action so that each islet poked above the lapping tide with the shape of a giant's doorknob. Each was crowned with vegetation like an afro haircut. "Keikano says tourists named the place Mushroom Bay; you can see why," said the youth.

Far beyond the bay, the north end of Fundabora sortied out into the ocean again, and there, starkly etched against the sky, tendrils of smoke hovered lazily, dark fingers pointing down as if to pinpoint Fundabora's exiles. Lovett hailed Keikano and pointed toward the smudges. "They don't try to hide their fires," he said.

"If anyone comes, they know," Keikano said simply.

"How do they know?"

"They know," Keikano repeated with an apologetic smile. "Wrong—Long ago, they learned it was necessary."

Lovett noticed the quick glance of Mel Benteen, who had been scanning the lava scarp behind them. She caught his eye, smiled, shrugged and looked away again. The late sun lit the planes of her face wonderfully and Lovett could easily imagine Melanie Benteen as a purebred island woman, one who had somehow avoided the tooth decay and a tropical sun that hammered wrinkles into the flesh from an early age. Island girls could be gorgeous at twelve, and crones at forty. Mel, already in her forties, could still give a man thoughts of—*will you knock it off? She's mean as a pet squirrel and she's not interested,* he snarled at himself. If anyone had a shot with Mel, it would be Reventlo. He did, after all, share the same bed with her—probably, Coop had said, in the same way he might share it with a sore-footed sled dog.

The footpath stood out clearly now, winding through declivities between jungle and the steepening lava scarp that was scoured too hard by the wind to permit anything more than tough grasses on its flanks. Far ahead of them the path descended, then rose again along the base of that rock spine they'd almost struck in their overflight. Palms and other growth crowded into small ravines that had captured windblown soil. Lovett wondered for a moment how a coconut palm could become rooted that high on a rocky slope. Then he thought of typhoons with winds so powerful they could literally hurl a coconut a thousand feet up like a flung baseball, and wondered no more. Along the isthmus, below that rocky spine, vagrant sunglints through palmetto thickets proved that the salt swamp cut the island almost in two.

And suddenly Lovett knew how it was that those northern outcasts could avoid surprise visits from Pelele's gang. A landing in the bay would be damned dangerous with those stone mushrooms creating crosscurrents. Anyone advancing in cover would do it through a mile or so of trackless swamp. Anyone advancing without it would have to use the path; and a single sentry, hidden somewhere in the rocky northern minarets, could give the alarm long before trouble could reach his village. A subtle movement on a nearby slope drew Lovett's gaze. He peered hard, then smiled. "Someone's pet pussycat," he said, pointing.

Keikano saw it, a slim graceful creature with markings like an ocelot, before it slid from sight. "They are wild, except for a very few. A pet like that must be raised from a baby or—," he said, and made claws of one hand, miming a furious swipe.

Lovett exchanged a glance with Chip and sighed. He hadn't come this far to waste time taming one of Mayday's distant cousins.

The sun had touched the horizon when Lovett pointed behind them to the southern spires that overlooked councilhouse, airstrip, and beach. "Keikano, does Jean-Claude keep sentries up there?"

A pause, and a mystified frown. "I do not think so. There is no path there. Why would he want to? He has nothing to fear."

"Just wondering." Lovett continued to gaze toward those dizzying pinnacles he'd seen daily from the other side, wishing he knew enough geology to understand the structure of a lava chimney.

"I bet we could see a lot from there," Myles said, wiping sweat from his forehead.

"There is no path and it is very dangerous," Keikano said with a finality that was almost brusque. "Especially after dark."

Vic Myles grinned through his beard at Lovett. "Maybe some other time during daylight," he said.

Keikano pointed his chin at a sun that had already half-submerged into the Philippine Sea. "Will you have time to do these things?"

"As much time as we want," Myles said.

This was plainly not what the schoolteacher wanted to hear. He forced a bright smile and said, "We must return now. Soon the path will not be friendly to your feet."

"It must be tough for you at night," Reventlo said casually, leaning against an outcrop, studying the heights.

Keikano, just as casually: "Why would I take such foolish risks?"

"I'm not sure why," said the Brit, smiling, "but I'm sure you do. Keikano, we already know you visit back and forth, and I don't think that meets with Jean-Claude's approval. It seems pretty clear you must do it in darkness."

"I do not like to speak of this," Keikano said, and there was iron in the soft voice. "Will you come back with me now?"

"Not just yet," Lovett urged. If Keikano was this anxious to leave, maybe Reventlo was right about the bats.

"But—it will be dark soon," Keikano said.

Reventlo: "We all have pocket torches." He pulled a compact Maglite from his pocket, twisted it to obtain a beam. Then he consulted his map before leaving the path for the uneven footing of old lava. "We should fetch up on the cliff above the airstrip if we keep circling the pinnacles this way," he said to the others.

In that instant, an emerald flashbulb filled the sky and, in the next second, dusk enfolded their world. Every one of the party paused in homage to the fallen sun. "Ohh," Chip breathed in awe. "What was that?"

"I've seen it before," Lovett replied, placing a hand on his grandson's shoulder. "The green flash, they call it; happens now and then when sunset is lensed through a wave, and conditions are just right."

"Rad. Why doesn't it happen in Santa Cruz?"

Shrug. "Beats me, kid. Maybe it does." And with the briefest of mutual shoulder pats, their moment of intimacy passed.

Moments later, Reventlo put hands on hips and surveyed the scarp ahead. "Bloody path's in shadow now, and I don't fancy a tumble down to the trees."

"What path? Listen, the teacher's right," said Myles, glancing nervously ahead. "We gotta start back."

The Brit was looking up and to his right, toward the pinnacles, as he said, "Forget what we came for, did we, Vic?"

"No, I—wup! There goes one," he said as a tiny scrap of blackness wheeled silently overhead like torn tissue on some unfelt breeze: a bat. Then he noticed Reventlo's hard glance in his direction. "What?"

Reventlo, acidly: "Would you like a megaphone, Vic?"

"Sorry."

Now they were all gazing around them, watching those scraps of sentient tissue flicker though the dusk. That was when Chip, facing the pinnacles, head thrown back with the grassy downslope behind him, took one step to the rear. "Where d'you suppose," he began to Keikano, and then lost his footing. "Wha, OOooo, *bummerrrr*," his cry dopplering down as he slid, now rolling onto his back, arms out as he accelerated down the slick grass.

"Chip! Chip," Lovett cried, watching in horror, unable to help as the youth plummeted to a terminal velocity that should have had a mach number attached. And when he reached broad-leaved undergrowth a hundred feet below, he simply kept going, his progress marked only by fainter and fainter shouts of, "Shit, shit, shit, Oh, shit . . ." Then silence.

They all called, Lovett and Keikano beginning to search frantically for some safe way to follow. Lovett said, "I've got to get down there some—" and stopped as a blond head poked out of the greenery.

It had an arm, and it was waving. "Whoa, dude, did I rip that one or what," floated up to them. In truth, Chip was no more than sixty yards away.

"God*dam*mit, Chip, you might've—this isn't a surfing run, idiot!"

"That's what you think, Pop. Yow, bitchin'," he shouted his delight. "Man, but I'm amped."

"Chip, will you get back up here before you kill yourself?" Lovett's shout was quavery with relief.

"No way," said the youth. "That grass? I think Pilau must've oiled it. It's not so steep down below, why don't you guys come on down?"

"The way you did?" Reventlo laughed aloud. "I would break every bone in my arse. Not a stellar plan." He turned to the others. "Any other mental cases care to try Chip's carnival ride to oblivion?"

"Maybe not," Myles said, stroking his beard.

"Absolutely not," Benteen agreed.

"I must go," Keikano blurted to the Brit. "Please, you must go back with those lights and please, please, stay on the path."

"Surely," Reventlo began, "you're not going to," but by that time he saw that the slender Keikano *was* going to.

Chip saw the long slide began, feetfirst, fanny down, and called, "Go for it, but look out for the lumps."

Keikano began the descent more slowly using arms and feet with care, but then gravity did what gravity does. With a yelp of what could have been fear or delight, the schoolteacher went hurtling down the slope, head bobbing, clods flying. Keikano disappeared into the jungle for only a few yards before the top of a broadleaf sapling waved merrily, Chip scrambling off to help, or perhaps just to view the remains.

When the little party on the scarp could hear laughter from below, they vented sighs of relief. "We'll take the long way," Lovett called, and heard an amiable reply float up from the jungle.

"And people ask me why I didn't have kids," Mel Benteen said.

Reventlo snapped on his flashlight and turned back the way they had come. Every few paces, he stopped to scan the air. "I'd bet my flight pay there's a cave entrance somewhere about," he said.

"Look for something like thin smoke," Myles said. "That's how a bunch of bats look against the sky from a distance when they first come out."

Lovett snorted. "Now you're a bat expert."

"Betcherass, Wade. Congress Avenue Bridge in Austin; one million Mexican free-tail bats under it, give or take a dozen. Nightly local event."

"Why am I not surprised," Benteen chuckled.

"Don't offend him, it's the Texas state bird," Lovett joined in.

"Spin around on this bird, Lovett," Myles suggested, with a one-digit salute and the peculiar good nature of a man who has grown calluses on his state pride.

"I'm not seeing anything like your smoke cloud, Victor," said the Brit, picking his way carefully back, still searching the darkening sky. "Any more useful tips?"

"I got one for Lovett," said the Texan.

"Enough with the straight lines, Cris," Lovett said.

Myles, imperturbable: "Mex free-tails may not be like these but they say you need an air supply in their caves."

"Bats must breathe, I should think," from Reventlo.

"Sure, but they can take the ammonia and you can't. The ammonia's from their guano, batshit. Great fertilizer, used to be mined for black powder nitrates."

"So if we smell ammonia, we could be near our cave," Benteen mused aloud.

"So they say," Myles replied. "Stinks like a dungeon full of used diapers."

Now they regained the footpath, remarking on the few bats they did see, less optimistic about their tactic with every step. Several times they were treated to an oddity that, at first, raised hackles: phosphorescence in rotting vegetation. The glow was dim but broadly suffused, like some eldritch candle hidden beneath layers of lime-green cloth.

When they had made their way back to safe and familiar ground, Lovett hurrying ahead the sooner to see his grandson again, Benteen voiced one last question. "Myles, why do they call them free-tails?"

" 'Cause," said the Texan, "the lucky little boogers get all the tail they want, and they don't have to pay for it."

"You had to ask," Reventlo said mournfully, then raised his voice. "I say, Wade, lower your flaps. You're leaving us behind."

The entire crew set up a vigil on the veranda, some picking at bits of fruit, Lovett pacing back and forth. When Chip trudged within sight he was alone and from the beach, not from the direction they expected. Lovett let go the deepest sigh in his collection at the youth's hail and returned it.

Chip should have been exhausted; his hair was rumpled, clothes torn, smears of dirt on his face. His face glowed with delight.

"Christ, kid," Myles said, "you look like you've been—never mind," he subsided.

"That grin of yours is a dentist's advert," Reventlo said, shaking his hand. "You had us worried, lad."

Lovett, peering toward the beach: "Where's Keikano?"

"He peeled off after we got to the airstrip. I knew where I was by then and just followed the beach. But, uh," he paused, shaking his head, still grinning. "Could we discuss it in the plane?"

Reventlo frowned, nonplussed. "It's quite late. You mean, in the morning?"

"If you want to wait that long," Chip said, his manner insinuating a great deal. "I don't think you do."

Reventlo's expression shifted gears instantly. "Well, I'll defer to your judgment—barring your unique way of getting down a mountainside."

"My leg's still a problem," Coop said. "Think I need to go?"

"I really do," Chip said, and his grin continued to say more. "It's about some deposits. If you don't come along, I think you'll wish you had."

They trooped out to the moonlit aircraft. Chip circled it as the others moved inside, then pulled the cargo door shut behind him. The cabin light threw his face into hard shadow as he said, "Nobody out there listening, I guess. I'd hate for them to find out before we're ready. But I guess that's up to you."

"I trust all this mystery is in aid of something major," said Reventlo.

"*Yesss*," Chip said, with a raised fist, and looked around him, his grin refreshed. Then temptation overcame him and, enjoying his moment, Chip Mason became sly, primly secretive. "Let's see: there were supposed to be, what, six Japanese planes?"

"Roughly," Lovett nodded, tired and grumpy and not enjoying this catechism in the least.

"In a cave, preserved like new," Chip went on.

Lovett drew a deep breath and jabbed a forefinger in his grandson's direction. "I don't know if you're still spankable, Chip, but the impulse is growing."

Chip abandoned his game, throwing both hands into the air. "Well, it's true about the airplanes. All of it!"

18

Keikano had seemed to arrive at some major decision, said Chip, after becoming convinced that his new friends had presented him with a sort of Catch 21, just short of a Catch 22. Having promised to take him along when they all left Fundabora, now they were in no hurry to leave. Leading Chip around the base of the rocky scarp in gathering darkness, Keikano had made his way unerringly between almost invisible goat trails, moving as if holding to some personal schedule and never needing to backtrack. Evidently Keikano's trail markers included a couple of those luminous mounds which, Chip said with an abashed look, took a bit of getting used to.

They had stopped for a breather after an hour and Chip, only half-stunned by the moonrise over a Pacific island shore, realized they had circled to a position overlooking the old airstrip.

There, as the American youth leaned against the cliffside while the Fundaboran rested in a squatting position, the schoolteacher saddled Chip with some friendly questions. Exactly how long, he wondered aloud, did the crew expect to stay on the island? And what were they really after?

Chip said the length of their stay wasn't up to him. They hoped to find something worth exporting.

And the sooner they found it, the sooner they'd take Keikano away? Chip said it looked that way. The group had brought no shovels on this trek, Keikano pointed out, but had shown great interest in bats. Why?

Maybe, Chip said carefully, they hoped bats would lead them to mineral deposits. Keikano had taken a long time to form his next question. Would they be just as happy, he asked, with more relics of aircraft?

Chip had seen that his guide seemed to know exactly where he was going along those animal trails, and when to leave them. Now he believed that it was no accident they had emerged on a prominence overlooking the moonlit swath of second-growth jungle marking a Japanese airstrip. And given such a leading question, Chip replied that his elders might be very, very happy with aircraft relics—provided they were in much better condition than the stuff they'd already found corroding in the jungle.

Chip recalled the next question verbatim, virtually whispered. "And if they were in condition to fly?"

Chip had laughed aloud. "They'd probably forget about minerals," he'd burbled. "But that's impossible. Isn't it?"

Chip's guide half arose but paused at his last phrase, comically bent as if wondering whether to make some vast, decisive leap.

In what he later said was a flash of intuition, Chip applied the goad to Keikano's backside. "Yeah," he said smugly, "that's totally impossible."

And that is when Keikano straightened, took a half-dozen steps, and knelt in moonshadow, straining at an upthrust of rock as if to move a ton of stone. And when it *did* move, Chip realized it was a thin slab balanced to permit its rolling to one side. The hole it revealed was shoulder-high, blacker than night, and Keikano had disappeared through it in an instant without hesitation.

Chip used his Maglite to enter the same hole, afraid to do it, yet buoyed by the soft scuffings of sandals just ahead. And hey, anything Keikano could do, . . . He found himself following down steps chiseled into soft limestone. A few steps ahead and below, Keikano's flashlight made a moving ellipse of light that splashed against a wall of naked gray bedrock on the right. Chip kept his shoulder brushing that wall because to his left was only the edge of those hewn steps and, beyond, pure velvet blackness.

After they had descended perhaps thirty steps, Keikano stopped, redirected his flashbeam outward and down, then twisted the device for a tighter focus. Ten yards below them, shining in the light—but softly, softly—a metal wingtip stood out in stark relief. Under Keikano's control the beam crawled farther away, outlining the entire wing, then the fuselage of a single-place aircraft, its canopy intact, its tail surfaces apparently undamaged. On the fuselage, a circle of red a yard wide proclaimed the rising sun of a Japanese fighter plane generations old, and Chip Mason was briefly awash with goose-pimples.

"Will this make them forget minerals?"

"What minerals," Chip had asked, their mutual laughter echoing softly in the cave.

They went no farther down the steps than that, Chip admitted to the silent crew. "There were two or three more like that fighter—radial engines, Zeroes I think, and a big twin-engine job that may have been green or black. It was hard to tell in that light. Maybe five planes, all told," he added. "I asked if Pelele's gang knew about it. Keikano said no, and if they ever found out *he* had known, they'd hunt him down like a goat."

"Oh Jesus, ohh, Jesus," Myles crooned, hugging himself, rocking to and fro. "Kid, if you're putting us on—"

"The little dogsbody. He knew all the time," said Reventlo, accepting Chip's account for the moment at face value.

"Oh yeah, but I don't think he realizes it's why we came," Chip said. "I think we should keep it that way. For Keikano's sake, this has got to be something we found without help."

Lovett rubbed his temples with fingertips, nodding to himself. "Of course. Walled up at the end of the runway; easy access, no long tow job. I should've figured this. Okay, okay, they're in a cavern. How the hell did they get in there?"

"Screw that," Myles retorted. "How do we get 'em out?"

Lovett said, as if to a small boy, "It's the same question, Vic. You know damn well they didn't assemble the planes in there, so there's got to be a larger entrance."

"If there's not, I'll make one," Myles promised gruffly. "If my TNT bricks aren't enough, Cris can bring us some plain ol' sixty percent dynamite."

Mel Benteen had been listening quietly, studying the men as she might study zoo specimens. Now she said, "Are you insane, Myles? I'm no expert, but—set off high explosives in a cavern? I've heard you can make them collapse with a loud yell."

"Excuse me," from Chip, "but from what I saw, it didn't look like a regular cavern; no stalactites hanging down or anything. No bats that I saw. The light was pitiful but it just looked like they'd carved it out of limestone."

"That'd take a long time," Coop objected. "Something weird about all this."

"It's probably academic," Reventlo said. "They had to have a safe way of bringing the planes out. We'll simply have to find it."

Gunther shook his head dolefully. "Wish I was as sure as you are, Cris. Who's to say what orders those crazy fuggers were following?"

The Brit sighed. "Coop, they all had one motive: protecting the home islands. The Nips began to collect everything that would fly in the spring and summer of '45 for the suicide armada they intended to fling at us. For years after the war, Japanese aircraft were turning up in underground hangars as far away as Taiwan. One Zeke was found in decent shape, on Guam back in the early sixties—not all that far from here—and restored. And there's that story about Atsugi."

Lovett: "The old base near Tokyo?"

Reventlo nodded. "Back in '68, I think. They say a bulldozer was crossing a taxiway when the concrete collapsed into a sinkhole, bulldozer and all. There were several fighter planes down there, nicely preserved. Not many people know about it, but that's why I was primed to believe old Elmo's story from Day One."

"So how'd they get 'em out," Myles asked.

"I wish to God I knew," the Brit replied.

When the schoolteacher failed to show up the next morning, no one was in a mood to wait for him. The existing road near the south beach brought the entire crew, chugging along on three Cushmans, almost to the airstrip. Their rope and battery-powered spotlights fitted, just barely, beneath the passenger seats and they carried a pair of shovels as window dressing. Lovett had expected Coop Gunther to decline the trip but, "Miss the unveiling? I'll crawl if I have to," the old fellow had said.

Chip located the faint upward path he had descended more or less blindly the night before, a goat track virtually hidden by lush undergrowth. The moment Myles unlimbered his machete, Lovett put up a restraining hand. "Hey, let's not build a freeway, or sing any goddamned marching songs. The quieter we keep this, the better."

"I wish that little fart, Keikano, was here," Coop muttered, using his shovel as a walking stick.

"I can get us there," Chip said.

"It's not that," said the old fellow, with a sad little smile. "I just need somebody to beat the shit out of, every time my leg twinges; and you guys are all bigger than I am."

"Thanks a load," said Benteen, who was the smallest of them all. Her smile reassured Coop. Lovett had never seen her in such good spirits. For Mel, he saw, this meant more than money and adventure: nothing less than the final validation of old Elmo Benteen.

In some places the climb was steep and Lovett, peering closely at the stone underfoot, noticed the subtle rounding and polishing of projections suggesting that, at some time or other, this soft limestone had known many a footstep. They moved around a low ridge, still rising, then returned moments later so that the airstrip came in view again. It was clearly visible from here as a line of least vegetation arrowing toward the beach and the breakers beyond.

Then Chip Mason stood at the top of that sheer drop off, arms akimbo, frowning at the vine-covered rampart he faced. And for one long, goose-pimpled moment, Lovett wondered if this were all some elaborate hoax by his grandson. *I'll boot his ass over this five-story bluff,* he swore silently. *I will!*

But after a moment of intent scrutiny of the stone embankment, Chip fitted his fingers into a seam; hauled sideways at the apparently immovable rock. An oval slab, no more than two inches thick, rolled away under its thin camouflage of live creeper vines, and the youth turned back to them, grinning. "Miz Benteen, it seems only right for you to go first."

Mel Benteen waved her hands before her as if polishing a mirror. "No, no, caves aren't my strong point, Chip. I'll follow you."

"Hey, listen now," Myles said, shuffling forward quickly. "Let me do it, okay? I've got an editor to impress." He unlimbered his little camera, took a shot.

Reventlo got there first, pausing at the entrance. "Not a good enough reason, Victor."

"Wait, wait! Okay then. A hundred bucks, Cris." Myles put his right hand up to God.

"Still not good enough," the Brit said, implacable.

Myles ground his teeth. "Son of a—*two* hundred," he pleaded.

"Apiece," Reventlo said pleasantly. "Those were very expensive mosquito nets you sold us, Victor."

"All right, goddammit, deal. Now get out of my way." And so saying, survivalist guru Victor Myles pocketed his camera, ducked into the hole, and missed the step, sprawling headfirst into the dim recess.

Chip caught the Texan by a trouserleg, warning him about the lack of handrails as Myles regained his feet cursing tunnels, steps, and folks who snickered at folks who fell down. Moments later they were crowding the inner wall in single file, flashlights washing the cave with errant beams. Now their progress was marked by echoes in oppressive blackness. Still in the lead, Myles paused halfway down and let his flashbeam play over the booty spread below. "The kid's right, they're Zeroes," he boomed, as "zeroes, eroes, eroes," mocked him faintly.

Reventlo stopped so suddenly that Benteen collided with him. "No, wait," he said. "Let's have all those torches together." They plied the beams over the nearest fighter, oohing and aahing, until Reventlo slumped against the wall. "My God," he said softly. "Oh, my very dear God."

"What's the matter?" Myles seemed ready to believe the worst while gazing at the best.

"Not Zeroes," said the Brit.

"Yeah," Lovett mused. "Canopy's different; tailcone, too. And something about the cowling. I don't know, the later models—"

"Tojo," said Reventlo, almost in a whisper. "It's a sodding Nakajima Tojo. Tie me kangaroo down if that isn't a Shoki; Tojo, Ki-44, same thing."

Gunther had caught up with them now and said for them all, "That's bad?"

"That is not bad, not bad at all," Reventlo crooned, "and there are four of them in here, lads and lass." Now the proper Brit astonished them all with an impromptu dance step, then leaned back against the wall again with a long, low whistle. "The twin-engine there is an old friend, if I may call it that: a Mitsubishi G4M, alias a Betty bomber. But—*four* Tojos? Out-bloody-standing!"

"You're starting to piss me off," Lovett said.

"That's because you didn't do your homework," his friend rejoined. "There are records of surviving Nip aircraft, Wade. A few Zeroes are still flying. Go on, ask the next question."

"You're saying the Tojo is rare," Benteen prodded.

"Not rare. You're at liberty to guess how many Tojos made it through the war." No one spoke. "Zed. Zip, and if you'll pardon the expression, zero. They were thought extinct. If these old beauties can be made to work as well as they look—well, it could be closer to two million apiece. You are looking at the only surviving Ki-44 Tojos on the surface of the globe."

"Under it, you mean," said Coop, at Myles's shoulder. "Why are we standing here when we could be—hey, just a froggin' minute here. Smell something?"

"Just hangar smells. No ammonia, if that's what you mean," Myles said, then continued with due caution.

Coop began to descend again behind Myles. "Right. Fuel, lubricant, rubber. After fifty years?"

Until that moment, Lovett had taken the familiar odors for granted. Now his mind reeled, and gooseflesh toured his arms as he followed Coop down those steps. A long disused hangar had its own sad, unique stinks: the sweetish odor of old Plexiglas, sometimes the dry tang of corroded aluminum. Rarely, the scent of old lubricant. But gasoline after fifty years? *No way*, his gooseflesh chanted in unison.

An instant's burst of blue-white light flooded the cave, setting Lovett's night vision back to square one. "Victor, why are you blinding us at a time like this," Reventlo asked with a courtesy they all knew could be deceptive.

"Proof positive," said the Texan. "This little Polaroid is gonna bring me a best-seller."

"Kindly warn us from now on, there's a good chap," Reventlo pleaded. One by one, they reached an uneven stony floor that, Lovett found, was old coral filled in by cement. Their discovery had become so enormous in Lovett's mind that, for the moment, he had to focus on something more easily grasped. So, as other flashbeams played over the hidden aircraft and more impatient fingers thumped aluminum hides, Wade Lovett walked in a squat, following his flashbeam toward the juncture of floor and cave wall.

When he had studied the tool marks on the floor as far as the juncture he moved his flashbeam up, following a gentle curvature innocent of tool marks to the point where it became an overhang, then a natural ceiling that swept forward to meet a front wall lost in shadow. "Hell, this was ordinary wave action," he said aloud, gazing at the smoothly contoured roof. No one paid attention, Coop and Reventlo talking a mile a minute as they clambered onto wing roots and slid canopies back. Wade Lovett stood up and strode to the opposite wall, nearly braining himself against a wing trailing edge in the process.

He needed only a moment to discover that the front wall was man-made; not limestone but cement, rising vertically from a foundation of debris to a height of perhaps thirty feet before it met the natural limestone roof. "Oh boy," he muttered to his gooseflesh; the entire forward face of the cave stood poised, awaiting exactly the right jolt—one that any vagrant earth tremor might have provided during the past fifty years.

"I've found the other one," Chip yelled, his flashbeam touring the underside of the lone twin-engined bomber. Lovett's hand lay against the cement wall, which vibrated at the youth's high-pitched shout.

"Stop, stop it, *quiet*," Lovett begged, but trying to shout without shouting was like trying to hammer a nail quietly. He hurried across the undulating floor surface and arrived at Chip's side as Myles dropped to his haunches beneath the bomber's belly, the better to see what Chip had found. "Please knock the noise off," Lovett begged as the others converged on the new find. "I've been checking this cave out, and believe me, it's not all that stable."

"Been here a long time," Myles countered.

"Not with a convention of Swiss yodelers bottled up inside, hooting their empty heads off," Lovett reminded him. "When my grandson yelled, I could feel the whole front wall shake. And I'll bet my share of this operation that it's about as thick as the film on your teeth. Yeah, we want it to come down—but maybe not while we're inside, okay? So let's hold it down to a dull roar unless we want a reeeal sharp one."

"It's that thin? Doesn't make sense," Reventlo said, sending his flashbeam to the featureless front wall.

"It does," Lovett said, "if you're a Japanese detachment sealing up aircraft under a big limestone overhang. We're standing on old coral smoothed out with modern cement. That says, about the time of sabertooth tigers, the sea level was a bit higher here. Waves undercut the limestone cliff over the coral; then the sea level eventually dropped away, roughly when humans quit swinging through the trees. My guess is, the airstrip was built where it is precisely because there was an overhang of limestone ten feet thick and deep enough to provide a natural hangar. Then when they got orders to hide it, they only had to create one wall."

"So all they had to do was run up some reinforcing mesh and plaster it with cement," Reventlo mused.

"By mesh you mean re-bar? That's assuming they had any, Cris. We won't know 'til it comes down. But that's cement, all right, and I'll give you odds it was designed to come down in a hurry."

"Lemme tell ya," drawled Myles, "it sure would if that thing under the Betty ever goes off." And with this, he swung his beam under the bomber to show them something most military pilots knew, if only from its legends.

The wings of the staunch old Mitsubishi bomber spanned perhaps eighty feet, main landing gear extending down from its engine nacelles. A man could walk under the wing and could ordinarily have ducked beneath its belly. But not beneath this one; half-submerged in the bomb bay, as if grafted to the bomber, lay a long, spume green bomb. No, not just a bomb, for its fins were short straight wings, and it had miniature tail surfaces as well. What they saw was a tiny long-nosed aircraft, its canopy almost hidden within the bomber, but it had neither propeller nor jet intake. "Who wants my share of this," Lovett muttered, because he knew what it was. And Chip was practically huddled against its long forward section. "Chip, get away from there."

"Wouldn't matter where he was if it decided to let go now," Myles chuckled.

"Ohka," said Reventlo with something like reverence. "And it's still linked up, ready to go."

Chip had moved back now, tapping at a stubby wing that was less than seven feet from the fuselage to wingtip. Its entire wingspan could not have been over seventeen feet. "The wings are wood, Pop."

"We've got a Baka bomb," Reventlo said. "That's what the Allies called it; a fool bomb, as if cursing it in Japanese would stop them from dropping it. Yes, the flight surfaces were wood. But the entire nose section was about a ton of high explosive."

They studied it silently for a moment, its twin rudders flanking the bomber's fuselage, a pinkish five-petaled emblem painted against its pale green hide. "But it looks like a guided missile," Chip said at length.

"It was," said Lovett. "A glider with a difference; for its dash to the target it used internal rocket boosters. Subsonic, but faster than anything we had. But see that little canopy sticking up into the bomb bay? That's where the guidance system sat."

"Oh, jeez," Chip said softly, understanding half of it. "You mean a guy sat in there and steered it until time to bail out."

"He sat there," Myles put in. "But he didn't bail out. He didn't have a chute, kid."

"The Nips called it the Ohka; cherry blossom," Reventlo said. "The idea was to train teenagers to guide them down against Allied warships. One Ohka, one ship. Ever see cherry blossoms dropping in a spring breeze? Like a blizzard. That's the blizzard of Ohkas they intended to drop, taking a generation of their youngsters with it. Worked all too well, when they could get within twenty miles of a ship. I'm told the problem was, the Betty bomber there was too slow when carrying an Ohka like that. Our lads shot most of them down before they got within range."

"And no chute," Chip said, marveling. "That was some gnarly shit for their high-school kids."

"Nope, no chute. And no landing gear either, and engines cheap as skyrockets, 'cause that's what they were," Myles said, flopping down to throw a beam up the exhaust port of the little Ohka. Now his voice took on a softer echo, as though from within a stovepipe. "Well, folks, this 'un's ready for the Fourth of July. Three little JATOs packed in here. Wait a minute," he went on, shoving his arm far into the aperture, grunting.

"Victor, I'm sure we'd all appreciate it if—" Reventlo began.

"Getcher fuckin' paws outa there," Coop snarled, to short-circuit the Brit's languid rhetoric. "That's all we need, you setting off a booby trap in here with a rocket on one end and a one-ton bomb on the other."

But Myles had pulled out a length of bamboo with an oily rag spiked on it. "Somebody tried to do something right, to seal the nozzles," he said, shining his light on it, then resuming his scrutiny of the tailpipe. After a few seconds: "Oh, balls. Powder grain is cracked. No surprise after storage for so long."

Reventlo tried to attain brevity: "Is it more dangerous that way, Victor?"

"Only if you fire it. Anybody got a match? Just kidding," he said to the chorus of heated replies, replacing the cloth wad. "A solid booster propellant needs a certain shape; that's what controls the burning rate. Cracks can't help but increase the burning surface. Lots of things happen then, usually bad. Blooey," he added simply.

"Well, that's one thing they couldn't keep pickled for fifty years," said Lovett.

"Maybe the only thing," Coop replied.

"What do you mean?"

"I mean it's spookier than those goddamn glowing lumps in the jungle, Wade," said the old fellow. "Me and Cris have been checking in the cockpits, and I'll bet that bomber is just like the Tojos. There's a decent workbench at the base of the steps; looks like Philippine mahogany, big vise and all, under an oiled tarp. Big old cracked mirror behind it with a pair of hurricane lamps that, I'll bet you, are still workable. There's even a spare twin-row engine showing through a packing crate against the wall. Cris thinks he knows what kind."

"Think, your backside; I can read the spec plate," Reventlo said. "It's a late model Nakajima, the same article bolted in these Tojos. Put out upwards of two thousand horses, it did. This one, I'll wager, has never been run."

"There y'go," Coop said. "They set this place up so they could make the planes ready to scramble on short notice. Cockpit leather's still oiled and flexible, rubber's not too bad, even the cowl flaps and stuff are workable. No battery power of course, but there's a scavenged fuel tank against a wall that smells like there's a gasahol mix in it, and an APU—well, lemme show you."

As he let himself be led through an obstacle course of closely spaced aircraft, Lovett said he failed to see anything unnatural about it. Shut off from the tropical sun, from salt spray, from virtually all inclement weather, an entombed airplane might survive this way indefinitely. The proof was all around them, he said.

"Yeah, but even mixed with alcohol, would gasoline last this long?" Coop knelt near one limestone wall, and Lovett saw that he was pulling a wooden plug from the fuel tank of a small air-cooled engine. The engine was bolted to what might have been a pump but, when Lovett saw the long coils of cable and the wheeled cart, he knew better. It was an auxiliary power unit, known around the globe to airmen as an APU. With an APU, you could recharge a battery—or get your airplane started without one.

Coop ran two fingers into the tank and pulled them back glistening; held them up for Lovett to sniff. "That may not be avgas, but it's fuel," said Coop, tapping a larger tank cannibalized from some ancient wreck.

"Probably gone 'off' long before this," Reventlo said. The pilots all knew gasoline tended to fume off its best components in time.

"I know a good way to find out," said Coop, who was now happily fiddling with a rope-coil starter that looked handmade. "One'll get you five this sucker turns over."

It fired on the first pull, ran on the third. Coop shut it down quickly because of its noise, after generating sparks from the cables. "Gents, we've got us a live system," he said as the echoes faded.

"It's fantastic," Reventlo said.

"It's spooky," Coop repeated, rubbing dust from a specification plate on the generator. "Aw well, shit, what did I expect? I can't read this thing."

Reventlo hunkered down, took reading glasses from his pocket. "Most of it's a mystery to me," he muttered, "but even in the thirties the Nips used Arabic numbers. It's a twenty-eight-volt system. Too bad it wouldn't serve to start our LeTourneau."

"Who says it wouldn't," Coop scoffed. "This is a higher voltage but it'd run hell out of that starter motor. 'Course you don't wanta keep that up for more'n fifteen seconds at a time. Good idea, Cris. I'll keep it in mind."

Mel Benteen had scarcely said a word the whole time but, as Lovett moved his flashbeam past her, he saw that she stood calmly, arms folded, basking in distant memories. "Wouldn't it be something," she said now, "if we could fly these old beauties out."

Lovett had reconditioned a lot of planes in his time, and knew the odds. "No. Even if we got one running, it would be insane to take off without a battery in the system. And what am I saying? Starting up an old APU is one thing, but these," he swept his flashbeam across the cave, "would need hundreds of gallons of fuel assuming they did run."

"Even money on that one," Coop said. "I can't tell you why, and I know it's weird. But I got a feeling about it."

"A good feeling," Myles probed.

"I didn't say that. But a feeling these old buggers would fly, just as they stand."

19

Climbing down from the belly hatch of the old Betty an hour later, Reventlo viewed this relic with mixed emotions. "I'd forgot how narrow this hatch is," he said, looking back into the bowels of the craft. "The one I ferried in '46 seemed roomier."

"Maybe you weren't so roomy then," Benteen joked, steadying his arm.

"There's that," the Brit conceded. "At least I can still read the controls. This old bird is—well, if I didn't know better, the only proper phrase for it would be well-maintained. Now if only we can get her out of here in the same condition. What does Wade say about that?"

While Reventlo toured the innards of the Betty, Lovett and Myles had checked out that wall of cement that sealed the cave. Benteen and Chip, with Coop Gunther, had begun an inventory of the equipment stacked here and there along the walls. Hearing the question, Lovett made his way back through the obstacle course of wingtips. "I think I found the way Elmo got in. There's a place at ground level that used to be a hole up to about waist high. It's plastered up with mud and rubble and doesn't look like the rest; my guess is, old Elmo filled it in himself."

Reventlo *hmmmed* that over. "Perhaps we could begin by opening it up again."

"Yeah, but we don't know it was Elmo's work, and it's at foundation level. The Japanese were great at booby traps. If we dislodge one fragment too many, we could be sorry in a hurry."

"And what does that say about using explosives?"

"Myles doesn't think the wall was intended to be blown down," Lovett confided. "I'm inclined to agree. The American way is to push a button and blast everything halfway to Palau. The Japanese way—beats me," he admitted.

"Nibble it down," said the Brit. "For Japanese in those days, hand labor was still cheaper than anything else. Given a hundred soldiers with hammers and chisels, working around the clock—a couple of days at most. If we had enough sturdy hands or enough time . . . but perhaps Victor will have a solution."

"Sure he will," said Coop. "And it won't be quiet, and it won't be safe."

"I heard that," said Myles, his flashbeam preceding him across the floor. "Coop, don't forget I have as much to gain, or lose, from this as you do. You think I wanta drive a hunk of cement through a million-dollar bird?"

"Lemme put it this way," Coop replied; "there's six of us and six airchines. Whichever one you cover up the worst with rubble, bubba, that one's yours."

"Gentlemen, please," Reventlo said quickly.

"He's on," Myles said. "Like the man said, it may not be quiet, but I'll take that damn wall down like Joshua."

"Blowing your horn all the way," Coop grumbled.

"If we're going to stand around snarling at each other, why don't we do it outside, and save our batteries," Benteen said plaintively.

"I can't think why not," Reventlo sighed, and led them up those steps long ago chiseled into limestone.

Mindful of whoever might be watching them outside, they emerged cautiously and rolled the entrance cover back into place before finding places to lounge above the cement cliff, letting the sea breeze bathe their faces.

Chip, leaning out past the natural overhang face downward, seemed in such danger of falling that Lovett warned him back. The youth obeyed, then sat staring toward the distant surf, rubbing his fingers together. "Why," he asked suddenly, "would they have oiled the overhang?"

Myles thought it was to make it too slippery for snoopers. Coop suggested it was residue from dumping used engine oil after the cave was sealed. "Nips didn't waste oil, in my youth," Reventlo said. "They'd have filtered old oil and used it for lamps or cooking fires. They never wasted *any*thing. Ever see one of their dumping grounds? There was nothing anyone could possibly use again, ever. At the prison camp, they didn't mind if we picked through their dump; even the mice weren't interested."

Chip shrugged. "Maybe, but there it is; just like that layer over all their junk in the cave." And he wiggled his fingers for Lovett's inspection.

Lovett grasped the proffered hand; sniffed and rubbed Chip's fingertips. "Not much here, but—wait a sec." He tossed a perplexed frown in Coop's direction, then gave a wry grin. "Nah."

"Nah what," said the old fellow.

"Nah, even if they used to run up those engines inside, all that oil-rich exhaust couldn't get through solid cement."

"That's as good a 'nah' as I've heard recently," Coop confirmed. "Assuming the cement is solid all the way across."

Myles: "Why wouldn't it be?"

Chip: "Vents to get rid of exhaust smoke. Isn't that what we're talking about?"

"To vent that damned oil-rich exhaust," Lovett echoed, brightening. "Thank you, Chip. I couldn't get high enough on that cement wall to see, but there might be vents of some kind there."

"Should've asked us," Coop put in. "Mel tried to tell me a length of giant bamboo on the floor was a ladder, but damn if I can see how you'd shinny up using those little holes on the pole."

"Wade mightn't," said Reventlo. "But the Nips of my youth could stick a big toe in those holes and nip right up it, so to speak. Anyone care to try?"

Searching glances and negative shrugs said a little about caution and a lot about advancing age, because all eyes eventually fell on Chip. "Oh sure, try it on the dog," he complained. "I'm not keen on doing a face-plant off a bamboo pole in pitch dark, guys. Why not lower me on the outside instead with a rope?"

Reventlo's tone was emollient with sweet reason. "Because the rope's in my scooter, and we're up here."

Muttering, Chip disappeared down the trail alone, leaving the others to study the half-mile of jungle that must be cleared before they could tow any aircraft as far as the beach. Myles naturally preferred primacord. Lovett asked him how recently he had towed a multiton aircraft across three thousand feet of shattered tree trunks. Coop thought the earthmover might help.

Chip puffed back to his elders presently wearing a put-upon expression and, over his shoulder, a hank of the cargo plane's nylon tiedown rope. Myles surprised them all with a surge of expertise, tying several loops of one-foot diameter near one end, testing each loop using his foot as though in a stirrup. Then he did the same at the other end. Fifty feet of nylon had quickly become twenty feet of cordage loops. "There," he said, tossing the rig to Chip. "Footholds and handholds, and loops for us to belay you with. Grab hold, everybody."

It wasn't quite that easy, but by easing himself feetfirst backward over the cliff with a death-grip on one loop and his foot thrust into the last one, Chip allowed them to lower him from sight. Lovett was nearest to the edge, but they could all hear the youth a few feet below them. "Lower. Looower—another foot; okay." Bits of vegetation at the verge moved suggestively as he went on: "These little vines kind of hide the underlip but—*whoa,* shit," he exclaimed softly.

"Chip!" Lovett's imagination treated him to a vision of the youth dropping forty feet.

"It's cool, Pop," floated up to them. "I just tried to move some soft stuff like rope, and my hand went through. Jeez, Louise, that's some breeze," he went on. "There goes some more. It's solid in some places and stuffed with crud in between. You getting this?"

"Every word," Lovett replied, wishing he could see over the lip.

"The cement's about three inches thick at the top. It's not solid cement, there's little bits of rock and, uh, coral I guess, mixed in. Where I pushed the crud inside, it makes a slot I can't quite get my head into. But the air coming out of there smells like the cave. Ah—Pop? Can I come up now?"

They hauled away immediately, bringing a familiar grin into view. "That was way cool," Chip grinned, scrambling to his feet. "It's a vent, all right. I bet if you were inside, you could see the slot."

This proved to be the case, when Lovett and Reventlo followed Chip into the cave again. A shaft of light streamed across the cave's sloped ceiling, and at the thickened foundation of the cement wall they found what proved to be a mat of woven fibers Chip had dislodged from the vent.

Reventlo knelt to inspect it; grunted in satisfaction. "Old-time Japanese handwork, probably local bark fiber. In Burma we had to make pallets this way. I'd say it's as good a caulk for that vent as you'd need."

Chip, meanwhile, trained his flashbeam on the huge bamboo pole they had found earlier. "This is one humongous hunk of grass," he said to no one in particular. "Pop, I think I could make it up this thing if you guys can hold it in place."

"What changed your mind?"

"There's enough light now; I can make out the holes and get a grip with my fingers. I'm not saying I could stay up there long, but we could give it a try."

Erecting a thirty-foot pole in semidarkness was no simple task, but at its base the bamboo was the diameter of a cantaloupe, and it did not flex as Lovett had feared. He reminded himself that many an Asian skyscraper had been erected with bamboo scaffolds, and with Reventlo, gripped the pole as Chip began his ascent.

The youth started up three times, emitting surfer curses softly, laughing when he failed. On his fourth try, wiping his hands on Reventlo's jacket—"Oh, thanks for nothing," the Brit mumbled—he gripped harder with his legs and grunted his way up and up, finally becoming a half-illuminated figure almost at the limestone roof where it met the wall.

Soft fibers began to rain down on Lovett's face, followed by a roll of matting. More light flooded the cave's roof but, as Lovett dodged the mat, he allowed the pole to twist. "Hey, hold it still—Pop*lookout*," Chip cried, as Lovett stood manfully, blinking and half-blinded, hands up to break his grandson's fall.

Reventlo tried to prevent the pole's sidelong fall to no avail, cursing as it clattered down. Then, when Lovett realized that he was not to be hammered senseless by Chip's fall, both men stepped back to survey the tableau above them.

The second vent hole was larger, perhaps five feet wide, and instead of falling back, Chip Mason had managed to thrust head and shoulders through to the outside world. Now he hung there, legs limp, and whatever he was shouting, Lovett knew it was not a poem of ecstasy.

"Well, this is a proper bag of arseholes," Reventlo said, and watched in the half-light as Lovett raced toward the steps. "Where are you bound, Wade?"

"To lower the fucking rope," Lovett panted, already halfway up the incline. "Come on!"

Because the overhang placed the rope beyond Chip's grasp, it became an engineering problem. They tried to solve it this way; with all but the end loop loosened, they had nearly fifty feet of rope. Lovett thrust a leg through that loop to his crotch and made the others lie with legs braced, then had them lower him to Chip's level, a man's height below. With Chip's hands to push on his grandfather's knees, Lovett began to swing forward and back until Chip managed to grasp the rope above the loop. The crew above called out profane warnings that, as Chip hauled on the rope, their combined weights were too great to be held by three old farts and a woman. And the drop might not kill Lovett outright, but it would surely ruin his day.

"Then start lowering me. Make it slow," Lovett called, and told Chip to let the rope pass through his hands as his grandfather, feeling like a toy monkey on a string, slowly moved down the face of the cement wall.

After an endless minute or so, when Lovett was still nearly ten feet from the base, Reventlo called down: "That's the lot, Wade. Getting dicey up here."

"Pull me up, then," Lovett called.

A derisive hoot from Myles: "You a comedian, Lovett?"

He tried frantically to undo the knot at his crotch; no go. Then he began to wriggle until the loop was halfway along his thigh; breathlessly untied his boot one-handed; failed to pull it off.

Both Reventlo and Myles were calling for him to hurry now, and Lovett could feel the rope dropping in little jerks—from, he decided, big jerks. A younger man might have pulled up hand-overhand to free his leg, but that was no option for Lovett, who let go with his hands and swung head-downward, trying to urge his leg free. It caught, of course, at his boot, which began to slide off his foot.

"I'm sorry, Pop," was the call from Chip, who could see what was happening and was actually trying to help pull. Then the boot slid off and Lovett, by now dangling only six feet above the low vegetation, covered his head with his arms. He hit on his shoulders among shrubbery and rolled heavily away, gasping for breath. It didn't help when his own boot crowned him a good one.

Chip, still grasping the rope, was mostly supported by the wall, their plight still invisible to the belaying team. The youth called, "Can you haul in a few feet?"

In answer, Reventlo's group was able to recover some rope because Lovett was no longer a pendulum on the end of it. Lovett heard Coop call, "Whatever you do, do it fast." Feeling older than Elmo Benteen, Lovett staggered to his feet, chest heaving, black spots before his eyes. Then he saw Chip writhing like an eel, hauling furiously on the rope, and gravity helped as the youth half-fell from his perch, still gripping that rope, kicking away from the wall.

After that it was a fast swaying, hand-over-hand descent for Chip who dropped the final ten feet and bounced up again to face Lovett, merriment dancing in his eyes. "You can pull up the rope now," he called.

"No we can't. Love your confidence in us though," called Mel Benteen, as the rope slithered down to lie in a heap at Chip's feet. And briefly, the little man-made cliff echoed with inane cackles of relief from above and below.

With infuriating energy, the youthful Chip went bounding back up the trail, bubbling with ideas and optimism. Lovett got his boot on and started up right behind, but lagged a good deal off the pace, still aching from his fall but determined not to show it. He found his grandson chattering excitedly to the others, who lay about and wheezed at him like dotards, half amused, half angry.

"Your grandson," Reventlo said to Lovett, "bids us leap up and belay him again. Look at me," he continued, holding up a pair of reddened fists. "I can't unclench my hands, and this witless nipper is ready to have another go at it."

"I'll take him away and have him destroyed," Lovett grinned.

"Would you?" There was humor in Benteen's request, but it was lurking deep.

"At once," the Brit added, beginning to chuckle in spite of himself.

Coop only sat and looked at the youth, shaking his head and flexing his callused old hands. "Now what's this about knocking down the wall, kid?"

"I'm trying to tell you, it's not solid cement," Chip said, and recounted how, in his struggles, he had kicked fragments of the wall loose.

They had fruit and MRE lunches, but forgot them once they'd recovered enough to find anchoring vines for the rope—something they should have done previously. A stout stick tied at the rope's end made a seat for Chip, and knots made gripping easier so that a gangling youth might climb down a few feet and up again without exhausting his elders in the process.

When Chip explained his needs, the group made still another foray into the cave because no one wanted to return to the workshop, perhaps to be sidetracked by some request by Jean-Claude Pelele. Now the cave was only gloomy, not wholly dark. Oiled canvas bundles and brass-bound boxes lay near the mahogany workbench. The boxes contained old uniforms, meticulously packed. When unrolled, the bundles turned up tools and spare parts that mechanics had once used.

"This isn't bad stuff," Coop mused, testing a pair of cutters on a roll of braided, string-slender control cable. "Not like most of the pot-metal-and-tinfoil crap the Japs turned out before the war."

Reventlo, lounging beside him, knew why. "They had good metal, Coop; but it all went to the military. Shipping, tanks, aircraft, and good tools to maintain it. In Burma, our Nip guards were goggle-eyed at my father's tobacco packed in steel cans because of the implied waste. They made do with wood and oiled paper. But their rifle barrels were good steel. They didn't skimp on the essentials. These Tojos prove my point; they'd climb with the best, and in case you haven't noticed, they carry wing cannons."

"There's an idea," Chip offered. "Just aim at the top of the wall and shoot a few times."

"And the echo alone could bring this whole bloody cave down on us," Reventlo laughed. "You've never heard a forty mike-mike fired, I take it."

"No sir. But you've never hung four stories up on a little bitty rope and nibbled a cement wall down. Or have you?"

"Touché," said Reventlo, because Coop was laughing at their interchange.

Chip knew what he wanted, and no one was better equipped to provide it than handyman Coop Gunther. While Coop began to make a logger's loop splice in a length of cable and the others sought particular tools, Lovett attacked the upper end of that bamboo pole with a hacksaw. He brought the yard-long, three-inch-diameter tip to the workbench where Coop, using a miniature brace and bit Myles had located, bored holes at its midpoint. He passed the length of cable through, stuck the free end through the loop, then made a similar logger's splice in that free end.

Chip loosened his belt, passed the loop through it, retightened the belt. Now the bamboo cylinder was linked to him by six feet of cable and Chip announced that, given a maul or even a claw hammer, he was ready. The nearest thing they found was a metalworker's double-headed hammer, and they trooped back up the steps to emerge where, as Chip put it, they could all catch some rays while he vandalized the wall. The bamboo staff, as all knew, would be shoved to the vent and propelled through it to form a sort of grapple. By hauling in on the cable, Chip could swing back and forth enough to clamp an arm through the vent. Later they could improvise a better perch but this would give them an idea whether the wall could be nibbled away. And if it fell, Chip would sit safely above.

As Chip eased himself from sight on the rope, hammer stuck in his belt and the staff hanging free, Reventlo closed his eyes and faced the sun with a huge sigh. Myles stoked his pipe contentedly, and Benteen simply smiled toward the distant surf, perhaps savoring the Benteen legend. Coop watched the vines anchoring Chip.

Lovett rubbed the knot on his noggin and moved near the silent Reventlo, one ear cocked to judge Chip's progress. Only when he heard, "Sitting down now," did he release the breath he held.

"Penny for your thoughts, Cris," said Lovett softly.

For a moment it seemed the Brit had not heard. Then, "I'm wondering where I'll find another C-47, fast. And a seagoing barge big enough to ship a twin-engined Betty—minus the flying bomb strapped to her belly, mind you."

"Call Quinn for the money," Lovett shrugged.

"I very much doubt it'll stretch that far, Wade. Leasing may be the way to go; the barge will need a crew. I suppose I hadn't really planned for success of this magnitude."

From below, a hollow clatter and a "dammit." Lovett asked, "Will it take long? Given enough time, Pelele may decide to renegotiate the deal."

"It could take weeks, but he's not my chief worry. We'll need a barge crew we can trust, and piracy comes readily to mind. Some Lascar skipper could decide to relieve us of our cargo, once taken aboard. It's not unknown in these parts, even today."

The sunlight abruptly faded, and Lovett squinted toward a towering mass of cumulus to the west. "Weather front, from the look of it," he said idly.

"That's another thing," said Reventlo. "We're getting into the wet season. If we haven't had a typhoon or a serious blow by August it's a vintage year. Entire islands get swept into the Philippine Sea now and then, Wade. How would you like to be on a bargeload of flying antiques when it happens?"

"Isn't that over the Mindinao Deep? Let's talk about something else," Lovett pleaded, uneasy at the very idea of water seven miles deep. Nearby, from below, came an echoing *thok*.

"Swinging in now," Chip called.

"I'm thinking we might do better to disassemble the planes," Reventlo went on. "We could fit them on a smaller boat. Make several trips if necessary."

"To the Philippines, or Guam?"

"It's six hundred miles or so either way," the Brit said. "I used to fly Air Mike into Yap, which has its own commercial docks. And it's half the distance, due south of us. That's less than two days on the high seas by slow barge."

"Or an hour and a half by C-47," said Lovett.

"Not to mention forty-five minutes in a Tojo," Reventlo added wistfully.

"Fly a Tojo? You're . . ." Lovett began.

"I said not to mention that," Reventlo interrupted, deadpan. It did seem a stretch, even as a joke.

"Enough with the Benny Hill imitations already," said Lovett, grinning anyway. At that point he heard the first taps of a hammer echoing below, and knew that Chip had begun the long process of disinterring a treasure hidden for half a century.

In an hour, Chip had tapped away several square feet of the wall, enough that they could plan a more efficient attack on it. By now it was clear that the wall had been put up as two thin shells of ochre-tinted cement with a bit more mortar securing a lot of rubble—bits of coral, wood, even bamboo segments—between the inner and outer shells. The fibrous parts of that rubble made up the only internal reinforcement they had found. That this tender barrier had stood so long was a marvel attributed to Japanese cleverness. The ochre was its crowning achievement, lending subtle shadings of color to the wall that had made it seem natural.

All agreed that they should bring more tiedown ropes the next day. By anchoring ropes outside and passing them through the vents, they could create loop ladders with stick seats to be climbed from inside the cave. Then, Lovett and perhaps Myles could join Chip in knocking away that wall piecemeal. Myles tried to hide his disappointment at being denied his own brand of demolition work and grudgingly admitted it was too risky. Primacord might be fun, but money was his toy of choice. In the interests of bringing delicate aircraft out intact, quietly tapping away that wall from the inside was the only way to go.

When the first rain squall sent them all inside the cave, Chip announced that he'd done all the dangling he could for one day. "I'm thrashed, Pop," he said, combing cement dust from his hair with dirty fingers, as rain pelted the foliage outside the cave entrance. "The wall gets a little thicker, the lower down you go."

"Probably a foot thick at the bottom," Lovett said. "As a structure, it makes sense." They descended the steps again to the cave floor, where Coop was taking a more thorough inventory of the place. The cave was still shadowy but, with a hole the size of a telephone booth near top center of the wall, they could dispense with flashlights. They could also grumble that, as soon as they began to bring the wall down, errant wind gusts speckled the nearest Tojo with raindrops. "Principle of physics," Lovett observed; "water flows to where you're working."

Before leaving the cave, Reventlo called his fellows to that spare engine. "What do you think about moving this little beauty out," he said.

"Little, hell," Lovett responded. Its diameter was roughly four feet, its outlines that of a huge basket with cooling fins staggered about its rim. "Maybe not as big as some of ours but it'll go a half-ton at least."

"You didn't think we'd leave it," Myles said.

"I mean, chaps, move it right away; ship it in the C-47 when I take off—which I intend to do as soon as humanly possible," Reventlo reminded them. "Just in case we should need more financing, I cannot imagine a more tantalizing proof of what we've got here."

"Not 'til we've punched a hole to get it out," said Coop. "An extra day, even if I cannibalized the APU cart for a dolly."

Reventlo's glance was sharply hopeful. "You can do that?"

Coop snorted. "Is the Pope Polish?"

"Then let's get to it tomorrow. Wade, I trust you can persuade your master mechanic, Pilau, to lend that half-track lorry of his for an hour."

"It's Merizo's vehicle, but we can find some excuse," Lovett said. "Right now let's get those fiber mats unrolled topside, so we can tie them in place over the vents. And then—I don't know about you, but I'm going to sleep for a week."

Climbing the steps for the last time that day with one end of a mat in his arms, he saw Myles move near Chip, who was carrying the other end of the mat. The survivalist seemed troubled. He said, suspiciously, "The Pope's a Polack?"

"For a long time now," Chip said. "You're kidding, right?"

"Yeah. Yeah, I knew that," said Myles, and hurried on.

A moment later, Chip glanced back at his grandfather. "Don't they have newspapers in Texas? This man's a published writer, Pop!"

"Some guys are pretty focused, Chip. Vic Myles is just focused tighter than most."

"Or more loosely wrapped," the youth said.

It was on Lovett's tongue to caution Chip about showing scorn to his elders, but he kept silent. Such things had a way of working themselves out.

20

Lovett awoke after dark in his room, as freshets of rain swept the roof. It was not the rain that waked him; in the light of a kerosene lamp an arm's length away, Chip was in whispered, urgent discussion with little Keikano. Lovett lay quietly and listened. It seemed they hadn't been talking long.

"Knocking it down? Is there no way to repair it now?" Keikano's whisper was almost a squeak, as if agonizing over what he had set in motion.

"They don't want to, Kei." *Now it's "Kei,"* thought Lovett. *As in Kate, as in kiss-me-Kate. This little prettyboy is definitely romancing my grandson. Or vice-versa. And Chip seems to be comfortable with it. Well, he's old enough to make his own decisions.* "That's the only way to remove the planes," Chip went on. "I thought you knew that."

"I did. I—had not realized how serious this would be."

"To Pelele? Merizo? Who?"

"They? They are in the village planning the leadership games. I am afraid I will lose the respect of—Fundaborans. I am afraid that—I am afraid," he ended simply.

"When we go, we take you along," Chip whispered. "What's to fear?"

"But I will return. It is a matter of respect. You cannot understand this, Chip Mason."

"I can if you explain it. Try me."

A silence. Then, "I cannot. I have already done a terrible thing."

"Is that what you think, or what other people think?"

"Others, certainly. I—do not know what I think. I did what I thought was right. Now I do not know how to undo it."

"You can't shove the Genie back in the bottle, Kei," Chip whispered, not unkindly.

"Jeannie? A girl's name. Your Jeannie?"

"Uh—no. It's a kind of magic person that lives in a bottle and gives you what you ask for. And you'd better be sure you want it. I'm not certain I can explain it."

"You see? My problem, too."

"Are you saying you're in danger, Keikano?"

"Not to my body." A half-snicker, almost a chortle: "At most, nothing that will not heal. But I wish there were something I could offer your elders, some trade. Pearls; I could put my hands on many of those."

"Your pearls, Kei?"

"Well . . . what would they care?"

"Uh-uh. No, you're trying to get yourself seriously killed, Kei. Anyway, I know our guys, and they're amped on these planes. They wouldn't care if you owned your weight in pearls. I'm sorry, but that's how it is. And you helped work up that agreement with Jean-Claude yourself; those planes are ours now."

"Your grandfather is a reasonable man," Keikano began again.

"Not where those old planes are concerned. He'd sooner die than give them up now. The others, too."

"I hope you are not foretelling his future," Keikano replied.

"Someone might try to kill him?"

"It is possible; him or any of you. I hope I can keep that from happening. Your people could bring awful power to bear. That would be understood. I hope," the whisperer hesitated, then added, "There is an old saying: *'When you wake a sleeping giant, you may fill him with a terrible resolve.'* "

"I heard that old saying somewhere. It's not Pelele or his guys, is it?"

Another silence. "You are not going to leave the cave in peace," Keikano whispered dolefully. "What is done, is out of the Jeannie-bottle. I see that now. Chip, there are many ways to urge your Jeannie back into her bottle. I must not say more than this: all of you be very careful in the cave, especially when I am not with you, from this day; what you move, where you step. I fear for you."

"Booby traps, you mean."

"I do not know how boobies are trapped. I know that if your

Jeannie has accidents, she might want to go safely back into her bottle."

Now abandoning the whisper, Chip laughed gently, his voice gruff, almost manly. "I keep telling you she's not my genie, Kei. I don't even know if genies *have* sex."

"Then how do they," Keikano began in puzzlement.

Chip broke in with, "I didn't mean that. I meant—huh, maybe that's what they do in those bottles, how would I know? Anyhow, I haven't got a Jeannie at home, either; it's just an expression. Okay?"

"I am amped," said Keikano softly. Deep inside Wade Lovett, something small and vulnerable began to shrivel.

"I'll pass the word on," Chip promised. "Hey, where were you all day; in the village?"

"The village, yes," Keikano agreed. "And I must go back again now. You have no idea," he said sadly. Then: "What is that thing you do with your hand?"

"Pick my nose," Chip laughed. "You mean this," he added. Lovett heard a mild slap of hands and knew that his grandson was instructing this fey little fellow in the ways of the High Five.

From near the doorway: "Dangle free," from Keikano.

"That's 'hang loose.' You, too," Chip said, and released a long sigh. After a moment he said, "Pop?"

Lovett rolled over, yawned for effect. "Yeah, Chip."

"You weren't asleep," the youth accused. "How much did you hear?"

"All of it, I think. That is one troubled youngster."

"He's a mixed batch, all right. Mostly he seems worried about us. Man, I am flogged, hammered, thrashed." Chip leaned over and blew out the lamp.

"We used to say we felt shot at and missed, and shit at and hit," Lovett chuckled. "More fine nuances for your mom's society gatherings."

"I'll be sure and use it for von Wart, just to watch his expression," said Chip, sounding half-asleep.

"One thing, Chip: how'd you know I wasn't asleep? I was inert as a statue."

"That's why, Pop. You roll around when you sleep like you were practicing for the hammer throw. In the past ten years you've kicked my slats out a dozen times. It's always been a mystery to me how you can burn up mifty krillion calories all night long and wake up full of energy."

"You never mentioned that," Lovett said.

"What for? A man can't help what he is," said Chip, mumbling it. "G'night, Pop."

Lovett said gently, in an old exchange lovingly quoted, "Sleep tight, Chip." But Chip needed no encouragement for that.

Their work parties changed for the next two days, Coop Gunther reconditioning the LeTourneau with Pilau's help, Mel Benteen serving as his combination go-fer and translator to Pilau. This was a stratagem deftly chosen by Reventlo for her safety, after Lovett reported on the booby-trap scenario. Using two motor scooters, the cave party carried hammers and other tools from the maintenance sheds, tiedown ropes, and gourds of water to the cave's hidden mouth. After pulling away mats heavy and damp with residual rain, they set about tying cordage loops, fitting stout sticks, and sending Chip down to insert the rope ladders so that they dropped down inside the wall.

They moved into this phase of the job with care, assuming now that someone else besides Keikano knew about the cave. Myles prodded suspiciously at anything that looked as if it might be rigged for unpleasant surprises. Nothing blew up or shot darts at them, and while Chip proceeded to the top of the wall, the three older men began to excavate that breast-high plug of debris at the lower edge of the same wall. It turned out to be mostly a local form of adobe—mud, weeds, and bark fiber. It turned to clods quickly, and before noon it was only a memory as they continued to widen the hole, spitting dust and confirming that the wall was over a foot thick at its base. When the new passage was five feet wide and six high—Coop had warned that the engine's dolly would require extra headroom—they broke for MRE lunches.

Squeezing cold pork chow mein directly from its plastic pack into his mouth, Lovett essayed a snile—something between a sneer and a smile—in commentary. "Like eating Jell-O that's been lost in the jungle for thirty years," he added.

"Quit bitching, it beats hell out of going hungry. You'll need your strength, hanging on that rope," Myles replied, through a mouthful of chili with beans.

"Tomorrow, maybe. After lunch I'll try to disconnect the APU from that cart. Coop isn't the only A & P mechanic around here. That leaves you and Cris with Chip on the ropes."

"Chip on the ropes," said the youth. "That's about the size of it. No, I'm okay. Really," he said, noting Lovett's concerned glance.

"Now Lovett's giving orders," Myles said to Reventlo.

"Sounds sensible to me, Victor," said the Brit. "Or would you rather I gave the quote order unquote?"

"At least it's the chain of command we agreed on, and I still don't fuckin' like it."

"I'm not much of a wrench Boffin. I doubt you are," Reventlo explained with the patience of a man knowing he should not have to make such explanations. "Three ropes, three men. What different order would you give, Victor?"

Thus challenged, Myles sucked more of his lunch down before replying: "You and the kid on ropes, Lovett playing with his Jap tinkertoy, and me marking the trees and stuff we gotta take out to move a half-ton cartload of engine as far as the road. How's that for orders?"

While Chip kept his head down, unwilling to engage in this petty bickering, Lovett and Reventlo swapped gazes. "Works for me," Lovett shrugged.

"So long as you're, ah, gainfully employed," Reventlo said to Myles.

As the afternoon wore on, Myles proved equal to his self-appointed task, cutting small blazes on trees and using a shovel to ascertain where limestone bedrock was near the surface under an accumulation of only fifty years of decaying humus. With a ground-level entrance now, and another of the shovels they'd brought to the cave, they developed a routine. As they worked across and down the jagged upper lip of the false wall, Chip and Reventlo called for rest breaks now and then. When they did, Lovett left the cart and took a shovel to the growing heap of rubble that ranged along the wall outside. It would have to go sooner or later anyway.

A simple calculation gave Reventlo a rough idea of the time they'd need to finish. The wall was something less than a hundred feet across, slightly over thirty high. Three thousand square feet of wall to demolish, and they'd spent a total of roughly sixteen man-hours hanging from ropes to take down about three hundred square feet of wall, yielding a guess of a hundred fifty man-hours before that primitive hangar lay wide open to view. The job was doable, Reventlo said, during the time he'd be gone.

At last, when the sun dropped below tree height and the cave became gloomier, Reventlo eased himself down the loops again, followed by the equally dust-covered Chip. Sweat had carved rivulets down the dust coatings on their faces, as Lovett straightened from his own work and accompanied them outside for a rest. "I find my body a rickety sort of construction," said the Brit, pulling off his gloves. "Don't bruit that about to La Benteen, there's a good lad."

Lovett only grinned understandingly but, "She could be your daughter," Chip said in surprise.

"Not in this incarnation. I quail at the thought," Reventlo laughed. "I met Elmo's wife once, thirty years ago; didn't know she had a daughter then. Avrile Benteen was an island girl, the purest article. Body of a goddess, mind of a clam. And she chewed betel nut, which places Elmo among the very bravest of men, or the most desperate. Chipper lad, do you know what betel nut portends?"

As he admitted that he didn't, Chip squandered a gourdful of water on his hair and face. "Why do I get the feeling you're going to tell me?"

"Because your education is not complete until you've seen it. Haven't spotted any devotees here but—very well. The betel palm has a nut, mottled brownish, hard as my—um, fairly hard. In Asia and Oceania they boil the nut, slice and dry it, then wrap it in a kind of leaf. Then they chew it."

Chip squinted quizzically. "Candy?"

"More like snuff; alkaloids, y'know. Calming influence. Half a billion people use it, I would guess."

"You're hiding a punch line, Mr. Reventlo. Cancer, I bet."

"No. It merely induces the user to spit vast streams of red spittle, turns the teeth black as a coal-scuttle, and dyes the mouth and gums a nice, horrid brick red. Makes a young girl look as if she's been eating the hemorrhoids out of a camel. Fair takes your breath away, it does. Your appetites for dalliance or dinner, too. There's a goodly number of ladies who may be my daughters and not know it, but none of them could, by any stretch of the imagination, be Avrile Benteen's. You may trust me on this," Reventlo said with dark assurance.

Lovett chuckled softly and endorsed Reventlo's account. "Maybe that's why so many people do it with their eyes closed," he offered.

"I would hazard a guess," said the Brit, "that Elmo and Avrile pioneered the practice." A shudder. "Let us pass on to some more agreeable topic."

"Looks like Myles is knocking off," Lovett observed.

"I said, something *more* agreeable," Reventlo groused, but managed a wave and smile for the survivalist.

"You guys work fast," Myles said, scanning the wall as he approached, nodding his approval so that drops of sweat fell from his beard. "Listen, we won't have to do much blasting to clear the airstrip. Soil's so thin there, most of the trees and stuff can barely get a grip. All we gotta do is put fifty men to work pulling stuff down to drag away."

"Or one belly-scraping LeTourneau," Lovett observed. "We won't have to renegotiate for that."

"Man, what a D-8 Caterpillar could do," Myles said.

"It's a nice thought, but even if I found one I'm not sure I could get it here," said Reventlo.

"Do what you can," Lovett said, brushing off his trousers, collecting empty water gourds.

"But first I must launch from Fundabora. If you don't mind a new directive, lads, we should spend tomorrow clearing a path for that nice new antique engine."

Myles: "Getting antsy, Cris?"

Reventlo: "If you think I'm anxious, try and imagine the mindset of a certain digger in Alice Springs. They've heard of handcuffs in the Northern Territory, too." His tone said he was half in earnest.

So their last hour of labor that day was spent learning how to clear undergrowth from bedrock. It appeared that they might clear a narrow path as far as the road in one day, provided they could use their crew from the maintenance sheds.

They found Coop and Benteen already picking at the buffet provided nightly in the councilhouse lobby, using sections of some broadleaf as plates. Evidently the staff had decided to provide more everyday fare on this night. When Benteen referred to the leaf as breadfruit, Reventlo objected that breadfruit leaves had fingerlike projections.

"At the end of the branch, yes," Benteen said. "Not at the base."

"I won't debate you on islander expertise," the Brit smiled.

"I was raised on breadfuit, *in* breadfruit, and *under* breadfruit," she confided. "A shady tree that makes good canoes, bark fiber mats, a nice bland mush like yam, and a decent place-setting if you don't like washing dishes. Try it like poi," she said, using two fingers to spoon some of the stuff to her mouth.

Chip pointed to another mass of mushy food in a huge clamshell. "I thought this was breadfruit," he said.

"Taro's a root," she said; "dug up like turnips, only better."

"Great. There's paste, and there's paste," he said.

"I forgot; the breadfuit sap makes glue, too," she said, laughing. "Ignore the taro and breadfruit, then, and have some fried bananas."

"That's different; *fried* paste," Chip said with patently false enthusiasm, reaching for a handful of some crackly protein.

"Oh, shut up and eat your grasshoppers," Benteen said, giggling as Chip snatched his hand back. "Use your eyes, Chip. Those are just funny-looking shrimp, actually," she went on, popping one into her mouth. "And this is crab over here, and there's coconut milk, too. Or would you rather tear into an MRE?"

"Gah," said Lovett, helping himself to the taro. "I'll take these Guamanian grits, thanks."

They took their meals out to the C-47 to discuss their progress. Coop brightened at the idea of working in the cave. "I won't mind a break from the sheds," he said. "Couple of days more and we may have Benteen trying out the LeTourneau. Meanwhile the sheds are like an oven in the afternoon and I'm welding in there. 'Course, where our friend Pilau is, comic relief ain't far off."

"We're going to need him and that half-track," said Lovett, "so be nice to him."

"That's getting easier to do," Coop replied, "even though there's dumb, and there's dumber, and then there's Pilau."

"What's he done now," Lovett asked.

"Not as dumb as Coop thinks," Benteen countered. "That pluperfect little bureaucrat Merizo has been lusting after the scooters; you knew that." Lovett nodded assent and she went on: "So this morning he came to the sheds with a couple of his TV wrestlers and insisted we show him how to drive a Cushman. So I had to leave Coop to give lessons."

"Nothing wrong with that," Myles said.

"I suppose not, but given the fact that we know how Pilau got those stripes on his back and legs, you can't expect me to enjoy Merizo's enjoyment when he's ripping up and down the drive at top speed with me for a passenger."

"I'm jealous," said Reventlo, grinning.

"Oh, yes, he looks for bumps. I think he likes it when my front bounces off his back."

"The cad," Reventlo said, enjoying himself immensely. "And he dresses as such a gentleman! I take it he didn't crash and burn with you."

"Not with me," Benteen said, now smiling at her thoughts. "But he said he'd be needing to take a drive alone later. And he did."

Reventlo blinked. "And," he prompted.

"And his bullyboys bodily carried the Cushman back to us later," Coop put in, "front fork bent to shit, headlight busted, splashguards like pretzels. I'm fixing it, though. Seems that Merizo had driven out to the village and was terrorizing everybody for about thirty seconds—until he decided to turn around and do it again. For that, he had to use the brake."

By now, Lovett had already begun to laugh. "And Pilau had oiled it again," he managed to say.

"You can really kill a punch line, Wade," said Coop. "That's what happened. You could see Merizo was cruising for a bruising the way he gunned away from the shed. And he got his bruising; went ass over teakettle right in front of his peons in the village, laid himself out cold. I checked the scooter out and asked Pilau the big question. He denied it, but hell, I could see and smell the evidence. I backed him up anyhow; Benteen convinced the big guys that Merizo's brakes had just plain failed. Nobody's fault that Merizo got a broken arm."

"I love it," Benteen said. "It was not an innocent mistake. Pilau gets his revenge, and his victim's none the wiser."

Reventlo, the only one to hear of Merizo's spill without obvious satisfaction, shook his head. "I'm glad you're glad, but before you shred your sleeves laughing up them, remember we've been warned that someone may be planning nasty surprises for us. What if Merizo is behind that after all?"

"Our side got in a preemptive strike," Myles grunted.

"But not a decisive one, which would only leave him more determined," said Reventlo.

"He won't have much time for that for a while," Benteen said. "Cris, you have to understand that these people are getting ready for a big annual celebration, and Merizo is the ringmaster. I don't think Jean-Claude will take kindly to excuses, merely because Merizo made marmalade of himself. As long as he can breathe, he still has his job to do."

"I hope you're right," said the Brit, who then described the work already done at the cave, and what remained to be done. He ended with, "If there's one good thing to come from this public-school foolishness of Pilau's, it's this: we shall have the use of that half-track, without question."

"Say again," Coop requested.

Reventlo's smile was bland. "Even if Pilau *didn't* sabotage the scooter, your claiming he did would send him poling off toward the horizon on the nearest raft."

"You mean blackmail him," Chip said, not too pleased with the idea.

"Reason with him," the Brit amended.

"Make him an offer he can't refuse," Chip insisted, with a glum expression. "I saw the movie. That sucks."

Lovett coughed for attention. "The question is whether we want to be perfectly circular assholes about this."

"The question," Myles corrected, "is, do we want six or eight or ten million bucks worth of airplanes, or don't we?"

Reventlo turned toward the bearded Texan. "Victor, I have never heard you so eloquent. My answer is in the affirmative."

Lovett felt troubled knowing that if it came to a vote he, too, would side with Reventlo and Myles on this. To salve his conscience he said, "Look, let's catch our fly with honey if we can. Let me talk to Pilau; if we select some heavy stuff in the cave and tell him we need to move it to the sheds, and then divert him to the plane to load that engine, we might avoid bad feelings."

"You mean hold back the threat as an ace in the hole," Myles said.

"That's not what I meant, but it might work out that way," Lovett admitted. He could tell that Chip was making some pitiless judgments about them all, now, and wondered how he was judging his own grandfather.

It was decided that, because the entire crew should be able to create the necessary path in a day, they would suspend work in the sheds. They would ask Pilau and Keikano to help, citing the movement of heavy hardware to the sheds. No one had seen the schoolteacher that day, but perhaps he'd been pressed into service for the upcoming celebration. Usually, said Chip, Keikano dropped in for a friendly evening chat. He might even be waiting now.

Another brief rain squall found the councilhouse later, but Keikano did not. Vic Myles dictated his version of recent events in a whisper while Chip dutifully fed them into his computer and Lovett visited Reventlo's room. Though he sensed an odd reserve in Benteen and the Brit, Wade Lovett didn't tumble to its meaning at first. Finally, after Reventlo used the phrase "odd man out" for the second time, he realized that he was the odd man, and that his old buddy Cris was wishing he were out.

Lovett returned to his room thinking that over, realizing that if Mel Benteen was to develop a soft spot for any of them, it would most likely be Reventlo whose spot might not be soft, but the old boy claimed it was still dependable. Chip was alone now. Sighing, Lovett arranged his mosquito net. "Ready for lamps out?"

"Sure," said Chip. When all was in darkness, the youth said, "Pop?"

"Drop it on me," said Lovett.

"Pilau's a good guy. He shouldn't get his butt in a crack."

"I know that." Chuckling: "But he should be more cautious, a man his age."

"Like you and the others? Uh-huh. Anyhow, you did the right thing. Thanks."

"You mean as an asshole I'm not quite complete?"

"Well—not as perfectly tubular as some I could name. You still have some sharp corners."

"Speaking of sharp, where d'you suppose Keikano is?"

"I'm clueless, Pop. And I kinda miss him."

"I know you do." Lovett would have liked to say more.

His tone must have said that, for Chip laughed softly. "Don't sweat it. I know what you think, and to some degree you're right, I guess. We'll talk about it sometime."

And long after Chip's snores signaled the sleep of the not-quite-innocent, Lovett lay awake wondering what he would say when "sometime" came.

21

It was only because Coop had suggested pulling down some of the shallow-rooted little palms with rope the next morning that Chip scrambled up the incline at the cave to untie their ropes. And if Chip hadn't found one anchoring root almost completely severed, somebody could've taken a nice long fall the next time he climbed that rope. As soon as Victor Myles heard of it, he huffed up the slope to make an expert appraisal.

The root hadn't been cut, Myles noted as he studied this subtle sabotage; it had been worn away, abraded as if by natural causes. But Lovett had checked the anchorage the day before. The abrasion was all new—overnight, in fact. That's when Myles decided to take the interior steps back down, rolling that cement cover plate away from the upper cave opening; and *that* is when Chip walloped Victor Myles aside with a body block, his warning shout half-lost in the ensuing slither and a rattling crash like that of a dozen bowling balls.

"Goddammit, kid, what're you trying to do?" Myles's glare was furious as the youth pulled himself off the older man's chest.

"Trying to keep you alive," said Chip, pointing to the pile of stones, some the size of a melon, that now rested in front of the cave opening. Trickles of dirt dribbled tardily from above. "Sorry 'bout that, Mr. Myles. Next time you want me to think it over first?"

Myles, grumbling about smartass kids, dusted himself off and then attended to this second little surprise. Having heard the commotion, Lovett hurried up the slope in time to see Myles identify the trigger stick. While Chip explained what had happened and helped

Lovett roll those little boulders down the slope, Myles studied the telltale wooden piece, something even simpler than a hunter's deadfall trap. He displayed the hardwood rod with its short *Y* tip. "He hid that critical rock under those big leaves and balanced it so it was barely held in place by the *Y* end of the stick, with the stick hidden under leaves and its plain end wedged against the cement cover. The other rocks were stacked behind the first one. Move the cover a little; stick comes loose; first fuckin' rock comes down. Followed by the others. Slick," he commented, hurling the telltale trigger rod far out over the cliff. "If you didn't know what to look for, you'd think this was accidental. But the little fucker didn't count on Vic Myles," he said to himself, as if testing the phrase for his publisher.

Lovett and Chip traded jaundiced glances. Because there was no point in reminding the survivalist that his survival had depended on the instant reaction of a youth, Lovett said, "Why not 'big fucker,' Vic?"

" 'Cause Kei-friggin' kano *is* a little fucker."

Chip was appalled. "You're sure it was Keikano?"

"It was somebody small enough that he couldn't lift anything bigger than about fifty pounds. Big guy would'a balanced a single rock that'd squash you like a bug. And who do we know that knows about the cement cover? Keikano." He lowered his head so that he had to look up to meet Chip's eye; took a pace to one side; took one to the other. *He's wasting his time*, thought Lovett. *Chip probably never saw Perry Mason on TV*. "Like Agatha Christie proved a hundred times, it's always the one guy it couldn't possibly be. And who's the last guy on earth we'd suspect?"

"Why, uh—you are," Chip said pleasantly.

"Get serious," said Myles.

"Seriously then," said Lovett with some heat, "that's the silliest deduction I ever heard. You're offering drawing-room mysteries as the real world, Vic. Sure, it could've been Keikano, but somehow I doubt it."

"Somehow he doubts it," Myles said to the sky. "Why?"

"Because it might just as easily have been Chip who moved the cement cover," Lovett said, the implication making him unwilling to meet his grandson's gaze.

"Yeah," Myles said, an unpleasant smile tugging at the edge of his beard. "That's a complication—maybe one he didn't think of."

"Riiight. Okay, you just keep your eye on Keikano, Myles, but for God's sake don't let him know what you think. If you're right it puts him on guard, and if you're not it could drive away the best friend we've got here."

"Shit, your kid couldn't drive him away with a stick—but from what I've seen, he probably ought to. Whaddaya say about that, kid?"

"Nothing you want to hear. Let's hope these are the only traps *Keikano* set," Chip replied, stressing the schoolteacher's name.

"Most sensible thing I've heard today," said Myles, who then stumped off down the interior steps alone.

When he had gone, Chip glanced back at the foliage where those stones had been balanced so perilously. "You think Keikano would've done that, Pop?"

"Not for a second. There's a kind of paranoid logic in what Myles says, but it'd be simpler to have poisoned our food."

"But then there'd be nobody to fly him off the island," Chip reflected.

"Spoken like a true paranoid," Lovett said, and winked. "Let's get these ropes loose; I can see Reventlo standing down there, waiting with all the patience of Captain Bligh."

Reventlo kept a jaundiced expression on first hearing what Myles and Chip had to say, but took the small acts of sabotage more seriously when Lovett confirmed that serious injury could have resulted. Sighing, he said that he'd thought about a rotating sentry duty, and that perhaps they should do more than just think about it. Then they fell to work on the cart path.

By making the path somewhat sinuous to follow the path of least work, they saved a great deal of time, using machetes against shallow roots as they pulled a few young trees down and cleared underbrush. Coop Gunther had decided that he would try to use that APU to start the LeTourneau, and loosely reattached it to the cart with two bolts. "This load only weighs about four hundred pounds. But if we get it as far as the road, we'll have a good idea whether we can do the same with that big engine," he said.

And they found a few soft spots on the way, and left Mel Benteen to fill them in by hand, embedding flat limestone slabs in the thin soil. By midafternoon the crew had trundled the cart near enough to the road that Coop reckoned Pilau and his half-track could do the rest.

Except that, when they puttered back to the councilhouse leaving

Reventlo and Myles to off-load the APU from its cart, no one could locate Pilau around the building; nor Jean-Claude nor Merizo, for that matter. "He's probably in the village. We should've asked first," said Benteen, when the maintenance sheds proved untenanted.

"Then we'll ask second," said Coop. "Merizo will know where he is."

"Merizo may not be in high spirits right now," Benteen cautioned. "He should be in the village, too, and it occurs to me that we really ought to make a sympathy call. I hope I can keep a straight face."

"Let's give him a bottle of scotch," Chip said.

"Jean-Claude will only take it away from him," Benteen objected.

"So? Not our problem, and we get two good-guy points instead of one," Chip said. When Lovett grinned and nodded, the youth trotted away toward the C-47.

Hands on hips, Benteen watched him enter the aircraft. "There goes a budding diplomat," she murmured at length.

"Careful how you talk about my grandson," Lovett joked.

"You could use some of his subtlety," she said, with a sidelong glance.

"Meaning?"

"Oh—he knows how to intuit how people will react. Call it a sensitive nature."

Thinking of his concern over Chip's odd relationship, Lovett bristled. "Bullshit! I'm sensitive. Jesus Christ, Benteen, I'm sensitive as hell!"

"Toss in a few more ear-burners while you're at it, Wade," called Coop, who'd been standing nearby quietly. "That'll convince 'er real good."

Lovett turned to his old buddy. "Benteen *wrote* the great international dictionary of curses," he said hotly.

Her reply was soft: "Do as I say, not as I do."

"If I want to be a goddamn diplomat?"

"If you'd like to be more—attractive to people," Benteen replied so gently that Coop could not have heard, then waved as Chip came in view again.

Thunderstruck by all that this might possibly imply, Lovett did not say another word until the four of them had scootered to the village, and the festive changes in the place made him forget Benteen for the moment.

Everyone, including the children, seemed to have an appointed job in turning the village's central plaza into a showplace like a primitive county fair. Lovett realized that, as an annual event, it had developed its traditions: a huge tree trunk brought in for some unknown purpose; a circular area the size of a large room with a rim of stones that were being whitewashed by children; even sets of steep bleacher seats flanking the plaza, made from poles lashed to more poles.

"I hope Jean-Claude doesn't expect people to climb up in those things without footrests or seatbacks," Coop said, indicating the bleachers.

"Jean-Claude expects his villagers to do whatever he wants," Benteen said. "If he wants them to stand balanced on one foot atop those stupid poles, then they'd better learn. Ah, there's Merizo, with those women braiding cordage." They left the Cushmans and, taking the bottle from Chip, Lovett cradled it in his arm. He even remembered to put a concerned look on his face as they approached the frog-voiced little man. *Sensitive, that's me*, he thought.

The village women sat beside piles of brown bark fiber, twisting the stuff into skeins of thick rope that lay in their laps. Merizo was inspecting the work of each, greatly hampered by the fact that his right forearm was swollen to the size of Popeye's, cradled in a mat slung from his neck. If Merizo was sepia, his arm was polychrome. He'd picked up a few scabs on his cheek and chin as well. The hand of his good arm looked as if it had lost three rounds against a rotary grinder.

After seating herself cross-legged in approved fashion, Benteen looked up at Lovett. Very fast, she said, "Tell me something to say, oh glorious male. I'm only a poor female vessel, remember."

Lovett nodded at Merizo and said, in sepulchral tones, " 'Twas brillig, and the slithy toves did somethingorother and gimbal on the whatzis, and I forget what the borograves did but it was probably a felony."

She gave him an adoring look and said, "Thank you, Mr. Sensitivity. Make me laugh now and I will dice your cojones." Then she put on a long face and to Merizo she began, "Me fella stop longhouse belong Jean-Claude, lookoutim Merizo. Savvy Merizo bigbig hurt." There was more, most of it gibberish to Lovett, but he understood her final, "You awright?"

Merizo was not all right by a damned sight, and told her so for minutes, full of gestures with his good arm.

"He says he hurts like hell. That Cushman was out to get him and only his mana, big spirit medicine, saved him. Says you must paint the bad machine with evil dots—could be an old reference to smallpox—so he'll know which one to avoid," she finished.

"Tell him okay, but they all have the same evil tendencies, and that we've brought our own medicine for him, out of the goodness of our sensitive hearts," Lovett said, and offered up the scotch.

Merizo, who knew from experience what was in that bottle, brightened considerably as he took it while Benteen translated. He made as if to open it with his teeth while Lovett, with gestures, made him understand that it was exclusively for Merizo and his arm. Soon Merizo had taken a healthy gulp, and then another, eyes watering from the sting.

"Coo-wull," Chip murmured. "This is one bottle that the big guy won't get."

"Give him a little time for it to take hold," Coop Gunther said. "Ask him how the big annual bellyrub is coming along."

This she did, and translated the answers. "It might help put him in a better frame of mind," Chip said presently, "if you told him Mr. Gunther's putting their big earthmover back in shape." Which Benteen did, earning a faint smile from Merizo who vented a subterranean belch and swigged again.

It did not take long, Lovett saw, to fill a guy of Merizo's size to the scuppers. He turned as if to leave and then said abruptly to Benteen, "Okay, now I have my sudden afterthought. Tell him we intend to salvage some of those old airplane parts, stuff we found in the jungle, but we must transfer some heavy parts to the sheds to make the, what is it, bigbig machine, to run. We need the half-track and Pilau to drive it," he urged.

Benteen managed to convey their wants. Merizo waved vaguely toward the jungle and used Pilau's name in his reply, then stoppered the scotch bottle and shoved it into his waistband. When he reached down to grasp a length of cordage, he missed it twice.

"He's a busy man, he says," Benteen reported. "Let's go before he falls on his face and decides to have spots painted on you, Wade."

As they strode off Coop asked, "All I wanta know is, do we get the floggin' half-track?"

"We get it if we can find it," she said. "Pilau's with a work crew up the creek a ways, cleaning the pond."

Soon, proceeding on the scooters, they noticed fresh treadmarks in the rutted track near the creek. It wasn't long before they found Pilau by the pond, tinkering with the half-track's engine. To Lovett it was transparently obvious that Pilau was working hard to keep from working. Four villagers pulled, shoveled, and carried an assortment of branches and muck from chest-deep water to be deposited in the jungle. Though smeared with yuchh they did not seem to begrudge Pilau his apartheid; perhaps, thought Lovett, because he was gaining a certain status from helping Coop in the sheds.

Benteen explained their mission. Pilau did not show much enthusiasm until she mentioned that Minister Merizo, cradling a bottle of firewater, had blessed the idea. Suddenly, then, he began with a right good will to prepare his crew for the new location. The natives washed themselves down happily enough before piling into the big vehicle which, compared to its previous condition, was now running like Deion Sanders.

"What Pilau told them," Benteen said to Lovett as they led the half-track on their scooters, "was that Merizo's on the sauce, and the farther they can get from that, the better."

"I take it there were no dissenters," Lovett said.

"Not one. I believe they understand their honchos pretty well."

"Bunch of new-age sensitive guys, huh," Lovett teased.

"Screw you, Wade," she said.

"First let me find some bumps to ride over," he said. "It worked for Merizo."

"Watch the road," she commanded, but she was laughing nonetheless, those fine breasts pressing against his back in a most satisfactory way.

They found Coop and Reventlo taking a break, having disconnected a man's weight of engine accessories from the aft face of that big Nakajima engine. They'd covered the gaping orifices with tatters of old aircraft fabric from what they referred to as the jungle junk piles. A generator removed from an engine was one you could carry away later, Coop observed. When Pilau backed his brutish vehicle to the cart, Lovett saw an excited exchange between his friends and hurried to them, wondering what their elation was all about.

"Five more guys, Wade," Coop beamed. "I've already unbolted the APU. If somebody'll keep 'em here 'til we can haul the cart back, we can get that flakin' engine aboard now. I mean *right forkin' now!*"

The APU was not much of a load for four stalwart Fundaborans, another who took one look into Lovett's face and decided menial chores were the better part of valor, and the always-energized Chip.

Once she understood the drill, Benteen set the Fundaborans to dragging felled trees into deeper jungle so that they wouldn't follow the men with the cart. The Boffs hauled that little cart away at a virtual trot, Chip carrying their tiedown ropes. Because the path was twisted, there was no immediate view of the cliff or its new openings.

There was then only the small problem of loading a half-ton of engine in close quarters onto a metal cart scarcely larger than a wheelbarrow. They managed finally by rolling the entire crate onto its side, and onto the cart in the process. "This is one tippy bitch," Coop said, affixing both ends of two ropes to the top of the crate. "Let's see if we can get it out of here without killin' somebody."

The shadows were long and tempers frayed before they strained and cursed the overloaded cart two hundred yards down the path. The engine swayed horrendously, though steadied by the ropes, and finally began to tip despite men fighting its inertia. It fetched up against a small palm and heeled over at a perilous angle, the cart with two wheels in the air, the other two now bent.

"That does it," Coop said in disgust. "It'll take hours to fix those axles."

"We're more than halfway there. I'll get Pilau's guys; they can't see where we started from here," Chip panted, looking back up the path.

Lovett complained that as a dead lift, that load would be too much even for their ten men. Reventlo said he'd seen astonishing weights carried by islanders, as long as they could somehow take that load on a pole over a shoulder, and asked Chip to bring in Pilau's reserves.

They succeeded, at last, by cutting five sapling trunks for poles and lashing the poles beneath that crate. Pilau's crew showed no misgivings, but squatted below their poles and, with cadence called by one of them, began to stand erect while the Boff crew helped all they could. Then the ten men slowly centipeded forward down the path, muscles knotted, taking small steps.

"I'm not a lotta help," Coop muttered to Lovett.

"Me neither," Lovett managed. He noted that all the gasping and grunting seemed to be from the visitors; the damned cadence-counter did not shut up or vary the pace until they had reached Pilau's half-track.

Engine, accessories, cart, and APU all fitted easily into the half-track's open cargo bay and Pilau's men stood watching as Coop roped the engine in place. Lovett's exhaustion faded the instant he turned from his Cushman seat to see the old vehicle churn forward behind him. Chip was grinning, Reventlo was grinning; even the face of the surly Myles glowed with elation.

Dusk came as they waved Pilau back toward the C-47, their prized antique engine lurching against its lashings like a petrified sumo wrestler, Reventlo swinging the cargo door wide in anticipation. They imagined that their little problem in transportation was solved until after Pilau, having backed within inches of the plane's tender hide, helped pass engine accessories to Lovett and Chip who now stood in the C-47. Then he got his men to tip the big engine so that one end of its crate lay inside the plane. At that point, Pilau explained to Benteen why their job was complete.

His crew would not be of any further help in this enterprise, he told her. Jean-Claude Pelele had invoked terrible punishment for any villager who so much as touched the big aerocanoe, and that was that. His expression said, "game over."

Male curses and Benteen's most piteous imploring did no good. The only way to get further help would be through the orders of Jean-Claude himself; and this, Reventlo would not hear of. "It's borrowing trouble," he said, "and I want no further complications."

Then, despite a few inches of upslope: "We can do it," said Coop, who flung himself hard against the crate. Reventlo and the others, including Benteen, followed suit. Crate boards creaked; an inch was gained.

"No, we bloody-well can't," Reventlo wheezed at last, as his bootsoles skidded along the half-track's flooring.

Coop looked around him, breathing heavily. "Any ideas?"

Pilau did not understand the words, but he understood the situation. And while he was far from the fox of fable who knew many things, he *was* the hedgehog who knew one very, very important thing. Smiling shyly, he produced a beer bottle full of used crankcase oil from beneath the driver's seat; mimed smearing it on the floorplates and the crate's wooden skids.

Coop Gunther slapped a palm against his forehead with the clap of a gunshot. "I've done that a hundred times," he cried, snatching the bottle, patting Pilau's shoulder.

"You'd have thought of it," Reventlo surmised. "Tomorrow."

The crate went in as though on wheels, proceeding more slowly as they oiled floor plates and hauled the engine further forward, still upslope, at Reventlo's urging. Lovett understood perfectly; a C-47 was a forgiving airplane but a half-ton mass far to its rear during flight would not make it happy.

Without explanation, they passed the remainder of their stowed goods out to Pilau's men to be stored in a maintenance shed, then closed the plane up again. Pilau's last stop was the shed where everything, including the APU and its much-abused cart, was removed. Handshakes and smiles all around, and then the two crews went their separate ways.

Though the others gorged on the lobby buffet, Crispin Reventlo drank only coconut milk and jotted notes as they talked softly. "I'm more wakeful on an empty stomach, and tonight I'll be a crew of one," he told them.

"You could wait and launch at first light," Lovett suggested.

"Not my style," said the Brit, with a romantic old-bold lopsided grin for the attentive Melanie Benteen. "I intend to be refueling on Yap or Koror before double-ought-dark-thirty. Wherever I am, I'll no longer be worrying about whether a certain largish Fundaboran gentleman wants to interfere. Then it's on to Darwin by noon. I know there's secure storage there."

"Don't forget batteries; aircraft quality," Coop said.

"Duly noted," Reventlo assured him.

"And a trunkload of those sleazy videos," from Benteen, "and a few cases of cheap booze, for His Nibs down the hall." A nod.

"And the medicine Keikano wanted," Chip said. "The blood-pressure stuff, too."

"Look here," Reventlo said. "I haven't forgotten a jot or a tittle, any of it. Perhaps you nice people can help me think of things like fuel octane additives, battery acid, an inverter to recharge Chip's computer, a drum of aircraft cable, hand torch batteries, a water purifier—things of that sort."

They settled down then, able to think of little that Reventlo did not already have on his list. Finally, when their mental batteries had flagged, Myles said slowly, "Maybe a cheap little Polaroid flash setup, Cris."

"What's buggered with yours then," Reventlo asked.

"Nothing. I'm thinking of something disposable I can stash where it can't be found, that might show us for certain who's our little friend at the cave."

"If it's a tripwire, he can follow it to the camera," Chip said.

"Not if it's done right. Just do it, Cris."

"Good on you. That's the kind of thinking I like," said the Brit, scribbling again.

"And a fax machine," said Chip, "and Fritos."

Coop brightened. "Fritos! The old-fashioned kind, and beer. Jesus God, how I miss—"

"I believe we've come to birthday lists now," Reventlo interrupted, his hand up to stem the tide. "I'll try, but please remember that I'll be busy enough merely locating some kind of hull that might, with prayer and fasting, make it to Fundabora. Oh, and when you see anything on the horizon, in air or afloat, try your comm gear. It may be me."

Lovett and Coop accompanied the Brit to the plane in darkness, leaving the others to present a business-as-usual appearance. After a shamefully inadequate preflight inspection and a more careful check of the cargo lashings, the men scrambled about removing wheel chocks with only a flashlight. Soon they were treated to the familiar homey sounds of one C-47 engine cranking over, then a second. It made a hell of a racket but no Fundaboran committee came rushing out, and five minutes later Reventlo advanced his throttles, landing lights throwing the sandy beach approaches into sharp relief. The tide was out, giving Reventlo a broad, gently sloped runway. Lovett did not realize his fingers had been crossed until he uncrossed them, watching a huge shape ascend eastward before banking in a graceful arc toward the south to disappear into blackness.

"Now I can die happy," Coop said in a choked voice, when all they could hear was the surf.

Lovett agreed for form's sake, but he felt a curious sense of detachment as they walked back toward rectangles of lamplight in the distance. Now, *if* Crispin Reventlo didn't fall asleep, or ditch in a million square miles of Pacific, whatever else might happen they had earned themselves a footnote in aero lore, recovering a valuable piece of equipment buried in a cave for half a century. There was a term for that: they had demonstrated proof of principle.

Yet somehow, his sense of accomplishment fell short of elation. This was only Round One; there remained the problems of getting the planes out intact, loading them onto some seaworthy craft, and bringing them to a modern hangar. And all of this while someone was trying to sabotage everything they'd worked for.

22

There is no way you can sneak a C-47 into the air. As Lovett and Coop Gunther walked into the lobby they found Jean-Claude Pelele, barefoot in what could only be described as a skirt of circus-tent dimensions, asking the other crew members about the hellacious racket outside. He scanned the newcomers' faces and fell silent. After a moment, when it became obvious that Reventlo was the missing man, the big fellow spoke. "Ol' Cris he fightim aerocanoe cross salwater no takim youfella. Wichway?"

Lovett knew by now that "wichway" meant "why." The huge Fundaboran showed no irritation, but that might mean nothing. He was probably capable of wringing a man's neck, smiling all the while. "Cris went for more supplies, Jean-Claude. He told us to keep working until he returns with what we need to repair the machines." As Benteen began to help translate bits of this, Lovett donated a big smile and added, "Medicines, too, and a lot of boy-girl movies; everything you wanted him to bring."

From Jean-Claude's quick change of expression, it seemed that he understood more standard English than he spoke. He also understood, probably from Pilau's report, that Reventlo had taken off carrying some machine from the jungle. Wichway?

Because, said Lovett, they had found it and brought it from underground, in accord with their agreement. That, he said, was wichway ol' Cris was flying off—to repay Fundabora as agreed. Pressed for details, Lovett finally conveyed the main ideas: they had found old machines underground. Some they hoped to sell elsewhere; some could best be used right here by Jean-Claude's own people, and instead of flying off with them Reventlo had donated them. Pilau had already brought some of those machines to the nearby sheds. Would Jean-Claude like to see them sometime?

Indeed he would; his phrase, a startling addition to traditional pidgin, was vintage militarese: "fuckin' A, John." Lovett's intuition said that this was in the nature of a veiled challenge. And Jean-Claude would like to see them right now. Did he mean right now, tonight? In his reply, Jean-Claude again referred to naughty John.

The visit to the shed was so informal that Jean-Claude disdained his bearers, walking with Lovett, Coop, and Benteen who all carried flashlights. The big shed was cool now, the Cushmans ranked together except for the one that stood propped, awaiting repairs. Coop immediately excused himself and began to rifle through the supplies they'd off-loaded. "Looking for that silver dope," he said. Fabric and its necessary paint "dope" had been among Lovett's supplies, in case the C-47's fabric-covered control surfaces became damaged.

Jean-Claude Pelele became a lot less suspicious when Lovett showed off the APU and the cart. "This engine generates electricity so we can start the LeTourneau. Explain that, Benteen."

She did, saying small machine drink burnwater made lightning, by and by made bigbig machine work. If Jean-Claude harbored any doubts that the generator had come from underground, he kept them to himself. Probably, Lovett decided, the big man did not think in those terms.

Presently the sweet tang of aircraft dope made Jean-Claude sniff in appreciation. Was it, he asked hopefuly, something to eat? Or better still, to drink?

Lovett turned his flashbeam on Coop, who was carefully painting circles on the old Cushman merely to have something to do while entertaining this mountain of a man. The smell, he told Benteen to say, was merely paint. Nogoodim drink; allsame good to paint evil machine. Wichway, asked Jean-Claude, was the limper putting little full moons on the pootpoot machine?

When Lovett told him of Merizo's order, the shed echoed with the headman's guffaw. That was really stupid, Benteen translated, when everybody knew *all* of the pootpoots hated Merizo. He had a history of trying to ride them; trying, and ending up beneath them, or hurled off. But if he wanted moons on this one, he should have them. As for Jean-Claude: give him the bigbig machine any day.

It would certainly belong to Fundabora, Benteen translated, when they left. No, the big man explained, he wanted to learn to drive the thing! At this, Benteen's eyes widened and Lovett knew what she was seeing in her mind's eye: Jean-Claude thundering around the island at top speed in this multiton velocipede, a brontosaurus on wheels. The mind simply boggled at the idea; it would take three of the councilhouse merely to contain the walking wounded.

Coop explained that the LeTourneau would have to be modified for an operator of Jean-Claude's heroic size, but he would think on it. Perhaps something could be arranged but first the great machine must be made to work properly. And if it did not like its operator, he said, it might grow angry.

Jean-Claude announced that he was not afraid of any machine alive, meanwhile thoughtfully sidling away from the LeTourneau. Then he changed the subject, and Lovett was compelled to list the items Reventlo had promised to seek for the island. Finally satisfied, Jean-Claude decided he had spent enough time in the shed and marched them back to the councilhouse. Benteen declined an invitation to visit his quarters, climbing the lobby stairs with her menfolk.

The five crew members, feeling like castaways, met in Lovett's room to confer, heads close, in tones near whispering. "I know what you're feeling," Benteen confided early on. "Me, too; it's like our ship came in, and then sailed without us."

"Part of the job," shrugged Coop, a man who was used to being alone.

Lovett nodded, knowing that they must not continue to focus on this new sense of vulnerability when they were vulnerable on other fronts as well. "Poor pitiful us, marooned with our treasure cave on an island paradise. Well, we can sit around fretting as if we'd just missed the last rowboat out of hell—or we can get on with it like sensible folks." As he spoke, he was tearing little streamers from notepaper.

Myles said, "Right now I'm for a swig of scotch. Be with you tomorrow, bright and early."

"Or maybe tonight, dim and late," Lovett replied, holding up one fist so they could see the tips of the paper streamers protruding.

Myles: "What's that for—oh, hell. I think I know."

Chip: "I sure don't, Pop."

"Sentry duty at the cave. Whoever draws the shortest piece stays there tonight, and so on." He saw their dejection and went on, "Look, I don't like it any better than you do but we know it's got to be done unless we want to get snookered again some night. I'll take the piece that's left since I know which is shortest. What could be fairer?"

Reluctantly, they consented, Myles studying Lovett's face for long moments before he made the first choice, as though it were a poker game. Chip took the next piece, then Benteen, and finally Coop, leaving Lovett to display his own. To Lovett's dismay, Chip drew the shortest streamer.

"He gonna go by Cushman and warn ever'body away, or hoof it and maybe catch the bastard? There's arguments for both ways," said Coop.

"I can walk," said Chip, fetching a bedroll. "If you don't mind, Mr. Myles, I'm borrowing your flash camera." No one seemed to care any longer that they weren't keeping their voices down.

He wants to catch the guy in the act, Lovett thought, *just as I do.* Then the implications of that flooded in. If Jean-Claude was listening and understanding, the hell with it. "Let's think about what you could be walking into, Chip. Without a weapon—"

"You mean like this?" Myles drew that horse-choking .45 of his, handed it to Chip. "You were saying, Lovett?"

"Even with a weapon," Lovett plodded on desperately, "we're asking a lot from a ki—a seventeen-year-old. Maybe I should take the first night."

"Don't do this, Pop," said the youth, working the automatic's slide, his face dark.

"You don't know what could happen, Chip," his grandfather pleaded.

"Nobody does. And if it's who some people think, it's more my job than anybody's," Chip said stubbornly, doing a great imitation of Vic Myles as he thrust the weapon between his belt and the small of his back.

But his words instantly gave Myles second thoughts. "Oh, yeah. Well now, come to think of it, maybe that makes you the only one of us that shouldn't go."

When Chip stood fully erect, as he did now, he was taller than any of them. "But I *am* going, and right now before I let my big grommy mouth get me in trouble."

"Chip, it's not just the possible danger," said Lovett in one final rhetorical plunge. "Packing that damned forty-five makes it a huge responsibility."

"I know it," said the youth, pausing on his way to the door with a secret smile. His little secret did not last long. "How old were you when you first had to make a decision about somebody else's life, Pop?" He waited three beats as Lovett hesitated. "Sixteen, you said,"

Chip went on; "the guy hot-wiring the family car, and you threw down on him. Remember? How about you, Mr. Gunther?"

"Uh—fifteen," said Coop. "Crazy-drunk Klinkit backed my mom into the pantry. Well, he asked," Coop added to Lovett.

"Huh. I'm off to a late start, wouldn't you say?" And with that, Chip shouldered his bedroll, pocketing a transceiver and flashlight as he went.

They heard his footsteps on the stairs. "Kid knows his mind," Coop said gently.

"Never, *never* tell your grandkid stories of derring-don't about your own youth," Lovett said with a helpless chuckle. "Was that true about you and the Indian?"

"Yep. Lots of Klinkits are better men than most. That wasn't one of 'em. What I didn't tell Chip was, I sure 'nough shot the sonofabitch."

"So how'd it feel to kill someone at fifteen?"

"Right and proper, at the time. Guess you had to be there. Didn't kill him, actually; just laid him up. But I was trying, Wade. They gave me credit for that. Hey, relax; Chip will be okay. Sooner or later you've got to let go. And anyway, us old guys don't always have the best answer, we just try to tell the young ones we do. Well, don't we?" To this unpleasant truth, Lovett had no reply.

Myles heaved a long sigh and headed to the door. "I'm having that drink, Coop. Coming?"

The old man stood up, nodded, and stumped out leaving Mel Benteen alone with Lovett.

"He was his own man before this, Wade," said Benteen, watching him move about the room. "You're doing the right thing—by the way, what *are* you doing?"

"Looking for my machete. Got my little Maglite and netting already." They were talking in semiwhispers again.

"You wouldn't," she said, smiling sadly.

"Spend a night as Chip's backup? Damn right I would, Mel. He doesn't have to know it."

She began to laugh, a low throaty chortle, head thrown back to yield a fetching profile in lamplight. "And here I thought we could go to my room, talk, share some Drambuie I haven't told anybody about. You could tell me that story about the car thief when you were sixteen."

Lovett paused in astonishment, and said something stupid. "Cris Reventlo is my friend. Would he approve?"

"Absolutely not, but it's not his Drambuie, *or* his business."

"You mean you two haven't been, uh—"

She sat down on his bed and faced him squarely, honestly. "That's not *your* business, but since you ask, yes. Once. Oh, Crispin Reventlo is a charmer but the English, I have to tell you, seem to be more about style than substance. More power to them, I guess. Far more." And she smiled again. "He's still a good man, an old bold pilot worthy of my dad, a man I'm glad to know."

"Just not in the Biblical sense, hm," Lovett joshed.

She became serious now. "Is it necessary for me to ask you not to repeat any of this, Wade? Are you that kind of good old boy?"

Lovett knelt, putting their heads on a level, and took her hands in his. "Wild unicorns couldn't drag any of this out of me, Melanie—great name, lovely name, by the way." He searched her gaze. "Suits you. And if my only grandson weren't ten minutes ahead of me in a jungle that hides a goddamned saboteur, I'd already be sharing your Drambuie." And he stood up, knees popping like Rice Krispies.

"I'm definitely slipping," she replied with good humor, and followed him as far as the stairs. In answer, he shook his head and threw her an appreciative wink.

He followed the C-47's tire tracks down the beach until they disappeared, then stumbled inland to the perimeter road. On Fundabora, no haze interrupted the hard points of starlight that defined the path they'd hacked out and Lovett moved slowly to avoid noise. He half-expected to see errant beams from Chip's flashlight from the openings they'd made as he chose a recently felled sapling as a seat, very near the lower entry hole. Perhaps, he thought, Chip hadn't reached the cave yet. Then, only minutes after he pulled his netting noiselessly down over his body, he heard a soft thud from inside, and an irritable, "Ow, shit a fuzzy brick." One of Lovett's own expressions.

Then another sound, between a hiss and a whistle. A moment of silence, followed by one word. It could have been "Chip," with a questioning inflection. Lovett stood quickly and moved to the tunnellike hole.

An actinic burst of light caromed from inside. "Gotcha, dammit," Chip called. "Is it Kei? Don't you move; you hear me?"

"My eyes," came the unmistakable voice of Keikano. Lovett felt much the same way, his night-vision temporarily zapped by that little flash unit.

"Should've kept one of em closed like I did." With that, an ordinary flashbeam winked on, flicking across the aircraft. Lovett saw the beam stabilize on one of the Tojos where little Keikano sat leaning back against its fuselage, legs stretched out along the wing. "Don't move," Chip said again, and walked to the Tojo. Lovett could barely make out Chip's movement as the youth thrust his borrowed weapon from sight. In a voice Lovett had rarely heard from his grandson, Chip rumbled, "You've got some explaining to do to us, pal." Lovett could not explain why a wave of relief flooded him then.

Shading his eyes in the flashbeam, Keikano swung sandaled feet over the wing's leading edge. Chip dropped the beam a bit. "Let me see your hands, Kei."

A show of hands, open and empty. "I cannot hurt you, Chip. I would not."

"No, you'd just bring a rockfall down on me."

"Is that what he—were you hurt?"

"Do I look hurt?" Lovett warmed with pride; Chip was maintaining his advantage like a pro. *Where do they learn these things*, he asked himself. *Maybe from their mothers*, his internal imp replied.

"I cannot see you well, Chip. Was anyone hurt?"

"You'll find out. No thanks to you, either way."

"I warned you," Keikano said in a voice so gentle it made Lovett angry.

"Yeah, and then you came back to try again," Chip accused.

"No! I came here to reason with him. I thought, when I heard you enter, that you *were* him. I wanted to wait and surprise him but I heard no more, and then I waited longer. Then you made a noise and spoke."

"Bunged my elbow. Had no idea you were already here," Chip said, in tones less truculent.

"When I knew, I called to you."

"Smooth move, Ex-Lax. If you hadn't, I might've put a hole in you," Chip said. "So who's this *he*? Pilau? Merizo?"

"No and no. They are simple folk. Merizo, perhaps; but no."

"I'm going to find out, Kei."

"Not from me." Soft, but adamant. "And if he comes with you here—please, just go," Keikano begged almost as a woman might beg.

"I forgot," said Chip, and the light flicked from existence. "I've still got some rat-catching to do."

"You will not speak of him that way!" The shift from entreaty to a hissed command was abrupt.

"Any way I like," Chip said. "Whoever the hell he is. I'm still not sure it's not you, Kei."

Sullenly: "You will speak with respect of him—and to him. And you cannot!"

"Could if I wanted to," said Chip, like a child challenged.

"I mean that he would not understand you. Ah, this is not possible. My position is not. Chip, please, one thing: do not harm him. I could not live with that."

"Listen, little bitty buddy, if he tries to harm any of us again, *he* might not live with *that*," Chip insisted.

"Then I have no choice but to stay with you. If you force me to leave I shall wait outside."

"And do what," Chip demanded.

"Whatever I can to avoid harm. I set this in motion." And then small sobs in the darkness. *Oh, you slick little faggot*, Lovett said to himself. *You've even got me feeling sorry for you.*

"Cut it out, Kei. Look, I'm climbing up there with you and we're gonna be quiet as rats, okay? I'm in no hurry to shoot anybody but I'm a by-God sentry and these are our by-God airchines." *Lordy, he even sounds like a B.O.F.*, Lovett thought.

"You and your rats," Keikano said in petulance.

"Hush! Stop moving around," Chip said.

"Give me your hand then. I will not run," Keikano replied. And then, for so long that Lovett eased back outside the hole, the cave was silent. Once Lovett thought he heard Chip say, "Good God," and was tempted to make his presence known. But he had dealt himself this hand—each of them had, for that matter—and decided to play it through.

It could have been an hour later, or perhaps two, when Lovett realized he had been dozing on his log. The thing that waked him was a broadleaf stroking the net over his face, and from his place in the undergrowth Lovett could see a silhouette against the stars. A double-armspan away, someone stepped past him, moving with glacial slowness. A tiny *tink* as of metal on stone stopped even that movement for many seconds, and then the figure slid without sound through the hole.

Lovett waited for others to follow and was gratified when none ghosted past. He eased up from his seat, silently cursing himself when the machete made the faintest windsong against his trouserleg. Then he squatted in the cave entrance.

When he heard footfalls softly, unerringly climb the internal steps in total darkness, Lovett eased inside the cave absolutely blind, one hand held before him. He could not recall the exact position of each aircraft and was damned if he wanted to announce his presence by crowning himself—again!—against a wing. When at last he felt an aluminum leading edge, he moved forward, finally to kneel beside a landing gear strut. Chip and Keikano, he knew, were—or had been—sitting on another of the Tojo fighter craft. God only knew where they might be now. Gone, maybe; he hoped so. *Whatever they might be doing?* his imp asked. *Whatever*, he told it, *and now kindly bug off.*

His heart leaped like a rabbit when he heard another footfall because it was so near. Was it Chip? Should he whisper a warning? Caution ruled him; and a moment later he was glad it did. Small muffled noises suggested someone moving at the workbench, and then a series of brilliant sparks strobed the outline of a small figure wearing an odd cap, facing the bench, bent at some task. A sudden glow, prospering and paced by vitreous clinks, proved that the man had lit an oil lamp. As he lifted the lamp and turned, his face was illuminated for the first time, beard and all. Lovett almost cursed aloud.

"Hold it," Chip's command echoed through the cave. "Freeze!"

Instantly the lamp fell from the hand, and its wick extinguished as the man whirled in a crouch. Knowing every one of them was blind for the moment, Lovett stood erect and moved silently across several paces of free space. And when Chip's flashlight speared the man, he had grasped a rifle of really extraordinary length. With its thin-bladed bayonet, the thing was longer than its user as he swung it toward Chip.

A high-pitched yelp, almost a scream, erupted from someone; not Lovett or Chip because it was language, but none they knew. And also because Lovett was busy in his own language. Stepping in close from slightly behind the little man, Lovett laid his machete, edge-on, against his unprotected neck. "Drop it," he said harshly, and wiggled the blade when his order was not followed instantly. "Or you're a dead man."

And now, as the little man turned to view his ambusher, it was Keikano who leaped down from his perch, hands up, eyes wide. He rushed to the feet of the rifleman stammering out words Lovett could not follow; threw himself literally at the feet of this stranger; kept talking in a rush of gibberish, grasping the man's shins. As the man lowered his ancient rifle, Lovett flicked on his own flashlight to make certain of his first impression.

The little fellow finally spoke; and when he did, it was a word Lovett did know. "Hai," he said, lowering his rifle. It meant "yes," and with that word, from a distance of two feet Lovett realized he was gazing into the face of a Japanese in his seventies, perhaps older. The man's gaze was unwavering despite the flashbeams, and he spoke briefly with the stoniest of expressions.

"Get up, Keikano," Lovett said. "Chip, take the rifle."

As Chip kept his big flashlight trained on the little fellow, Keikano scrambled to his feet and hugged the old man around the chest. "He surrounds. Surrenders! He will not hurt anyone."

"Goddamned straight he won't," Lovett said as Chip took the rifle. "There should be another lamp over there." Then, because neither he nor Chip was a smoker, he said, "Keikano, make him light it."

Keikano gave a soft burst of Japanese and the old man turned, stiffly erect, to the workbench. His lighter was a curious little gadget that could have lit a bonfire on sparks alone. In a moment, the remaining lamp shed its glow on this ill-matched quartet.

"Jeezus *Christ*," Chip breathed, pulling Keikano back gently as he stared at this apparition from the past. Rail-thin, wearing leg-wraps to the knee, the old fellow with the wisp of beard was in uniform, short-billed cap and all.

23

Keikano would not step away until the old man gave a brusque order and after that, for a moment, no one moved. Though tears were now streaming down Keikano's face, the old fellow seemed in command of himself, standing at rigid attention. Yet he seemed to be gauging the distance to the bayonet affixed to that rifle Chip held, and Lovett's intuition briefly worked overtime. "Chip, put the rifle away," he said, patting the old fellow down. He found a small caliber automatic pistol under the man's shirt and pocketed it. He also took a small canvas bag of what felt like rifle cartridges, tossing it to Chip. As he did, the old man turned to face him, and Lovett flinched. Either the oldster kept a stash of Limburger cheese, or he had the worst case of halitosis since buzzards were invented. Lovett demanded, "Keikano, who the hell is this?"

Keikano said something to the old man, who replied briefly, and the schoolteacher said, "He wishes you to know that he is Ohtsu Yohei, flight mechanic in the Army of Nippon. Attached to the Naval air arm in 1945 when supply lines were cut. You would say Yohei Ohtsu," the youth stammered.

"Tell him he can't be connected to something that hasn't existed for fifty years. He's retired. Honorably discharged."

Keikano spoke in Japanese. Old Ohtsu's gaze flickered, and though he said nothing, his expression said he wasn't buying it.

"Is Ohtsu one of the people taking care of these planes?"

"No. For many years, he has been the only one. It was the responsibility given him," said Keikano.

"And he thinks he's still fighting that war?"

"He continues to do his duty," Keikano said.

Lovett recalled the stories of Japanese soldiers and even civilians with children hurling themselves from cliffs rather than surrender. No wonder this old guy was studying the bayonet on his own rifle. "Tell him he has covered himself with honor and that we're amazed. Tell him Japan and America are at peace and no one wants to hurt him."

Keikano, blinking tears away, began to translate. The old fellow's reply was much shorter, and Lovett had heard that phrase before, a famed example of polite disbelief: "*Ahh, so desukaa,*" he murmured, meaning *Is that a fact, and I don't believe a word of it.*

Lovett smiled and shoved the machete into his belt. "Ask him to relax, Keikano." On hearing the translation, Ohtsu smartly shifted his left foot forward and out a half-pace, arms still at his sides, in a motion that might have simulated his version of the military parade rest.

"This isn't what I meant. Tell him there is no need to act in a military way. I was an officer in our Air Force but at present, there—is—no—war. I am now a civilian. And whether he likes it or not, so is he."

Now Keikano embarked on his rhetorical mission to the past, nodding briefly as the old man made a few comments. Finally Keikano said, "He has heard these things, but one hears many things that are not necessarily true. But he wishes to know, in that case, why you captured him and are trying to steal property entrusted to him."

Whoa, that could be a tough one, Lovett thought. He moved back to the workbench, hopped up to sit on it in an attempt at informality. And at last Ohtsu slowly sat down cross-legged to face him with an air of expectation. After a few moments to gather his thoughts, Lovett said, "After your ministers signed Japan's surrender on the deck of an American battleship, we shipped some of Japan's warplanes to America. The Japanese helped us destroy the rest. A few more airplanes were found hidden later, and now they belong to whoever finds them." Not always true, but whatthehell . . .

Keikano explained, and the old man replied. Keikano said, "He says that if this is true, he wishes you to know that because he found them first, naturally they are his."

This, Lovett felt, was not going well at all. He tried again: "If they are his, what does he intend to do with them?"

This time the old fellow took his time answering. "That is not your affair," Keikano said nervously. "He has his orders."

"Then let me tell him about those orders. Everyone knows now that Japanese officers expected to wait with their great kamikaze armada until America attacked the home islands. Then they would tear down the cave wall, fly the planes to the nearest American ships, and dive into them. Tell him, Keikano."

The old man's face fell as he heard Keikano but his reply was stolid. "If you knew, he says, you did not need to ask," Keikano said.

"This is crazy. Look; those pilots of his who aren't dead, are probably owners of Japanese companies, driving expensive German cars, wearing expensive Italian shoes, and selling expensive electric gadgets to Americans!"

Keikano translated but Ohtsu remained impassive.

All but shouting in his frustration, Lovett blurted, "No eighty-year-old Japanese pilot is ever going to come to Fundabora and demand to fly any of these planes! They all think the kamikaze armada was shameful now. Even if one did come, he couldn't fly across an airstrip covered with small trees, even if the planes could still fly, which they can't."

When the translation and its reply were complete, Lovett understood the knowing smile now on Ohtsu's lined face. "Of course the planes will fly. It was a simple matter to a master mechanic. The most difficult part has been finding fuel to run the engines."

Lovett squinted in perplexity at Keikano, though this stunning revelation explained some more peculiar facts. "He still runs up the engines? When?"

Without consulting the old man, Keikano replied, "Every year during the leadership games, when all the people in Pelele's village are out of their minds with drink."

"You know all this without asking." Not a question.

"Of course. Someone had to help him," Keikano shrugged. "Before me, it was my father."

"And how does he find fuel," Lovett said, smiling.

"He knows where it is, because I tell him. A drum of Jean-Claude's fuel can be rolled into the jungle with ropes, and from there we move it bit by bit," Keikano admitted.

That told Lovett how relatively fresh gasoline came to be in the cave. It didn't explain a hell of a lot of other things, though. "Does he start the engines with that generator cart we took to the sheds?"

"Yes. He will not be pleased that you took it."

"Yes he will," Lovett said. "Tell him we took the cart away to help start that earthmoving machine in the sheds. With that, we can clear the runway again." And it was truly interesting to see the waves of consternation, suspicion, and hope that chased across Ohtsu's face.

"He wishes to know why you want to clear his runway," Keikano said.

"We intend to fly an airplane in here soon," Lovett said. It was a half-truth at best but it left the old man trying to hide a glimmer of hope.

From Chip, who had been standing near, eyes like saucers: "Pop, you think these planes will actually fly? Just as they are after all this time?"

"Somebody found a 1911 experimental seaplane boxed up in Minnesota, a few years back," Lovett told him, "and it was flyable. But these—I dunno. He sure thinks so," he said, nodding toward the old Japanese. "It's academic, because we're going to ship these out."

"Even though they belong to him," Keikano interjected.

"I thought I explained that."

"Not to him, I think," Keikano insisted. "I had hoped to avoid trouble if you took the planes quickly, because I knew they will never be of use to him as they are. But he can still walk many miles in a night to make an occasional inspection. Even though it may kill him. I think he should not have such excitement as this."

Chip laid a gentle hand on Keikano's shoulder. "Kei, is this who the blood pressure medicine is for?"

A nod, while gazing sadly at the old man.

"You've taken some big chances for this old guy. I don't understand why you'd go to such lengths for him," Chip persisted.

"That is odd. I have no difficulty understanding why you would go to such distances for *your* grandfather," Keikano said.

Lovett looked from Keikano to the silently watching man. "This old soldier's your grandfather?"

"And the head of my village," Keikano said quietly, proudly.

"This is the damnedest thing I ever," Lovett began, then stopped. "Is there a village of Japanese soldiers on Fundabora?"

"Only my grandfather now," Keikano replied. "Many years ago when Fundabora was abandoned, the Japanese left five men to care for the planes. When the islanders broke free a few days later, they hunted the soldiers down like animals."

Lovett knew why, but this was not the time to say that what goes around, comes around, and he nodded for Keikano to go on. "My honorable grandfather and one other had made friends among the islanders with food and kindness. One of those friends became my grandmother. They were very young, very brave. They went away with their few friends to the north end of the island. As you have seen, Fundabora is almost like two islands and it is easy to defend the north end, easy to see war parties approaching. Finally the south village stopped making war and accepted Europeans with their hotel. Grandfather felt that it was best to stay forgotten so that he could do his duty. The Pelele faction would never tell Europeans of a small village they could not defeat, only a few miles away.

"The other remaining soldier died before I was born, but by then it was understood that visitors and Pelele's villagers were still not welcome in the north. Still, there was some trading by canoe; there still is. The rice terraces are all on the north end. We trade for the modern medicines and machines that traders bring to the south village."

"What kind of modern machines," Lovett asked.

"Drills for metal," Keikano shrugged, miming a hand-operated brace and bit. "Food grinders. Things to replace those that have worn out. My grandfather's food must be made soft and he does not want my mother to spend hours each day preparing special food."

Chip saw the implications of this immediately. "Kei, your family still lives in the north village?" A nod. "But not you. Why not?"

"My father was a fine sailor of canoes. Because his mother was islander he could pass as one of them, and my mother was islander, too." At this point Keikano said something to the Japanese and, for the first time, Lovett saw the old fellow smile. It was a gentle smile, full of memory and rotten teeth, and he said something very softly. "When I said I was speaking of my father, Grandfather said he was a bird, skimming his canoe. When he died of an infection, the village mourned for a year." And Keikano fell silent.

"Don't stop now," Lovett urged.

"Most of my mother's kin chose to stay among Pelele's people, and it was a simple thing for me to spend weeks at a time among my kin in the south village. One or two others did the same. Jean-Claude's father, Matai Pelele, knew it, I think. I believe he thought it was a good thing.

"As a small child, I enjoyed the rich tourists. During my visits here in the south I learned English and showed tourists the south village. Once I met a Japanese tourist and tried to interest him in a visit to the north. He was very much interested in the fact that I also spoke Japanese, but I could not tell him why."

"I don't see why not," Lovett said.

"Grandfather had forbidden it," Keikano said. "Just as he insisted I must not play with other children in the south village, or take part in the leadership games. If I dressed and acted like a *gaijin*, a tourist boy, Grandfather felt I would not become a south villager. His wisdom protected me in many ways. He did not trust the things he heard, and would not risk a personal visit. For him, the war was still real. He alone had responsibility for the airplanes, you see, since the others had died."

"And all this time he could have kept Jean-Claude's machines running," Lovett said.

"Never. Certainly not after old Matai was killed and Jean-Claude took over," Keikano said. "Jean-Claude is a bad man. He takes any woman he likes; that is one reason why the tourists left. Several women came to the north village to escape. But the children of the south village needed a teacher, someone who understood how things stand."

Chip's short laugh made Keikano stiffen. "That's why you've lived this way," he said.

Keikano turned quickly, eyes burning with intensity. "None of it was my idea, it was a decision among my southern elders. And what I reveal to you must not be shared! What others do not know, they cannot tell. I beg you, Chip. My life is in your hands."

"Hey, no problem," Lovett said, as much taken aback as Chip. "So you became a sort of go-between for the two villages, helping your grandfather when you could. Jean-Claude sure won't hear it from us, but unless I tell my friends they won't trust you."

A long silent gaze between Keikano and Chip, and then the American youth nodded. "He has to tell them that, Kei."

"I cannot stop you," said Keikano in dismay. "I cannot stop anything, it seems."

"You'll feel better when Reventlo brings the medicine for your village," Lovett said, and nodded toward the old Japanese. "Does he know about that?"

"Why tease him with promises? I will tell him when I see it."

Guess I can't fault Keikano for not trusting our promises, Lovett thought. "Tell him that, in return for these airplanes, we will bring him medicines for his ailments. That's our promise and I'll be responsible."

"Yet you have already promised that to me," Keikano pointed out.

"But some of it's for him, dammit! You knew that, even if we didn't."

Lovett could see that this stuck in Keikano's craw, but he addressed the old man again. A brief but lively dialog ensued, and Lovett knew the outcome before Keikano said, "He wishes you to know that the trade is unequal."

"One of these days we'll have a talk about Japanese-American trading, and inequality," Lovett gritted. "Meanwhile—Keikano, ask him if he accepts that his war is over."

Keikano hesitated, then complied. Ohtsu responded. Keikano finally translated, not very happy about it: "The enemy is strong, and he is more clever than a simple man."

"That's not much of an answer," Lovett said.

"Mr. Lovett, he does not wish to say that you are lying. That is his way."

"Shit, I remember now. They didn't like to say 'no.' "

"He has no difficulty saying it to me," Keikano remarked with a trace of humor, "but to an enemy officer he is more polite."

There it was again; Ohtsu's conviction that he was a prisoner of war. It seemed that if any progress were to be made, it would be by following old Ohtsu's world view. Then a simple solution made Lovett brighten. "Keikano, ask him this: does he believe an American officer has captured him?"

The one-word reply to Keikano's query was a reluctant "*hai*"; evidently it was acceptable to say yes. "Very well. Does he accept that these airplanes are captured, too?"

Another query from Keikano, another *hai* from the old man.

"Will he, as my prisoner, obey my orders?"

This time, old Ohtsu replied only after some internal debate. "He wishes to remind you that it is dishonorable to be captured, but a prisoner's honorable duty to escape," Keikano reported.

"Okay. It is my duty to see that prisoners are well-treated," Lovett said, with a smile for his "prisoner," and as Keikano rattled off his translation, something in Ohtsu's gaze seemed to soften. He made no reply however. "I will treat my prisoner well if he promises not to harm us or our captured property. If he promises that, I will not punish him for honorable intentions."

With this translated, Ohtsu regarded Lovett with fresh curiosity, and his reply was lengthy, terminating with a brief bow. Keikano said, "He bows to an honorable captor and will abide by the terms. He wishes to know if his weapons will be returned."

Lovett wanted to comply and when he looked at Chip, the youth said, "Sure, Pop, why not? What's he going to do?" Somehow that sounded childishly naive.

And if that was naive, maybe Lovett was courting the same mistake. "Shoot us, maybe; the guy's a soldier, Chip. No, Keikano, in his time you didn't give a prisoner a loaded weapon. I think he's testing the system. Tell him." This Keikano did, and the old fellow reacted calmly, silently, as if to a move on a chessboard. Then Lovett added, "Now tell him to go outside and wait."

Keikano translated. The old man took a few steps toward the new entrance, then turned as if waiting. Lovett waved him on.

Chip asked, "Should I go with him, Pop?"

"Certainly not," Lovett grinned.

"But he'll just—oh," said the youth.

"Right," Lovett said, seeing Ohtsu still eyeing them as he left the cave. "If he hasn't sailed off the island in fifty years, he won't do it now, and we're not in the prisoner business. Hell, we both know where he's going. If he goes back on his word, his ass will be grass. Keikano, you can go with him if you like. Tell him that if he leaves us in peace, I'll see that he gets that medicine."

Keikano swallowed hard. "I will see to it that you will not be sorry for this."

"I'm just doing myself a favor, getting him out of here before I barf, Keikano. Maybe old soldiers never die, but my God, their teeth sure do. Your old grampa's breath would gag a maggot," Lovett said, as the schoolteacher hurried from the cave with a final imploring look toward Chip.

A moment later they heard Keikano's voice raised outside, calling through darkness to the old man. Lovett let the cave's silence deepen, thought about Mel Benteen, then said, "This has been one night full of surprises." Chip gave a distracted nod as if lost in thought. "Under the circumstances, Chip, we may as well sleep back in our beds."

"Not me. We agreed this was my duty and I intend to do it, Pop. You go on. I want you to."

"Christ, you're worse than that old man."

"Same to you. Hanging out like that, checking up on me like I couldn't do a man's job."

"You sorry I did?"

"A little, but I might be sorrier if you hadn't," the youth admitted. "You going to radio back to Coop and the others?"

"No point in that. But I'm going on one condition: any more of this wargames horseshit tonight, and I want you on the radio on the double."

"Sure." When Lovett continued to look daggers at him, Chip said, "Yeah, okay! What's the matter, I said yes."

"The matter is, you didn't do it before."

"That was different," Chip said, failing to meet Lovett's gaze. "Just like your coming out here."

Lovett smiled. "I guess we both know more'n we did an hour ago," he said, and Chip rolled his eyes in silent agreement.

Lovett stood before the door to Benteen's room for so long in indecision, he damned near fell asleep on his feet. *I can see me now, starting to snore at the crucial moment*, he thought. *Not the cleverest of strategies.* Instead, he found his own bed, put his radio next to his ear, and tried to raise Chip without success until he fell asleep after twenty seconds. They would learn later that their little transceivers would neither transmit nor receive from inside the walled-up hangar.

Lovett was wakened by the half-track's clatter and thrumm as Pilau urged it along the crushed shell drive. It was already midmorning, and Lovett didn't need to dress because he hadn't undressed. He managed to raise Chip by radio immediately, because the youth was already perched outside the cave wall, hard at work. "No more problems, Pop," he said. "Mr. Myles brought me a mango. You gonna sleep in today?"

"Smartass kid; I'll be along. What've you told Myles?"

"Nothing. I'm gonna tell him you released a saboteur? You tell him. I'm tired of getting yelled at. Over."

Lovett punched off and tried Coop's frequency. Benteen answered in the maintenance area; Coop was cussing one of the LeTourneau's tires as he worked and ". . . I thought my dad taught me every phrase in the book but Coop's giving me a postgrad course," she said with a throaty laugh. It set Lovett's nerves to tingling.

"Tell you what, Mel: when you break for lunch, bring some food to us at the cave. Coop should come, too."

"You can't get your own? We're getting close to a trial . . . ," she began.

"It won't take long. You'll both want to see this," he promised.

She agreed, grumbling, and Lovett took the sole remaining scooter, jouncing down deepening ruts to the road's end. He was peeling a late-breakfast mango as he arrived at the cave.

Poor Chip was still walloping away at the wall, hanging from a rope while Myles, shirtless and gleaming with sweat, dumped the debris into the underbrush. Even though it was clear that Vic Myles avoided going up on a rope, he'd chosen heavy work that needed doing and, try as he might, Lovett couldn't bitch about the division of labor. It seemed to suit Chip, who was whistling—*whistling!*—as he walloped.

By now, a good ten feet of wall had fallen across its full width, yet Lovett could not see any sign of an aircraft from ground level. It occurred to him that, given the slight downslope, the cave wouldn't display its secrets to a visitor at any distance until that wall came down another six feet or so, which gave them more time before someone told Jean-Claude exactly what was inside. Sure, they'd told the big bastard they'd found more machines. They just hadn't told him those old machines looked brand-spanking new. When he found that out, sure as hell he'd decide he'd had the raffia cloth pulled over his eyes. If he didn't find out for another few days, maybe he'd be too busy with the annual leadership games to care.

And there was another major job to be done before the planes could be pushed, towed, or—*Jesus, maybe even taxied!*—to the beach. "Hey, Vic," he called, tossing the Texan a mango as he approached the cave.

Naturally he took some flak for tardiness, and sustained it philosophically. "Didn't get much sleep last night," he called down as he settled onto a rope perch. "Tell you why when the others get here." Then he began to methodically bash his way toward Chip, whose lank muscles shone beneath a patina of rock dust as he worked.

Benteen radioed at noon, and presently they heard the tubercular chug of a Cushman expire in the near distance. Benteen brought salted fish and coconuts for them, with Coop plodding slowly behind, still favoring that leg. "This better be worth it," he called as Lovett slid down from his perch. He was not to be disappointed.

The first thing Lovett displayed was the little pistol he'd left with Chip. "Hell, that's a Nambu," Coop said as soon as he spotted it. "Saw some of those in May of '43 after our guys took Attu." He handled it gently with those callused fingers, shaking his head in remembrance, then returned it. "Found a stash, did you?"

"You could say that. You see any infantry rifles on Attu?" With that, he picked up Ohtsu's rifle with its overlong bayonet and the canvas ammunition pouch now linked to its sling.

"By God, that's one of 'em," Coop said, laughing. "You *did* find a stash!"

"Yeah, but the guy was still using 'em." It was Chip, who couldn't wait for his grandfather to draw the moment out.

With a look of disgust toward the youth, Lovett sighed. "Punch-lining an old man; God will punish you for that, Chip. You see if I don't." He turned to the others. "Well, he's right. We caught the guy who's been setting traps for us. Chip disarmed him. Turned out he's Keikano's grandfather, who claims he's kept these damn planes in condition to fly."

This, in one great lump, was simply too much for any of them to swallow so Lovett had his fun after all. It took a full half-hour to satisfy Coop, Myles, and Benteen as to the details. Coop strained hardest at the idea that a Japanese soldier-mechanic had stayed hidden for so long; Myles had trouble believing that Lovett had actually let him go.

Benteen found all of it somewhat easier to accept. "That makes Keikano a quarter Japanese; no wonder he had trouble pronouncing his *L* at first, he was rusty on English but not on Japanese. He doesn't have the, what is it, epicanthic fold? The little Japanese eyelid, but I should've suspected anyhow. The little snip," she said, and laughed, adding that she'd known islander kids before who'd become passable linguists at an early age.

Keeping a sentry, they decided, was still the only safe course. "Somebody ought to put the word out," Myles said grimly, "if I see either one of 'em during my sentry duty, he'll have a hole in him you could throw a bear cub through."

"Worst thing you could do," Lovett told him. As things stood, he added, they might learn much about servicing the airplanes from old Ohtsu, especially when Reventlo brought the medicines he'd promised. As for Keikano, no one on Fundabora had been so helpful.

Coop's view was similar. "I'd prob'ly have trussed the old Jap up myself, or shot him maybe, but it seems to me Wade and Chip did okay. I'll say this, though: if he comes creeping around here again the least I'll do is hog-tie him. He'll understand a kick as well as the next man."

"Nobody kicks Keikano, okay?" Chip said softly.

Coop gave the youth a level glance. "Giving orders, sonny?"

Even under his tan, Chip's flush was evident. "I'm asking. He's not—he doesn't deserve that," he stammered. "I know him better than anyone here, and you weren't with me when that old guy snuck into the cave, and Keikano was, and—he could've screwed us up and he didn't, that's all. If you see him around, chances are it's for your own good. That's all I'm trying to say. Let's keep him on our side."

"That's a little more like it," Coop said, "but I wonder if Wade sees it the same way."

Lovett thought about that for a moment, swigging coconut milk. Finally: "I think he should be warned away from here outside business hours," he said at last. "Though I've got to tell you, that little confrontation could've gone downhill in a hurry without Keikano to smoothe things out. I'd say handle him gently. Much of what we've learned, we got from him."

Myles didn't like the consensus, but grudgingly accepted it and then changed the subject. "How's the LeTourneau coming?"

It ran, said Coop, but it filled the metal shed with diesel smog. By the day's end he hoped to have the tires fixed. The belly scraper blade could not be adjusted until corroded parts had been cleaned. "Another day and we'll know whether the brute's in business," he finished.

Lovett waved an arm toward the gentle slope of overgrown runway. "Does that mean you could give it the acid test on the airstrip?"

"Not tomorrow. Next day, maybe," Coop judged.

That, said Lovett, would work out nicely. He stated his case for leaving the wall half-demolished until they'd cleared a broad path for the planes.

"I s'pose that was about half bullshit, what you told the old guy about clearing the runway for Reventlo," Coop ruminated. Lovett could only shrug, with a guilty smile. "I thought so. But actually, why couldn't we?"

Myles blinked and stroked his beard, eyeing the jungle growths downslope. "Could we? That'd depend on what you could do."

"What *she* could do," Coop responded, with a nod toward Benteen. "Whaddaya think, Mel?"

"Whoo," she said, eyes slitted, gazing over the job. "Not in less than a week. More like two, and that's if we can wheedle enough fuel from Jean-Claude. A LeTourneau guzzles the stuff, guys. You're asking for a swath two hundred feet wide, half a mile long, aren't you?"

Lovett said he thought so. There was no way to know whether Cris Reventlo would arrive with another C-47 or something smaller. Whatever it was, it wouldn't take kindly to landing on stumps or a field of potholes. The largest of their treasures, the twin-engined

Betty, was almost the size of a C-47 and would need a clearing a hundred feet wide merely to be towed to the beach.

"All I can say is," Benteen concluded, "I'll give it a shot and see how the strip packs down. If Coop gets the LeTourneau well and truly cranked up for me, when I'm operating here it'll be loud enough to be heard from the village. So one thing we can expect is a bunch of native kibitzers."

Benteen was thinking of jobs she'd had on other islands. She was not thinking about Jean-Claude Pelele and his demands on the village.

24

The luck of the draw had slated Melanie Benteen for sentry duty, and after their dinner buffet she tucked her own little pistol into her bag before gliding off the verandah to set off down the beach.

"Want me to go partway? Not that you really need it," Chip added hurriedly.

Before she could reply, Lovett said, "Oh hell, I'll do it, Chip. I need to take a closer look at that old bomber anyway."

Myles ignored them, watching tendrils of smoke curl from the bowl of his corncob as he sat on the veranda, looking after the vanished sun a la General MacArthur minus a shave. Lovett made a show of reluctance as he moved off with Benteen.

"I am perfectly capable," she began a bit haughtily as he caught up to her.

"I know that," he muttered. "Just wanted it to look good for the troops."

"You may not have fooled them, but you fooled me," she replied more gently. "So I'm an old bomber, am I?"

He laughed softly. "You've gotta admit, you sure dropped one on me last night. Dead bang on target, too."

"Oh, don't say 'dead bang,' Wade. Not 'til you know me better."

He chuckled again, then said he supposed she hadn't thought to bring that Drambuie; and she said he supposed right. By the time they reached the turn-in from the beach, Lovett learned that old Elmo had sent her to pricey schools in the States, not all of which appreciated her, and the feeling was mutual, and that while she'd been treated as an only child she wasn't sure how many half-siblings she might have. "Maybe half of Fundabora, if I know my Dad," she sighed. "He was marooned here for quite a while."

In turn, she learned that Wade Lovett's older brother had been with the 6th Marine Division, killed in action on Okinawa late in the war. "In case you're thinking what I'm thinking, I'm pretty sure this old Ohtsu guy couldn't have been there," he confided; "and I don't intend to ask."

She said that was wise of him and then chose a surf-abraded log to lean against and sank down on dry sand that was hardly cooler than skin. He copied her, taking her hand, reacting at her swift hissing intake of breath. "What'd I do?"

"Not you. Try using a wire brush on rusted fittings all day and see how many pricks you get," she told him.

A moment's silence. Then he said, "You want to rephrase that?"

"You're shameless," she said, and actually giggled. "I like that in a man."

"That's a lie, Melanie. Cute, but a lie."

He could see her profile faintly against the sky as she shook her hair for the breeze and chuckled. "All right, if you know so damned much: what do I like in a man?"

He drew up his knees, elbows across them, chin on his arms. "Easier to say what you hate, since you always make that so terrifyingly clear. Let me guess by elimination. You want him gentle, a steady sort, maybe a family man."

"Hardly the type I always wind up with—but you could be right. My God, Wade, I think you *are* right!"

"I'm not finished. You don't want him too up-front."

"And what the hell is that supposed to mean? Of course I do."

"Well, you may want him that way, but you don't *need* him that way. Because if he is, you'll always be arguing. You'd like a guy with the social graces of a Crispin Reventlo, the basic decency of my grandson, and the sex drive of—of—say, Errol Flynn."

"Why an old film actor," she asked.

" 'Cause I didn't want to use Jean-Claude or Elmo as examples," he admitted. "That'd make it too personal."

"I don't see how you could get much more personal," she said.

"No?" He leaned back and cupped her chin in his hand. "Let me expand those horizons."

It was a gentle kiss, warm and unexpectedly yielding. "Mm,

salty," she murmured, and kissed him back, accommodating his tongue. After a moment: "You know, I don't think we're going to miss the Drambuie."

"Not if I manage to hit something else," he said, both of them fumbling in the darkness.

"Will you shut up," she encouraged. And he did.

There was something to be said, he remarked somewhat later, for pleasures more primitive than liqueur.

"Oh? Like sharing a warm shower," she said wistfully.

"I suppose, if we had one available. You know what I mean," he insisted, lying full-length beside her as the night wind cooled his perspiration.

"I know. When it's this pleasant, I second the motion," she said, stretching her arms gracefully aloft. "Even when it isn't this good, it's not all that bad. There's an old joke about that but it's too much trouble to recall right now."

"I know just how you feel," he said sleepily.

"Sensitive new-age man that you are," she chuckled. "How do I feel?"

"Firm and responsive," he said, misreading her for the fun of it. "You seconded a lot of motions, I'm happy to say. Must be that hot islander blood I've heard so much about."

"You're welcome. So now it's your turn. What else do you like in a woman?"

"Me," he said, and she kicked him lightly.

"I'm serious. You seem to understand me fairly well, and there was a time when I would've hated that. But now I don't mind; it's kind of nice, in an old-shoe kind of way. And I said it's your turn and don't make me guess."

He took so long she nudged him with a toe, fearing he'd fallen asleep. "Acceptance! Forgiveness, approval," he amended. "Jeez, give me time to think. Of course I like the physical things, all the things you have in abundance, my God but you must've been a town-wrecker at twenty."

"I was," she agreed. "Girls in my dorm called me the Tramp Steamer—but we're talking about you now."

"Maybe the word I'm looking for is endorsement," he said, "like countersigning a check. Maybe you don't know what I intend to do with it; maybe you know and wish I wouldn't; but you're willing to live with that difference of opinion and let me just—just follow my best judgment." More softly, now: "All my life, I have wound up with women who thought we had to resolve every difference. Compromise, meet halfway, every decision ratified."

"Whereas you want to be the top dog in your kennel," she said.

"Depends, Melanie. When I'm better qualified, you're damn right. Even when everybody's equally qualified, sometimes you have to agree on a top dog. Like the pilot in command, or the responsible surgeon. I had no trouble letting Cris Reventlo stand a pace ahead. And when we first got here, we joked about your being our Maggie Thatcher but I had no objection."

"You'd have played hell talking with the Fundaborans on your own," she observed.

"My point exactly. When democracy means all opinions are equal, that democracy's in deep shit. You might stumble along in a half-assed way but—somebody said that great airplanes aren't designed by committees. I'll go further; neither are great cars or great buildings or great anything else, with rare exceptions. When I thought my wife or my daughter was the expert, I was willing for 'em to carry the ball. When I was, they expected full veto power."

"I think that's part of the give-and-take of marriage," she said. "I'm not sure we should believe in experts."

Lovett's response was sly: "Is that your expert opinion?"

She laughed, seeing her dilemma. "Okay. My old man always used to say, 'Ain't no democracy in the cockpit,' and I suppose that means career pilots make lousy husbands."

"Suppose away. You won't get a rise out of me," he chuckled.

"Not again; not tonight," she said, sighing contentedly. "So that's it? If she has adequate goodies and agrees on a pilot in command for a given situation, you're a happy camper?"

"How would I know," he said. "I've never met her."

Her laugh this time was a series of little bleats, gradually subsiding; then a fresh outburst that set him off as well.

At last she stood up, rearranging her clothes, still amused. "I'm afraid you're incurable, Wade Lovett. But thank God, not inoperable."

"I still have my moments," he agreed, standing with her, sharing a hug that said more about friendship than lust. "But I suppose this was a moment we never had, right?"

"I hope you can deal with that," she said, snapping on her flashlight.

"We were just a passing fanny," he said, raising his voice as she strode away. "Just two ships that shrieked in the night."

"You're babbling," she laughed. "Go home."

No trespassers showed up either that night or the next, when Myles took sentry duty. The false wall was now half its original height and, being thicker near the base, became a slower job. After his solitary duty Vic Myles met his fellow crew members at the maintenance sheds, as agreed, for a crucial test. As he put it, he didn't want to miss seeing Benteen put an earthmover through the end of a building.

Except that Mel Benteen was as good as she'd claimed. Seated high and erect under the LeTourneau's protective cage, she waited until Coop Gunther linked the APU cables up, then nodded at his forefinger-in-a-circle signal. Obviously they'd done some dry runs; when Coop cleared the cabling away, the entire metal shed was already trembling with the rumble and snort of a big diesel, the air thick with a rich mix of exhaust.

The vast wheels turned, engines bellowed, and everyone abandoned the shed with hands pressed over their ears as Mel Benteen operated the huge vehicle by manipulating switches on her console. Standing near the leviathan as its eight-foot tires took it outside the shed, Lovett couldn't even hear the crunch of shell over the din, but he could hear electric motors and gear-trains, two motors to each wheel, doing an industrial-strength job as they'd done it a generation past.

For some minutes she put it through its ponderous paces, checking turn radius and scraper blade travel, and the noise made one corner of Fundabora uniquely American—Texan, in fact, since Coop swallowed his Alaska-sized pride enough to admit the brute was the proud product of Longview, Texas. When Benteen silenced her monster, she was rewarded with cheers and clambered down to plant a resounding kiss on Coop's brow. "Check the oil, clean the windshield, fill 'er up and point me at the freeway," she joked to further cheers.

"Lordy, I wish we could," said Coop. "This sumbitch will guzzle six or eight gallons an hour and I don't think she'll burn coconut oil, folks."

Myles: "We could try it."

Coop: "Sure we could. And try it in those Tojos, too. Then try and find somebody willing to disassemble the fuel systems to clean 'em out when it doesn't work, 'cause I sure-God don't want the job. The LeTourneau has injectors. Am I getting through to you, partner?"

"Just an idea," Myles said, hands up in surrender. Coop's wry smile said he wasn't sure you could call it an idea; more like a knee jerk reflex. Myles went on: "So how much fuel's in there now?"

"About half a barrel of kerosene, all we had, mixed with—what, six gallons of thirty-weight?" Benteen looked to Coop for a nod and got it. "It needs both. You've heard about vehicles that burn oil? Well, these old LeTourneaus are supposed to." She glanced around and saw the new arrivals from the village. "And if it burns a barrel of fuel every couple of hours, we'll need more of it from Jean-Claude," she said more loudly, deliberately exaggerating the fuel consumption.

Lovett looked around and saw why. The man-mountain stood near the shed with two of his guards, chest heaving, agleam with sweat. His broad grin said he was merely winded from trotting, not angry. Keikano arrived moments later, hands gray with what could have been soot, studying Jean-Claude the way a zoologist might study an anaconda. "Bikbik machine him talk too much," Jean-Claude said, but he seemed to be joking.

Benteen conferred softly for a moment with Coop before the old fellow started talking, running his hands over fresh weldments, feeling motor housings, keeping up a monologue not really intended to be understood.

Mel Benteen stood near Coop and appeared to be translating but Lovett had to bite his lip to hide a grin. Some of her speech was pure improvisation. As Lovett understood it, she said the huge machine was ready to rebuild the presidential roads. Here were the repairs made by iron stick burn broken iron, blah blah, and everyone who heard the LeTourneau bellowing across the island would hear in it the voice of the mighty Jean-Claude. Now the roads could be improved, blah blah, and a better landing strip created for Ol' Cris, who would need something more substantial than a beach when he landed his aerocanoe heavy with Fundaboran goods. The big machine's motors needed much slick water and, my, my, how sad if they quit working but of course Jean-Claude understood what his needs were. By the time Coop finally stopped rambling, Benteen had buried Pelele knee-deep in bullshit. She ended by saying that the big machine's voice—Jean-Claude's voice, so to speak—lacked only fuel now.

Not to be outdone by Benteen's rhetoric, the big man set off on a fanciful flight on his pidgin, circled the globe twice, and settled back to earth with a perfect landing. Benteen smiled and turned to Coop. "Ake-shay the man's and-hay," she said, and Coop let his hand be swallowed by Jean-Claude's, everyone now grinning like fools for a variety of reasons. The presidential fuel dump was at their disposal, said Benteen.

Keikano got a direct order to see that Pilau would provide the needed liquids before Jean-Claude set off toward the village again. "I would go with you," he said to Benteen, "but I must finish my task first."

Lovett took in the gray smudges and said, "What're you doing, sweeping chimneys?"

"The annual games require much play-fire. You have a word for it. The Chinese traders bring many kinds; pop, poof, pop," he explained, hands describing arcs in the air.

Benteen said, "Fireworks?"

"That is the word," Keikano said, brightening, turning to leave. "Pilau does not like such work. He will be happy to help you instead of me."

Myles burst into laughter. "Smart of him, kid. If that's black powder on you, you're a walking sparkler." Raising his voice as Keikano strode away: "What night will you shoot them off?"

"Each night," was the reply, with a wave, and then Keikano was trotting away.

"I—be—damn," Myles breathed, grinning. "That's something I wouldn't mind helping with. Firework displays are still an art, you know."

"Spoke like a man lookin' for an alternative to a little hard work," Coop said. "Let's just wait 'til that dumbshit Pilau gets here. We've got some fuel to transfer."

Presently Pilau arrived in the half-track with a pair of helpers and drove them all to the lagoon with its ramshackle dock. Across the lagoon, villagers swarmed over temporary structures made from palm logs lashed together with braided fiber. Benteen learned from Pilau that the local citizens were under the critical gaze of Merizo, which explained why half of them weren't splashing around in the lagoon, joyously watching the strangers sweat like Englishmen in the hot sun. For that matter, Pilau himself stepped up his standard pace, uneasy at being called away from his work in the village.

They did not begin loading fuel drums immediately despite Pilau's anxiety because this was the first chance they'd had to make a detailed check of the dock's condition. While Lovett tallied the drums of stuff stacked beneath thatching near the dock, Coop lay on his belly and used a machete to test the pilings.

Lovett's report came with a smile, Coop's with a rueful head-shake. "There's gasoline, too. Some of those drums have been tapped—you guess who—but there's at least two thousand gallons of kerosene here," Lovett said. "Let's grab some drums of gasoline, too. And some of those cases of engine oil stacked in cardboard cartons that're falling apart. Some of the cartons have stencils from the sixties."

"Doesn't matter," Coop replied. "If it was under the Arabian desert for a million years, thirty more won't hurt it. What worries me is, whether this dock will stand up to loading airplanes onto a barge." The pilings, he said, had been attacked by some marine borer, the equivalent of termites.

While Coop's team rolled and Pilau's lifted with Chip's help, ten of the drums found their way onto the half-track. Because motor oil had once come in tin cans, the corrosion of the tropics had actually begun to eat rust pits into those cans. "Christ, there's more oil soaked into the ground than there is in the cans," Myles noted, lugging an armload with care. "I know a wildcatter in West Texas who'd sink a shaft right here."

It was past noon before the second shipment of fluids was delivered, this time to the edge of the old airstrip. Now, with five hundred gallons in the sheds and a similar amount at the airstrip, Coop allowed as how they just might have enough. He worried about skimping on oil in the mixture but, he said, he'd think of something. After Pilau left, they slowly rolled the few drums of gasoline to the cave.

That afternoon, Benteen made her first foray down the perimeter road with the fully tanked LeTourneau, using its belly-scraper blade in the process. The result was more cosmetic than useful but it brought her to the airstrip, followed by admirers on Cushmans. "Now," she called over the stentorian burp of her great vehicle, "let's see how this buggy fights the jungle!"

There was simply no contest between spindly, shallow-rooted twenty-foot trees and a leviathan on eight-foot wheels. Lovett and the others spent some time in Benteen's wake, clearing debris as she sent her steed bellowing up the gentle slope to within a hundred yards of the cave. At last Lovett, sweat streaming down his face, realized that Coop and Myles were seated on a log like kids on bleacher seats, cheering Benteen on. At that point he and Chip collapsed on another log, but Lovett told Chip to save his breath. Benteen couldn't have heard them over the thunderous blatter of that diesel, he said, if they'd been the Mormon Tabernacle Choir.

Presently Benteen and her jungle-chomper outdistanced them enough to resume something like normal conversation. "Look at her go. She cuts a swath like a tank through those trees," Lovett observed.

"I bet she's imagining they're men," said Myles.

"Whatever takes 'em down," Coop said.

"Like I said," Myles replied. "But hey, so long as I'm not one of 'em."

Lovett bit back a rejoinder and winked at Chip. "She'll have it mowed like a lawn in two days," he said.

"Not by a damn sight," from Coop. "Before she can level and and pack down the surface we gotta get all these trunks hauled out somehow, and a belly-scraper won't do that. Too bad our old buddy Pilau's so busy building that crap in the village."

"But he's doing it with logs," Chip said. "Dudes, I think we can get him back here."

"Don't even think about it," Myles rejoined. "He was antsy as a cat in a kennel this morning; got Merizo's deadlines to meet, or face the usual consequences."

Chip sighed and muttered a few quiet sentences to Lovett, who patted the youth's knee and interceded. "Coop, those guys are wearing that half-track out, toting logs into the village. Here's an idea: have Pilau and a crew load as many of these logs as they can into the LeTourneau's hopper. Then Benteen can haul 'em to the village a hundred at a time. Works for them, works for us."

"By God," Coop said, nodding, then smiling and nodding again. "By *God!*"

Myles jabbed a forefinger at Chip. "You should'a thought of that one, kid."

"He did," Lovett said. "You told him not to think about it."

"He listens to Keikano," Chip put in to reroute the conversation. "I'll see if Kei will talk to him, try and get it arranged. That way, Miz Benteen won't need to make another address to the U.N. like she did this morning."

With that agreement, Chip set off alone on a scooter. At Coop's suggestion, the men began to carefully pace off the dimensions of the old strip for the first time, the better to estimate exactly how big a bite of jungle they had to chew. From cave mouth to beach sand turned out to be roughly twenty-four hundred feet, a hair-raisingly short distance for a warplane, even the lightweight craft the Japanese had built.

Lovett checked the strip's width several times alone; it came to a hundred and sixty feet, give or take a few. Stumps of fully mature trees, now chiefly visible as rotting waist-high lumps that fed jungle ferns, defined the limits of what the Japanese had carved out so many years ago. Even the LeTourneau couldn't bowl over giants like those, but it wouldn't have to. And because Reventlo couldn't depend on having an airstrip to land on, he would most likely come floating down in something that could handle beach sand. Surely something like a Caribou, or a Pilatus with a whopping turbine.

Surely. . . .

25

Night had fallen but, in the light of coconut-oil torches, the villagers continued to work because they knew better than to quit while Jean-Claude sat looking on. Adjusted for the vagaries of their pidgin, the President and his first minister discussed matters of state roughly as follows.

"Pilau claims that he has cleverly convinced the whites to help transport logs more quickly," said Merizo, gnawing a chicken bone. "I gave permission. It was probably Prettyboy's idea. He spoke with the white youth late in the day."

"Those people must be up to something," Jean-Claude replied, licking yam paste from his fingers. "Are they digging any deep holes in my island? Dealing with the north village, you think?"

"My watchers say not, though the whites have somehow beaten a great hole up on a cliff." His shrug conferred the notion that there was nothing especially curious about that. Outsiders did weird things; and holes were where you found them, or made them. "The giant machine has improved the road somewhat and they are stripping the jungle from that area where the aerocanoes once landed. I think they just want to make a better place for Ol' Cris to land."

"A new road, and a way to let traders fly in," Jean-Claude ruminated. "Fundabora will soon be a world power. But it is not like outsiders to work so hard without reward."

"Their reward seems to be the old machines they find, and by agreement we will keep those in the shed that they have repaired," Merizo pointed out. "Who knows why they love old machines so?

Perhaps they can sell them somewhere to islanders less advanced than Fundaborans. Or perhaps they are just crazy," he laughed in his bass rumble. "Let them be crazy, so long as they give us what we want."

"I still want that woman," said Jean-Claude. "I mean to have her, and soon. I will make her love me," he said, with the confidence of a man who had bedded many women without understanding the least thing about any of them.

"Ol' Cris would not love you. You would anger the very people who bring the other things you want?"

"Not until I have them," the big man admitted.

Merizo watched as a dozen villagers struggled to drag a raft of lashed logs as far as the lagoon. "That may not happen until after the leadership games. A wise man would wait until Ol' Cris has delivered our goods, and our roads are perfect, and someone like Pilau has learned to drive the giant machine."

"And then I take the woman," Jean-Claude persisted.

"Perhaps. But first only as a captive. Then we could make the whites do something they might never do otherwise."

The big head of Jean-Claude swiveled to regard the smaller man. "And that is?"

"With the aerocanoe and Ol' Cris to fight it, we would have a weapon that would make the north village yours," Merizo said, his rumble a near-whisper. "It could drop fire on their roofs, as we have seen in old pictures. You would become truly the President of *all* Fundabora."

It had always pained Jean-Claude like a carbuncle in his groin that the north village—in fact the northern third of Fundabora—remained a blank smudge on his personal map. *Fire on their roofs*. The more Jean-Claude toyed with this mental image, the more he liked it. He did not think about peaceful trade being better than warfare, nor about destroying the things he already got in trade. He thought about tiny antlike figures streaming from flaming huts, howling in fear; and he liked that most of all. Those old foreigners who had built the north village were supposed to be long dead. Keikano had said as much. "This may be one of the best ideas I have ever had," Jean-Claude mused. "But it is not a thing we should speak of, when Prettyboy is around."

"Until after we do it," Merizo said, torchlights reflecting from his eyes. "Then, we will not need that little snot."

"You never liked him much," Jean-Claude grinned, well aware

of Merizo's dislike for others who, like himself, lived by their wits. Wits were for those who needed them; with brawn, you could buy wits. "When that day comes, I give him to you."

"He will furnish us much entertainment," Merizo said, and walked away on noiseless feet. He had noticed one of the young villagers nodding off from exhaustion while tying knots. A stick across his shins would wake him nicely.

Lovett spent his night in the cave on schedule, familiarizing himself further with cockpits. The tiny flying bomb snugged against the bomber's belly was a miracle of simplicity, its cockpit reached from inside the Betty. Squatting in the bomb bay above it, shuddering at the very thought of climbing down into such a deadly little contraption, he saw that the pilot of an Ohka had few instruments, none at all for real navigation. *What for*, he asked himself. *When the poor bastard was dropped, he was already within sight of his target, and the ticket was strictly one way.*

To snug down in there without a chute it took someone of Chip's age and foolishness, brimful of misdirected patriotism and, to say the least, highly motivated beyond all rational limits. It was one of the ironies of war, Reventlo had said, that there were more of the little twin-tailed Ohkas in museums than of any other product of the Japanese war industry. Maybe they would just leave the Ohka on Fundabora. Hauling that thing off a barge in front of sharp-eyed longshoremen would vacate somebody's wharf like a mink in a henhouse.

Such thoughts were depressing, and Lovett moved forward to the Betty's cockpit. Maybe, one day before they sold it back in the States, they might actually fly it. Cris Reventlo had once known how; it would be enough for Wade Lovett simply to make a few gentle banks, maybe a modest wingover. But not, he grinned to himself, with that goddamned suicide machine shackled into the bomb bay.

Rummaging among the workbench supplies he found that someone, probably old Ohtsu himself, had carefully laid in a supply of virtually everything needed to maintain those planes. To maintain rudders and ailerons covered with doped fabric, Ohtsu had a supply not only of fabric but of dope, sealed in wax, gurgling as if still usable. Nearby were sailmaker's curved needles in oiled paper and what must have been a mile of heavy waxed thread. It looked like the cotton and linen stuff Lovett had used when reconditioning old puddle-jumpers, which gave the bleary-eyed Lovett an idea. He rigged lines across the possible entries and tied wrenches to the lines so that, when the line was disturbed, a wrench would scrape against a piece of flimsy aluminum sheeting. That racket, he decided, would certainly wake him—assuming that he fell asleep while sitting in the cockpit of a Tojo.

It was one of his better assumptions. The clatter and skritch of metal on metal brought him fully awake only when Chip blundered into the cord the next morning bearing breakfast. Keikano stood outside the cave, unwilling to enter now without an invitation.

By now the standard breakfast of a sentry had become the best and worst vittles available to the human race: a fat, ripe, multicolored mango and crackers from an MRE packet. Lovett found that the LeTourneau was already chugging into the clearing Benteen had made, Pilau and a half-dozen men piling out of the half-track to begin filling the LeTourneau's hopper with logs. The B.O.F. crew helped, wielding their machetes. As soon as Benteen headed for the village, the crew hauled remaining debris to one side of the clearing. Keikano tried to help Chip but chiefly succeeded only in getting in the way.

What made the entire log-skimming operation so ludicrous was that, for purposes of clearing the airstrip, those trips of Benteen's to and from the village were sheer wasted time. Given a half-dozen strong young men for a few days, Benteen could have simply hauled those logs off fifty yards to one side for dumping. But willing as he was, strong as he was, Chip alone could not make up for the fact that his partners comprised a woman and three aging duffers, one of them with a prosthetic leg. After all, Lovett complained, it was sad but literally true that the B.O.F.'s middle name was "old."

Still, "It's happening," Coop said, arms akimbo as he surveyed the mess, "and faster than I figured." With a wary glance toward the little schoolteacher, he said, "I hope they can use all the logs we can give 'em."

"And how many is that," Keikano asked.

Coop took that up with Myles, Alaskan and Texan roommates amiably arguing out a rough estimate. "Upwards of two or three thousand," Coop said at last.

"How many is that in hundreds," said Keikano.

"I thought you taught school," Myles said, not unkindly.

"Not numbers," was the crestfallen reply. "My honored grandparent helps me count with pebbles but—I think Pilau will be satisfied with ten loads like the one they have."

"Oh, shit, that's not half of what we'll have, not even counting twice that many little skinny saplings," said Coop, jerking a thumb toward nearby foliage. Interspersed with the palms and ferns were many more small trees, some as twisted as pool cues in hell and all so slender they resembled self-supporting vines with sparse broad leaves. They were no thicker than a man's wrist, yet they would have to come down.

"He's trying to tell you we need Pilau to take maybe thirty loads," Lovett put in, flashing him all ten fingers three times.

Keikano's eyes grew large, his lips moving silently. "No way, José," he said, Chip's jargon sounding comical from this willing linguist. "But this is something you need?"

"If we want to clear this airstrip for Reventlo—grab those vines, will you, Vic?—we need everything taken away," Lovett said, working as he spoke.

"That is far more than the village can possibly use," Keikano muttered. "Unless—let me think on it." A gentle smile began to play about his mouth. "No, they will not burn well. I thought maybe, but no."

"All that stuff in the center of the village? Whoa, don't get yourself bonked on our account," Chip said, appalled.

"I am always careful," Keikano protested, drawing himself up, the narrow shoulders straightening. "But thirty hundreds? No way," he said again.

"Way," Chip insisted. "Somehow, way." And with that, they fell to work again.

At the end of the day they had cleared away over five hundred logs, and by then Pilau was convinced that the entire idea had been his own. He even let Myles drive the half-track, which was a great help in dragging brush away. The slender polelike stuff was ignored for the moment, too big to toss around with ease yet not bulky enough to be of interest to Pilau's crew. Pilau chose some of the smaller poles and spent a few minutes idly hurling them into the jungle, as a boy might skip stones for amusement. Before leaving for the councilhouse the B.O.F. contingent simply stood and regarded this horrendous web of debris without much enthusiasm.

"What I wouldn't give," Coop muttered, "for a battalion of Seabees."

Chip brushed leafy bits from his hair. "Bees?"

"World War II would'a turned out differently without 'em," said Coop, the only man there who was old enough to have seen

Seabees in the Aleutians. "Navy Construction Battalions—Seabees. Said 'C B' stood for 'confused bastards' but in these parts, they built runways while under sniper fire, I shit you not. I hear even the Marine Corps put up signs in their honor—and gyrenes weren't known for their applause."

"So what would five Seabees without bulldozers have done with all these fuckin' pickup sticks," Myles asked, combing his beard clean as he surveyed the clearing.

"If I knew, I'd do it," said Coop, turning away. They worried at the problem all through the dinner meal.

Coop, never very agile afoot, left the lobby buffet alone after dark and took a Cushman to the cave for his turn as sentry that evening. Keikano, whose job as fireworks technician was far from finished, said that he must work at night to make up for time lost.

The schoolteacher was overjoyed when Vic Myles offered to help with it. "You expect to work with black powder at night by torchlight? You're out of your friggin' mind," said the Texan, grabbing a big flashlight.

"I am always—" Keikano began.

"Careful, yeah," Myles laughed. "Tell me that when you're passing over Manila as a loose assortment of pieces, kid."

"That sounds almost responsible," Benteen said. "You never cease to amaze me, Victor."

"Around a sizeable pile of that stuff, you're either responsible or unrecoverable," Myles replied. "What black powder lacks in efficiency, it makes up for in unpredictability. I've known some so-called expert powdermen with hands missing, eye patches, big gouges outa their hides. Some experts! See these?" He held up both hands, fingers spread. "Count 'em. Nothing missing, and that's how I mean to keep it."

Chip, in tones Lovett recognized as far too casual, said, "I wouldn't mind watching, if nobody cares."

Lovett was tempted to object, but relented when Myles said, "Better ask your grandpa."

"Precious little I have to say about it," Lovett said wryly, knowing it was the only right answer. "See you later—preferably intact."

"Well, if you don't mind," said Chip.

"Aah. I'll stay here, sit around with Benteen and listen for a big bang."

Benteen waited until the Cushmans fired up outside the councilhouse. Then, "Hmm. Coop's away, Chip and Myles are playing with fireworks, and I believe that Drambuie is still hiding in my bag upstairs," she purred.

"I suppose," Lovett said judiciously, "we could listen for the big bang up there as well as anywhere."

She pursed her lips in a smile loaded with prurience. "But as long as that damned audio circuit of Pelele's is working," she said, "let's not let him hear our *little* bang."

"You're on," Lovett said, following.

"I will be," she countered, hips rolling gently as she preceded him up the stairs.

The next several days passed in flurries of success and frustration as the second-growth jungle was stripped away. Big wheels and tracked cleats compressed the earth enough to resemble something like a rough landing strip down the exact center of the old runway; a landing strip, that is, for any aircraft that could land in a clearing forty feet wide. Since this was obviously a tactic for a lunatic, they continued to widen the strip daily with the LeTourneau and kept their radios handy, expecting Reventlo at any time, knowing that expectation was asking too much. It was Coop Gunther's turn again as sentry the night they reminisced over the days when fireworks were part of the American experience.

The Fundaboran fireworks, Myles reported, were years old but as good as new and must have cost a small fortune—but since Jean-Claude liked them, a hut had been specially thatched to store them safe from moisture, near the dock facility beside the lagoon and across from the village. "Remember when you were a kid," Myles said that evening, packing his pipe on the veranda, "and you got a couple of bucks to squander on firecrackers?"

"Yeah," Lovett said, smiling into old memories. "You could get a funny little four-pack of Chinese crackers for a penny, wrapped in crinkly paper with a cover label that said, 'Black Cat' or 'Yan Kee Boy.' I wondered where Yan Kee was 'til a big kid said it meant us: yankee boys. A teenager would show off by setting one off while he held it between his thumb and forefinger. I tried it. Once."

Chip urged him on with, "So what happened?"

"I was ten; I cried is what happened. Stung like hell and numbed my fingers," Lovett said with a sad little smile. "Big red firecrackers called 'baby giants' were two for a nickel, and they'd send a tin can halfway to Nebraska; nobody held those in their fingers. A cherry bomb cost more, but it'd unwrap that can like it was tinfoil. When you unrolled one of the little Yan Kee Boys that hadn't gone off, you could see it had been made from Chinese newspaper. All those little ideographs; we used to think it was secret code, like, 'help, I'm held prisoner in a Hong Kong fireworks factory.' "

"The real secrets were in the complicated stuff," Myles confided. "Roman candles; rockets; those aerial salutes we called Dago bombs, especially the big ones, fat cardboard mortar tubes on wooden bases with big warnings, 'light fuse and GET AWAY FAST.' I used to collect the stuff that hadn't gone off, spray it with water and then take it apart. Had a faint stink like a boiled egg left in the sun too long. Hell, I even liked the way they smelled.

"When I was twelve I could make the simple ones myself. Most fun I ever had, though, was with what was left of a big cardboard mortar tube after I knocked the wooden base off and tucked both ends closed. Ever hear of a Mills Bomb? An early Brit grenade. I called mine the Myles Bomb. It was a foot long, two inches in diameter. Still had the colored paper on it but it was empty; couldn't hurt you. But try telling that to a bunch of kids after you stuck a live fuse into one end, lit it, and tossed it underfoot. They made more noise than a real grenade would've. I mean, it got their absolute undivided attention better'n a hornet's nest. Some big kids got to calling me Gonna-get-you Myles, but you know, somehow they never got around to it."

Chip, admiringly: "Quick on your feet?"

"It wasn't that; if they *did* get me, I think they worried that the next Myles Bomb underfoot might not be empty," the Texan winked.

"You should've been arrested," Benteen said.

"I was. Got my butt warmed. But whatthehell, in one respect it was the safest firework in Texas. Kids got hurt every year, no question about it, so eventually a lot of do-gooders made fireworks illegal. Now every year on the fifth of July you read about all the kids that drowned, or fell off their motorcycles, the day before. Those were kids that would've been better off spending the Fourth with fireworks. Like these islanders."

"How would you rate Keikano as a powderman," Lovett asked.

"Careful," Myles said in grudging endorsement. "He's got enough common dynamite fuse to surround Fundabora. You know the stuff? Orange, thick as a pencil, waterproof. He cuts into it to link up a bunch of aerial salutes, so he can line up two dozen starburst mortars he's lashed on a raft and float it all in the lagoon. That's what some of the rafts are for. Seems the kids have games, too, and the winners get to swim out carrying little torches in one hand, and light the fuses."

"Two dozen aerial salutes? Every night?"

"Two dozen every couple of minutes! I'm telling you, when I saw all the waxed cartons of that wonderful old shit stacked up high as my head, I decided maybe Jean-Claude really is a rich man. Christ almighty, if that grass storage shack ever catches fire, you'll think it's a fuckin' heavy mortar attack."

"I'm losing track of the days," Benteen sighed, stretching becomingly in the moonlight. "How long before we get to see all these festivities?"

"Three days," Chip replied. He looked around casually, then went on in softer tones: "And Pilau may need some more logs. We'll know in the morning. I'm, uh, meeting someone in an hour to see about it."

"I don't like the sound of that," said Lovett. *In more ways than one.*

The others exchanged glances. "If you're up to some kinda high-school fuckaround, we'll need particulars. This is a team operation, kid," Myles told him.

"Well, basically it's not our team, okay? Not my idea, either, but if it works, we score. I'm just gonna scope it out."

"Kid's out of control, Lovett," Myles grumped.

Lovett bridled. "Yeah? And who was the goddamn genius who smuggled him aboard the C-Fort in the first place?"

Benteen's tone had more resignation than anger in it: "Oh, *will* you stop?" More softly, she said to Chip, "At least tell us where you're going."

And in a wondrous softly snarling, nasal parody of a man he had seen only in classic films, Chip said, "Meeting a guy down on the waterfront, Sweetheart. No place for a dame like you," breaking into laughter as he finished.

"I give up," Benteen announced. "Wade Lovett, you created a monster, once removed."

"I tried to remove him again at Mejit but you knew better," Lovett reminded her, then nodded toward his grandson. "Just remember the Fifth Flying Commandment, Chip."

"Thou shalt have a damn good reason the FAA will buy," the youth quoted. "Got it. The fed you mean is the size of a barn." With that, Chip gave them a half-salute and slouched off in the general direction of the maintenance sheds.

Myles began to chuckle. "You taught him your own Ten Commandments, did you, parson? What were the others?"

Lovett stood up, looking after the departed youth, feeling a thousand years old. "I'll give you one more. Avoid restricted areas. You're in one now," he added, and headed for his room.

He had heard the soft knock, presumably Mel's, and ignored it because this was one night he needed to be alone. When his luminous watch dial said it was past ten, he eased out of bed and ghosted outside with a comm set in his pocket. He kept to the verge of the tree line, taking his time, and reached the edge of the wharf without seeing anyone. His only alarm en route came when he kicked a land crab by accident and it grabbed his trouser leg. The damned things were big, nocturnal, and generally edible, at least until you stomped it to marmalade while high-stepping an impromptu jig in pitch darkness. Ants and land crabs were worse in some respects than mosquitoes. Both kinds of critter tended to find you if you hunkered down for long. The ants were worse in one way because they gave you no warning until you felt those tiny hobnailed boots tromping up your leg. The crabs rustled fearlessly along giving you plenty of warning; but if one of them said howdy with a big claw, your reply was likely to wake the dead.

A few villagers were still at work in distant torchlight across the lagoon, the pale flickers dancing like antic crescent moons on the silently flowing water. The wharf's wooden surface had been built to last, and did not give him away with creaks. Here, the channel had been dredged long ago to accept trading craft with shallow drafts. Lovett waited for some sign of Chip, biding his time by imagining how the place might have looked on a sunny afternoon when FunIsle's tourists and phosphate rock were still the chief industries on Fundabora.

A little coastal steamer, or perhaps a graceful tall-masted ketch, might have been warped with hawsers to the—what, bollards?—big posts projecting from the wharf's edge. A couple of dumpy, middle-aged geography teachers on vacation would have the time of their lives paddling a rented outrigger, or swimming the hundred yards between the banks of the lagoon which, Lovett knew, was really a misnomer. It wasn't a coral-fringed lagoon but a widening of the island's major creek into a tidal pool, bringing salt water in during high tides, flushing it back out in slack tides.

Some retired broker would be rubbing suntan lotion on the back of his bikini'd darling, many years his junior, as she sat on a towel away from the hustle and bustle of loading at the wharf, studying the play of muscles on half-naked stevedores through her half-closed lids and thinking idly about—and a fish flopped downstream from the wharf, and Lovett's little fantasy evaporated. But was it a fish?

And again, more of a swirl, barely audible. And then a series of rhythmic whooshes that gradually increased in volume, and Lovett knew he was hearing the steady breathing of a tired swimmer. Sitting against a bollard, Lovett might have been part of the gray on black that was the wharf itself.

The swimmer's breath came in the long sighs of one who had been out there for a while, and his emergence onto breakwater stones beyond the wharf was almost noiseless. It was at this time that Lovett realized a second swimmer was closing in, making a bit more noise as he eased up from the water. Something was whispered, too faint to be understood from any distance. Then the two dim silhouettes embraced, a soft chuckle shared, and though he could see very little, now Lovett knew the slender silhouettes had to be Keikano and Chip who were now hurriedly putting their clothes on as they sat together on the big stones.

I didn't want to see this, he told himself, thinking of that embrace against the stars. *Maybe not*, himself replied, *but if you keep spying on the kid you deserve what you get*. With great stealth, Lovett began to inch his way back to the darker black of old fuel drums at the wharf's edge until he brushed against one. And because it was empty, it made a sound like stroking a bass drum with a broom. To Lovett's subjective ear it seemed more like the tolling of a gong.

Instantly the small sounds from the near distance ceased. A moment later, the unmistakable sounds of flight, footsteps swishing through rank grass, fronds clashing softly as bodies rushed away. And now Lovett was alone, and could stand up and make his way back, this time by way of the sheds. He strode into the councilhouse as if he owned it, and beat Chip back to their room by a good half-hour.

This time, when Chip disrobed, his grandfather didn't feign sleep. "So where the hell—cancel that." It wasn't even an honest question; he knew bloody well where Chip had been. "Got any news, Chip?"

"Not yet. We'll see tomorrow," was the whispered reply, sounding suspiciously hoarse with exhaustion. And if Chip wasn't asleep in thirty seconds, he was a superb faker.

26

The next morning, Chip deflected questions with, "If there's news, somebody will tell us," and they'd been hard at work for an hour before they heard the half-track clamoring along the perimeter road.

Keikano rode with the native crew, explaining that—surprise!—they would need several more loads of logs as replacements, and more still for spares. Somehow, he said with exaggerated innocence while Pilau looked on, their log rafts had broken loose during the night, floating out with the creek's flow as far as the breakwater. Now they were just so many logs again, flotsam thudding around in the surf. It would be quicker to have Benteen transport a few more loads than to recover the rafts that had already broken up in rolling waves.

Myles again borrowed the half-track to move debris. Chip and the schoolteacher studiously avoided much interaction until, an hour later, Benteen went thundering off down the road again with the native crew, minus Keikano. Chip threw an arm around the shoulder of the smaller youth, watching the LeTourneau disappear, and both began to laugh. A gentle High Five followed.

Lovett did not want to admit that he knew the reason for their elation; he'd have to face Chip's accusing look when he did it. Instead, he waited until Coop asked what the joke was as they loaded brush into the half-track.

"Rongi said the rafts should not be floated so soon," Keikano replied, with a look of dismay so deliberately bogus that no six-year-old could have missed it. "But Merizo insisted. Now Jean-Claude will be angry at the delay and he will direct it at his minister." Eyes twinkling, he suddenly favored them with one of those gorgeous smiles. "I suggested that, in addition to replacing the rafts, an extra supply of logs should be left near the lagoon. Merizo liked that."

"In case more rafts float away," Lovett nodded sagely. "Good idea, Keikano. But I think it could be very suspicious, in fact downright damned dangerous, if any more logs head for the surf." More sternly now: "You understand me?"

"Oh yes," said Keikano brightly. "It was I who said that someone should sleep with the new rafts, to be sure they do not seek the sea again."

"So of course you couldn't have shown them how to seek it," Lovett persisted.

"It would be normal to think that way," Keikano agreed.

Lovett's glance toward Chip was accusing. "Okay, it worked, and thanks. But I'm going gray—all right, dammit, my roots are getting grayer—worrying about the pranks you two play on King Kong."

"Kei would've done it alone, Pop," Chip said. "As long as I couldn't argue him out of it, I could help make the job go quicker. Actually we had to make sure those rafts would get all the way to the surf. If they got hung up I was afraid Pilau could've used the half-track like a mule to tow everything back this morning, and I didn't want to crow until the eggs hatched, so to speak."

"No more jobs like that, Chip, unless you want to risk being a capon, okay?" Lovett waited for a nod, and Chip gave it to him.

"You swim as my father did," Keikano said admiringly to the tall youth. "I had no idea. But you do make too much noise, Chip."

"Tide going out means fresh water in the stream. I'm not used to working that hard to stay afloat," Chip explained.

Keikano's shrug implied that anybody who would use such an excuse was, perhaps, not really at home in the water. Lovett realized that while Chip thought himself a regular Evinrude on a surfboard, islanders might as well have gill slits.

By the day's end, long after Keikano had left with Pilau and his final load of logs, they could look down a long swath of runway to the beach itself. The rough strip was now about the width of the Betty's wingspan, its upper reaches terminating in that untouched stand of trees hiding the cave's half-demolished wall. Benteen, who had been chauffering logs and natives for much of the day, learned about the rafting scam later, as they were laboriously refueling her LeTourneau. Tropical rain fell in little spits and spats, though the late sun still shone. "We're topped off," she called to Coop, and replaced the fuel cap. From her commanding height, she squinted toward the cave. "Tomorrow I might get another twenty feet mowed. Then what?"

"Keep mowing," said Myles who, like Lovett, had flown enough in Southeast Asia to intuit the problems Reventlo might have in landing. "Even if we don't get it all taken away, Cris will need enough clearance for wings."

Chip brightened suddenly. "A big helicopter would be cool. Can he fly one?"

"Dunno if he's qualified, but he's not coming in a helo," Myles said. "He knows we couldn't fuel it and anything with rotors uses more fuel than a blast furnace."

"Pilatus Turbo could make it, I think," Lovett mused.

For once Myles took Lovett's words for wisdom, nodding. "You could grease a little Pilatus down on this strip just as it stands, but whatever you're flying, get yourself a crosswind gust and those trunks would take your wing off like a chicken-plucker."

"Or he could dig a wheel into a soft spot in this crap," Lovett said, kicking a clod, "and get a ground loop out of it. Same result. A lot depends on what he's flying; how slowly he can float 'er in with full flaps."

Coop reminded them that Reventlo wasn't expecting a runway anyhow and would most likely be prepared for another beach landing. "I don't mind telling you, I expected him back by now. If he's bought a very damp farm out there somewhere we sure won't read about it in the *Morning Fundaboran.*"

Benteen, trying to mother a sourdough thirty years her senior, reminded Coop that their missing Brit had a lot of details to cover before his return. "He might have had trouble raising Quinn back in the States, or transferring the money," she said, looking to Lovett for support.

And getting it. "Don't forget, the barge and crew could take, Jeez, I don't know how long," Lovett chimed in. "For all we know he'll come chugging into the lagoon from the breakwater on a barge with a crane."

"Uh-huh," Coop said. "And then we—what, tow those freakin' Tojos behind my LeTourneau all the way down the beach?"

"My LeTourneau," said the proprietary Benteen.

"Pelele's LeTourneau," Lovett reminded her.

"What-effin'-ever," Coop said, unconvinced, inventing a scenario for effect: "Hi there, Jean-Claude, mind steppin' aside so's our shiny new fifty-year-old bomber doesn't grind your fat ass to lard while we load our property on a barge? What say? Oh, yeah; well, some airchines turn to shit when buried in the jungle, and some just get shinier. You'll buy that, won't you, ol' buddy? You won't? But hey, we've got a signed contract. Oh, you can't read, huh? Well, trust me, you can't violate that contract without the gummint's say-so.

"Ahh, you say you *are* the gummint, and—whaddaya mean, 'impound'? Whaddaya mean, yours?" By now, Chip and Mel Benteen were grinning openly, and Myles might have been smiling behind his thicket of beard. Lovett put up his hands in silent surrender, and old Coop nodded with the satisfaction of a vindicated pessimist. "That's what keeps me awake nights, anyway."

Myles: "You been snoring like that, and you wide awake?"

Coop ignored him. "I wish Cris was here, that's all. Wish I knew what options we'll have once we unveil these old beauties. You think we could get 'em loaded some night while ever'body's skunk-drunk during those games?"

"Not a chance; you know better than that," Lovett said. "Look, sooner or later Pelele's crowd has to find out. Their annual bash may be over long before Cris gets back. Besides, it'll take time to move those planes so that we don't collapse a gear strut or something, and the middle of the night is not—that—time."

"Well, they can let us scarf their food and haul their logs with everbody smiling and all, but the later those guys find out about our goodies, the better," Coop muttered.

"No argument there," Myles said, tamping his pipe with a dirty finger. They moved off toward the Cushmans, making plans for the evening. Chip had sentry duty; Myles said he'd endure Keikano's company just to fiddle with the fireworks display again; Lovett had promised to find a receptacle in the councilhouse kitchen to recharge the battery in Chip's little computer; and Melanie Benteen agreed to help Coop work on one of the scooters. It smoked worse than Myles, and her eyes worked better in lamplight than Coop's did though, she claimed, half the time as Coop's helper she had no more idea what she was doing than the much-maligned Pilau.

More days passed with no sign of Reventlo, and the crew became moody with tension. On the afternoon when the games finally began, Benteen admitted she was fighting a great temptation to knock off early. She had seen that huge tree trunk erected in the central plaza with its tiny platform a dizzying fifty feet up, and recognized it for what it was. "I just hope they don't test it with kids first," she said with a shudder.

"Aah," said Myles, "those kids all climb like monkeys, Benteen. They won't fall off that platform."

"No. They jump," she replied, and set her big vehicle in motion again, leaving Myles and Lovett to swap awed glances. Suicide leaps? She had to be kidding. *Or maybe not*, those glances said.

The cave wall was now completely removed in the center to ground level, leaving parapets on each side as high as a man might reach. They had piled brush and fronds in the entrance to the same level, but any native who got near enough could have seen what was in that cave. By now, however, the village resounded with the beat of log drums that resounded faintly down the perimeter road. Evidently no villager had the slightest interest in what went on anywhere but in the central plaza.

At last Benteen made her final pass of the day, getting an OK sign from Lovett, silencing the rumble of her leviathan near the cave. "The hell with this," she announced.

The drumming had stopped long before they puttered to the village plaza, and the sounds that greeted them reminded Lovett of a Little League playoff. Instead of Cokes and hot dog stands, they saw coconut milk and skewers with smoked pork, mystery meats, baked fish, and fruits lying on mats here and there, visited by a steady stream of noshers. Those pole bleachers were packed with citizens in their colorful, best attire and the newcomers strolled near to stand with the overflow crowd.

Sitting at front center on his inevitable cushioned bench, surrounded by his retinue of teenybopper wives and beef trust offensive linemen, Jean-Claude Pelele gave a hand signal and a breechclouted boy separated himself from a half-dozen others, all holding cane javelins. The lad hefted his weapon, dancing lightly as he gathered his concentration, then hurtled forward, releasing the javelin behind a line of whitewashed stones. The cane missile arced high though not very far, landing short of several previous efforts, and Lovett saw that there was no target; this was simply for distance. The audience gave a lusty cheer anyway, and presently Jean-Claude signaled to another contestant.

Not far from the area where the javelins were falling stood a sort of easel covered by a tattered cloth mat. Worked into the mat was the lifesized—or more accurately perhaps, deathsized—figure of a man, a tan figure on green matting. "Mel, what's that all about," he said, pointing toward it.

Benteen spoke with the raven-tressed woman nearest her for a few moments. Then: "Lance target," she confided. "They've finished with that already; something they haven't done since the years they fought the North village. I gather my informant isn't all that happy to see it brought back."

Lovett studied the target, which seemed to have had the living hell poked out of it. "I'm with the lady," he said. "But better this than the real thing."

"Holdover from a warrior culture," Benteen said, her gaze following the flight of another cane spear. "Or new beginnings."

"My thought exactly," he said. "I'm gonna grab some of that fish; want some?"

"I'll get my own," she said quickly. "You don't want to get Myles to thinking, do you?"

"That'll be the day," he said with a wry smile and was soon slurping lukewarm coconut milk with Coop Gunther. As a final cheer went up, the winning boy was hoisted to the shoulders of his competitors for a tour of the prize ring. As Jean-Claude bestowed a garland around the lad's neck, Lovett scanned the crowd but failed to see what he was looking for. "Coop, you see that grandson of mine anywhere?"

"Nope. But we both know how to find him."

"Say again?"

"You want me to spell it out? Look for Twinkletoes," said the old fellow.

Galling, but true. Two hundred yards from the crowd, Lovett found the youths together, separating one of the log rafts from the linked series moored with ropes across from the wharf on the village side of the lagoon. Lovett counted eight rafts, each with its cargo of fireworks: rockets with guide sticks, what looked like Roman candles, and an array of cardboard mortar tubes, all fed with thick, old-fashioned dynamite fuse. As Chip returned Lovett's approaching wave, Keikano thrust the chosen raft into the languid current, holding its moorage rope as he walked downstream. Lovett said, "Time for the finale, is it?"

"After the swimming and canoe races," Keikano called. "It will be near dark then. I will release the raft and the winning child will swim out with his torch to start the fuse."

Hearing more cheers, Lovett turned to see a dozen boys pelting around the plaza in a footrace that looked from a distance like a ghetto rumble. Tripping was okay, elbows were fine, and tackling was "in." The winning kid was the best hurdler, leaping over sprawled bodies to pull up before Jean-Claude, bleeding from scratches as he knelt for his garland of pale blossoms. Lovett shook his head. "Are the adult games pretty much like these, Keikano?"

"Men's games are rough," said Keikano, binding the moorage rope.

"If they're much rougher than that," said Lovett, jerking a thumb over his shoulder, "you must get some casualties."

"You mean injury? Always," said Keikano, with a vexed glare toward the throng that was pure elitism. "Or worse." Lovett only nodded, thinking about sour grapes. If the men's races were rougher than what he had just witnessed, a little sprite like Keikano would've wound up getting rendered for tallow.

"I was going to see if I could enter the men's swim meet," Chip said ruefully, "but according to Kei, I'm not eligible." Peering past Lovett's shoulder, he added, "Hey, here they come. What happens now?"

An excited babble began to grow from the near distance, villagers trooping toward the lagoon, boys sprinting in pairs for small canoes with single outriggers that lay overturned at the waterside. Most of the kids were antic with haste, flopping their scaled-down log canoes over, outriggers slapping heads and shoulders with abandon. Only two of the pairs seemed casual, last to thrust their mounts into the water. "Where are they racing to," Lovett asked.

"They will begin at Rongi's order," said Keikano, pointing far downstream, "and will race to Jean-Claude." Motionless on stones, far away near the breakwater, standing tall in the late sun, was a solitary figure and, from the broad shoulders and slender waist, Lovett knew it was Rongi. Jean-Claude had taken his position at the terminal curve where the creek fed into the lagoon. Nearer, the paired teams were spurring one another on with urgent little cadenced cries as they paddled frantically toward the distant figure of Rongi. All except those last two pairs, who took their time getting underway.

"So they're not racing yet," Lovett said, smiling.

"No. They are boys," Keikano replied, smiling back as if to say that explained everything.

Chip was half amused, half disgusted. "Don't they know they're wearing themselves out before they start, Kei?"

"They are boys," said the schoolteacher again. "All spirit, no brain. Some learn sooner than others. My—part cousin?—Tanil is in the last canoe. He listens," said the schoolteacher.

"To you," Chip persisted.

"To me," said Keikano with quiet pride.

"What tricks did you teach him?" The last of the little dugout canoes had now diminished to toys in the distance, with tiny manikins flailing graceful paddles in fading sunlight.

"Those my father knew," said Keikano. "Paddle as one. Note the water's motion. Do not spend yourselves too soon. Keep your balance float out of harm's way. Be wary of other paddles on your near side."

Lovett said, "You mean those kids will be fighting each other like in the footrace?"

"You will see," Keikano said, as though Lovett's question were the height of naivete.

The tiny outrigger canoes were still jockeying for position when Rongi apparently gave some signal. Three of the seven little dugouts shot forward, two others veered sharply together as if choreographed so that one outrigger flew up and over in a capsizing, and the final two began to skim along the edge of the lagoon just off the pace. Keikano scurried to stand atop a boulder, shading his eyes.

The short paddles, their blades shaped like flat exaggerated spearheads, flashed in the sun at a startling rate, at least one stroke per second for those in front. Lovett laughed as he saw Rongi make a flat expert dive toward the two entangled craft. The hapless boys were now swimmers, still using their paddles, but now for combat. Whether Rongi intended to break up the fight or serve as referee seemed moot.

Villagers were cheering, some trotting along the water's edge toward the oncoming speedsters, and at midpoint one canoe had forged a half-length ahead. Now approaching near enough for Lovett to make out details, the canoes were moving at the pace of a long-distance runner. At that moment, the forward paddler of the second-place canoe swung his paddle wide, so that it caught the aft outrigger brace of the leading craft. And again. Each time that happened, the second craft narrowed its deficit by an armspan. And now the lead canoe's aft oarsman made a wide sweep of his own, sending a perfectly directed gout of lagoon water into the face of his competitor and, not incidentally, fetching his opponent's paddle a solid whack. The third pair of canoeists steered wide of this foolishness and, as the leaders became spearmen instead of oarsmen, nosed ahead. *No wonder the tips of those paddles are pointy,* Lovett decided. The islander blade design may not have matched the curved blades of a Brit collegiate champion for sheer efficiency, but as a weapon the damned thing could poke your lights out. Maybe that had been the original idea in the islands . . .

And now, as the early leaders became brawlers egged on by hundreds of yelling spectators, the new leader swept well past; but Keikano's gaze was still fixed on one of the laggard craft that sped along in the shallows on the near side. It wasn't lagging so much anymore, and Lovett could see that while others were beginning to flag, this pair was one of those that had saved all that boyish energy for the time when it counted. They actually picked up their cadence a bit, pulling abreast of the leader as both craft passed by, drawing a glare of helpless fury.

And a desperation tactic that would've had the tiring pair drawn and quartered in any Western contest. Because the lagoon was a hundred yards wide and the shore-hugging canoe well beyond paddle-reach, it seemed the winner was a foregone conclusion—until the glaring oarsman of the fading pair quickly made a sleight-of-hand gesture one-handed, and a slender cord unfurled in midair. It was a fishing line complete with hooks, in an unerring toss that covered the ten yards that separated the canoes and caught the outrigger of young Tanil's craft. Tanil, kneeling forward in the bow with his paddle, lost his balance and cannonballed into the shallows. A great shout went up from the crowd and Lovett watched in slackjawed amazement. This was legal?

Then Tanil's partner veered his little craft into a deliberate collision, riding his prow over the opponent's outrigger, and Lovett found himself laughing helplessly at this donnybrook by children, only a few hundred feet from the shore where Jean-Claude Pelele stood to greet the winner.

So why, Lovett wondered, was Keikano's distant cousin scrabbling so hard to the shore with his paddle still in hand? The boy came out of the water like a beaching porpoise and began to sprint, scant yards from the yelling throng that lined the shore. He reached Pelele as another oarsman was leaping from his craft; knelt, paddle erect like a pole, before the big man; and received the garland to renewed cheering. The other boy, foiled by one second, looked at his paddle as if it had betrayed him.

Tanil and his partner were taking their ride around the official circle, the crowd filtering back to the plaza, before Lovett could make himself heard to the smiling Keikano. "If he could just run to the finish line like that, why not come ashore earlier," Lovett asked.

"Someone would have tripped him," Keikano replied. "Running is not fair unless you have been held in some way."

"So why didn't those other kids do it, at the first?"

"They tried," Kaikano explained patiently. "Why did you think they were holding on to each other?"

Lovett shook his head, hands up in mock despair. "Damnedest rules I ever heard of. At least your cousin won."

"Only because he kept his weapon. His paddle. And of course, he stayed near shore where the water flows more slowly."

Chip, who had been listening to this interchange: "Don't the other boys know all that, too?"

"They do, when they are thinking. They are—"

"Boys, yeah, I hear you," said Chip, with a rueful grin. The three of them strolled back to the plaza where six finalists, including Tanil, stood inside the prize ring awaiting another signal from their hulking President. Log drums beat, the crowd began to chant, and at Jean-Claude's gesture boys began to grapple as the chant became white noise.

Tanil and one other lad were flung beyond the ring of stones almost immediately because each was attacked by at least two others. Keikano writhed in disappointment at this but, "All's fair in love and war," Chip called to his little pal.

"This is not love," Keikano called back. The wrestling contest ended only when the pair that had almost won the canoe race ganged up on the third remaining lad and bodily dragged him to the edge of the ring. As the lone boy struggled, one of his attackers disengaged himself and then delivered a brisk kick to his own pal's backside. His pal and the third boy both fell across the stones, leaving little Master Betrayal alone in the ring.

The crowd roared its approval and Keikano turned his back on the spectacle, hurrying off toward the lagoon.

Lovett heard a gruff familiar voice in his ear above the cheers. "Fuckyerbuddy week," was Coop's laconic view.

"Makes you wonder about the contracts they sign," Lovett replied, watching the flower of Fundaboran boyhood as he was carried about on willing shoulders.

Then, with dusk hanging heavy as incense in the air, Jean-Claude handed the boy a small lighted torch. With blood still clotting on his scratches, the boy trotted away a bit unsteadily toward the lagoon where a barefoot Keikano was pushing one of the rafts into the current, following it out with powerful leg kicks.

The boy eased into the water, holding his torch aloft easily in one hand. By the time Keikano had emerged ashore, dripping, the boy had reached his goal and the villagers had taken up some new chant in unison, sounding more like a benediction than an exhortation. Lovett thought it was just as well, because that kid was just about all used up for one day. Served him right, Lovett decided.

The torch flickered at the raft's edge, the crowd fell silent, and moments later a hard little blue flame with pinkish edges stabbed out. The boy began to swim back, and it was that precise instant when the air became filled with a shattering roar. Directly overhead, something passed down the length of the lagoon toward the breakwater carrying a familiar thousand-horsepower snarl with it, disappearing as it banked away. From every villager with a voice: white noise again. For a few frozen heartbeats, Lovett was as stunned as any of them.

He stood still for only a few seconds, patting his pockets. He yelled toward Chip: "Got a radio?"

A headshake and, "Myles has one," and then they were both ducking through the crowd that had fallen silent again, caught between anticipation and awe as every eye followed the small lights that winked like eyes from wingtips that were turning lazily.

Then, far out beyond the breakwater, brighter eyes flicked on, settling lower, turning until staring toward them. "Myles, Myles," Lovett screamed. "Use your radio! He's about to land on those fireworks!" Lovett had noted the blunt shape of the fuselage that passed no more than three hundred feet above the lagoon, and knew it was an amphibian. It could land directly on the lagoon. Crispin Reventlo had made a perfect choice for a landing—at almost any other time.

Vic Myles did not hear Lovett but some things, he would say later, even a Texan can figure out for himself. Lovett snatched up a torch from its socket and raced toward the lagoon, trying to estimate the raft's location through the murk. Chip copied him, perhaps without knowing why, and stood by as Lovett threw his torch overhand as hard as he could. It made a flaming arc that extinguished in the lagoon ten yards behind the raft. The blocky amphibian, its landing lights now distinctly separate points, was very low near the breakwater and still boring in. Chip made his own toss, a far better one, that flamed out bare yards beyond the raft. And then a flare erupted from the raft like a distress signal, a crimson ball the size of a bushel basket, rising up and up, flaming out while still rising. And a green flare, two seconds later, like some demonic antiaircraft battery warming up to intercept the plane.

Lovett began to leap and wave, arms crossing back and forth. Chip Mason did something more risky but also more likely to save one life while taking his own: he dived into the lagoon, hard overhand strokes knifing him toward the raft which now emitted sparks every time it belched. Now it was firing something nastier than simple flares.

The sound of twin engines suddenly firewalled came to Lovett as Chip reached the raft. High above the lagoon, with a soft *pooom*, a great spherical burst of blue points spread across the sky as another hollow belch and its shower of sparks trailed a second mortar shell in its vertical rise. The amphibian twin came so near touching the lagoon that it left a furrow of roiled water, then steadied with its lights sweeping over that raft, a lethal obstacle if they touched, Chip kicking hard in his effort to tow the whole thing to the shallows where Keikano was now plunging in to help, calling for others.

And then the big twin roared past in its cataclysmic rush, louder than before as it strained to rise, another colorburst rending the sky directly above it so near that the lowest of the fireballs shattered into roiling tubes of green fire in the prop wash, the plane now with enough speed that its pull-up and shallow bank toward the sea cleared the tallest palms by a good three feet.

And those goddamned mortar salutes just kept coming, now a twinned red-and-green combination with one vast white wink that brought a thunderous concussion a second later. Lovett lost his footing on his way to aid Chip, hit and rolled to the water's edge. He sat up groggily and shook his head. Surely to God, after flying directly through one airburst of fireworks display, Reventlo wouldn't make another such pass anytime soon.

Sitting on a stone beside him, tinted from time to time by bursts of star shells in red, white, blue, yellow, Vic Myles was calmly talking on his handheld radio. "Naw, those suckers are patched together, Cris. You gotta wait 'em out." An evil chuckle followed this. It made Lovett want to kick him.

A thin voice, muffled because Myles held the set to his ear, said something Lovett couldn't hear. "Current's only a couple of knots and they've pulled the raft ashore," Myles reported. "You'll be clear." At that point, Lovett saw two figures kneeling on the raft, one frantically pulling unspent mortar tubes from their powder train, dumping them into the lagoon; the other—Chip—pulling off his T-shirt.

Lovett and Myles both saw what happened next, Chip stuffing his cotton shirt into the open mouth of that remaining mortar, and Myles was first to react. He bellowed, "Mason, *jump*, you fucking idiot!"

Chip, still kneeling, turned toward Myles. A muffled *thump* beside him trailed sparks and carried his T-shirt twenty feet up. Chip followed it with his eyes—but as he did, Keikano grabbed him by that mop of long hair, peeling off into the channel side of the raft carrying Chip with him.

The T-shirt, with a two-pound star shell inside it, flopped back onto the raft. And disappeared in a blinding flash that spewed lavender points of light the full width of the lagoon, villagers ducking for cover. Another five seconds passed before Chip's head bobbed to the surface with Keikano following. Safely beyond the danger radius, Jean-Claude Pelele was roaring with laughter and Lovett, luckily, could find nothing handy to throw at him.

27

Reventlo's landing, like most water landings, wasn't a thing of beauty; it was the sort of controlled, wounded-goose flop the old Grumman amphibian had been built to take, straight up the lagoon with room to spare. With a blunt fat body and pair of small, noisy radial engines perched high on its short wing, the Grumman boasted all the charm of a snarling hunchback and had been saddled with its name, Goose, from those plunging water landings.

Coop Gunther literally rubbed his hands in glee to see it; the tough, reliable little Grumman Goose had once been a mainstay in Coop's Coast Guard squadron. It was half the size of a C-47, just as slow and five times as ugly, but *amphibian* meant that when you dropped it into the water it didn't sink. In a pinch it might carry eight or ten people.

With natives bearing torches and Reventlo's friends streaming onto the dock weak with relief, his greeting committee soon dissolved into a series of hugs and questions. Cris Reventlo, with an armful of presents and his white hair sweat-plastered to his forehead, didn't look like a man who had taken off fresh from Yap two hours before. From his last-second radio contact with Myles, he knew that aerial blitz had been purest accident. "I've heard of a flaming welcome, mates—but *really*," he said, eyebrows knitted, spotting the head of Jean-Claude above all the others. Raising his voice: "Since Fundabora's juvenile delinquents failed to shoot me down, I bear gifts as promised. Keikano, I feel curses coming on, so I leave it to you to massage that into a proper greeting." Whiskey in one hand, a pair of videocassettes in the other, he handed them over to Jean-Claude.

Keikano and Merizo flanked the big man, whose jaded glance said volumes as he took the tapes. Then Reventlo explained that there was much, much more of the same inside the plane, and at Keikano's translation Jean-Claude began to smile but remained rooted to that spot. He wanted it all. Now.

The unloading took an hour; a Goose's lone hatch behind the wing needed a raft for the job. In that time the B.O.F. crew learned that a small ship was under charter, easily capable of taking a pair of the Tojos and possibly the Betty on its deck. A small leased Kubota bulldozer would be aboard. That was the good news. The bad news was, it wouldn't reach Fundabora by way of Port Moresby and Yap for two weeks.

When at last the Grumman was properly moored and Jean-Claude's precious porn carton had been hauled away with his other loot to the councilhouse, Reventlo accompanied his friends with their own boxes of cargo to the big maintenance shed. Item one, an unmarked box toted by the tired pilot himself, was a case of Thai beer still chilled from its ride in the Grumman's nose. "Singha," Lovett breathed as he used the opener of his Swiss Army knife. "Consider yourself kissed, Cris." And for a few minutes they all simply relaxed, sharing excellent beer and the Aussie equivalent of potato crisps, toasting one another.

The C-47's owner, said the Brit, was so happy to see his property in Alice Springs he forgave its tardiness. "I'd already put our Nakajima in storage in Darwin. Handlers' eyes were big as saucers; they knew what it was before I told them. Still have a mate or two in Darwin; lived there for dingo's years, y'know; and hired an agent to round up our needs. By the time I got back there from Alice Springs the rumors were flitting about like bumblebees. I'm afraid you're all part of the mythology now, mates." It was remarkable, Lovett thought, how a week or so in an Australian port city could infect Reventlo's accent again.

Benteen tended to think more strategically. "I gather you got hold of Curran Quinn," she prompted.

"How else could I have funded that charter boat, not to mention our Grumman." He eyed Lovett shrewdly but Lovett didn't bite on the Benny Hill line this time. "Ah, Victor. Quinn got a rocket from your editor, fellow named Beacham; imperative you call, he said."

"Shit. Thinks it's a wild-goose chase, no doubt."

"Not anymore, I daresay. I called New York. Told Beacham you were unreachable, marooned on an uncharted island with gun and camera and a lovely half-caste, guarding a secret squadron of priceless warplanes from a hidden saboteur." The others were smiling now, half embarrassed at this description straight from a supermarket tabloid, but realizing that none of this was actually misleading. And by the time Myles got through with it, the story would be embroidered like Irish linen. Benteen groaned, put fingertips to her cheeks and shook her head as if waking from a nightmare.

Myles, of course, was unembarrassable. "That's about right. Becham liked it, did he?"

"Gibbering with excitement, Victor; simply gibbering," he said, with a turn of his head and a wink that only Lovett caught. "Oh, and your flash camera is in one of those cartons."

"Thanks," said Myles and nodded toward Lovett. "Only I don't think we're gonna need it. We know fucking well who our saboteur is, but Wade let him walk."

Reventlo let his eyebrows ask for details, and Lovett supplied most of them with some help from Chip. Before they had finished he was grinning in amazement. "Ohtsu, you say? Now there's a chap I'd like to meet," he said. "Hasn't shown up since?"

"Not that we've noticed. We're still pulling sentry duty and since the little fella knows that, his old grampa prob'ly does," Coop shrugged.

"You know, I'll bet Keikano puts a lot more miles on his sandals than he wants anyone to know," said Reventlo.

"He gets around," Chip said. "Did you bring the books and medicines for him?"

"In a ten-kilo carton with his name on it," said Reventlo, searching among the taped cardboard boxes. "But I don't see it. If that goddamned sumo wrestler's taken it," he began darkly, then sighed and shrugged. "Well, time enough to track it down tomorrow. It's not as if they could read." He began to cut into the cartons. "Some of this is pricey stuff, and weighty as remorse, but I've even brought a filter for our water. Anyone fallen afoul of the dreaded gyppy tummy from the sludge you've been drinking?"

No one had, and they rummaged among their new goods like kids around a Christmas tree. Batteries of several kinds with electrolytes, cable, fuel additives, even a chainsaw; and a carton of chocolate bars that disappeared into pockets within seconds.

Junk food and Singha stoked them through a spate of story-swapping but finally Lovett declined a third bottle with, "But save it for me. It's my turn in the big dark barrel again, so to speak."

"Aw, Pop. Does anybody really think that's still necessary?"

“Folks *I* don’t trust are still out there in the toolies,” said Myles, and treated them all to a ripe baritone belch.

“Folks *I* don’t trust are still around nearer than that,” Lovett rejoined, and waved as he pocketed radio and pistol. The perimeter road was now beaten into submission, star patterns serving him as a narrow directional bearing overhead as he walked. After a full day of hard work and the hours of excitement that followed, he found himself curiously buoyant. *Guess I’m getting whipped into shape*, he mused as he trudged upslope to the cave. They were all in far better shape than they had been two weeks before; Mel Benteen was cinching her belt two notches tighter, which didn’t hurt her silhouette any. Even the big belly on Myles had hardened, ridges of muscle showing faintly now when he stripped to the waist. And as for Chip: well, the kid was—the only apt word was *beautiful.*

Lovett rigged his cable alarm again, knowing damned well he’d fall asleep in a Tojo cockpit. When the secret of the cave was known to all, they might have to double up on sentry duty.

Reventlo was plainly delighted when he arrived with the crew for work. Mango-smeared, biting into a cookie the Brit had brought him from their new stores, Lovett strolled with him down the old airstrip. “Think you could goose your Goose in here, Cris? I’ve noticed the prevailing wind is pretty dependable.”

“Not with those little tires,” Reventlo said. “Rough water is one thing, but it wasn’t designed for this kind of abuse. Tojos couldn’t make it either, I suspect. The Betty, now—but we’ll have time to build a scaffold and pull her wings; that should make it an easy tow job with that Kubota tractor. I’m thinking that’s our next step: crowd the Tojos so that we can move the Betty forward, set up the scaffolding, and remove her wings. Oh, yes, and that goddamned monstrosity suckling under her belly. That’ll have to go. They aren’t rare in any case. After all, who in his right mind wants to fly them?”

This was a job to challenge any mechanic. They spent the morning in the cave, measuring clearances and discovering that the old bomber couldn’t be moved to the entrance until one of the little fighter craft had been rolled outside. “Look,” said Coop, who would shoulder most of the responsibility for doing it right, “I’ve never taken a Japanese plane apart, and they didn’t put ’em together the same way we did. I’m not too gung-ho on starting with the big one. Why not pull the wings on that Tojo we’ve gotta move first, before we roll it out? We can rig supports easy, and the six of us should be able to lift a Tojo wing."

He got some heavy arguments on the idea but one fact would not go away: better to risk a mistake on one of four small identical planes than on the lone, priceless Betty. So, while Coop spent his afternoon poking into the guts of a Tojo wing, the rest of the crew set about demolishing more of the wall. It was Benteen who suggested dragging that long workbench into position below the wing of the Tojo.

In one respect, they were in luck: only the outer halves of a Tojo's wings could be removed. Since the wing cannons and landing gear were mounted solidly on the inner segment, they could still tow it, and each outer panel was less than ten feet long. Excitement built as Coop called on Lovett for help; then Revendo, then Myles. Finally the entire crew abandoned their other work until, in late afternoon, they lowered one aluminum wing by hand onto the mat-padded workbench. It was only minutes before they carried it out of the way and repositioned the bench.

"You guys take off. I've got sentry duty tonight," said Coop, squinting at that other wing. "I can have this sucker almost ready when you yuppies show up tomorrow."

"The adult games have already started," Benteen reminded them. "Don't you want to watch awhile?"

Coop loosed one of his raspy laughs. "Listen, this Alaskan has been there, done that, ate the T-shirt. Every Seventeenth of May in Petersburg, they celebrate Norwegian Independence in ways Fundabora couldn't touch with a ten-foot Swede. I've seen guys so lubricated they tried to steal a Viking longboat off a trailer, pilots shanghaied right off a commercial airliner by ladies carrying booze and spears, naked women sashayin' past the post office—I don't suppose these guys can top all that for sheer celebration. You go on; I've oh-deed on weirdness with the folks who invented it."

So only five of the crew showed up in the village plaza in time to see the finals of the spear-toss. Jean-Claude, splendid in a feathered cape, lumbered a full step across the line before hurling his javelin, yet no one seemed willing to complain. His toss was mighty though, Lovett noticed, his trajectory was too flat. Rongi looked like an Olympian and put his superbly muscled torso into a higher toss that soared six feet further. The crowd cheered him as if the contest were already decided.

Until Pilau, all knobby joints and intensity, began his run. Lovett expected good-natured laughter from the villagers but, he realized, they apparently knew something he didn't. After all, Pilau didn't have a gram of fat on him, and he couldn't have reached the finals by incompetence. The usually ungainly Pilau did not advance with his javelin held high in a warrior's threatening position as the others had, but held it by his side, big feet flapping harder, gradually accelerating until his pace surpassed that of the musclebound Rongi. With every step Pilau looked less inept and, gathering as if for a leap like a long-jumper, he brought his lance up, his long slender arm flashing forward, in a toss that sent his missile up in a perfect ballistic arc.

Pilau's javelin soared as if rocket-boosted. Evidently his long skinny arms were a real advantage, and the whoop from the villagers told the story. Pilau had won by four arm-spans, and Lovett thought he saw moisture glistening in the man's eyes as, with great dignity, he allowed himself to be carried around the winner's circle. Those casual practice tosses he'd been making with poles at the airstrip hadn't been so casual after all.

When the footrace contestants lined up, the visitors thought they were hallucinating. Each contestant selected a net bag of stones, the bags seeming roughly of equal size. Most of the men chose to sling the bag around their shoulders so that the loads fell like huge brassieres at their sides. Pilau was one of those, hands gripping the loads to keep them from swaying. Rongi carried his high around his hips, forearms curled at his sides to support the load. Jean-Claude simply slung his one-handed over a shoulder as if it was an overstuffed pillow. Each of those loads had to be over a hundred pounds.

"I don't believe it; Jean-Claude's load is the same as everybody's," Lovett muttered to Reventlo, watching some of them stagger around. "Now there's a handicap race with a difference."

Benteen broke off her pidgin with a woman nearby. "Just wait," she urged wryly. "I'm told it gets better—or rather, worse."

"That would be a tall order," Reventlo said, just before Merizo dropped his flywhisk.

And they were off. One poor bastard, not built for carrying such stuff, was well and truly off from the start, managing only a few steps before he was jostled by another man and went careening away to fall in a heap. Rongi took an early lead, swinging his weights with forearms so that his hips moved like a woman's, surviving one effort to trip him. In the pack, Jean-Claude moved in a fast graceful shuffle, and God help the man who lunged within reach because that man—two, in fact—took an elbow the size of a tree stump in the gizzard and promptly lost interest in further proceedings. The others surged safely around Jean-Claude, using those stone weights like bumpers among themselves. Lovett decided with some regret that it wasn't fair to single out the gigantic Jean-Claude for curses when everyone else was cheating just as hard, tripping, jostling, head-butting with abandon. Everyone except Rongi, who'd had the physique and the good sense to lunge out alone in the lead.

At the halfway mark, contestants were strewn along the path like victims of a highway wreck, the determined Pilau well behind Jean-Claude who had moved into second place through sheer attrition. Somehow Pilau was slipping along among his fellows while staying clear of trouble. But Rongi's stylish sway had begun to look more like a gallop now; he was tiring, yet Jean-Claude plodded behind, inexorable as a battle tank and gradually gaining ground. Within twenty paces of the finish line, Rongi's stride faltered. He struggled to regain his rhythm, knees buckling.

"Shot his bolt too soon," Reventlo said. Lovett, turning to agree, saw that Benteen had opened her mouth to reply, then thought better of it and only smiled to herself.

And now Jean-Claude pulled abreast of Rongi, and Lovett waited for the big man to bowl his rival over. He was almost disappointed to see Jean-Claude move ahead as cleanly as if the Marquess of Queensberry were watching. And really disappointed when Rongi fell forward, grasping Jean-Claude by one ankle in a shoestring tackle.

The crowd loved it. So did Jean-Claude, who staggered free, spinning around with a kick that just missed its target, then continued to trot backward, shouting encouragement or perhaps ridicule to the desperate Rongi. The resurgence of wild cheers told Lovett it was the cheating, not the race, that the crowd had come to see.

Rongi was up again now, no longer stylish but still game. A heavyset fellow thundering along in third place butted him squarely in the back, which only propelled him a little faster, and when they tangled it was Rongi who stayed erect. The blocky man went to one knee to maintain his balance, struggling up again.

Pilau, gleaming as if bathed in sweat, moved like a marionette but when he drew alongside the blocky man, he was grabbed. The heavier man's grip failed and he tried again. And failed again, hands slipping away as Pilau plodded ahead.

In the end, Jean-Claude Pelele won handily, lungs heaving, and welcomed Rongi and Pilau as they arrived in a dead heat. It took all of his beef trust to carry him around the winner's circle and Jean-

Claude, who could afford a show of sportsmanship now, insisted that both Rongi and Pilau be carried as well.

For Rongi it was a problem; he was too limp for an easy carry. For Pilau it was a different problem; no one could get a grip on him. Good old stolid Pilau, who knew one very important thing, had wiped himself down with engine oil.

Lovett edged off toward the lagoon in search of Chip as ceremonial torches were offered to the evening's winners. He saw several figures in the gloom, guiding rafts out to the sluggish current, and knew Chip would be among them.

Vic Myles found him at the water's edge; pulled two bottles from apparently bottomless pockets of his bush jacket. "Saved you a Singha," he said, and handed one over.

Lovett had swilled two Singhas the night before, and he could divide twenty-four by six as well as anybody. He opened the bottles, knowing that by rights they both were his, shrugging it off. Compared to the outrageous cheating that Fundaborans took for good clean fun, Myles's little swindle over a warm beer couldn't be viewed without a microscope.

The two men sat and watched the swimmers carry their torches out to the rafts one by one, Myles grinning like a schoolkid as fireworks filled Fundabora's slice of heaven with bursts of light, bathing their upturned faces in delicate shades of color. Lovett found himself listening with interest at the *oooh* and *aaahh* from so many people who spoke little or no English. Beneath a fireworks display they sounded exactly like an American crowd. At some very basic level, he thought, perhaps the language of emotion was the same everywhere.

At some point Lovett saw Pilau scrubbing himself down with sand and, later, Jean-Claude in earnest conversation with little Merizo while his guards stood by. Later, he sought Chip but saw no sign of him. Keikano too was missing. *It figures*, he told himself, strolling back to the councilhouse with his friends. He knew Chip would come padding in late, and would be full of vim and vinegar in their room the next morning.

But then, in his sixty-odd years Wade Lovett had known a lot of things that weren't true.

28

If Chip had returned in the night, no one saw him do it. He was absent when Lovett awoke and none of the crew could say where he was. Mostly, their gazes said, *we don't want to say what you don't want to hear*, but Myles reached Coop Gunther by radio.

Coop's answer was distracted. "Naw, he's not here but I could sure use him. How long before I can get some help dropping this other wing? It's ready."

"Relax," Myles said. "From the sound of it, they're starting the goofiness early in the village today. I don't know about anybody else but I intend to play hooky and watch for a while this morning, Coop."

Lovett agreed instantly. That had to be where Keikano would be; and where Keikano was. He let the thought trail off as he fell in step down the stairs. No fresh fruit had been set out, but in the village plaza they'd have to step over piles of it.

The sounds from the crowd in the plaza suggested a different note, almost one of reverence, among the throng. Reventlo was first to see why as they putt-putted near the plaza, thrusting an arm up and out as he braked. "Stone the crows, that man is mad!"

Lovett nearly ran into a tree when he saw the man—it proved to be Rongi—jump. He had climbed a rope ladder affixed to the very top of the naked tree trunk that towered over the village, finally to stand stripped to the waist on the tiny platform six or seven stories high, a few yards below the apex to which the ladder was tied. When Lovett looked up, a pair of villagers had run off fifty feet tugging on a cord tied to the ladder, so that it hung in a long curve like a loose guywire, and the tiny figure that was Rongi had already taken flight—

but falling slowly, arms stretched wide as if to embrace his own death, a slender rope tied to his ankles. The rope had been wound around the great pole so that, instead of falling as a bungee-jumper would, Rongi was circling the pole as the rope unwound. It took perhaps two or three seconds to make a full revolution, to the accompaniment of a low drumming and a toneless *aaaahhh* from many throats that was almost music.

Lovett trotted ahead, stumbling because he kept staring upward, lost in awe of the physics involved. With every revolution the jumper descended some four or five feet, and as he did, his bindings became longer. That meant his spiral became wider too, a full revolution taking longer so his downward velocity actually dropped. Lovett realized that while Rongi was now dropping more slowly, the poor devil's circular velocity was increasing. By the time he reached the ground he'd be circling faster than a man could run, faster than a scooter could scoot. Fast enough that when he hit bottom he'd be in far more danger from friction than from impact.

One of those patented Fundaboran cheers went up as Rongi descended to a point where Lovett couldn't see over the crowd, but he saw palm fronds flying and wondered if Reventlo had brought enough merthiolate to paint a man from head to foot.

Benteen shook her head like a schoolmarm. "With the leaps I've seen, it was a religious ceremony, but they used slip-knots and fell straight down, and missed the ground by a foot. I've heard about variations like this, but I've never seen anything quite like it before. I wonder how many people died before they got it right."

"Right? It isn't right, it's lunacy," said the Brit.

They watched as a triumphant Rongi arose on willing shoulders, arms still wide. "Jesus, looks like he came up smelling like a rose. This is one for my book, but nobody's gonna believe it," Myles said.

"Palm fronds will slide over each other like cardboard over grass," Benteen said. "There must be a circle of fronds on the ground where we can't see them. I'll bet he didn't even lose much skin."

"The man is still barmy," Reventlo insisted, his British sense of propriety outraged.

Myles, in contrast, was merely amused. "They're all nuts. Welcome to Fantasy Island," he said to the Brit.

They watched as Merizo paced off a distance from the pole to the spot where, evidently, Rongi had touched down. "I get it. The competition is to see who hits farthest from the pole," Lovett said.

"The competition is to see who's the biggest idiot on Fundabora," said the Brit. "And as if there were any doubt, look who's climbing the pole."

"Omigod," Benteen breathed. Swaying on the rope ladder that now lay alongside the pole, hauling his great bulk up like some hairless bear, was Jean-Claude Pelele.

"Give him points for guts," Myles said.

"He'll have them scattered all over the plaza if that rope doesn't hold," Reventlo replied. "I mean, the fellow's a ruddy villain but I'm not sure I'd want to see that."

At that point, a beeper in Myles's jacket sounded. He drew the radio from his pocket, free hand over one ear, and responded.

Having reached the tiny platform that swayed alarmingly, Jean-Claude selected one of the ropes coiled around the pole and tied his ankles as the ladder was again pulled aside. "Hey, Wade," said Myles, "Keikano just showed up at the cave with Coop. Wants us ASAP."

Lovett nodded, craning his neck upward. "Tell him I'll be along shortly," he said, distracted by the spectacle.

"I think we'd all better go," Myles said, loud enough to get Reventlo's attention.

"Right you are," said the Brit. "But whether our vast fool balks or no, this is not to be missed."

Myles spoke again, softly, and put away his radio as Jean-Claude stood on the swaying platform, then fell outward to a chorus of drums and voices. Just why it was that he began to spiral as widely as Rongi, Lovett couldn't decide at first; the important point was that the rope seemed to be holding. The man's huge belly seemed to move toward his chest as he swung around and around, head downward, the tree trunk visibly flexing.

"The pole's flexibility is giving him help. It's a setup for the heaviest guy," Lovett said suddenly.

"Why am I not surprised," Benteen remarked.

"Hell with this," Lovett said suddenly; "you see one showoff with a death-wish, you've seen 'em all." He turned his back on the still-rotating Pelele and lifted the Cushman's kick-starter.

Myles, watching over his shoulder, hurried to get astride the rear seat, knowing that it was either ride with Lovett or walk. Reventlo and Benteen waited until they concluded that Fundabora's President was not going to splatter himself far and wide before they followed on the other scooter.

They were able to ride all the way to the cave by following the LeTourneau's spoor, and found Coop at the entrance looking grim.

"It's just our folks," Coop called into the cave. A disconsolate Keikano peered out from the edge of the fallen wall, beckoning to Lovett. "He wouldn't tell me anything," Coop said, disgusted. "If you never saw a pale Fundaboran, take a good look at this one."

As they crowded into the cave mouth, they could see that Keikano was trembling and perhaps a shade or two lighter than usual. "Hey, it can't be that bad," Lovett said, laying a hand on the delicate shoulder.

But Keikano shrank from the contact. "Not for me, sir." The throat worked convulsively. "For your sonson." It seemed that Keikano was so frightened his language skills were suffering, too.

Lovett spoke first. "What's happened to Chip?"

"I don't know, after they take him. But they take him. *Took* him," he corrected himself, visibly struggling with the urge to panic. "I think all are dangered. You, me, you especially," he nodded at Benteen.

"The sonofabitch that grabs me is in worse danger," she said.

"Now calm down, lad," Reventlo pleaded. "You're with us and we have guns, Keikano." He glanced at Myles. "Where are they, by the way?"

"Grease gun's with my other gear over there," Myles said, jerking a thumb toward the shadowed recesses of the cave. "Sentry takes Ol'—uh, the forty-five. Got it, Coop?"

Coop silently displayed the big pistol, and Myles took it back.

"My grandson," Lovett burst out. "Who the hell took him and when, and where the hell did they take him and what the *god*damn hell have they done to him?"

"It—was last night, at the last of playfire—the fireworks," Keikano said. "Jean-Claude's men came while we dried off from swimming. I saw them come. I not know why but I know those ugly pigs. I tell Chip to follow and swim off. Chip turns to meet them. He calls, 'Tell my Pop, Kei,' and they knock him down."

"Oh Jesus *Christ*," Lovett said, half turning away, then facing the little schoolteacher again. He felt Benteen's hand on his own shoulder and wanted to slap it away, but curbed the impulse. Melanie Benteen was not the enemy. "Did they hurt him?"

"I did not hear clubs. They have a special sound," Keikano explained.

"I'll sodding bet they do," Reventlo gritted. "Why would they arrest you? Did you two give them any reason?" He turned to Lovett:

"Sorry, Wade, but we need particulars. What reason might they have had, Keikano?"

"None that I knew then. But I watched and followed them to the councilhouse."

His mouth set in a furious hard line, Lovett said, "But you couldn't find us during the fireworks? Or come and tell us later in our rooms that he's being kept under the same roof?"

"Not if I followed to see where Chip was taken." Keikano's expression said that whatever he'd done he would be damned for it. "After the celebration, lookouts were posted near the councilhouse stairs. I saw them and crawled through a kitchen window. What I heard later—Minister Merizo wants me now. I fear for myself, sirs."

"Okay, you're probably right. What we do now is march in there and get Chip back," Lovett snarled.

Keikano put up both hands as if warding off the idea. "I heard much in the night, with my ear to the wall. If you found him, you would have to kill every guard; their orders are plain, and Chip would be killed. They have guns, but few bullets. And I do not think he is still there. I also learned that Pelele and Merizo want me. They want you," he went on, nodding at Benteen. Facing Reventlo, he went on, "You brought what Jean-Claude wanted and what he wants now, you would not give unless he has prisoners."

"And beside you and our formidable lady, what might that be," asked the Brit, dangerously calm.

"That was not clear, but they are agreed. I think they want you to fly somewhere."

"I'd be bloody pleased to push off at this juncture," Reventlo said, "but not without all our members."

"Sirs, they know you have a *kokutai* here. Someone reported it," Keikano said.

Coop: "A what?"

Reventlo translated instantly. "Nip naval aircraft squadron," he said distractedly, then nodded to himself. "Yes, we do at that. So why aren't they here to raise hell about it?"

"They don't have to. They have my grandson while they finish those crooked games that keep Jean-fucking-Claude in the driver's seat," Lovett answered. "I wish I thought—Keikano, is there any chance that Pelele *won't* win as usual?"

"I do not see how. By midday, the leaders will fight to see who is last in the ring of stones. By now they will be drinking for courage, and to make them foolish," said Keikano.

"And that big lummox should be able to drink anyone else into a coma," Benteen said. "Don't they know that?"

"It is tradition," said Keikano helplessly.

"And when they've finished, you can expect 'em here, drunk as congressmen," Coop inserted, suddenly galvanized. "Gents, you gotta help me finish pullin' that Tojo's other wing right now!"

Benteen was aghast. "At a time like this?"

"Can't haul that airchine out and point it until we do. Couple of machine guns in the fuselage and forty mike-mike cannons in those wing stubs; explosive warheads. They look functional to me. Just the thing to give us some clout," Coop said, already moving toward the Tojo.

Without a word, the entire crew fell to work in haste to turn that aircraft into a credible weapon. Twin forty-millimeter cannon might not win a war, but every little warhead that struck a stone or a sapling would spew shrapnel far and wide. Fifteen minutes later they rolled a stub-winged Ki-44 fighter downslope and bodily lifted its tailwheel onto stones to aim the guns low. Thanks to shortages faced by Japanese designers, it weighed no more than an average Buick.

"All they've got to do is move out of the direction of fire," Myles observed.

"We know that, but maybe they don't. And there'll be some hot little bees singin' off to the sides," Coop said, rigging wires from a new aircraft battery he had installed in the fighter plane.

"If you can fire 'em," Lovett reminded him.

"Yeah. God, right now I wish that old Jap was here."

"You think he'd help us," Myles said with deep sarcasm.

"He might help Keikano," Lovett said. "But it's probably academic, he's not here and if he were, he might enjoy seeing us run off the island. I don't guess I blame him."

"You do not know him, sirs," Keikano said quietly. "His fondest wish is to see Jean-Claude Pelele leave Fundabora. I believe he might wish to help."

"The enemy of my enemy is my friend," Reventlo quoted.

"Yes, but also the man who ends my pain is my friend," Keikano said. "He has some relief from his teeth now, thanks to you."

"You took that carton? I thought Jean-Claude's people got it," Reventlo said with a quick smile.

"He thought the same. I saw my name on it, and I acted, sir."

"Got that heavy carton across the island by yourself at night, did you? Well, don't let the old fellow wolf those blood-pressure pills like sweets," the Brit cautioned. "One a day, I think. Tell him, Keikano."

The little fellow's stare was ripe with friendly challenge. "Would you tell him yourself?"

"If he were here."

"Or if you were there," was the reply. "I believe that will be the only way. He is an escaped prisoner, you understand."

"Go; do it," Lovett pleaded. "You even speak his language, Cris. We've got to get some options here, before I take Myles's burp gun and let the air out of Jean-Claude."

"But you must come, too, sir. My honored grandfather is your prisoner."

"Shit! We can't all go," Lovett said, exasperated, waving an arm about him. Benteen divided her attention between them and the pair working feverishly on the fighter plane. Myles, sitting in the Tojo's cockpit, was taking instructions from Coop Gunther who knelt at an open panel of the stub wing.

"No. Only the officer who took him prisoner, and the pilot who brought his medicine. Tradition is strong here," Keikano said.

"I'd rather wait right here for Jean—" Lovett began.

At the single concussive *blammmm* only twenty feet from him, he dropped to his knees. The echo thinned away and lost itself in the heights like one of Pelele's biggest aerial salutes, but not before a second report reached them from somewhere among the palms near the beach. While Reventlo spun and ducked, Mel Benteen leaped like a gazelle. Keikano was more direct; he simply sat down hard and fainted.

From Coop Gunther, now sprawled on his back halfway off the Tojo's wing, an agonized, "Whatthefuck, Myles? What in the goddamn crossed eyes of Texas did you do in there?"

Myles, frowning down at the controls, called, "I just held this switch down like—"

"Well *don't do it again*, f' Crissake, feed mechanism nearly took my forkin' finger off!"

"But don't forget what you did, old man," Reventlo called, with a nervous giggle. "Oh, that was capital; *cap*ital! Hard to believe the bleeding thing still works. I wonder if they heard it in the village?"

"Could've heard it on Guam," Coop said, rubbing his ear. "I hope Pelele did hear it; might make him think twice."

Lovett stood up again. "I feel a little better about leaving here for a hike across the island now, Keikano—uh, Keikano?"

The response was groggy, but game. "Was anyone hurt?"

"Nope. Just one of your grandfather's guns, making a report to the nation," said Lovett.

Their preparations were brief, Benteen detailing herself to the hidden upper entrance to camouflage it with foliage while Myles and Coop set about preparing for what might become a siege. "Keep a radio outside in case the reception is dicey," Reventlo said, pocketing one of the units. "Let us know if you get visitors."

"Oh, you'll hear it," Myles promised, digging into a duffel bag he had stashed in the cave. "You think that little forty mike-mike was loud, wait'll I get my toys in order. You ain't heard nothin' yet."

Reventlo paused as Lovett followed Keikano up the steep foliage-covered path. "Ah—Victor. Grenades aren't choosy, and some of those poor buggers may be innocent, staggering drunks. Don't let's jump-start the war ourselves, right?" He got an abstracted nod and hurried after Lovett.

The sun was at its zenith when Keikano, striding along an unprotected trail high on the narrowest part of the island, abruptly began to climb along the rocky stones to one side of the path that wound along the rocky spine overlooking the sea. Lovett stared ahead, seeing faint marks of split hooves that went straight forward. Keikano had warned them to do exactly as he did, but this seemed like a silly maneuver. "What the hell?"

"Mantrap," Keikano said evenly. "A goat may cross, or a child. You would fall through." And he resumed his scramble, hopping lightly back to the path twenty feet farther.

With Reventlo peering over his shoulder, Lovett dropped to one knee and studied the trail's surface. He still saw nothing but dirt and stones.

"Lord love us, look down there," Reventlo murmured, pointing. Two hundred feet down, amid stones fallen in some earlier rockslide, lay a human ribcage scoured by a thousand winds, bleached gray by a thousand suns. Farther down: more human remains. "Another one of those stone balances, I'll warrant. It just gives way and hey presto, down it all goes with you. Tell you what, old cock: let's do as the lad says."

They scrambled across the rocks until they had reached Keikano, who then set off at a trot without a word. Soon afterward the little native left the trail again, this time amid shrubs windcarved into oval shapes. And this time the Boffs followed suit, scanning the area fruitlessly for any sign of danger. They paused to rest as they began their descent into carefully tended rice paddies strung along the island's contours like slender parallel canals, and here Lovett asked about the second trap.

"Earth seems firm but it is not," Keikano said, and went on with evident discomfort. "Very sharp spikes just below, smeared with—pekpek, human waste. It goes through your foot, you fall. More go through your body. You may not die as soon as you like."

"Punji stakes," Lovett nodded. "I've seen that before."

"Nasty beggars," Reventlo muttered.

"The traps are moved from time to time. Pelele's gang has learned not to visit. There is a trail near the water," he said, pointing to the swamp. "Different traps; more of them." He stood up again and began a quick choppy stride that, Lovett found, kept him from losing his balance on the steep downslope. Below them to the north, beyond the swamp, lay a group of thatched roofs with a stream that had been channeled by human hands. There was no real clearing; the place could barely be called a village and it existed among the foliage. Tendrils of smoke curled from two roofs, the very picture of tranquil island life. Over Lovett's right shoulder were stone pinnacles more than a thousand feet high, and far below to his left lay the blue Pacific. It was a picture worth sitting down to enjoy, but not on this day. Each time Wade Lovett thought about Chip, brutalized by Jean-Claude and his taciturn thugs, the blood began to pound in his ears again.

During a brief rest, Reventlo brought out his radio and found to his delight that he could talk with Benteen. He reported their location and asked, "Any sign of trouble?"

"Nothing yet. I guess Jean-Claude expects us to come to him."

"Perhaps we shall, my dear, one way or another. Keep the home fires burning." With that, he put the radio away.

As they neared a stone outcrop a half-mile from the tiny village, Keikano cupped hands at his cheeks. The staccato bleat of a goat floated on the air, and another. It was so realistic, Lovett needed a moment to realize Keikano was the goat. A child's head popped up from among the rocks with a similar bleat, and Keikano called down a brief message. The child sprang off and down the slope without a response, disappearing finally among the houses.

Lovett glanced at Reventlo who said, "Japanese. I'm a bit rusty but something about officers coming in peace."

Keikano led them more slowly now, and Lovett noted what might have been a small garden shrine near a sparkling little pool made by damming the creek above the houses. Something was very different about this hamlet, and Lovett smiled when he realized it was the utter cleanliness of it all; houses on pilings with tin-can skirts to deter rats; no debris. And no bustle of natives. The only friendly native seemed to be a half-grown cat which padded to Keikano like an old friend, tail held like a flag, and wound around his ankles. It had a coat similar to the one they'd seen on the heights one day, golden with umber markings. When Lovett knelt, it regarded him solemnly for a long moment before it approached, allowing him to scratch its cheeks before it ambled off again as Keikano watched in silent surprise.

"This must be one of the friendly cats you mentioned," Lovett said.

"Only to a few," said the schoolteacher, in smiling puzzlement. "I did not think he would do that."

Now Lovett could see that the village people were near, peeping from window frames. The person who met them was Yohei Ohtsu, dressed in his uniform so hurriedly that one of his leg-wraps was awry.

Keikano's bow was a peculiar one, his voice a rapid singsong to the old man who only nodded before Keikano stepped backward a few paces, clasped his hands; bowed again. Then Ohtsu bowed and spoke.

Reventlo bowed as well, and nudged Lovett who made a clumsy try at it. "My honored grandfather welcomes you to the north village and thanks you for the medicines," Keikano said.

Reventlo smiled. "I heard him. He also apologizes for his escape." When Keikano looked up, startled, the Brit went on: "I told you I was in a Japanese prison camp, remember?" Then he began to speak, haltingly, in Japanese. The old man's face began to lose a few of its frownlines.

Lovett kept silent in the interchange that followed, his anxiety level rising. At a pause, he said, "What's going on, Cris?"

Reventlo turned to Lovett. "I've told him he can thank us all equally for the carton I brought. Wanted to know if I can speak for you; his way of finding out who's senior man. I told him we are equals in our decisions." Both men saw Keikano listening and nodding. "I doubt he's used to democratic process, but he's just going to have to accept it. The way I have to accept his breath. If I'm any judge, someone's put the poor old punter on a carrion diet," Reventlo finished with a grin.

"Let's get on with it," Lovett urged, with a glance at the sun.

"Not that simple, old man. This fellow is caught in a time warp from—" He turned to Ohtsu and spoke briefly, getting a longer answer. "The last modern city he saw was Manila in 1942—the year 2602 by prewar Japanese reckoning. If we want something of him, we damned well observe the culture he remembers and keeps."

At this point Keikano began to speak with soft urgency to the old man, whose wrinkles went through some interesting gymnastics.

"Keikano told him we didn't come to imprison him; we're in a great hurry because, uh, his boyfriend, well, let's say his best friend, not to put too fine a point—"

"Forget you're a Brit and cut to the chase, Cris," Lovett interrupted brusquely.

"Right," said Reventlo, trying not to look offended. "His friend is held by Pelele for no good reason and you're the lad's family patriarch and we don't have bags of time. He was more circumspect than that, but the old boy knows we're time-bound."

"That's more like it. Thanks, Keikano."

But Ohtsu was already motioning them to follow him toward the perfect little garden beyond the houses, Keikano following behind the visitors. Lovett, his inner ear hearing the clockticks of fleeing seconds, thought he was going to begin yelling from frustration when old Ohtsu took his time leading them to low handmade benches in the garden.

Keikano had disappeared into the largest of the houses where a distant conversation ensued. Reventlo made what were obviously complimentary remarks about the place, which looked like exactly what it was: Japanese homes imitated fairly well with Fundabora's materials.

Presently Keikano arrived in the garden and served tea from a service clearly fired from local clay, then stood quietly in the background. Reventlo seemed nonplussed at first. But Lovett played "Simon says," imitating Reventlo, and soon the old Japanese began to show less formal reserve. After one exchange, the Brit said, "He knows it was Chip he met in the cave, and wonders where his father is. He's really asking about your own relationship."

Lovett gave the basics in a few short sentences, ending with, "Chip's my one best reason for living, I guess. If anything happens to him, I'm gonna do a Rambo number on those bastards. That way I might be able to face my daughter."

From the tail of his eye, Lovett saw Keikano regarding him intently. As Reventlo explained in his halting Japanese, old Ohtsu's glance became more thoughtful as well. He replied slowly, and Lovett caught the word *seppuku* in it.

"He agrees; it is better to take enemies with you than to die a failure, by your own hand. He's assuming you'd suicide if we don't, um, well . . ." Reventlo paused and shrugged.

"Got it. Let him think what he likes; will he help us against Pelele?"

Reventlo needed some aid from Keikano now, and Lovett's anxiety level climbed up his spine like mercury in a thermometer. He didn't know why Keikano hurried away until the youth returned with a small polished wooden tray containing a cloth-wrapped package. The old Japanese took the tray and offered it to Reventlo, who accepted the little package gravely. When unwrapped, it proved to be two clips of rifle ammunition, and Reventlo made much of them as he pocketed the rounds.

"It's necessary for him to give me something special for all the goods I flew in for him. He says those bullets fit the rifle we took from him," the Brit said.

"Does that mean he will, or he won't, help us?"

"I'm not certain yet." And Reventlo resumed the negotiations as if he had all the time in the world. Just when Lovett felt his head would burst with frustration, his friend turned to him. "The old boy can see you're in a state, Wade. You've treated him honorably and he wants to respond in kind. He says his cat never makes mistakes about a man's character but he won't commit any of his people to your fight. Too risky for them."

"Then he won't help," Lovett said.

"He didn't say that. He just won't drag his own extended family into general hostilities. I believe he's sent them all out of sight to avoid letting us know how many, or how few, they are. They're all a lot of cousins to Jean-Claude's villagers, you see. As far as his own help: yes, he will," Reventlo said.

Expelling a huge sigh: "And how many years do we sit here jawing about it?"

"Rome wasn't burnt in a day," Reventlo told him, and resumed in Japanese, with Keikano supplying the occasional phrase. At length Reventlo said, "I've explained how we're using our wingless Tojo—

by the way, to him it's a *Shoki*, a devil-beater. He says he could pull one of the machine guns from the 'Cigar'—that's what the pilots called their bomber—without much trouble."

"I can see us hand-firing it like some movie hero. Knock you flat on your butt."

"These are copies of the Lewis gun, Wade, little thirty-calibres, not all that heavy."

"Whatthehell. We'll radio Coop and suggest it."

"And, um, there's one more suggestion he made. I hardly dare mention it, but he seems rather sanguine about it."

Lovett knew the old Japanese was watching for his reaction. "Don't keep me in suspense."

"He assures me the big cigar will fly, and it carries twenty mike-mike cannon as well as that dreadful fucking suicide bomb. If worst comes to worst, it's practically an air force."

"That's it? He wants us to strafe a village full of drunks?"

"Not the south village itself—I think. But if we dropped the bomb on Jean-Claude's councilhouse, at the least he'd be just another fat man without a palace or a way to enjoy his pornography or, for that matter, those pathetic pretensions of his, and he'd lose ninety percent of his prestige."

"And at most we'd blow the sonofabitch to smithereens," Lovett nodded. "I like it. I wouldn't do it with Chip anywhere near it, but—oh, hell."

"What?"

"We're talking sheer bullshit, Cris. We're assuming this old guy's right, and that we could get that Betty in the air."

"And back down again, don't forget that. I'll grant you, it's a bit much," Reventlo said, "but don't forget to smile."

Both men turned to Ohtsu and made a brave show of teeth.

29

I feel like we've—wasted a day," said Lovett, his chest heaving as he leaned against a boulder high above the north village. Reflections of a midafternoon sun winked at him from the mangrove swamp far below on the island's western margin. "At least we should've—insisted Ohtsu—come with us."

Reventlo forced several hard breaths, a tactic that allowed him to speak with less effort. "I don't think he would've, absent force. We don't know what'd happen if we tried that. Certainly make at least two enemies we need as friends." He panted hard again. "Even if we're *gaijin* friends, definitely inferiors."

"I didn't get that impression."

"No?" A knowing chuckle. "You'll notice he didn't invite us into his house. Keikano had to retrieve that blood-pressure cuff so that I could show them how it's used. But I grant you, he was quite friendly for a thirties nip, especially a military man." More forced breaths as he hauled out his radio. "I say, Melanie. Crusoe to Friday, if you need call signs. Over to you."

After a moment the little comm set responded with Coop's voice. "She's making a tunnel out of fronds up on the bluff. Will I do?"

The Brit told him they were en route back to the cave, adding that the old Japanese had promised to help against Pelele, and passed on the suggestion about dismounting a machine gun or two. "Anything new from your end?"

"Naw. Me and Myles are startin' to wonder if it was really Pelele who snatched Chip."

"What? You think he wandered off and injured himself?"

"Nope. It's a possibility, but we have an eyewitness that says otherwise. And that's *all* we have—hey, is little lightfoot with you?"

"No. He'll be coming later with the old man."

"He hasn't got a radio? Wouldn't put it past him."

"We have two, you have two. That's the lot." Reventlo stood up again and began to walk, Lovett a stride behind. "Whatever can you be thinking of, Coop?"

"All we have is Keikano's word. What if he, or the old Jap, or some of their folks, are holding Chip? Bad blood between the villages for a long time. We go to Jean-Claude mad as hell, piss him off, we don't believe him when he says he's pure as the driven slush. Somebody gives the wrong order, somebody else raises a club, and both sides thin each other out some while the old Jap sits back and applauds. You thought about that possibility?"

"I confess I hadn't. Not a pretty scenario. We'll think on it, Coop. Reventlo out," he said, and pocketed his comm set. "You heard that, Wade?"

"Yeah. Didn't like it worth a damn," said Lovett, a pace behind.

"Then you don't think—"

"I think it could be true. Chip's the only one of us that wouldn't be in danger, and that just might suit Keikano. Hell, Cris, I don't know. My grandson is my life, and for the first time ever I've got a glimmer of how a kamikaze must've felt. Let me think."

They did not speak again until they reached the first mantrap, pausing to rest after going around the hidden punji stakes. Lovett leaned against a tree and asked, "If Keikano's people have Chip, where would they keep him?"

"Not where we might find him. And I can't believe they'd have trussed him up and carried him north. I hate to mention this, but they could have, um, put him down somewhere in the jungle."

"No. Keikano wouldn't let that happen. I know it, Cris, I goddamn *know* it."

"Hope you're right, old man. In any case, the sooner we face Jean-Claude, the sooner we may know."

Lovett agreed as they set off again, adding, "If Jean-Claude's innocent, we might just throw in with him; get him to help us lay siege to the north village. He'd love that."

"Mm, yes. We do know where the traps are," Reventlo mused.

"And Keikano knows we know. If he were guilty, I don't think he'd have shown us."

"It's a knotty one," said the Brit, picking his way toward the naked rocky spine of the island.

They found the cave a subtly different place as they circled around to its upper entrance in late afternoon. Benteen had covered the approach with fronds so that they found it possible to come down the stairwell without showing themselves at the top of the low cliff. It nearly got them shot.

"It's us! Jesus, put that thing down," Lovett said quickly, as Myles, hearing them, trained his little burp gun on the steps.

"You ever hear of a radio," Myles growled.

"My mind was somewhere else. I'm bushed," Lovett complained.

Coop was sitting in the wingless Tojo while Mel Benteen perched behind the remains of the wall with the old Japanese rifle. She hugged Reventlo, a nuance Lovett did not miss and, curiously, didn't really mind. "I hope we're wrong about what we've been thinking," she said.

Myles handed Lovett and Reventlo two tape-wrapped packages apiece, lumps the size of a child's fist with bright orange fuzes the length of a finger protruding from the tape. "Twelve-second delays, give or take," he said shortly. "Frag grenades. The initiator caps are down inside but I wouldn't get too playful with 'em. They'll stow in your pockets."

"And we don't know who to toss 'em at," said Lovett.

"We may, after we approach Jean-Claude," said Reventlo. "It's a fair bet he's not anxious to come here."

"Yes, but *how* do we approach him," Benteen asked.

"From a position of strength," Myles said. "The LeTourneau's hopper can take us all."

"Not a plan," said the Brit. "We're delicate eggs; we shouldn't tempt them by gathering all in the same basket."

"The goddamn hopper is bulletproof," Myles insisted.

"And let's say, for the sake of argument, they decide to toss some of those bloody fireworks inside," Reventlo replied. "I for one would come out of there like a flipping tiddledy-wink."

"You think they're that smart," Myles sneered.

"I think the score is one to zip, and we're the zip. You decide who looks smart, so far," Lovett said. "Cris is right, but somebody has to go. I vote for me."

"I'd rather have my pistol than this rifle, if I'm going in there," Benteen said, offering the rifle to Myles.

"You can't," Reventlo said, aghast.

"Oh? And who else can drive the LeTourneau: you? Coop? Anybody at all?" She looked about her, showed her open hands in an enormous shrug. "The LeTourneau is power, all right, but I'm the only driver. End of argument, guys. And," she said with sweet softness, "if you want to worry about someone, worry about a certain randy gent who's the biggest target on Fundabora. I will put numerous little holes in people if I have to. Count on it."

"Not from more than twenty yards. That's no target pistol," Myles warned.

"Then we'll just have to get closer," Benteen replied smoothly.

The general silence hinted at misgivings as Lovett clambered up to perch near Melanie Benteen on the looming LeTourneau. The nervous glances among all of them suggested that each crew member was hoping someone else would think of a better tactic at the last moment. Because no such brilliant idea came to any of them, Benteen could only wave as she put her rumbling vehicle in motion, Lovett scanning the jungle's verge. He'd decided against carrying a weapon, but at least he could furnish an extra pair of eyes. He might as well have kept them shut; they saw no one during the ride.

Benteen let the LeTourneau expire near the councilhouse with a last flourish of engine noise. As a pair of Pelele's burly guards caromed off each other in the doorway, Benteen made her way to the ground with Lovett, stuffing her pistol into a hip pocket of her slacks. "Stupid gomers are drunk as skunks," she observed.

"Only makes them more unpredictable," Lovett replied, and tried to look pleasant as the two of them mounted the verandah. Benteen's curt pidgin to the guards parted them like a wedge and all four of them strode directly through the lobby, then down the hallway. "You are one gutty lady," Lovett muttered to the woman pacing beside him.

"I am about to foul my scanties," she murmured back without looking at him.

Merizo may have been sober; it was hard to tell. Jean-Claude, with a bottle of Reventlo's rotgut in hand, was getting a rubdown from three of his teenyboppers but sat up straight on the edge of his vast bed to welcome his visitors. The look that passed between the President and his minister was a smug "told you so" in all known languages.

"Tell him we assume the best man won and is still undisputed champ," Lovett suggested. Benteen's pidgin brought a slack grin to Pelele's features as he replied.

"Ever the generous winner, he's not through celebrating, so we're invited back to the village," she said.

"We'd just adore it, but my grandson is missing," Lovett said. "We may show up after we find him and does His Nibs have any idea where he might be?"

Benteen duly pasted this into pidgin. Broad shrugs and a wave of sausage fingers around the big room as Jean-Claude replied. Benteen said, "He takes care of his, you take care of yours. Did we think he was here?"

Instead of hurling himself on the great oaf like a pomeranian on a bear, Lovett took a long steadying breath and made his face pleasant. "We thought His Grossness might be playing a joke. Ask him again if he has any idea where Chip is."

Benteen's question elicited another look between Pelele and Merizo, who had so far said not a syllable. Then, "Maybeso chief hide boy belong Lubbet, no make fun," Merizo said in his sepulchral basso.

"You get that? If they were hiding Chip it wouldn't be any joke," said Benteen. "That's about the best you can do in pidgin to get around answering a question."

"Let's cut the bullshit," Lovett said, his face growing darker. "Are they holding him captive?"

Benteen straightened her shoulders and asked.

Jean-Claude looked at Merizo, who took his time answering. Benteen nodded; turned to Lovett. "They have no free men as captives during this celebration. It would not be the same for criminals."

While Lovett considered this, searching the little minister's face, Merizo began talking again, Benteen nodding occasionally, her expression hardening. Jean-Claude put in his two coconuts' worth at the end of this spiel.

"Ooh, boy," Benteen said. "Merizo says they'd be happy to help search for Chip, but they'd want a favor in return, and Jean-Claude likes it but you aren't going to. Or maybe you will."

"Not if you don't effing *tell* me, for God's sake," Lovett gritted.

"Set fire to the north village using our plane," said Benteen, unwilling but determined to do her job.

Lovett stared in amazement, even though similar ideas had

passed through his own mind. "What plane? Our Grumman isn't a goddamned bomber. What for? Ask them that."

Both Jean-Claude and his minister answered Benteen together, Merizo's voice cutting through the big man's. North villagers were nogoods, criminals, and evidently that was that. The aerocanoe float along water, Lovett realized, had to be the Grumman. Benteen explained the main idea: drop bundles of fireworks on the little settlement and Jean-Claude's picked men would take care of the survivors.

"Yeah, take care of them like Serbs and Moslems take care of each other," Lovett said. "Ask if they've thought about losing some of those picked men to traps."

As Benteen translated this, Merizo spoke quickly to Jean-Claude, then replied to the woman. With no show of excitement she said, "First he tried to slide one past me; told the Michelin Man our little friend has been telling things and that they should bury him a piece at a time when they catch him. Then he told me they know there are traps, but as long as the celebration lasts, a few casualties won't stop them because they'll have the airplane as an ally."

"He means as long as they're still tanked on booze," Lovett said. "And it'd probably work. Look, now that they put it on the table, it looks like the inside of a drunk-tank bucket. Tell them some aerocanoes—shit, now they've got *me* doing it!—some planes can drop fire, and some can't. The Grumman isn't rigged for it and I've never flown one. Tell them thanks for nothing, we'll just have to look for Chip on our own."

Jean Claude began to chuckle before Benteen had finished, the huge belly pulsing with obscene mirth. His reply was offhand, dismissive.

"He says the Grumman is under guard anyway because he considers it not covered by agreement. It floated into the lagoon, so it's his. Well, don't look at me, sweetie, I'm just the anchorwoman for these little bulletins. Said it might be returned to us if we found a way to use it against the north village. In fact, he said it so casually I think it's probably his crucial ploy."

Lovett fought to keep his patience because he could see that both Pelele and Merizo were getting a big kick out of the way their scam was unfolding. "We'll pass their kind offer on to Reventlo. Let's get the hell out of this place, Mel, before I say something I regret."

He half-turned, waiting for her to translate. Merizo waited until she had finished, then put a smarmy little smile on and said a few short sentences. As he fell silent, Jean-Claude belched, took a pull on his bottle, and added, "Allsame bigtits." Benteen's eyes flashed angrily. "The son of a whore," she said, "just told us they might, just might, find Chip if we brought Keikano to them. He didn't say what for. He didn't have to."

Lovett put up one hand as she started to back away. "Correct me if I'm wrong, but I think Mr. Cholesterol said you'd do as well as Keikano."

"Do I dignify that with an answer?" Beneath her natural complexion and her tan, Melanie Benteen was blushing.

Lovett shook his head. "But we may be getting close to the real, no-shit nub of it, Mel. Ask them who *would* be captives, if not free men?"

Benteen asked as bidden, and got her answer from Merizo. "He says, people who violate great taboos. People like Keikano."

"And what cosmic injustice has that poor little sprite done, beside trying to help everybody? Put it any way you like, Mel."

On hearing the question, Jean-Claude gave a pervert's laugh, held the bottle between his knees, made a tight circle of thumb and forefinger, and thrust his other forefinger into the circle several times. "Disfella make pushpush datfella," said Merizo primly, as if the gesture wasn't clear enough by itself.

"Oh, Jesus Christ," Lovett groaned. "I got it, don't rub it in. And who did Keikano do this with and when?"

Merizo evidently didn't need a translation. "Sonson Lubbet."

"Does this mean Chip isn't a free man?" Benteen asked, her voice icy.

"Maybeso, maybeno." said Merizo. Jean-Claude said nothing, his little eyes glittering between half-closed lids.

Lovett himself said, "Sonson Lovett nogood?"

Again: "Maybeso, maybeno." Merizo smiled at Jean-Claude, secure in his power base.

"God*damn* this cat and mouse game! What happens to Chip if he's a nogood?"

According to Merizo, said Benteen, Chip would be released—after the raid on the north village. Otherwise he would be punished as a criminal.

"I'm wondering why we don't just ventilate this pig-fucker right now," Lovett said softly.

"Look at those gomers with clubs all around us. That's why," said Benteen, her voice catching a quaver.

Lovett folded his arms. "If they have Chip, let me see him right now."

Benteen translated; Merizo looked sly and replied. As Benteen massaged it for Lovett, he saw that she was beginning to lose her composure. "He says if they have him, you'll see him after their war. Personally, I'm sure they do, Wade. And he demands that you make your decision now."

Screw it, I'll say anything I have to, Lovett decided. "Tell them okay."

Her mouth dropped. "What?"

"Okay, yes, we'll do it!"

Momentarily she forgot the audience. "I won't help," she hissed furiously. "These shitheads will lie and cheat, can't you see that?"

"I'm fighting fire with fire," Lovett told her grimly, hoping she would understand.

Jean-Claude Pelele seemed almost jolly to see the two arguing, and chose this moment to say, "Bigtits allsame sonson Lubbet."

Lovett turned sharply to face the big man. "You're asking me to trade her for my grandson?"

Melanie Benteen waited no longer, drawing her little automatic and waving it toward the nearest targets, which happened to be two guards. "You'd do anything for Chip—but I won't," she said to Lovett, mouth trembling. "Back out, Wade. I'll come behind you."

Lovett had a firm policy of obeying whoever happened to be waving a loaded pistol, and he moved quickly while the guards were still looking blearily for their own orders. Then Mel Benteen, her little weapon at the end of a fully outstretched arm, began to sidle toward the hall only a few steps behind Lovett. Jean-Claude's eyes darted here and there as if searching for a crevice large enough for him to squeeze into.

Then Merizo barked an order. Some of those tanked-up guards looked at one another and made no move. But one began to stalk Benteen instantly, and two others followed suit.

"Shoot the nearest gomer, then the big guy," Lovett said quickly. "Do it, Mel. *Now!*"

That was probably the best advice he would ever give. But though the pistol wavered with her intent, poor Melanie Benteen had just discovered something about herself. "I can't, Wade," she said in a strangled moan. "I thought I could, but—"

"Hand me the pistol," he demanded.

Benteen spun on her heel but, as she tried to pass her weapon to Lovett, she was jerked backward by her free arm. The pistol clattered to the floor as she was gathered up in a bear hug, Merizo's orders booming like gunfire in the room.

Wade Lovett's decision came unbidden; without a weapon, with the gomers rushing forward while Benteen fought and scratched, he was about to be borne to the floor by sheer weight of numbers to become a captive, perhaps with a club against his skull. He'd be of no use then, just another spent pawn. He ducked under a clumsily swung club and raced into the corridor, already damning himself for cowardice, expecting to see beefy enemies fill that corridor at any second.

But the gomers were all crowded into that room, hopeless amateurs at real showdowns, grunting as they followed on big unsteady flat feet. Lovett amazed himself by managing a sprint through the lobby, overturning rattan chairs in his wake, taking all the veranda steps in one leap. He took three steps toward the beach before deciding he'd make better time on the perimeter road, veered in a new direction as he heard urgent shouts behind him.

Seconds later he heard the cough and clatter of a Cushman scooter around the first bend of the road. Dusk had come like a drawn curtain and, expecting Reventlo, he was shocked to hear a different voice. "Where's Benteen?" It was Vic Myles who stood astride the polkadotted scooter that had injured Merizo and, ever since, tended to veer off on its own like a spooked horse.

"Gomers got her," Lovett husked, swinging onto the scooter. "Some of the big bastards are lumbering along back there behind me."

"Any firearms?"

"They have Mel's."

"If I bagged a couple they could make her pay. Hang on," said Myles, and put the Cushman in motion.

They took one spill and remounted. The second time, they darted cursing into the undergrowth. Now Myles simply abandoned his mount, a chugging, wheezing decoy ten yards off the road in gathering darkness. "Fuck this, we'll double-time it," Myles snarled. "Let 'em beat up on the damn velocipede."

They were more than halfway to the airstrip by now, Myles pounding along in the lead, the little burp gun bouncing on its shoulder sling. Their stamina leaked away as they trotted up the final slope, Lovett calling the only code word he could think of: "Mayday, mayday!"

Coop hailed them from his sentry position in the wingless Tojo, joining them as they stood, lungs heaving, in the cave with Reventlo. The Brit asked several times before Lovett caught his breath enough to say, "Major fuckup. Gomers grabbed Benteen. . . ."

Shortly after dark, Myles noticed movement in the brush near the airstrip. When his hail was not answered he took careful aim and sent three rounds into the foliage. The range was extreme for his weapon and it seemed unlikely that he had hit anyone, but with that short burst he made a point: close surveillance against these crazy old men would not be a safe employment.

Despite anything his friends could say, Wade Lovett took the setback as a personal failure. "I should've known," he said, pounding a fist on his knee for emphasis. "If I'd carried that grease gun, I'd be the President of Fundabora right now."

"If it's any help, Wade, I wouldn't have loaned you my heavy hitter," Myles admitted. "Not many guys will actually squeeze off a clip and waste a dozen people. And in a closed space, ricochets would be like teeing off a golf ball in a tile bathroom."

This was the blunt truth, and one he hadn't considered. Still it was no comfort to Lovett. "Poor Mel was so sure she could squeeze off a round at a blackhat, and when push came to shove she got buck fever. Could happen to anybody. And I should've known," he moaned again.

"Why wouldn't she convince you? She'd convinced herself," Reventlo replied, keeping watch at the cave entrance. "What the Boffins call paper empiricism. We ask what a chap would do, *if*, and he tells us, and hey presto, we jot it down as gospel, when actually he hasn't the foggiest idea."

At least, said Coop, now they had less reason to suspect Keikano. The one thing they did know was that, with the kidnapping of an American woman, Fundabora had become a fit target for a squad of U.S. Marines.

"Not until we can get the word out," Myles said. "That means a lucky radio transmission to some passing commercial airliner."

"And how many contrails have we seen," Reventlo asked. "This isn't on any direct route I know. Lads, it's time for us to sneak aboard the Grumman. We can raise Guam with that set, or fly to Yap and make our case in person."

"And leave two of us and the haul of a lifetime to be bunged up by club-wielding gomers? Go ahead," Myles growled. "You guys boogie out of here if you want to, and I'll stay here and take 'em out one by one."

Lovett studied the bearded Texan in the lambent glow of a lamp wick. Victor Myles had always been a man you could depend on to look out exclusively for Victor Myles, while tooting his own horn harder than Maynard Ferguson. But recently he had begun to show signs of—of—well, call it decency. Nobody had forced him to move that doddering old Cushman into position as a backup. That had bordered almost on the verge of courage. Now he seemed willing to stake his life on his ability to hold off Pelele's gomers alone if necessary. Or so he said. *Paper empiricism*, thought Lovett. Maybe that was one scenario they should avoid.

Reventlo jumped like a cat when his handheld unit beeped. He knew who'd taken that fourth radio. "Melanie? Come in, luv."

"Don't give me love, give me respect," was the soft reply in a near whisper. "I've spent the last hour keeping my virtue, but not my pistol."

"Are you all right? Did you get away?"

"Not even faintly funny, Cris. I'm in a storeroom with some lovely bruises and a ton of toilet paper they don't seem to know what to do with. They didn't rough me up too much; I think Jean-Claude wants me—oh, hell, you know; functioning. His little bimbettes won't talk to me; afraid to, I think. Fundabora Fats put a round from my pistol into the ceiling trying to figure out the safety. Sorry to tell you he didn't kill anybody."

Lovett crowded near the mouthpiece. "Any sign of Chip?"

A sigh. "Sorry, no. But I can't get near the harem rooms; they may have him there. I'll try to get a dialogue going with someone and let you know."

"If we knew where everyone was, I could start blowing it down by sections," Myles said.

"Well, you don't," she said.

"Wish I knew what to tell you," Myles went on. "You can usually make a weapon from something, Benteen. For close work, you know? When Jean-Claude decides he wants to play."

"He already decided that. Guys, it turns out that I seem to lack the killer instinct, so don't count on me for it. I'm better at bullshitting. I convinced Merizo that you'll need me to modify the Grumman to drop things, and if Jean-Claude took my honor, you guys will be in no mood to help fly against the north village. Oh, those two had a hell of an argument about it. They think I'm lying but they don't know for certain. They still have this fixed idea that you can be coerced into their little war."

Coop leaned close to the radio. "Benteen, have you checked out every window, every wall? You can start a hole through some walls with a hairpin."

"I've tried. The window is too high to reach and the walls are concrete block, and it's dark in here. You try climbing up in the dark on a bench made of gooshy toilet paper rolls and see how much good it does you." A long pause. "So tell me something good."

"We're thinking of an assault," said Reventlo, shrugging at the others because he could think of nothing better to boost her spirits. "Are you alone there?"

"I can hear a couple of those bozos grumbling in the next room. Jean-Claude and Merizo were talking about another appearance in the village, but for all I know maybe they're corraling a bunch of drunks to make an assault on you. Is it near dawn yet?"

"Oh God, Melanie," Reventlo said, near to weeping. "It's hardly ten o'clock."

"Time flies when you're having fun," she said, with a pathetic catch in her voice.

Myles put out a hand for silence. "Heads up. Somebody's out there," he whispered, and began to edge outside the cave with his submachine gun. Lovett cocked the big colt. At least they could make surveillance very, very costly.

30

For a moment there was no sound from the jungle. Then a soft hissing whistle that nibbled at Lovett's memory. "Over there," Myles whispered, aiming his weapon. "I'll send a few—"

"Wait," Lovett muttered, and heard the whistle again. Now he recalled a stealthy signal he'd heard while Chip was on sentry duty. He called with soft urgency: "Keikano? Who goes there?" It sounded idiotic.

It also brought results. "Sirs? My honored grandfather is here." And with collective sighs, the men put away their weapons as Keikano slid noiselessly from the underbrush only yards away with his skinny patriarch. It should not have surprised Lovett to see that Ohtsu carried a twin to the rifle he'd given up.

"Our old duffer doesn't know you, lads, so let us make haste slowly," the Brit murmured.

"That's a limey for you. He wants delayed gratification," Myles remarked to Coop, "and he wants it *right now*."

But at Reventlo's look of reproach, Myles stood glitter-eyed and unbending in the distant lamplight. Coop Gunther made no great show of welcome either, having served on a spirited welcoming committee in the Aleutians once upon a time. Reventlo and Lovett exchanged bows with the old fellow. The handshakes that Reventlo urged in the western tradition were tentative but, within a few minutes, much of that cautious reserve began to melt away on all sides. It was Keikano who did most of the translating as the men explained how their predicament had worsened during the past few hours. Reventlo then said, in Japanese, that they needed to discover exactly where young Chip was being held before they could take action.

The old man gravely agreed, and said that it was very, very bad for the woman to be taken. It was his opinion that, whatever Jean-Claude Pelele might promise, he would try to capture all of them as opportunity arose. He also pointed out something that had been a large question mark among the B.O.F. contingent: the lack of firearms among Pelele's people. In fact, Ohtsu claimed, they had a score of Japanese rifles but, unlike a trained Japanese soldier, had never known how to preserve them against the island's salt air. Naturally, they had given up on such finicky weapons, especially when they had used almost all their ammunition in earlier skirmishes. Then Keikano and his patriarch lapsed into a conversation that was not pleasant for either of them.

"The lad's making a case," said Reventlo softly. "Duffer doesn't fancy it. They're going too fast for me."

Presently, the old man came to some glum decision and, with a couple of head-bobbing *hai, hai*'s Keikano turned to the others. "It would be unthinkable for Jean-Claude himself to be anywhere but the village on this special night; on that we are agreed. But the councilhouse will be guarded now, perhaps by men outside as well. Sirs, none of you has the experience you need to slip into the councilhouse. I am the only one who could do that. My honored grandfather has taught me how to move quietly, and he agrees that you must not try."

Reventlo, with a wry smile: "But he doesn't half like the idea of your doing it, does he?"

A hard swallow. "He does not like it, but he believes that only I can do it."

"He means we're all too goddamn clumsy and noisy," Coop said. "But a little noise might help him, from the right quarter."

"Diversion," Reventlo said, nodding.

"The kind that'll kill a flock of birds with one stone. I was flying a Grumman Goose when it was just an egg, and I'm not good for much else with this bum stump. If Keikano can get me through the jungle to the plane, then he can sneak back to the councilhouse and I'll goose the Goose. How much fuel's in her, Cris?"

"Enough for Yap plus reserve. Not enough to orbit over Fundabora 'til dawn, and believe me, Coop, you do not want to put her down in that bay full of stone mushrooms at night. I've seen it."

"Weather's good. Hell, I can just taxi out past the breakers, shut her down, call for help, and wait for first light before I taxi back to that bay. I'll be home free."

"Sure you will," said Lovett. "The damn plane is guarded, Coop. You going to shoot your way in?"

A grin, and a shrug. "That's one option. There's others more friendly for a few tanked-up gomers. I'll take a bottle of booze, the .45, and a couple of Myles bombs; see which one rates the most respect. Way I see it, ol' Lady Luck wants me in the air before she cashes me out. One way or another, there's gonna be some prime noise from the Grumman and that's when the Twinkie here will have his chance." He looked around him. "Well?"

"Well, you're fucking crazy," said Myles with a laugh. "Tell you what, though. If you set fire to the fireworks shed, you'd have a diversion for *your* diversion. Maybe I should go along, Coop."

Keikano had been looking earnestly from one of them to the other. Now he said, "Sirs? Please. I might bring one of you quietly by my own path. Not two."

"It oughta be me," Myles grumped. "Trouble is, I've never flown a Grumman."

"Besides which, I have an idea we'll need you here, Vic," Lovett said. Keikano softly translated these interchanges to the old man as Lovett went on. "Let's say everything works to perfection; Keikano helps our hostages sneak out, and Coop radios for help while he's floating around with a sea anchor waiting for dawn. What do you think Pelele will be doing before sunup?"

"Rounding up every poor rummy numbnuts who isn't too drunk to walk and hoping they can overrun the cave by sheer numbers if they can't talk us out, which they can't," said Myles.

"I never expected to say we think alike, but there you are," Lovett replied. "Even at best, we need you here, Vic."

"And at worst, Victor," Reventlo said, "we shall well and truly need you here, not plunging about in the bush like some crazed survivalist."

"I'll say this once," Myles said, flushing darkly. "A real survivalist isn't some asshole who looks for ways to risk his neck. He's a guy who intends to pull through and avoids heavy risk when he can. Why the hell I catch myself taking voluntary risks now, when I'm surrounded by solid gold airplanes, is beyond me, maybe I *am* going nuts. Maybe that's it, but if there's one thing it's not, it's survivalism.

So you talked me out of it, boys. Me, I'm gonna hunker down and wait for Coop to call in the Marines."

For a long moment the only sound was Keikano, murmuring to the old man. Then, "Gotta go fiddle with my leg. How soon you think we should go," said Coop, easing his rump up on the workbench.

"Ask Keikano," said the Brit. "He's our expert, God save us."

Coop took the .45, a pair of Myles bombs, and a bottle of awful scotch when he limped off with Keikano around midnight. With some reluctance Keikano accepted a long Japanese bayonet from his grandfather. Other than that he was unarmed.

To avoid a case of jitters, Crispin Reventlo organized a work party. It was now possible to trundle another of the Tojo fighters—Ohtsu stubbornly refused to call it anything but *Shoki*—to the cave mouth as a gun platform without removing its wings. Sweating, panting, they were entirely ready for almost any suggestion when Ohtsu engaged the Brit in a brief dialogue.

Reventlo chuckled and wiped his brow. "He wonders why we don't just start it up and taxi it outside. He's started it many times with only one helper."

"Oh yeah, sure," said Myles, in tones of a man claiming a belief in the Easter bunny.

"I'll try anything at this point," Lovett said. "Can't be harder than this."

The old man wasn't too happy with the way his hardware had been vandalized by these *gaijin* ruffians, but presently he stood on the wing with Reventlo at the controls, repeating a few instructions several times. He eased his spavined joints down from the Tojo's low wing, ducked around to a maintenance panel near the engine cowl, and sang out a phrase.

And the propeller jerked with a whine of protest, jerked again, now beginning to turn, and then Ohtsu called out once more and Reventlo, watching his instruments intently, did things with his hands and then a furious *ka-chuff* of white vapor erupted from the huge exhaust stack on one side, and another fuel-rich *chuff* from the other side, and then came a familiar beat of big pistons steadying into a rhythm, a few ounces of fuel urinating from the cowl onto the coral floor as though from some great startled beast. Standing at attention near the wing, the impassive Ohtsu caught the eye of Reventlo and made the slightest bow toward him that just might have had a touch of mockery—*told you so, round-eye*—in it. Off to one side, Myles stood and stroked his beard. Lovett folded his arms, shook his head in disbelief, and grinned like a fool.

The brakes tended to grab but Reventlo coped with it, the propwash hurling bits of debris into the cave as the old fighter, wingtips jouncing, moved downslope a good fifty feet. Reventlo did not chop the throttle until the craft turned to face across the strip, guns pointing into the jungle.

After another palaver with Ohtsu, the Brit helped his friends lift the tail wheel for a flatter trajectory. "Old fellow tells me these forty mike-mikes have very short range, only a few hundred meters. No possible way they'd reach the village. I suppose that's a blessing."

Myles, who had fired one of the little cannon already, sat in the cockpit and discussed the guns with Reventlo. Lovett made his way up around the low cliff through the tunnellike camouflage Benteen had created, carrying the rifle he had originally taken from Ohtsu. Without his flashlight, well past midnight, it would have been dark as the inside of a python. He sat peering out at the starlit night and tried to relax, imagining what must be happening across the jungle to his right.

When the first sign of a glow rose above the treetops, Lovett moved higher, wondering if Coop had managed to set fire to the fireworks shed. He strained to separate the faint sounds in some meaningful way without much luck. But when the muffled explosions echoed and, a long minute later, the fireball climbed into the sky, Lovett called below. "We've got some action!"

"We hear it," Myles called back cheerfully. "Music to my ears. But damn shame they had to use up all those goodies at once."

The glow diminished within minutes, finally fading out as Lovett sat above the cave trying not to enjoy Coop's triumph prematurely. If he were Jean-Claude, he thought, right about then he would be rousting warm bodies for a vengeance raid.

Ohtsu was first to hear Keikano's code whistle, and responded with another. Lovett nearly fell headlong getting down from his post, anxious for news of Chip. Little Keikano puffed into the cave sodden wet, bowed to his grandsire, and looked into the group of grinning faces.

Lovett: "Did you see Chip?"

Reventlo: "Did the plane get away safely?"

Myles: "We heard the fireworks go up."

"No, no," said Keikano, catching his breath. "Men around the councilhouse. I could not see a way. Knew I must return to report. I am—dishonored, sirs."

"Hey, it's okay," said Lovett. "How did Coop make out?"

"It was not the shed that burned," Keikano said, head down, adding something in Japanese for Ohtsu.

"Oh, Lord God," Reventlo whispered. "He says it was the Grumman."

For one thunderstruck moment, no one spoke, then everyone did. Keikano knelt before the old Japanese, who bent to touch the quivering shoulder. Keikano struggled up again, hands waving before him as if to push the voices aside. In a halting voice he described the disaster.

Coop Gunther had moved among deep shadows with Keikano, near enough to the Grumman that they saw a pair of beefy gomers sitting at the lagoon's edge with torches stuck into the turf. Keikano had slid into the water, severing cords that kept the plane against the shore, without alerting the men. When he reported back to Coop, the Alaskan asked him to try creating some kind of noise to draw the men off. This Keikano did, circling around, then calling out taunts in a child's falsetto.

When this merely made them rise and shout challenges, Keikano tossed stones. Only then did the gomers surge off with their torches in search of the truant, and Coop actually did make it to the plane—which by this time had floated a few feet from the shore. Coop finally managed to climb aboard and the gomers did not realize this until one of the twin engines coughed to life. Before Coop could get the second engine running, the guards were pounding back to their post, shouting and waving their torches. And when one of them hurled his torch out at the Grumman, now twenty feet from shore, the disaster was triggered.

"He overprimed it," said Reventlo, when he heard that the water below that engine had burst into flame. "All that high-octane pissing out of the engine into the water. Go on, Keikano. That wasn't your fault."

Keikano had hurled more stones to divert the men, rushing to a better vantage point, but soon others came hurrying to the lagoon and he melted into the shadows. Meanwhile the Grumman's props surged, evidently in an effort to blow out flames that now licked into the engine nacelles. When the fabric-covered trailing edge of one wing began to burn furiously, Coop had gunned both engines, trying to drive the floating bonfire onto shore.

Because the cargo door was now hidden from Keikano, he could not say whether poor Coop Gunther had got out before the first of the fuel-fed explosions that had been visible across miles of treetops. Keikano had ghosted around the councilhouse to find the place crawling with alert, if juiced-up, gomers. Then he had returned to report that the stalwart old Grumman Goose was no more, its parts spread flaming across the lagoon and its verge.

"I will shoot the first man who tells me our Goose is cooked," Myles said grimly.

No one smiled. Hands at his temple, Lovett said, "Oh, shit."

Reventlo nodded. "Shit forsooth," he agreed.

"Bummer," Keikano added, borrowing from the missing Chip. Before Lovett could curse him, Reventlo's radio beeped.

Benteen's first words were, "Did you know Coop is here?"

"We knew they burned the plane," Reventlo told her. "Is he hurt?"

"I can only see through a little hole I've scratched through this damned door," she said, her voice low. "His shirt is half burnt, but—" and now she was sobbing softly, "that's not the worst of it, Cris. Give me a minute." And she tried to choke off her bleats of misery. "I don't think Coop is badly hurt. They were pretty rough on him. Kept shouting in pidgin, and he kept shouting back that it's all his fault. He doesn't understand them. What he did understand was—oh, hell. They opened a door and flung him into another room and—and oh, Cris," crying harder now, "I could see Chip's body lying on the bare floor."

"Chip? How is he," Lovett crowded near the radio. "Could you tell if—"

"Wade? I'm—you know how sorry I am, Wade. I wish you weren't there. How do I say this?" Now Benteen was gulping with the effort to speak. "Chip wasn't moving, and before they shut the door Coop dropped down beside him. He turned and tried to get up, and I've never seen a man look so wild. They slammed the door and Coop was pounding on it and he was—he was screaming, 'Dirty bastards, why did you have to kill an innocent boy?' Oh Wade, Wade, I'm so—"

And briefly, they heard only her broken sobs, and then her transmission ended.

Lovett's body went slack with a cold that was bone deep, and he knew, when the others turned to look at him, that he would lose consciousness if he did not do something right. And this was no time for weakness. He put his head on his knees, drawing deep breaths, willing himself to avoid passing out because there were people who needed his help and now, other people who needed a touch of extinction. He could hear Keikano explaining to his grandfather in tearful Japanese, and in his mind's eye he could see his own daughter Roxanne staring at him in speechless accusation. He sat up straight, stretched a hand out to Myles. "The burp gun, Vic. I have some unfinished business."

"We all do," Reventlo said sharply. "I understand how you feel, Wade, but—"

"Do you? You have any idea what it is to feel a howling cold black wind where your insides were? To know you let your only grandchild walk into a trap set by murderous savages?" Lovett's eyes were dry and hard, his gesture toward the stuttergun a silent demand.

Reventlo placed both hands on his friend's shoulders. "Look at me, Wade; *look* at me. That's better. So far we've let our people saunter off by dribs and drabs, and that hasn't worked well. Ohtsu says his aircraft radios have been useless for dog's years, so now we have no way to get help. Melanie and Coop are prisoners, Chip is—lost to us, and we need to plan our next moves to make best use of everyone. Someone said revenge is a dish best served cold; that means you must remain cool. We came here as a team, and it's important that we act as a team. Are you with me?"

Lovett squeezed his eyes shut, and let a shudder of revulsion rack him. Then he stared into the Brit's face and nodded. "So long as it means cutting off the head of this—this annex of hell, yes."

Keikano's murmured translation had kept the old Japanese informed. Now Ohtsu replied, and Keikano seemed caught up in horrified fascination at what he was hearing.

Reventlo patted Lovett roughly on the shoulder, frowning as he tried to follow the discussion. "Old boy says we have the best way there is to force Pelele to release the hostages. I'm not quite sure I get this; '*kokutai*' is a naval squadron but none of us can fly a Tojo, which was an army plane anyway. I'll have no part of that; it would be suicide to try." He waited for a pause, then asked something in Japanese.

In answer, Ohtsu Yohei, late of the Imperial Japanese Naval Air arm, came to attention and raised his right arm. It pointed straight at the gleaming twin-engined naval Betty bomber. When he saw that

Reventlo understood, he began a dialogue in tones that had a noticeable note of authority, if not command.

To help his friends understand, Reventlo spoke in English and let Keikano translate. Yes, he'd told the truth when he said he had flown a G4M Betty—a "cigar" in Japanese slang. But he'd had a flight engineer to help. Ohtsu Yohei could serve as both gunner and flight engineer? Well and good; but how could they safely remove that dreadful thing under the plane before flight?

Ohtsu told him, and Reventlo's expression tipped Lovett off before he heard the Brit reply, "Take off with the sodding thing? You'd actually sit inside and careen down a rough airstrip hoping I could stay between those trees with a ton of high explosives ready to bounce loose beneath us! I doubt it would take off at all with such a load, let alone drop one. There'd have to be a third man to make sure the bomb shackles worked, too. You understand there's absolutely no question of landing again, with that—that *thing* slung under our belly."

Myles evidently imagined a vast firebloom halfway down the runway. "Whoa, Jasper," he said, his eyes wide. And Vic Myles *enjoyed* explosions, as a rule.

"I like it," said Lovett, imagining a concussion wave with its center on the councilhouse. "But how do we get Mel and Coop out?"

Reventlo gave Lovett a quick nod, then faced Ohtsu, who was responding to Keikano's translation. When the old fellow fell silent, Reventlo said, "Yes, Benteen could give them our ultimatum, and with the tanks holding only an hour's fuel the gross weight should be manageable. But Pelele may simply dare us to drop that awful device on our own people. He should know damned well we won't." He listened, and rubbed his chin, and looked doubtful as he replied, "Possible. I could fly while you strafe from the nose or upper turret; that would certainly get his attention, prove we're serious—assuming we haven't spread ourselves all over the island. In any case, the councilhouse won't be a prime bombing target; we mustn't hit it with our people inside, and if they're released we're honor bound to leave it intact."

"Honor," Lovett snorted, but nodded grudging agreement.

Keikano had been translating this but now suddenly he broke off. "Sirs," he said, "the villagers would not remain in their homes after you passed low over them, firing guns. Especially if I slip in earlier to tell them you intend to destroy everything." He spoke quickly to Ohtsu, whose ghastly dentition showed as he made a smiling reply. Then to the others Keikano said, "My honored grandfather wants to do this because he knows that Jean-Claude has always sworn he would let nothing unpleasant happen to his village. If an Ohka warhead struck the plaza, the honor of Jean-Claude would be lost forever."

"And the fucking village with it," Myles agreed. "But you're not gonna drop it there, are you?"

"Minimum loss of life, maximum loss of face," Reventlo replied. "Perhaps we might. It's a credible threat, and that's important." He passed a hand across his face and sighed. "Listen to me, blathering on as if I thought we could actually do this. No, mates. Put it out of your minds. If it were just me—but I'd be responsible for two more of us."

As Keikano spoke to his grandfather, Lovett said, "No you wouldn't. This old guy has already volunteered, and I'm my own responsibility, and a decent mechanic, too, and if I had to chew those shackles loose I'd do it. Don't try to smear your chickenshit on me. If you won't, then that's it. But don't use me as an excuse."

Something like an instant of rage flickered across the face of Reventlo to be replaced by tight-jawed control. He spoke to Ohtsu.

The old fellow straightened again, barked "Hai," and nodded at Lovett with great satisfaction.

Lovett's grin was more than feral. It was ferocious. "Even I know what that means, Cris. Can you take 'yes' for an answer?"

For a long moment, Crispin Reventlo stood and stared at the old bomber, then at his evidently suicidal friend. Then, with a calm that bordered on the comatose, he said, "Well then, so much for sanity. Plan A: Melanie gets the ultimatum to Jean-Claude, and our people are released down the road with Victor covering their escape. We jettison the Ohka and hope to land here. That failing, Plan B: we send the villagers scattering and drop our calling card on the plaza to burst Jean-Claude's leadership bubble before we land. Comments, Victor? If things go bollocks-up, this could leave you alone on an island crawling with enemies."

A faraway light shone in the Texan's eyes. "Yeah. Hot damn, what a yarn that would make. But I know you, Cris, you'll screw everything up and get back in one piece."

Reventlo's headshake consigned Myles to a mental ward. "We'll have to work all night, lads."

Several calls to Benteen went unanswered, but this did not slow the process of getting a bomber with ninety feet of wing moved by inadequate light to the cave entrance. As with the fighters, the Betty weighed only a fraction of an American craft of the same size, and they did not transfer the added weight of fuel into the plane until it stood with its nose protruding toward the runway. The cave stank of spilled gasoline. At last Reventlo calculated they had a bit over an hour's fuel aboard. "We'll try to taxi her out now before we're exhausted. If we can't, it was just one more good idea gone to seed. If we can, I'll have an idea how good the engines are. Oh, and one more thing: in case the bomb shackles fail, it might be best if everyone took a walk into the jungle while Ohtsu and I do the taxi test."

Ohtsu took pride in waving the others away while he helped Reventlo start the engines. Lovett, with Myles and Keikano, hurried off halfway down the runway to stand peering from behind trees. Landing lights speared into the night after the second engine settled into a steady rhythm and Lovett, seeing the winged suicide bomb shudder in sympathetic vibration with its mothership, suggested to Myles that they weren't nearly far enough away.

"Hard to say," the Texan replied. "If it dropped only a foot or so on its belly, impact might not set 'er off. Those rocket propellant grains could shatter, but I knew that weeks ago. Warmed up some tarry Japanese wax and sealed the propellant cracks one night, on sentry duty. Figured it should reduce the risks a little when we had to move it. Never figured on moving it this way."

"I'm glad I didn't know what you were doing," Lovett said.

"Wish I thought you knew what *you're* doing," Myles replied. "You realize, to reach those shackles in flight you'll be kneeling over a bomb bay with no doors and when the shackles release your load, that whole fuckin' bomber is gonna jump like an elevator, so be ready for it—wups, here we go," he broke off, as the Betty's engines roared.

The whirring rush of engines was curiously muted to Lovett, who dropped down on his knees at the base of a tree. He didn't realize for a moment that he had his face pressed into the soil with his hands over his ears. It seemed like the thing to do at the time.

When he felt a hand patting his shoulder, he stood up to find Keikano at his side. "I knew it would work," he said.

"Nothin' beats dumb luck," Myles replied, and they trudged back to the plane as its propellers ticked into silence. Keikano and his grandfather took their success matter-of-factly but the others shared an elation that could not last.

"We've an hour or so until dawn," Reventlo said. "I suggest we three flying fools try to catch a wink." And with that, he stretched out on a workbench that was now strewn with debris blown into the cave by his twin-engined tornado.

A few hours later, Lovett struggled back to awareness only because Keikano was shaking him, holding a radio before his face. "Wha—it's full daylight, we should be feet wet by now," he said groggily.

But as he shook Reventlo awake, he could hear the voice of Melanie Benteen from the speaker: "—war council early this morning; the taste of Jean-Claude's toe-jam must still be fresh on Merizo's tongue. I don't think they cared whether I could hear. Are you there, over?"

"Lay it on me," he said. "We're here, Mel."

Benteen went on, "Their idea is very simple. It would be. Since we told them about the charter boat, they have to hunt us all down and disappear us before it gets here. They'll say we all took off in bigbig aerocanoe, and if we don't return, who would like to buy a few of their nice shiny machines? Friendly smiles, innocent shrugs. End of story. Who's to argue?"

"For one thing, a shell crater the size of Sumatra," Reventlo put in, fully alert already. "We'll have to drop the thing now, if only to dispute that tale in the event none of us make it. Preferably in a spot where it can't be missed."

"Hi, Cris, and what are we dropping?"

Reventlo told her, ending with, "So when you hear our engines overhead, Keikano will be trying to alert the villagers without getting himself bagged, and it will be time for you to come forward to Jean Claude with your radio. Can you manage that?"

"I think so. What if I can't?"

"We'll strafe around the village and then put the biggest divot in creation slap in the middle of it. You could get some collateral damage even in the councilhouse, I'm afraid. But that might knock some walls down. I hope you and Coop can deal with that; burrow under all that bumwipe if you can, luv."

"You've got my vote. I don't know where Coop is, but I'll try to negotiate for him. It sounds better than the alternatives I've been having nightmares about."

"You must've done; we couldn't raise you during the night," Reventlo said. "Expect us within an hour."

"That, or a concussion wave from here," Lovett reminded them.

"That's our Wade, always a ray of sunshine," Benteen said wryly.

"You want the facts or don't you," Lovett said. "If that happens, try to convince Jean-Claude we're just testing our brand of fireworks, and that we have more."

"We do have more," Myles put in. "Not a patch on the ass of that thing you'll drop, but if I can still toss a Myles bomb, bit by bit I could make the councilhouse look like a bad day in Beirut."

"Please do, Victor," Benteen begged. "I don't know why, but I trust you of all people to do it right."

"We're terribly late, Melanie," said the Brit. "So it's pecker-up, and all that."

"Ah—guys? In case I can't tell you later: I'm glad you're doing this. Hugs to you all." And her transmission ceased.

Ohtsu had dug out flying togs too large for him from the storage boxes, and similar outfits for Reventlo and Lovett. The grayish brown coveralls were too small for the others, but the Brit managed to shrug his slender frame into a brown leather jacket with a sheared fur collar, his pale arms sticking out comically. The old Japanese explained that the parachutes had been cannibalized long ago by his friends. When Reventlo passed this on, Vic Myles sighed and brought his little surplus chest-pack chute from the cave. "You'll be hanging over a hole, Lovett," he said, and handed the thing over. "You'll want insurance, right?"

Lovett couldn't resist as he began to adjust straps. "How much you want for the rental, Vic?"

"Whatthehell, we're millionaires. Ten large, but only if you deploy it. And fuck you, by the way." He turned his back on them and trotted off. Lovett smiled to himself, thinking, *Vic Myles is the only man I know who can say "fuck you" with tenderness.*

Minutes later, they paused at the Betty's fuselage hatch before swinging up into its interior. Lovett pocketed his little radio, smiled wanly at his Brit friend. "We won't be high enough to get cold so I'll be okay. But if Myles tries to take a picture of you in those duds, shoot him quick," he said. "Hey, where's Keikano?"

"Off in the bush, waiting for us to clear the turf before he slips into the village," said Reventlo. "I promised him I'd make a low pass for the punters before we open up."

"And Myles?"

"Get your arse up in the Betty and quit asking questions," Reventlo replied shortly. "In his place, I know where I'd be: far from here, looking for a foxhole. Nothing he can do here now."

Ohtsu, dealing with switches in the cockpit, called a question down. Reventlo's reply sounded like a macho, "Ee-eh, Ohtsu-san." He swung up and inside, speaking over his shoulder. "He wanted to know if we had any doubts about this. I've always found, past a certain point of insane risk, a thing is easier to do if we look past what we're doing, and bear in mind *why* we're doing it."

"For Chip," said the American, pulling himself up. "Tomorrow would've been his birthday. What's your excuse?"

Reventlo fairly howled with laughter as he swung into the pilot's seat. "I haven't," he said, "the foggiest fucking idea."

31

Lovett strapped himself into the seat of the bomber's dorsal turret, almost directly above the glide bomb's canopy which protruded up into the bomb bay. That little turret, with its 20-mm. cannon, was a bubble like a tiny observatory that gave him an unimpeded view of jungle, rough runway, and the bowl of sunny sky above. As the Betty's engines warmed up, he took one look down between his knees and saw the deadly Ohka, influenced by the shudders of its mothership, vibrating under its shackle mounts. After that, he tried not to look down there again.

He energized his radio, knowing that Reventlo had one, too. "Should the Ohka be shaking like a leaf?"

"Everything will, except us. Think about something else, old cock; if it goes up we'll never know it." And then, as the engines roared into full emergency power, Lovett heard Reventlo launch into what might have been an Aussie version of a death song, at first in tones like a low moan but rising to mix with the song of engines.

But it was just Crispin Reventlo, thinking about something else. "Whoa, oh, ohhhh," and now he released the brakes, the Betty moving downslope, riding hard over the rough strip, "Once a jolly swagman," (bounce, *whump*), "camped by a billabong, under the *shaa*aade of a coolibah tree . . ." It was Australia's unofficial national anthem, a "go to hell" flung like a challenge in the face of probability, and as the tail wheel lifted, Reventlo was belting out, "You'll come a-*waltz*ing Matilda with me!" Lickety-*whop*, went one main wheel over a bump, and, "Down came a jumbuck to drink at the billabong," Reventlo thundered, voice shaking from the vibrations, and Lovett tried to watch the trees sliding by faster every second through Reventlo's next stanza, trying *not* to notice that they were veering slightly to the left, nor to see the towering trees their port wingtip seemed destined to find, and he wanted to join in the refrain but his vocal cords weren't having any, thanks.

And now the solid bounces weren't so solid, the broad wings lifting hard, Reventlo straightening the Betty so that they might not catch those top fronds on the left, yelling "You'll never catch me *alive*, said he-e e." Lovett wishing to Almighty God those words didn't sound so much like prophecy as he saw what seemed to be rushing at them dead ahead and knew that, even though the horrendous rattles of the undercarriage had ceased and they were actually airborne by inches, they weren't going to be borne high enough to clear the treetops after all, but the word *abort* had no meaning now as gravity hauled down on Lovett's innards and, "Waltzing Matilda, *waltz*ing Matilda," reverberated through the fuselage, now a weird duet because Yohei Ohtsu had heard the refrain and caught the spirit of the thing and was yelling, "Owaruzee Matiruda, *owaruzee* Matiruda," like a lunatic, and Lovett decided they should go out as a trio, and found his lungs finally up to the task even though slipstream winds were whistling in the bomb bay now and above the calamitous roar of big engines, three crazy old farts stared into those onrushing trees howling, "YOU'LL COME A-WALTZING MATILDA WITH MEEeee!"

And at close to a hundred miles an hour, committed absolutely and inevitably to a pair of treetops in the way, both of those tall trunks shuddered as if they'd been struck by Paul Bunyan's axe, beginning to fall away with agonizing slowness, a dust ring visibly spreading with the shock wave at the base of each tree, and Lovett had time to realize why Vic Myles had disappeared when he did, and where he'd gone to: the end of the runway, no place for a survivalist but directly below the path of the Betty, where primacord-wrapped tree trunks could be disintegrated as an extreme measure.

And they might have made it cleanly over the trees, buoyed by the Brit's resounding, ". . . His ghost may be heard as you pass by that billabong," but for the spread of the Ohka's stubby wing, which happened to intercept a load of palm fronds that wedged between the two aircraft with a grinding hiss.

Then they were past trees and beach, feet wet over a low surf and banking gently to the left, and Reventlo could be heard inventing a stanza of curses even as he fought to maintain a perilous hundred feet or so above the water. Familiar noises suggested that the main gear was retracting, though slowly. "Picked up something. She wants to roll, Wade; you may have to bail," Reventlo said, his voice tight.

There was only one chute on that plane. "Wait one; maybe not," Lovett said, cramming his radio between his breast and the chute. He found footholds, with no problem getting down to the bomb bay where green fronds whipped and scratched furiously against the Ohka's plywood wing, making one hell of a racket. His chute wouldn't deploy at such a low altitude anyway, and it was like a hard sofa pillow against his chest but it would take too damned long to shuck the thing so Lovett wriggled down, pushed the Ohka's canopy back, and dropped into its seat, fumbling in very close quarters for that Swiss army knife in his trousers.

"Got a saw blade here," he said, seeing that Ohtsu had come aft, almond eyes astonished as he watched this American madman begin to saw at the hissing, whipping palm fronds while sitting in the cockpit of a kamikaze bomb. "Narrow envelope here," Reventlo's voice came hoarsely. "Rate of climb minimal, but I think we might orbit the island."

"Hit one of those peaks and—we'll orbit the solar system," Lovett replied slowly, fighting greenery that wanted to fight back. One fanlike branch fell away, gone instantly as if it had never existed, and Lovett's free hand stung as he grasped the butt of another bunch, and as he sawed away he could see, from the edge of his vision in a narrow slit between the mothership and its flying bomb, the shoreline of Fundabora slipping past a half-mile distant. It seemed as if Reventlo's control of the Betty was slowly improving but Lovett's surge of strength began to ebb now, and he slumped for a moment, grimacing up to meet the gaze of Ohtsu.

The Japanese peered at the varying clearance between the fuselages, then jerked around and shouted something. "Ichi-ban idea, I'll try to jink her, Wade," said Reventlo. "Ready?"

"Does it matter?" But as the entire length of the bomber yawed and rocked, the clearance slit dilated again for an instant. With the rushing hiss of a bad steam-fitting, another bunch of fronds magically disappeared. Now Lovett caught at the last bundle and began to tug sideways on it, the slipstream now helping, now hindering. The bundle slapped against Lovett and then vanished, leaving a bloody welt on his arm.

"Capital," Reventlo crowed. "Come home, Wade, all is forgiven."

But as Lovett thrust his body up, his head extended above the windscreen of the Ohka, and the canopy, of course, had to be open for his exit. The slipstream, he found, now hurtled unimpeded around him. A man might drop down unaided, but he needed help to get back up again. He held his hands up to the old man who was braced above him. Ohtsu saw what was needed and reached down to help.

And it should have surprised neither of them that a spindly old fellow in failing health was more likely to fall than to provide the necessary muscle. Ohtsu, with no chute, almost tumbled atop Lovett twice before the American waved him away. "Call him back, Cris, let him explain," he said into his radio, making himself more comfortable in the cockpit. He slid the little canopy shut and, free of that hammering wind, took stock of his situation as Ohtsu disappeared forward.

His narrow field of vision showed that they were now a thousand feet up, skirting Mushroom Bay at a speed of roughly a hundred and fifty miles an hour. "I don't think we'll drop you by accident," said Reventlo, "after all that. Let's make a low pass for the home folks, shall we? Give Keikano some credibility." And with that, he spoke to Ohtsu, beginning a gentle bank, trading altitude for speed as they dropped toward the lagoon breakwater. Lovett could see, directly above him, old Ohtsu scramble into the dorsal turret.

"By the bye, do you have your hammer for those shackles?"

"Nope. Slipped my mind, Cris, I can't imagine why."

"Romeo to Juliet," Reventlo said, now hoping to raise Benteen. "Are you there, luv?"

"I've been listening and you're scaring me to death," she replied.

A bark of laughter from the Brit. "I chewed a few washers from my shorts, too. Let's see who else we can scare. You may call the big dog now, my dear." He followed this with a shouted order in Japanese.

Lovett watched the lagoon streak past as they bored in just above treetop level, up the throat of the lagoon with a bank to the right, evidently to give Ohtsu a clear field of fire. The hammer of cannonfire sent perhaps a half-dozen rounds streaking out, but Lovett could not see the target.

He didn't have to. "Loverly shooting," Reventlo exclaimed, pulling up and away over the sea. "I saw hits against the councilhouse roof."

Without conscious effort, Lovett found himself lapsing into phrases he hadn't used since his tour in Southeast Asia. "Melanie, tell

His Nibs this is a dragonship, and we've got enough ordnance here to hose every hootch in the ville. We're starting with his, 'cause we're nice guys." To himself he added silently, *Gotta remember that's not her pidgin.*

Roaring back over the councilhouse, well above the treeline, they could see every hut in the village disgorging tiny figures, some fleeing into the jungle, some making for the beach. Ohtsu let fly with two more rounds, probably aimed at the ocean. Benteen had left her radio on and the confused shouts that became background noise suggested that, if nothing else, they had certainly got Jean-Claude's attention.

"About forty minutes' fuel, if memory serves," Reventlo said calmly.

Lovett, preparing again to try exiting the Ohka: "What, no economy cruise settings?"

"We can't land with the Ohka. I know it and Ohtsu knows it. Get out of there, Wade," said the Brit in tones that meant business.

"If I can, I will." And with the canopy open, Lovett tried again. And failed again. "Cris, I'm gonna have to ride her down and bail after you drop me. No choice; no kidding." It was pilotese for "absolutely out of options."

Reventlo was silent for a moment while he banked the big plane for another pass up the lagoon. "I'll have to give you some altitude. Don't thank me, mate, the concussion wave will shed our wings if I don't."

Now the old Japanese was calling excitedly to Reventlo, who banked the bomber into a circle encompassing the village, the councilhouse, and much of the lagoon. Lovett's view was awful, but he felt a surge of hope when the pilot said, "There's our prize arsehole, you can't miss him coming out of his den." Then, for one instant in passing, Lovett saw the giant Pelele hurrying away from the councilhouse afoot with a trousered figure in tow, and from the hairdo it had to be Benteen stumbling between the lagoon and the plaza.

". . . Mad as hell, Cris, and he dares you to go ahead," came Melanie Benteen's voice from the radio. "He's got a thong around my neck and he thinks you won't fire on us both. Show him he's wrong, sweetie."

"Not an option," Reventlo said. Evidently Melanie Benteen had never seen human remains struck by cannon fire.

Lovett upped the ante. "Mel, tell him what he sees under our dragonship is a bomb so big it won't fit inside. If we drop it near his councilhouse there won't *be* any councilhouse, just fifty more yards of lagoon. And the ville had better be empty 'cause we're gonna frag it. He won't have anything left to be President of. Either that, or let us see you and Coop coming alone down the beach in the next two minutes."

"Well said," Reventlo chimed in.

They could not clearly hear Benteen's conversation with the big man but, during their next banking pass near the councilhouse, Ohtsu cut loose again with his aerial cannon. Moments later, Benteen laughed. "Now you've really pissed him off, boys. Ruined his big music box."

"How can he tell from out there," Reventlo asked.

"If you ever heard a cannon shell hit a grand piano you wouldn't have to ask," she said gaily, then stopped as another voice gibbered in the background. "He says you won't hurt innocent villagers. I think he believes it."

Reventlo: "The slaughter of innocents is what war is all about. Tell him he taught us that, and we learned fast." Then the Brit called in Japanese to his gunner, and straightened his next pass to parallel the village.

Lovett couldn't see the result, but through his radio he heard the inarticulate howl of fury from Jean-Claude Pelele. As Reventlo resumed his circular pattern he said, "Right down the plaza of Mr. Fundabora Fats. But he's not to worry, Melanie. If he doesn't release you, in two minutes there won't be a plaza."

They were banking upward, yielding Lovett a sight of the councilhouse, when a portion of its outer wall erupted in a puff of debris. "We got a secondary, Cris," the American replied, wondering what might have set off that secondary explosion.

Bits of stone peppered the edge of the lagoon in little watery bull's-eyes, and Jean-Claude Pelele sprawled, perhaps feeling some of that debris. Before Lovett lost his view, he realized that Melanie Benteen was off and running. "I'm loose," she cried.

"Head for the cave," Reventlo urged, increasing the altitude of his banked circle.

For the first time, the voice of Vic Myles: "Take the perimeter road, I can cover you," he said. Nothing more. Monitoring those transmissions, Myles could have only the sketchiest idea of the action but apparently he had moved closer to the center of it.

"Someone—running from," Benteen panted. A pause, then a delighted cry: "My God. Coop! Coop, over here!"

Reventlo's view was by far the best. "Run, you old punter," he begged as if to himself. "Wade, our people are clear. Your choice of targets." He pulled the old bomber into a steep climb.

Lovett did not want to think of his grandson's remains buried in a Fundaboran grave. There was a better solution. Without hesitation he said, "Councilhouse. Villagers don't deserve this." What Lovett really wanted was to aim for Jean-Claude's navel but from any altitude high enough to safely launch this awful gadget there was no assurance that he could locate the man again; and the councilhouse was, after all, the local status symbol.

For maximum climb, the old bomber had to broaden its circle a great deal. Somehow during all this, Reventlo managed to keep Benteen in sight. "They've joined up, Wade. I had no idea a one-legged man could sprint like that," he said admiringly.

"I'll need a little more air to play with," said Lovett, settling himself in his seat, making sure the canopy was fully open again. "I don't know how this thing handles. Or whether."

"Rockets might give you some help. No guarantees," said Myles, still monitoring as he had from the first.

With his throttles firewalled, Reventlo continued his climb until he had a mile of air beneath the Betty. "Your call, Wade. Give me a heading."

"Come in from the lagoon breakwater and drop me halfway to the councilhouse," said the American.

"Wilco." The bomber began another steep turn. "And, ah—Wade?"

"Yeah."

"Don't be a bloody fool when we're winning."

Voice deadly with calm: "You can't begin to know what I've lost."

"We may need you, goddamn your eyes—initiating my run," the Brit broke off quickly. "Tallyho."

A faint burst of Japanese came to Lovett. "Ohtsu salutes the thunder god who treated him and his grandchild so honorably," Reventlo added. "Don't do it, Wade." Both men knew the old term the Japanese had used for kamikaze pilots sworn to die: thunder gods.

Lovett was considering a reply when he felt the shackles release cleanly, a tribute to Ohtsu's maintenance, and from that instant onward he forgot everything but the task at hand. The Ohka fell away nose-down in a steepening dive from perhaps six thousand feet, but a firm pull on the simple control stick brought it up to the horizontal. The huge bulk of the old Betty droned off above him, instantly forgotten, his view now remarkably clear to each side, wind whistling fiercely around the open cockpit. An Ohka had never been intended to fly with its canopy back and, horizontal or not, the drag was making him lose altitude quickly. Because he had drifted to the right, he used both pedals and stick to recover; found himself saying aloud that he was using full control deflections, ". . . Bangin' it on the stops," as if testing this terrible device for future pilots.

At least the little beast was stable, and at flight speed it seemed to glide perhaps five feet forward for every foot down. By glider standards this was awful; yet it quickly sent Lovett well beyond his intended target and a steep banking turn without power would only make the device plummet faster. He didn't actually think about firing those rockets; he simply did it, snapping the first of three firing studs Ohtsu had shown him near the center of the primitive instrument panel. The result was instantaneous, a rushing burst of sound behind him and a surge of thrust against his back. His speed increased steadily until the lift of the Ohka's stubby wings roughly matched the forces drawing him down, and as Lovett banked the monster he realized that he was almost over the runway, down to perhaps four thousand feet.

Too damned low, too damned far, he thought, and knew he must have more thrust. Well, there were two more rockets, two more chances for one of them to blow his backside off, and as he felt the first rocket subside he fired another.

And this was more like it, sizzling back over the jungle with the councilhouse well in view, still dropping but not losing too much altitude, but when he tried to stand up the wind shear force nearly took his head off, forcing him back.

Well, he'd known for ages—thirty seconds or so—that this would probably be the way his world would end; not with a whimper but with a God-Almighty bang. No time for self-pity, none for rage, and damned little for aiming himself while peering through that ridiculous aiming circle just ahead of the windscreen, but he might plant the Ohka's nose just beyond the councilhouse, where he could see two tiny figures on the roof, the taller one in a yellow cap; and then he saw the taller figure turn to peer at him, waving what might have been a pistol, and it wasn't a cap at all but a mop of sun-bleached hair, the only such hair on Fundabora; and with one-tenth of a second of decisions left to him the word, *Chip!* burst in his mind, and he hit the last of the firing studs as he horsed back on the control stick.

In absolute extremity to miss the councilhouse, it was possible to convert all that speed to stretch a glide, even to climb briefly, but the laws of physics said there was going to be a price to pay. Lovett streaked over the councilhouse with only three hundred feet of altitude, in a darting climb that would last for a few seconds at most. With the fact of Chip's unexplained survival, in the space of one second Lovett had shifted goals, and if he'd had the thrust to do it he would have tried to roll the Ohka, use gravity to help pull him out, perhaps live to embrace his grandson again. But that was no longer possible; that was the price he'd paid to the gods of physics. Instead, as he flashed above the lagoon he tried to cheat with aerodynamics. He wrenched the stick for a wingover to reverse his direction which robbed him of some of his newly gained height. With a convulsive movement he put both hands on the canopy rail, and planted one foot on the control stick. His height above the lagoon may have been as much as five hundred feet.

When he sprang away, the little Ohka responded, snapping its nose down as his foot forced the stick forward. In a sense, the little brute simply ducked its head and flung him out. Men had lost their legs that way but Lovett was already clawing at the *D* ring on his chute, flipping over and over, expecting to be slammed into marmalade by the Ohka's horizontal tail.

Spread-eagle, commanded some old memory, because you fell more slowly that way and he didn't want to be found tucked into a ball, and a mass of white stuff erupted at his chest but chutes didn't open that fast and he was falling, tall palms rushing up for him, the world whirling around, and fronds slashed past his feet as the awesome wallop of an opening chute squeezed him breathless. You were supposed to relax, he recalled. *No problem.*

His compressed sense of time was disorienting because, as the ground rushed to meet him, he truly was falling more slowly, then not at all, swinging eight feet above a big fern as, two hundred yards distant, the Ohka pancaked into the lagoon, having obediently regained its level attitude the instant his foot left the control stick, but still losing altitude fast.

Lovett could not even cover his face, helplessly dangling, and saw the Ohka bounce flat, shedding one plywood wing that flipped away while the little monster spun furiously, skipping like a child's boomerang along the lagoon. And because the old fuze in the Ohka's nose did not strike the water with enough force, Lovett waited in vain for the explosion.

The remains of the Ohka slid near the shallows, its fuselage now a huge, flattened, buckled aluminum toy, and the entire one-ton nose section quickly sank, breaking away so that the aft end of the bomb protruded just above the surface like a buoy. Lovett was astonished to find that, among the emotions that flooded him, the primary one was disappointment.

The laughter behind him had a tinge of mania in it as Jean-Claude Pelele, having watched the Ohka destroy itself, drew near enough that he might have reached up to grasp Lovett's kicking legs. The chute had no single-point release and, grinning up at his helpless enemy, Pelele shook his finger cheerfully. "Lubbet plenty fun byandby," he promised, and began to bellow toward the village, actually beating his chest before he trotted to the shallows where the Ohka's debris lay.

It didn't take a genius to realize the big man's agenda: call his people back, show them he was still the alpha male, exhibit Lovett as a trophy before dragging him down to have plenty fun with him. Wade Lovett was digging into his trousers for his knife as Pelele strode bravely into the water.

A few faces peered from foliage near the village and Jean-Claude, to embolden them, held up a shard of floating plywood as he shouted encouragement. He was laughing as he stroked out to the base of the warhead, hugged it, slapped a big meaty hand down on one of several protruding studs.

Evidently the Ohka had impact fuses fore and aft. The shock wave generated by two thousand pounds of high explosive blew down trees, lifted a geyser hundreds of feet into the sky, and tore Lovett's chute completely free.

32

Almost everyone involved knew the fate of Wade Lovett before he did. Reventlo and Ohtsu knew because, circling far above and beyond the blast radius, they cheered the sudden blossoming of his chute just above the treetops. Benteen, Coop, and Myles knew because they could hear Reventlo's play-by-play reportage. From such a distance, the Brit could not identify a given person and didn't figure out why the Ohka's muffled blast and attendant waterspout were delayed so long, or where Jean-Claude had gone—"Everywhere," Keikano was to explain cheerfully—until the mutual debriefing later.

With only a few minutes of fuel left after that fearsome blast that cratered the lagoon, Crispin Reventlo had lowered his landing gear and made a single straight-in approach to the runway, knowing he would not get a second chance. With no heavy fuel load, no cargo, and next to no crew, he should have made it down cleanly. He very nearly did.

It could have been the surrounding water that allowed so little metal shrapnel to tour the deserted village. As for Wade Lovett, stunned but otherwise untouched hundreds of yards from the epicenter, he needed two minutes to unbuckle the chute harness and thrash his way out of his blanket of waterlogged palm fronds, and two days to lose the persistent tone in his ear. Later, when he whistled the tone for Chip, the youngster frowned and shook his head. "E natural. You'll never be a composer," he said in some joke all his own.

For an hour after he stumbled toward the crumbling councilhouse to be met by his grandson and Keikano, Lovett had found himself half-deafened, poised between anger and delirious glee. Chip sat with a beaming Keikano on the steps beside him and replied to Lovett's confused muttering. "I keep telling you, Pop, Coop was half right. They held me down and poured that shitty scotch into me to keep me quiet. I *was* dead—dead drunk. I must've been dishrag-limp, hardly breathing I suppose, and I guess poor Coop just took one look and jumped to conclusions."

"He could've let Benteen know later," Lovett mumbled, still coping with a mild case of shell shock.

"How could he know, after they moved him? He'd smuggled the forty-five in somehow, and by the time I came to, they'd taken him away. Found out the lump under my back was the gun he'd stashed under me. I couldn't aim it or stand up straight for half the next day; I was wasted, Pop. First time I tried to shout, it felt like the top of my head was coming off. I didn't try that again."

"So how'd you get out, Chip?"

"Keikano," said the youth, and hugged the doe-eyed native. "She sneaked in and talked to Pelele's wives after the big bastard hauled Benteen outside, and she found out where I was, and pulled the hinge pins out of the door. Would you believe Pilau had oiled them? Anyway, I had the pistol so we snuck up on the roof. I was gonna nail the fat man as soon as he got close enough; honest, I was ready to shoot him, Pop, but here came this twenty-foot skyrocket and I had no idea you were in it, and then . . ."

Lovett, who still had trouble focusing and considerably more trouble deciphering this babble, put up a hand. "She? You said *she*, dammit. You mean Benteen? Talk sense."

Chip slid his glance to the silent Keikano, and they shared a gentle kiss. "No, I mean Kei. I should've known sooner, Pop, but I didn't 'til the night we waited for her grandpop in the dark, and she put my hand on her chest and—well, anyway . . ."

"Keikano's a girl," Lovett said stupidly, and Chip merely nodded.

And now the young Fundaboran did speak, and when allowing her voice its natural timbre it was even more musical and as girlish as a giggle. "Several families raised their first girls as boys, sir," she said. "The Pelele tradition is to make child wives of eldest village girls. I am not the only one. The wives know it. They envy me, I think."

Lovett put his head down on his knees and rocked it to and fro. Muffled between his hands: "You know what I thought."

"Sure, Pop, but this was serious stuff. I swore not to tell, and a promise is a promise. If anybody gave the scam away and Pelele's bunch had found out, a dozen village girls would've been in deep trouble, same as Kei." He paused, cocked his head. "Somebody's coming in the half-track," he said. "Let's get out of sight."

They didn't show their faces outside the councilhouse until convinced that Pilau's mission was peaceful. The formidable Rongi commanded the half-track, his spear adorned now with Merizo's bedraggled little flywhisk, his face and breast streaked with hastily applied paint. He looked warlike and grimly satisfied. No wonder: trussed in the half-track's cargo bed lay three of Jean-Claude's burly guards with little Merizo for lagniappe, like a goat tethered among a trio of surly hogs.

Keikano spoke with Rongi for a time, then called her friends out of the ruined lobby. When Rongi rapped out a question, Keikano pointed at Lovett native fashion, with her chin. Rongi, his face split in a grin, leaped from the half-track and enfolded Wade Lovett in a sweaty embrace while speaking the local argot, and Lovett looked to Keikano for help.

"You sent Jean-Claude to the great fire below," she explained, "and left his gang leaderless. Rongi will now decide yes and no in the village. That is his right. These, uh—pieces of *pekpek*," she went on, indicating the trussed captives, "will be disposed of in your honor."

Lovett traded swift looks with Chip. "Whoa, don't do it for me. There's been enough pain on Fundabora. If they're beaten, can't he just let them go in peace?"

Keikano put the question to Rongi, who seemed dumbfounded for the moment. Then, with a look that said he never expected to understand these pale strangers, Rongi climbed into the half-track and spoke rapidly for all to hear. Merizo's expression brightened remarkably in the space of a few moments and, as Pilau lurched his big vehicle away toward the village, Rongi raised his arm in farewell, calling back to them.

"All are invited to the celebration tonight. Pelele's gang will get a canoe and a week's provisions," Keikano explained. "If they are found on Fundabora after today, their sentence will be carried out." Lovett wasn't bloody-minded enough to ask about that sentence; Merizo's face had told him.

By the time the trio walked to the airstrip, Lovett ached in every sinew, too weary even to remark on the sorry state of the Betty bomber. Keikano was canny enough to whistle her signal to old Ohtsu; otherwise they might have been welcomed by a bullet. After all, no one else knew how quickly the villagers had taken advantage of the air raid and the brisk departure of Jean-Claude Pelele.

When the shouts of surprise and triumph faded at the cave, Ohtsu was especially pleased. He even saluted Lovett, the only man he'd ever seen who'd figured out how to fly an Ohka without paying an immediate visit to his ancestors.

Lovett was, in fact, the only one still harboring some irritation. "Coop, I was half-ready to augur that damn bomb in and me with it, 'cause I thought Chip had bought the farm," he said, glowering. "You made believers of us!"

"How was I to know Benteen passed it on," Coop fired back, rubbing his leg. "When I got a good sniff of Chip's breath I realized what must'a happened. I had widened the vent hole in my leg so I could stuff a grenade and the pistol barrel in, and I figured Chip needed the shooter more'n I did. Then those big bozos caught me asleep and drug me out; stuffed me into a room alone with one lousy high window. When I heard you guys strafing I knew it was time to pull that little grenade of Vic's outa my leg stash. Blew the window out with it. I ducked under some mats in a corner after I lit the fuse. Vic," he said, calling to the Texan who was scribbling in his notebook, "whenever I need a fireworks display, you're elected."

"Well, it worked out, Coop," Lovett admitted. "Thanks to my ten-thousand-dollar chute. But next time—"

Reventlo had been listening silently but now he sputtered, "Next time, Wade? As in, the next time you fly a live, fused suicide bomb against an island despot? Give us a break, mate." Reventlo had fallen into a dark mood, admitting that he was unable to reach a previously secret ambition. Halfway through a textbook-perfect landing, he'd struck a soft rut on the runway, nosing over with the tips of both propellers bent just badly enough to prevent his flying the Betty to Yap. "I wanted to refuel and ferry the old tart on to Darwin by air," he admitted glumly, knowing that Vic Myles was taking it all down, not much caring.

The village celebration turned into a three-day convention that began on Chip Mason's eighteenth birthday. It was attended by visitors who canoed from the North village, and Benteen did her best to explain to her friends what she only half-understood. Several of Ohtsu's visiting womenfolk spent much of their time reviving auld acquaintance, gossiping with their southern kin. Dressed in silk kimonos, they made it obvious what had happened so long ago to those missing Japanese parachutes.

Keikano could not do her usual interpreter chores because she took a prominent part in the pan-Fundabora discussions, dressed in an odd combination of silks. Seeing her without her breasts tightly wrapped, Lovett wondered how he had ever assumed she was male. Keikano, he had to admit, was something of a dessert dish after Benteen gave her a makeover that left old Ohtsu both amused and scandalized. As for Chip's reaction, Myles nailed the appropriate phrase: "horny as a Texas bull."

Yohei Ohtsu, finally accepting that all his wars were over, was happy with the new order in which all villagers would simply vote for their island's leaders, rather than accept the results of rigged combat games. He was happier still when he found himself voted First Minister to Rongi, though he thought it passing strange that the women should want to vote. After talks with Reventlo and Lovett, Ohtsu's first public recommendation was to commit all resources to preparing Fundabora as a resort again—at present, for senior citizens only. That would be necessary, he said, before they could entice an honest-to-God physician to the island—and to pay the doctor.

That idea passed by acclamation. The United Fundabora council ended with a wonderfully symbolic gesture by Rongi, who splintered his spear over his knee and tossed it, with the hated yellow flywhisk, into the council bonfire to thunderous cheers.

In days, the councilhouse was repaired, its lobby cleared of rubble. Chip, viewing the mound of piano parts, wondered aloud how they had ever fitted into the shape of a baby grand. When Reventlo suggested that a fund be set aside from the aircraft sales to import another piano, no one argued.

It was another week before the chartered boat arrived, a much-modified LCT with a handmade deck of scarred timbers, an almost flat bottom, and room—barely—to take the Betty aboard.

When they saw the LCT's whip antenna, the first thing Victor Myles did was to use the radio to call New York. Editor Beacham, no stranger to the Myles brand of blarney, wasn't satisfied until both Reventlo and Melanie Benteen vouched for the story. Benteen's father was, after all, a legend and no one could doubt the measured Briticisms of Flight Captain Reventlo.

Coop Gunther made a call to Petersburg, Alaska—for all the good it did him. Apparently the major source of local news was Radio KFSK, and reporter Glenn Michaels had known Coop for years. "No, where are you, really," Michaels asked, loud enough that the entire B.O.F. crew could hear. "Best I could do is broadcast that story as a muskeg message to your friends out the road; both of 'em." When Coop repeated the truth he was told, "Sober up and come home, Coop, and see if the Petersburg *Pilot* will print it." Laughing, Michaels had hung up on the fuming Coop Gunther.

After Benteen, Reventlo had his turn, and like a good businessman he called Curran Quinn. It seemed that Quinn hadn't been idle since Reventlo's call from Australia. He reported tentative offers for the Betty and two of the fighter craft, each for seven figures.

Chip and Lovett took deep breaths and made the call they dreaded. Chip began with, "Hola, Domenica, thought I'd check in.—Hey, what's wrong?—Aw, cut it out, of course I'm okay; sure, him too.— Um, well, we went a little farther than, uh, is Mom there?—He is, is he? I could care less but I'd better have a word with Mom." The radio-telephone was an old-fashioned device. He spoke away from the mouthpiece: "Jeez, you'd think I was the long-lost son."

"Actually, you are," Lovett reminded him.

Back to the mouthpiece again: "Mom? Hi, Pop and I have been out of touch awhile, sorry about— Well, I've got a great tan and a fiancee, and I guess I'm a millionaire.—Oh. An island; Fundabora. You never heard of it.—Ah, a ways off the coast.—No ma'am, not exactly. The coast of Australia, actually.—No ma'am, I haven't touched a drop." He listened for another moment, then made a face and thrust the instrument out to his grandfather. "It's for you."

For a long moment Lovett waited for an opening, but Roxy's conversation tachometer was redlined and he finally just cut through it. "*Roxanne.*" His most commanding voice; he hadn't used that tone with her since she was ten.

He found it still worked as a shock tactic. "Roxy, I want you to know that Chip is exactly where he says he is, because he followed your orders and he's taken very good care of me.—Sure, activate the speakerphone for von Whatzis; it's not as if he had any say in this. There's no extradition from here anyhow, and if there's a dim cap involved, von Wart should be wearing it. Our little mining venture has paid off, big time. You'll probably be reading about it, and Chip's a full partner.—You heard him right, her name's Keikano; a linguist and a schoolteacher. You'll love her. Chip certainly does, and I admire his taste."

He rolled his eyes for Chip's benefit. "All right then, yes; you could say she's a native girl. Also the granddaughter of the First Minister of the Republic of Fundabora.—Yes, Mr. Von, she's royalty of a sort. Chip's lucky to get her and in case it's slipped your notice, Roxy, your son is now eighteen, and I'm afraid he's gotten used to making decisions for himself."

He listened for half a minute. Then, "You'll have to ask him, Roxy, and my advice is to ask him very nicely. I'm urging him to make a trip home with Keikano before they tie the knot. There's talk of reopening a destination resort here, and several of us will be staying on as consultants.—I can't say how long, but I can say we're very tight with the local administration so I'm having my VariEze shipped here. Believe me, if the ship doesn't sink under our airplanes, I can afford it.—Nope, Chip wasn't kidding; I'd say he's got more assets than you do, Roxy. I believe he's bringing you some Fundaboran pearls."

After listening again for a moment he burst into laughter. "No doubt you're a financial wizard, Mr. Von, I must admit I've always found your advice to this family fairly unique. If it weren't for you, I wouldn't have had to bug out like that. I thank you; my grandson thanks you. My daughter may even thank you, but I wouldn't count on it.—Say again, and try not to stammer.—A position? Why not; as one of the impulsively senile, I'll be happy to employ you on the spot if, and only if, you can answer one question here and now: who will give us the best deal on a matched pair of Shokis?" He spelled it out, Sierra-Hotel-Oscar-Kilo-India, and waited, loving it.

Presently he said, "Time's up, and I'm *awfully* sorry, but perhaps this work would be a bit out of your line. Our agent in Florida does know, and I've known him for forty years. A Shoki is an airplane, by the way. Nice try."

His laughter had brought his newest friend awake, and the tiny saffron kitten now thrust its head from his jacket pocket. He stroked its scruff gently. "Actually, Roxy, I won't be coming back anytime soon but you're welcome to visit. Invite Chip's piano teacher while you're at it; my treat.—Matter of fact, there's an islander I want you to meet. Name's Tasukete—Japanese for Mayday, more or less, and he's three weeks old. A gift from Minister Ohtsu.—Of *course* he's a cat, but he doesn't know it yet.

"Wups, captain's making signs I should wind it up. We've got airplanes to ship, and the sooner that's done, the sooner Chip will get a Qantas flight home.—Nah, he hasn't changed that much, but you'll have to get used to some tall tales from the world's youngest Boring Old Fart. . . ."